MAKE ME KING

Also by Keith C. Blackmore

Mountain Man
Mountain Man
Safari
Hellifax
Well Fed
Make Me King
Mindless
Skull Road
Mountain Man Prequel
Mountain Man 2nd Prequel: Them Early Days
The Hospital: A Mountain Man Story
Mountain Man Omnibus: Books 1–3

131 Days
131 Days
House of Pain
Spikes and Edges
About the Blood
To Thunderous Applause
131 Days Omnibus: Books 1–3

Breeds
Breeds
Breeds 2
Breeds 3
Breeds: The Complete Trilogy

Isosceles Moon
Isosceles Moon
Isosceles Moon 2

The Bear That Fell from the Stars
Bones and Needles
Cauldron Gristle
Flight of the Cookie Dough Mansion
The Majestic 311
The Missing Boatman
Private Property
The Troll Hunter
White Sands, Red Steel

MOUNTAIN MAN

BOOK 5

MAKE ME KING

KEITH C. BLACKMORE

Cover design by Podium Publishing

ISBN: 978-1-0394-4988-6

Published in 2023 by Podium Publishing, ULC
www.podiumaudio.com

MAKE ME KING

1

A damp mid-March cold enveloped Big Tancook.

Wet snow fell in miserable clumps and clung to the window. Gus scowled as another ball of white shit spattered against the glass and slid to the sill. A frosty marina sparsely populated with ghost ships and skeletal spars lay beyond the picture window. A ceiling of gray clouds hung over the wintry harbor, vacillating on whether to disperse or become a monster. Gus didn't want another storm. He'd barely been able to cope with this one, relying heavily on Scott and the others to clear the snow around his house when necessary. Gus walked with a limp these days, from where an unlucky shot separated the meat of his sole from his heel. Or a lucky shot, he supposed, depending on how you looked at it. The guy that tagged him probably thought it was a damn fine shot. A one-in-a-*million* shot. Not enough to kill, but, hell, it nagged the living shit out of Gus every damn day, and he considered that a win for the bastard. An ass-whooping stamp of approval, so to speak.

Then there was his ruined hand—the last two fingers had been blown off at the knuckles by ricocheting bullets. Maggie had worked Emergency Room magic on him, and he doubted he could ever repay the doctor enough. She got him functional again, but now it was up to him to live with an awkward grip and a buzzing in his foot for the rest of his life.

Wounds. He'd certainly gotten his share. And that was just the physical shit. The mental shit was just as bad. Or worse. Memories of Jerry still haunted him, tormented him at night. Ruined his sleep. Collie had advised him to forget about the warlord called Shovel, and to instead focus on the man before the apocalypse.

Easier said than done.

So very easy.

1

Clumps of snow continued to smack against the glass, melting as they slid down.

"She's here," someone said, and Gus turned away from the weather.

The conference room was a modest one, situated in the only hotel on the island. Tables and chairs were set up in a wide horseshoe around a small but ferocious wood stove that easily heated the whole interior. Nearly fifty islanders were milling about, their winter coats tucked away nearby. Some of them had brought their kids, who were now grouped together at the edges of the room, playing in hushed voices.

Scott and Amy were present, dressed in thick sweaters and jeans. Little Scottie was nearby, walking an invisible tightwire around them. Donny Buckle sat next to them, holding onto a cane and studying the weather outside with narrowed eyes. The Newfoundlander had warned them of Sheila's Brush, the last big storm of the winter, which was bound to strike up any day now. It was long overdue this year, and those dark clouds might as well have been giant billboards advertising its arrival. The martial arts instructor, Vick, sat next to Donny. Vick had already adapted to life with one arm, politely telling anyone who asked him if he needed a hand to fuck off. Vick resembled a bear awakened too early from hibernation—a burly man with dark rings around his eyes and a permanent scowl on his face. Gus had heard the story of how both he and Donny had been brutalized by a pack of road savages calling themselves Norsemen. The pair had survived the encounter, however, and didn't let their wounds slow them down.

Bruno was also there. He had stopped asking Gus if he needed any nudie books, but damn if the guy had gathered a sizeable collection. Bruno swore the magazines were purely for trade, but Gus didn't think too many of them got traded. He recalled their first meeting on the outskirts of Halifax, where he'd given the man a couple boxes of Kraft Dinner, as well as some packages of ramen noodles. The memory summoned a little smile.

The others at the meeting were survivors from all over, making the best of what they had, and what they knew. The conference room had become an unofficial nexus, where the island's sparse population met after the day's work of hard labor had been completed. The color beige coated the entire chamber, as if a bomb had gone off and wiped out all semblance of décor. Not the curtains, however, which were a festive red. They had been up since Christmas, and no one had bothered to take them down. They were warm and cheerful, and Gus had no trouble with that. He would've hung Christmas lights throughout the place if they could spare the power, just for the relaxing vibe the lights provided. Regardless, the conference room had become a place where islanders could wander in and chat, perhaps gaze out over the harbor, or sit and enjoy a hand of cards. Cribbage was the most popular, but there were a few boardgames as well. Sadly, Scrabble was not among them. Gus dearly wanted to find a board and kick some ass.

Faces watched him, and he remembered names and professions. It was good to see everyone together, even though he knew they all possessed terrible histories—harrowing stories of escape, fleeing the rabid outbreak. Frightening tales of survival. Gus kept a brave face for them all, but inside, he pitied them still, and wondered how they dealt with their memories, especially at night, when the wind battered their windows and made the bones of their houses creak.

They managed those ghosts, somehow, in their own way. They all did. And town meetings like this one helped them to cope with their pasts, by instilling a greater sense of community in them all. By sharing their experiences. By focusing on the present. And the future.

Maggie appeared in the doorway, pulling a winter cap from her head and shaking out her gray hair. "Getting mighty blustery out there, people."

"You slip and fall in the street?" Vick asked in that deep voice of his.

"Almost did in a few places. But I wasn't worried. I had Kevin. Give him practice, if I did."

A young man followed her into the conference room, smiling cheerfully while slipping out of his winter coat. Two weeks after Gus poured the Captain back into the Atlantic, he'd heard that Maggie had taken on a student. Which was a good thing. As the only resident doctor, her medical knowledge, skills, and experience were priceless in this new world. This knowledge had to be preserved, bottled, and passed on to future generations, for the betterment of their community. Kevin was average height, in his thirties, and originally from Boston. He'd moved up to Nova Scotia when he was in his twenties, chasing a woman whom he eventually married. His wife hadn't survived the apocalypse, which was a common story. He was friendly enough, certainly smart enough, and willing to learn the medical arts.

"Still waiting for Sheila's broom to show up," Kevin said, shaking out his dark head of hair.

"Sheila's brush," Buckle corrected.

"Broom, brush, towel," he said. "Whatever."

"Last storm of the season," Vick said. "That could be today."

"It'll be like any other spring," Kevin said. "Snow right up until the last minute, and then boom. Spring. Before you know it, it'll be heat like it was spraying out of a firehose. Where's the coffee?"

He spotted the table with the snacks and coffee jars. The coffee was instant, the cookies simple sugar and flour.

"We starting this thing?" Vick asked, looking toward the woman who'd called the meeting to order.

Colleen Jones, otherwise known as Collie, stood at ease, her hands behind her back. She'd positioned herself at the front of the semi-circle, in full view of everyone. Black, thorny vines coiled up her right profile and encircled her eye. The special forces operator indicated they'd wait a moment longer until Maggie and Kevin had a chance to settle down.

"They're not that important," Bruno said with a sly smile. "Go on. Kevin won't mind at all."

Kevin was too busy pouring himself a coffee to bother with the town's scavenger.

Collie scratched the back of her head. Her brown hair remained short, so everything was on fearsome display. She'd picked up some new scars since the battle of Whitecap, grooves that decorated her cheeks and drew the eye away from the missing tip of her nose. Other marks weren't so noticeable, but still very deep. She still missed Wallace, her husband laid to rest four months earlier. She admitted that much to Gus when their conversations would tug loose a memory and the memory would become words. At those times, Gus would listen, be an understanding ear, and offer words he hoped sounded comforting.

For all of Collie's ferocity, Wallace's passing had broken a part of her.

All Gus could do was stay close and try to be a friend.

All while hiding his own growing feelings for her.

"They're not that important, huh?" Collie directed at Bruno. "Think that's wise? To talk shit about them while they're in the same room? Even though you shovel out Maggie's walkway every morning?"

Bruno lowered his head.

"Thought so," Collie finished before silence stilled the room. She surveyed the group before her. "Thank you all for braving the elements and coming here today. Very much appreciated. I know there's no designated leader here, but a word from Amy, Vick, and Buckle seem to go a long way. So, with their permission, I thought it best to address you all for your thoughts and opinions about the spring. When we can reconnect with the mainland—*if* we can reconnect."

"That's not a problem," Buckle said. "We got sail power. And if we lose the sailboats, we can always row. If we have to."

"*You* can row over there," declared a woman named Shelly, a natural islander who once owned a convenience store on Tancook. "I'll stay right here, thank you very much."

No one challenged her. There were more than a few people who had no desire to leave the island. Tancook was safe, where no Moe, deadhead, or road crazy could reach. Not unless the crazies had a boat, and the means to power it. It was only two months ago when the islanders' own engines refused to turn over, signaling the last of the gasoline.

Collie waited a few seconds before continuing. "I've already mentioned this to some of you while on the mend here. Now, you know I'm military. One look and you can tell I've been in a few rock fights. After Whitecap, my partner and I were working recon with the community of Pine Cove, just before the townsfolk there were forcibly abducted."

She didn't mention Shovel specifically, and for that, Gus was grateful.

"Besides playing the role of guardian angel for the town, we were charged with finding survivors and bringing them back to Pine Cove. For several reasons. One, there's strength in numbers. Two, labor. We needed people to get shit done. Working the farms, managing livestock, fishing, harvesting, cutting wood. All the basic jobs to rebuild. The more people we have as resources, the easier life is for all of us. Three, we needed trained professionals. People to maintain and expand our skill base. Maggie's the best example of this. There aren't many doctors left alive these days, and I bet Maggie is one of the last. We can't just head into a medical school and look shit up if we need to."

Gus raised his hand. "I've done that."

"You've done that," Collie agreed. "You most certainly have. But you don't have to do that anymore. Maggie's with us now, and Kevin, God bless him, has volunteered to become her first official intern. But that's just the beginning. We need more skilled professionals. Not only to make use of their abilities, but to have them educate and train others so those skills aren't lost. Any functioning community knows that its greatest resource is her people. That's especially true for us. That was true for Pine Cove. Just one survivor can be a potential gold mine for knowledge, skills, and labor. And genes, I might add."

Amy cleared her throat. "We've been working towards that, but since we've come to the island here, our main concern has been food production. We've been sending Bruno out to scout for supplies and initiate contact with other communities."

"Just Bruno, right?"

"Well, yes, because there's just not enough of us to go around."

"Which is exactly why we need to increase efforts in finding and recruiting others. How is food production right now?"

"We're doing fine," Amy said. "We're on an island, so fishing isn't a problem. There already were some local gardens so we expanded upon those where we could. We've also built greenhouses and made use of root cellars for storage."

"How come you didn't try and recruit me to help you out?" Gus asked Bruno. "Back when I first met you?"

"I was warming up to it," the man admitted. "But you were on a mission. Looking for Maggie and the kids. I wasn't about to get in the way of that. I had this place to think about. At the time, I didn't know she was a doctor. All I knew was that you were going into some hard country. And probably meeting up with even harder company."

The hardest, Gus thought, but he kept that to himself.

"All I'm saying," Collie interrupted, "is sooner or later, we'll have to return to the mainland to recruit more survivors. We screen them and, if they're willing, bring them back. At the very least, we'll need to make contact with other communities and access their skill base if they have one. In turn, they can access ours. But, before we do this, we're going to need an enforcement arm, something to ensure we can handle ourselves during a potential threat. Buckle, you were a cop, and Vick, you and Amy have had some combat training. That's a great basis for a local militia."

This last bit was met with a resounding silence.

"You mean you want us to learn how to fight?" Shelly asked, leaning forward as if smelling a cracked septic line.

"No. Not all of you. But some. Eventually. To protect the rest. Here's what I propose. I volunteer to go back out there. In the spring. To continue what Bruno was doing. He can come along, too, if he wants. Anyone who's up for some exploring can come with me. We find other communities, make contact, determine if we're likeminded, and go from there. With an eye on bringing them back here."

"What if they don't want to come back?" Gus asked quietly.

"That's fine. We leave them alone. If they've already established a community, then perhaps we can discuss pooling resources. Open up lines of trade and services. Chances are, the smart ones will realize we're all on the same banana boat here. They'll be doing the very same thing."

"What about the not so smart?" Gus asked.

"And the much more violent?" Buckle added.

"That all falls under screening," Collie replied. "You leave that to me."

No one spoke for moments, allowing the wind and snow to batter the windows.

"We'd be safer to stay here," said Thomas, a cashier from Cape Breton who had recently become a farmer on the island.

"And watch our kids grow up," added Olivia, who was once a tour bus guide in Halifax, but was currently monitoring the island's root cellars and their stored provisions.

"Which will take years," Collie stated with a nod. "That alone will require a huge amount of time and energy. And while I'm sure they'll grow up fine, what about the generation after that? What about education? Sure, we can read a book, but we have to find that book first, absorb the material, and then try and apply it through trial and error. Much easier to have a skilled person on hand. We need new blood. Case in point, does anyone know how to replace brake pads?"

No reply.

Collie let all that sink in before continuing. "Think about it. We still have a month or so before spring. Then we'll need to get ashore to do any of this. And we still haven't considered the problem of transportation, seeing as our gasoline is finally flatlining."

"Ethanol," Buckle said. "We grow it then burn it."

"You know how to do that?"

"We've been working on it," Amy said. "And been successful, to a point. There's a problem, however."

"Let me guess," Collie said. "You have to produce a crop first."

"Well, yes. Food comes first. That'll take up most of the farmland available. Until we reach a population where we have to transfer production back to the mainland. Until then, however, for safety's sake, we stay here. And here we have to designate a portion of farmland for ethanol production, which is small. But there's another issue."

"The fuel itself?"

"Yes. Exactly."

"What's exactly?" Gus asked, his head starting to ache from the discussion.

"Ethanol burns faster than regular gas," Amy explained. "And we don't have access to the additives needed to stabilize or preserve it, which means…" She shrugged.

"What?" Gus asked. "Which means what?"

"We can't store it," Scott answered. "And we can't make it last. So we grow it, make it, and burn it, before it goes dead on us."

"Well," Gus said. "That's a pain in the ass."

"Major pain in the ass," Amy agreed. "We're on an island. We only have so much farmland to go around. We can't spare a lot just for ethanol production. But that's life in the new world. One big pain in the ass. All that and no pizza."

"I can make pizza," said Art, a short order cook from New Brunswick. "No trouble. Shoot me a moose or a deer and you'll have sausage on that thing, too."

"See?" Collie declared. "We're rolling already. Goddamn, I feel motivated."

"Wait-a-minute," Gus said, holding up a hand and squeezing his eyes shut. "We can't store the ethanol?"

"No," Amy answered. "Not for any great length of time. We use it or we don't. Anything we store will lose its buzz over the winter months."

"So how long to make it?"

"We have to grow the corn first."

"All right, how long until we can put it into a gas tank?"

"Months," Scott answered. He got affirming nods from those few in the know.

"Which means," Collie said, "we're without fuel for the first few months of spring and summer. So we already have mobility challenges. We have a limited timeframe and limited range, since we're probably the only ones around producing fuel. But there is a way around that. If we run out of gas, so to speak."

"You gonna have us all ride horses?" Vick asked.

"Not me. That's an option, though. And I think we all remember how to ride a bike."

"A bike?" Gus asked. "A pedal bike?"

"Mountain bike, if we got enough of them."

"Jesus, Collie. My ass is sore just thinking about that."

The operator smiled. "I know. We'll all be avoiding potholes, but it'll be worse for the guys. Long times in the saddle will adversely affect your sperm count."

Another round of silence, broken by Amy. "Can't have the boys firing blanks."

Scott frowned, pulled his son in close and quickly covered his ears.

"Anyway," Collie said. "That's all I have to say on that. Think about it before the snow's gone, and we'll go from there. There's one more thing, however, that gets top priority."

The population of Big Tancook shifted in their seats.

"The matter of security. Weapons. Any munitions people among us? Besides me and the cop?"

Her question was met with blank stares.

Collie exhaled. "Thought so. Figured I'd ask. All right. Given I can't go anywhere until the spring anyway, by which I mean the summer, since it'll take that long to grow enough to fill a tank or two—"

"Try the fall," Amy said.

"The fall?"

"Yep."

"Really?"

Amy nodded *really*.

"Well, shit. That sucks donkey cock," Collie muttered, ignoring the few dirty looks from the group. Scott's frown returned, his hands still covering little Scottie's ears.

Gus hid his smile. Collie had gotten that one from him.

"Okay," Collie said with a resigned shrug. "Can't control that, so I'll roll with it. But put me down for a few tanks and consider that an advance order. I'll need transportation for the other matter on my mind, which is returning to Whitecap. And securing the munitions there. All I need is enough fuel to get there and back. Whitecap's a top priority. We have two reasons to return there. One, we have a limited supply of ammunition, and no means of producing more. Whitecap has a sizeable stockpile of munitions, I mean goddamn sizeable. I need to get back to Whitecap, secure it, and, if I can, lug out every crate I can find."

That silenced the crowd.

"Can't you just leave them there?" Bruno eventually asked. "I mean, I've never been, but isn't that place way up in the boonies?"

"It is," Collie confirmed. "In a fucking jungle hellscape. The goddamn mosquitoes alone will stab for the jugular and then play in the spray like kids around a broken fire hydrant. In any case, I have to go back there. *We* have to go back there. A pack of crazies found Whitecap once, and I'm not willing to chance anyone else finding it. Someone *will*, eventually, and there's enough firepower there to outfit an army. Let that sink in for a few seconds. If we don't secure that stockpile, we run the risk of someone else securing it, and ultimately using it for their own ends. You know what it's like out there as well as I do. I sure as fuck don't want to go up against a pack of savages with military-grade weaponry and a mountain of ammunition to go with it. God forbid it's found by someone who's trained to use that shit. Or worse, has *experience* using it. That's a potential ass-reaming I shudder to even think about."

Gus winced.

"That's it, folks," she added. "Truthfully, we could spend the spring searching for other survivors, but I strongly advise returning to Whitecap first and securing the weapons and ammunitions there. We'll need them. And we can't risk *not* having them. You think on that one. Everyone good?"

No one answered.

Scott smiled weakly. "This where we say *hoo-ah?*"

"Marines say *hoo-ah,*" Collie said curtly while sizing up the crowd. "We say *fuck yeah, sir.* And we say that through clenched teeth."

Gus looked around to see if anyone was about to repeat those words.

No one did.

2

A proper burial is precious, Wallace's voice whispered in Gus's head.

Gus stood over the last of the graves and nodded in grim understanding. A proper burial was indeed precious in these times, and he wondered if he would be given that final courtesy. Aware of the time, he drove the shovel down into the moist earth and left it there, next to a makeshift cross. The grave was large, one of three, and contained the remains of Adam and the other farm folks, all of whom were killed by Shovel's pack of marauders. In one way, Adam had perhaps saved Gus from the same fate, by insisting he go off and search for the missing Talbert and his merry band of assholes. At least Gus had considered them assholes at the time. Talbert especially. After escaping Mortimer's mansion of horrors, however, Talbert turned out to be all right.

"Thanks, buddy," Gus whispered at Adam's shared grave. "For everything. Hope you're... at peace."

"What was that?" Scott asked a few paces away. Like them all, Scott had lost a lot of weight, and his tall frame had become a lanky, scarecrow thing. His blonde hair had thinned a little on the top, but his beard was full and thick.

"Nothin'," Gus said. "Just saying a few words for them, is all."

"Wanna be left alone?"

"No."

Scott glanced around at the other marked graves before studying the nearby corn fields. "This is all good. We'll have to come back here some time."

"For what?"

"Make use of those fields. This is the Valley, after all. Best ground in the province, from what I hear."

Gus cringed. "We buried people here."

"Buried them *here*," Scott said, gesturing at the fresh graves. "Didn't bury them over there."

"You probably pick blueberries in graveyards, too."

"Nothing wrong with picking blueberries in a graveyard."

"I sure as fuck wouldn't pick berries in a graveyard."

"Why?" Scott asked. "You superstitious or something?"

"Yeah, maybe a little. But then there's that thing about picking food growing from the same earth where dead people are. Right underfoot. Decomposing."

"Dead folks would want us to pick them. Be a waste, otherwise. And hey, dead people are all over. I bet if you dig down deep enough anywhere you have a fifty-fifty chance of finding dead people."

Gus stared at Scott, blinked, and cleared his throat. He shook his head as if coming out of a daze. "Yeah. Right. Good talk."

Scott held the silence for a moment, then said, "You sure you don't want to be left alone?"

"No. I'm good. Shoulders are achin' though."

"We did a lot of digging."

"Yeah, we did." Gus smiled.

Scott winced at the spotty display.

"What?"

"We need a dentist," Scott replied. "*You* need a dentist. Get you a plate. Or some chopped off piano keys. Something."

"I'm good," Gus said. "Feel good, too. About all this."

"You were saying."

"Glad we did it. Closure, y'know?"

Scott nodded that he did indeed know.

The air smelled of autumn, pleasant and mind clearing. Sweat glazed Gus's face and soaked his warm clothing, and he'd dropped his jacket nearby. His left heel, where the bullet had separated the meat pad from his sole, buzzed with pins and needles, as if he were standing on a live wire connected to a dying battery. Just after the battle of Whitecap, as the dust had settled and the dead were being gathered, Maggie had done what she could with what she had, and that wasn't much. In Shovel's makeshift clinic, she'd administered some disinfectant, given him outdated antibiotics, covered the wound with bandages and a tube sock, before finally duct-taping the whole thing together. It was a temporary dressing until she could properly work on it. In her professional opinion, however, she admitted she didn't know if it would heal or become infected. However, after they'd reached the island, both were pleasantly surprised to see the wound on the mend.

The nerves, however, didn't take so well, but Gus didn't blame Maggie for that. That was all on his ass. So he learned to live with the uncomfortable tingling in his foot. Some days were worse than others, but he had learned that being on his feet for longer than ten minutes would be enough for that buzzing in his boot to really take hold. An annoying sensation that cupped his heel and gradually crawled up to his ankle, until every step felt like stomping on hot needles.

The charred remains of the house distracted him then, and a knot of sadness hurt his throat. Once upon a time, a lot of good people had bunked down in that mound of scorched rubble. Memories of happier days then, of the two dozen survivors who lived and labored on the farm. Adam had begun plans to start gathering materials for extra cabins, so that some of the couples could have their own places.

Memories. The smell of freshly toiled soil brought Gus back to the present. There wasn't much left to the bodies he'd just finished returning to the earth. Mostly bones, really, but they dug the graves anyway, to an acceptable depth, and filled them with whatever remains they'd found.

"Yeah," Gus said and inspected the overturned earth one final time. "This is good. Thanks for coming along."

"Glad I did," Scott said. "It would've been bothering me, too."

Gus picked up his jacket and gave it a shake. "Let's get out of here."

Scott waited for him to go first.

"We'll be back, Adam," Gus promised the little graveyard. "Anita. Barney. Lisa. And the rest of you jokers. You… fine, fine jokers. We'll be back. We'll get this place back up and running. Get someone working those fields again. Away from here," he said, with a warning eye at Scott. "But close enough that you can see what's going on. It won't go to waste. Not if I have anything to do with it. I guarantee you."

Having said his peace, Gus returned to the three waiting pickups, his heel thrumming with that annoying electrical current. Dirt and dust stained the black exteriors. The rigs were large, with crew cabs, and two of them had their rear seats jammed full of supplies. The cargo beds were packed tight and covered. Collie sat in the driver's seat of one of the vehicles. One hand rested on the steering wheel while her left arm hung out the window. She wore coyote-brown army fatigues and a pair of cheap sunglasses. A rolled-up balaclava (really a ski mask but try telling a secret squirrel that) covered the top of her head.

Bruno stood next to her window, his hands inside the pockets of a long winter duster. A pirate's long stocking cap covered his head, with the end wrapped around his neck before disappearing over his shoulder. A wide pair of sunglasses hid his eyes while a trimmed tumbleweed of a beard graced his chin. Gus expected Bruno to say "*Arrrr*" at any time. He even tried it on him to see if it would take.

It didn't.

There was a third man nearby. Cory Shale from Cape Breton. Tall as Scott, just as bearded, but darker. He was dressed for a cold autumn, with a pillowy black jacket, blue jeans, and biker boots. In the old world, Cory was, of all things, a baker of pastries, and Gus secretly thought of him as Scott two-point-oh. He was still waiting for the two men to settle down and start swapping recipes.

Collie sat up as Gus approached the truck.

"All done," he told her.

"Good," she said. "Didn't take too long at all."

"Not with all of you. Thanks again."

"Well," she said, "that's that. Glad it's done. Now, back to the task at hand. We got about four hours of daylight left. I say we hit the road and see if we can't find a motel or something or other. Some place to hole up for the night. I don't want to camp outside for a second night in a row. Not with all of those perfectly good beds out there. Sound good?"

"Sounds good," Gus said.

"I thought the truck seats were fine," Cory said. "I mean, we had the sleeping bags and all, and when you lower the seats—"

"You still weren't fully horizontal," Collie said.

"We could've brought the motor home."

"The old girl would burn through our corn too damn fast."

Gus smirked. Corn was the pet name for the ethanol presently sloshing about in their gas tanks. And Collie was right. The crude, additive-free ethanol got shitty mileage, and the motor home was a four-ton hog with a square ass. The pickup trucks were much better for their mission, and the vehicles currently had their box beds loaded down with fuel, food, and other supplies.

"Besides," Collie continued, "we get to Whitecap, and we won't need her at all. You'll see."

"What is this surprise you keep reminding us about?" Scott asked.

"Reserved tanks of gas? Hidden or something? Or an electric car?"

Collie drew two fingers across her lips, zipping them up and tossing the imaginary key away.

"You're off the island now. I think it's time for the great reveal."

"Mmm," she said and shook her head. "It's a surprise."

"Thought you were doing that just to tease Amy and Buckle," Gus said, as curious as the next person.

"And Vick," Scott added.

"And Vick," Gus allowed. "We're here. Just us. The chosen few. It's okay to let us in on this little secret of yours."

"I know it's okay," Collie scoffed. "But I'm not gonna, all right? So stop with the nagging. You kids. Christ almighty."

"What happens if you get shot out there?" Cory pointed out. "And, like, we're left alive, and this surprise of yours is something really important to get into Whitecap?"

"Honestly?" Collie asked. "If I get shot…and croak… then you're fucked. Fucked, Cory. You're fucked. You're all fucked. But I do have good news for you. I don't intend on getting shot. Or croaking. Ergo, you shall remain un-fucked. Getting shot is not part of the plan. Dying is not part of the plan. Not for me or you. Just be aware there's a surprise waiting for us at the end of this rainbow and, by my recollection, if it's still there, all your pink parts will be pleasantly tugged upon and tickled. If you fancy a tugging, that is. And a tickling. So saddle up, boys. We got a long way to go. But I can guarantee you…if we find it—if it's there, you'll all be happy."

With that, Collie powered up the truck.

"This is it," Scott said to Gus and waited a few beats to let that sink in. Then, "I tell you, man, I wish—"

"You were coming with us?" Gus interrupted.

That took Scott back a bit. "What? No. Fuck no. I ain't going back out there. I mean… I have Amy now, and the little one. And another one on the way. I mean, it's not even up to me, anyway. Amy would have my balls if I even mentioned going along with you. I just came up here to lend a hand with the, all the, you know. So, no. I'm heading home after this. Sorry. What I was going to say is… I wish you didn't have to go out there."

Gus smiled and nodded. He'd meant the question as a joke anyway. It would've surprised him if Scott had said he was coming along. Like the man said, he had a family now.

And their little expedition here was taking them back into the wild.

"To tell you the truth, I feel a little nervous just being here," Scott admitted. "Even with you around, Collie."

Gus winced. "He didn't mean that, babe."

Collie aimed a gun finger at him. "Stop calling me 'babe'."

Scott wavered, saw that Collie wasn't going to say anything to him, and regarded them both. "Listen, I'm… we're all thankful that you guys are doing this."

Collie smiled and revved the engine. "Gotta go. This monster gets cranky once you start her up."

Scott reached out and gripped Gus's hand in a firm shake. "No man-hug, not today."

"Too much of that going around anyway," Gus said.

"There is. Or there was. Anyway, I'll save it for when you get back."

"Wahoo. Something to look forward to. Seeya in a week and a bit."

"A week and a bit." Scott nodded and stepped back from the idling machine. Gus passed around the front of the vehicle and climbed aboard. Once settled in, Collie turned to Scott.

"Get on home, now, y'hear?" she said. "A'fore I tan your ass. Make it all rosy and shit."

Scott gave her a weak smile, then raised his hand in farewell.

Collie put the truck in gear. Cory and Bruno followed the lead rig in their own truck, and the pair of vehicles rumbled out onto the highway.

When they were gone from sight, Scott turned for his own truck.

With thoughts of returning home to Amy and his son.

3

They cruised along the 102.

By noon, the rooftops of distant Truro crept into view. They drove by the town exits, heading for what would eventually become the 104 of the TransCanada. A concrete wall divided the highway along that stretch, and plenty of vehicles had, for whatever reason, bashed themselves against it on both sides, creating a briar patch of wrecked metal and rubber.

Gus grew noticeably quiet as they threaded their way through the corroding mess.

"Remembering things, are you?" Collie asked.

He nodded.

Ahead was the overpass.

"I can drive around," she offered.

"I'm okay."

But Collie drove around anyway, taking an off-ramp that snaked around the dreaded overpass. Sunlight glinted off the guardrails reinforced by wood and sheets of metal. Gun ports dotted their length, but no one took a shot at them. Comeau and his little pack of bandits were long dead, killed by Collie herself.

Gus leaned back when he realized where she was going.

"Sorry, babe," she said and meant it. "My mistake. I can avoid the overpass… but there's no other way to the 104."

"S'okay," Gus said, but his stomach clenched all the same.

Yellow grassland grew tall and stiff. Stamped across this wild field was a crossroads of pavement. A single set of traffic lights dangled above that treasure map 'X'. The tow truck was still there, dead and rusting and looking somewhat ashamed for being a part of recent history. A piece of cut rope hung from its boom, and the tire rim that once secured Gus's feet lay directly underneath.

Don't you worry, Gus projected at the truck. *Wasn't your fault.*

And it wasn't. Comeau's killers had strung him up there like a scrawny piñata and left him hanging. The bandit's overpass was some three or four hundred meters out. The sight of the fortified archway brought back a flood of memories, and none of them good. He'd been shot off the road and held captive, been questioned and smashed repeatedly. Then he'd been left outside in the cold, overnight, with just his soiled drawers on. That had been the longest, the coldest, and perhaps the most wretched time of his entire life.

Gus only spared it a glance before looking back to the tow truck.

There, standing at the corner of the vehicle, was a dark figure. It propped an arm on the hood, as if casually having a smoke. A dusty visor concealed most of the figure's face, but there was no mistaking that grimace of green-black teeth.

Before Gus could get a better look, Collie sped up and left that infernal place far behind.

Gus leaned forward, checking his side mirror, but the ghost was gone.

"See something?" she asked.

He settled back into the seat and stared ahead. "No."

Later that afternoon, the little motorcade rolled into a small town called Bassville. Dried brush and yellowed leaves scuttled across the pavement, driven by a crisp breeze. No one walked the sidewalks. A few cars clogged the street or were stopped on the shoulders, but nothing hindered the approaching trucks. The pickups rumbled through the deserted town, taking their time to get through the meager sights. Lawns had grown to savannah heights. Leaves gathered in ditches in thick, fiery curls. A large service station came into view, with its three bay doors closed. A chain fence surrounded one official-looking building that had its windows smashed out and the door left hanging from the frame. One house rose up behind a hay field of a front lawn, a car parked just to the right of a crumbling walkway. A small wall of mailboxes drifted by, several of their doors opened as if releasing birds.

Then came the bones.

Sprawled in open doorways as if they'd been cut down while escaping a pursuing horror.

"Well shit," Gus muttered, spotting a full skeleton.

"What?" Collie asked and applied the brakes.

"Over there."

"Those bones, you mean?"

"Yeah."

"Just bones. Gonna see them. Sooner or later. Little places like this shouldn't be too bad, but the bigger cities? Puh. Streets'll be clogged."

"Yeah," Gus agreed, turning his gaze to his lap.

"What? You gonna puke or something?"

"'Course not."

"Bones I can handle. Puking in the truck, not so much."

"Not gonna puke. I'm good."

"Well, all right then. Just let me know if you see any bullet holes."

He filed that request away.

The pickups moved onward, steering around the few abandoned vehicles. Twigs and branches crackled and crunched as the tires rolled over them. Potholes dotted the road, and several times Collie had no choice but to drive over them, prompting Gus to brace for impact. Ahead, an intersection appeared to have sustained substantial rocket fire, leaving shallow trenches. Chunks of pavement littered the area, all drizzled with dirt and dust. A manhole was uncovered, its iron lid tossed some ten feet aside and resting upon the sidewalk. A signpost had its top blown off, the message nowhere in sight.

"Jesus," Collie muttered, slowing to a stop.

"The fuck happened here?" Gus asked.

"I'd say something that got out of hand real quick."

Gus spied the ragged end of what appeared to be a subterranean pipe. "Maybe a gas line. Got ruptured."

"Maybe."

"Go that way," he directed, pointing to the right, where a post office stood on one corner and a hardware store just across the way.

"The things you see when you get off the main road and travel through the smaller communities," Collie said. "Hillbilly urban warfare."

"This pavement is shit."

"It is indeed," she said while checking her side mirror. The truck bounced through a significant crater, thumped over a sidewalk, and plowed through the tall grass before passing by the post office. They linked up with the street with a thump and a lurch as the truck dropped onto pavement again.

"Jesus," Gus gasped as he straightened. "Almost bit my tongue off there."

"And I was going slow," Collie said. "Cheap-ass pavement, man."

Bright lettering displaying the word 'MOLLY' came into view, the last 'Y' hanging at a precarious angle. Below that, the opaque glass of the storefront looked to be completely intact. Grass and weeds split the parking lot in places, but the asphalt wasn't nearly as pitted as the main roads. Shopping carts lay dumped on their sides all over the place—everywhere except the two empty corrals at either end of the parking lot. A few carts were sprawled over the wild lawns as if lifted and chucked.

Gus sighed. "People."

"What about them?"

"Two perfectly good places to park your carts, and they still can't be bothered. Fuckin' toss them wherever."

"Oh yeah," Collie said, getting up to speed. "Some people's children."

Gus squinted at the lot, hard enough to expose his missing teeth. "Town looks dead to me."

"Real dead."

"Might be some specials on at *Mollymart* there."

"*Mollymart?*"

"*Mollymart East.* Supermarket chain."

"Any good?" Collie asked.

Gus didn't answer.

"You wanna take a look?" she asked.

He shook his head.

Collie drove a little further before hitting the brakes. She killed the engine and gripped the steering wheel. Leaves skittered across their path, and overgrown lawns rustled.

"Bassville," Gus said in a tired voice.

"Been here before?"

"No. Never."

The truck behind them pulled alongside, and the passenger window lowered. Bruno, his pirate's cap still in place, leaned forward. "What's the plan?" he asked, wrinkling his nose with the question.

She pointed ahead. "I'm thinking we camp out over in that motel."

Just up the road past a jewelry store, a pizza place called *Larry's,* and a few decrepit houses, was the sprawling bulk of a motel. The building was almost camouflaged in a storm's aftermath of orange and yellow leaves. A sign at the mouth of the parking lot said, 'MERCER'S MOTEL', with the faded cartoon faces of a sleepy but grateful couple.

"You want to camp out there?" Gus asked.

"Thinkin' about it," she said. "Gonna be dark in an hour or so. I advise against traveling at night. Unless you know a better place."

"Nope."

"You good, Bruno?"

"All good here."

From the driver's side, Cory gave a thumbs up.

"All right then," she said. "It's decided. Goddamn, I love democracy."

She started up the truck and proceeded towards the motel. Gus eyed the tall grass along the sides of the road, feeling his paranoia increase as the machine crept along. Too many monsters had come out lurching and flailing at him from hiding places like that. He checked his side mirror and saw Bruno and Cory following.

"We used to do this all the time," Collie said while scanning the road. "All the time. Me and Wallace. When we landed in Pine Cove."

"Pine Cove?"

"Yeah, Pine Cove. You know. Phase two: Find new and exciting people and maybe bring them back to the settlement. It was like gathering a tribe, y'know? And every person we brought in, well, you just never knew what you were getting. Sorta like *Forrest Gump* and that line about the chocolates."

Gus nodded, keeping his eyes on the motel entrance.

"You know how we did it?" Collie asked.

"Find folks? How?"

"Well, you were different, obviously—you screaming your nuts off and all. Usually we had a map. Tried to be systematic. Methodical. Crossed off the towns we went through. Took our time, y'know? Stayed quiet, until we decided it was time to make some noise."

She turned onto the motel's parking lot, which resembled a patchwork of cracks threatening to collapse into a pretty big sinkhole. The surface held, however, much to Gus's relief. Two other cars were on the lot, their paint peeling in places but otherwise fine.

Collie parked the vehicle so that it faced the main road.

"You let people know you were there?" Gus asked.

"Yep."

"Seems to go against… everything I was doing."

"You weren't looking for people, honey. We were. And y'know the best way to find them? Bring them to you. With this."

She indicated the truck's horn.

That mortified Gus. "You're jokin'."

"I am not."

"You'd bring *everyone* if you did that."

"Only if they were around."

"I mean the good and the bad."

"Yup."

"The killers and the insane."

"Well," Collie allowed, "that's where it got tricky. But we managed. We only did it during daylight, usually in the morning, and we were gone an hour before nightfall. If people heard the horn, they'd investigate. And a lot of people answered the horn. Surprisingly. At least, I was surprised. They would wander over to the truck and we'd meet in a truce, and then we'd get talking. That was the first part of the interview."

"You ever get into trouble?"

Collie nodded. "Oh fuck yeah. The horn brought out the dead as well. Sometimes just one or two, sometimes more. They were easy to deal with, though, in comparison to the living dipshits. Bumblefucks gone total scavenger. And if something did go down, whichever one of us was watching would make themselves known. Make no mistake. We'd play nice until we weren't nice. Then we'd start shooting ass and tagging toes. Anyway. Those were the old days. These are the new."

She looked over at him and smiled gently. "Feel like a walk?"

"Where? In there?" Gus pointed.

"Gotta sweep the area. Make sure it's all okay."

He stared at the motel.

"C'mon," Collie said and patted her thigh, indicating the Sig Saur holstered there. "You got that Glock, right?"

"Yeah."

"Nervous?"

"Well…" Gus nodded. "It's been a while. And…" he held up his right hand, showing off the stumps of his missing fingers.

"Yeah, but you've been practicing. Two hands. Like I showed you."

"Yeah."

"Let's go then. Jump into the ring, buddy. Tag team. Time to work that ninja."

"Never was a ninja. My ass was too fat. And then there was that thing about being loaded drunk twenty-four seven."

"Fat ninja." Collie thought about it. "That could be a book. Well, anyway, you ain't fat now. You're lean. Sure as hell no FNG. And certainly no dogfucker. Not in my book."

That got Gus's attention. "FNG?"

"Fuckin' New Guy."

"Oh. And dogfucker?"

"That's a person who lets their buddies do all the work."

"I see." Gus's eyes widened as he absorbed that one. He studied the motel. Wasn't like it was a house or anything, although there were a few houses around, far back from the road and partially obscured by trees.

"All right. Sure. Let's go."

Collie smiled. "Atta boy. Proud of you. You're all cock."

An uncertain Gus pinched the bridge of his nose.

She lowered her voice. "Look, Gus, chances are there's nothing in the motel. No Moes. No meatbags."

"Let's go," he repeated and opened his door. "You gonna take the rifle?"

She patted her pistol. "I'll use this. My left arm's been fucked up ever since I took that bullet. It'll never be the same. So fuck it."

"Fuck it," Gus repeated.

"I like how you think."

They got out of the truck. Collie held her sidearm with both hands. Gus patted his own pistol grip, ready to draw if needed.

Bruno and Cory pulled up alongside and killed their engine.

"Hold tight here," Gus told them. "We're going to check things out."

Collie was already at the main office door. The motel was a thick, formidable structure, built of logs and shaped like an 'L'. There were perhaps twenty units total. Twenty surprise boxes just waiting to be popped open. The windows were mostly intact, with dark curtains drawn. Each unit had individual parking spaces, though the painted lines badly needed a fresh coat. Four vending machines stood outside the main office door, their colorful glass fronts smashed, gutted innards spilling out.

Collie eased up to the office window and studied the interior. Gus marveled at how carefully she opened the door and slipped inside, how graceful she moved when she was in stealth mode. She popped in and out of view as she searched the room. Gus checked on the other units, keeping a wary eye on the windows. He glanced across the street, hearing nothing. The houses were back there as well, with cars parked in their driveways.

"Hey," Collie said.

Gus turned as she held out a set of keys.

"Start unlocking," she said. "I'll go to the other end here."

She strode across the parking lot, minding the windows as she zeroed in on the farthest unit. Gus checked the keys in his hand. Unit number one was only a dozen steps away. As he headed to the door, he glanced back at the other truck and saw Bruno and Cory in the front seat, watching him.

"Yeah," Gus whispered with a note of resignation. He hesitated in front of the unit door, well aware that he was dragging his ass in front of the two men in the truck. He wiped his brow with a handkerchief and pulled the Glock free with his disfigured hand, nearly dropping the weapon. That little slip cost him the keys, which tinkled to the ground. He bent over and snatched them up, heat flushing his cheeks. Swearing at himself to get his ass in gear, he reached for the knob and unintentionally pushed the door open.

That caused him to duck and jerk back from the doorway.

Nothing jumped free of the opening.

"Fuck me," Gus muttered, seeing how far he'd retreated. "It's only been five fucking months. Six at best. I mean, goddammit."

He checked on Collie and saw her at the far end of the parking lot. He didn't dare look back at the guys. Gathering his nerves, Gus crept up on the open doorway. He entered the room, walking face-first into air reeking of mold and dust. The smell stopped him cold.

"Gross," Gus whispered, smacking his lips at the foul taste. He took aim at the darker parts of the motel unit. White walls, a box radiator underneath the main window. He pulled back the curtains and saw the sill frizzled with dust. Gus turned his attention on the unlit cave of the bathroom. The light switch didn't work, and he flicked it a dozen times before leaving it. He peeked into the bathroom, scanned the dark, oily shine of porcelain. Wash basin. Bare soap dish. Clean towels on hooks. An empty roll of two-ply on a dispenser near the toilet. A white shower curtain, half-torn off the rod, black, its base mottled with mold. In the sparse light, it looked like someone had wiped their ass on it.

Gus studied the main room again. He considered the television, the pair of chairs tucked under a table, and the little Bible on top of that. A set of glasses rested beside the book, along with a hunting magazine and an empty bottle of vodka. The bottle didn't interest him in the least. Back in the day, when he was shitfaced and stumbling around Annapolis, vodka wasn't his preferred sip of nerves and armor. Oh, he'd drink it, guaranteed. He'd guzzle that nastiness a third of the way down before stopping for air, but it was the last on his list, way below the other, better stuff.

Red carpet covered the floor. A little pill bottle lay underneath the table, barely noticeable from where he stood. Damned thing looked like a shotgun shell at a glance. He was just about to pick it up (and maybe the magazine) when he noticed fingertips sticking out from underneath the bed.

Four withered fingers, the skin gray and loathsome in the meager light.

The sight stopped him faster than a plank to the face.

He stood there, blinking at those wasted digits, aware of his racing heart. The tip of the thumb was there, too, just visible. Someone was under the bed. Someone had come into the motel room, crawled underneath to escape the monsters, and that's where they'd stayed. That's where they stayed until—and this wasn't a long stretch of the imagination—the vodka helped that poor bastard onboard the sleeping pill expressway all the way home. And that was that. It wasn't the first tomb Gus had violated, but it certainly was the most recent, and seeing those fingers splayed out against the carpet disturbed him. He'd almost missed the corpse completely, and if he *had* missed it, he thought he might've just sat down upon that bed in one great big squawk of springs. Heedless of the body underneath.

If it was indeed a body.

'Course it's a body, his mind scolded. *Y'fuckin' idiot. So get down there and check it out.*

His bad foot was starting to buzz, as if imprisoned in a boot-sized iron maiden, and the needles inside were hooked up to a generator. The light from the open doorway touched the tips of the fingers, and that just made the whole picture worse somehow. He wasn't about to get down there and check things out. Fuck that noise. That was when things grabbed dipshits about the face and held on, held on until blood flowed. That wasn't going to happen, obviously, not in Gus's mind, but he wasn't going to tempt fate.

And he sure as hell wasn't going to be stupid.

"I'm sorry," he finally whispered, and stepped on the fingers.

Bones crackled, as brittle as eggshell, and just as noisy. He didn't know what was worse, the sound, or that disconnected sensation of flattening a sausage. Gus pulled back and inspected the fingers, saw how a dull, gray matter had squeezed from cracks that weren't there before. There was no blood, just an oozing jelly that might've been raw meat, and that was enough for him.

Yup. You're dead. Whoever the fuck you are.

He left the unit and pulled the door shut behind him.

There he stood, one hand on the knob, shoulders hunched as if deciding whether to puke or not. Cory and Bruno were still aboard their truck, leaning forward as if readying questions. Gus fired off a rapid head shake, signaling them to stand down.

Which they did.

"You okay?" Collie asked from the far end of the lot, her voice goosing him. She stood before a darkened doorway. Her third, considering the two doors left open in her wake.

Oh yeah, Gus nodded, wincing a smile. As soon as she turned away, he sighed, righted himself, and again shook his head at Bruno and Cory, warning them not to say shit. He vowed to ensure that *they* took their turn checking things out. No reason not to share the fun.

His foot fully charged now and radiating an accordion's tune of discomfort, Gus headed to the next door.

*

While Gus and Collie continued their search, Bruno and Cory sat in their truck, the motor switched off. Cory had pushed back his jacket sleeves and Bruno was admiring the considerable artwork upon the man's arms. Artwork that extended up both wrists to the mid-forearm and probably beyond.

That reminded him.

"Been meaning to ask you," Bruno started. "Where you get all those tattoos?"

Cory's sunglasses remained pointed at the motel. "Here and there."

"They hurt?"

"Not much."

"Must've hurt a little."

"You get a little addicted to it, to tell the truth."

"To what? The pain?"

"Yeah."

"I'd rather be addicted to the ladies."

Cory shrugged.

Bruno looked ahead. "There was this rumor going around. That you were a bit of a hard case, right? Responsible for a few break-ins. Not that it matters now, of course. Not in this day and age."

Cory squirmed just a touch uncomfortably. "Yeah, that was me."

Bruno balked. "That was you?"

The other man nodded.

"Wanna share? Y'know… some details?"

Cory huffed. "Should've known better," he muttered in an unimpressed tone. "I know who told you. I only told one person. The one lady."

"Unless she told someone else. Who might've told someone else. Before I heard it. We're from a small town now. Things get boring during the winter."

"Well, who'd you hear it from?"

"Hey." Bruno held up a hand. "I don't reveal my sources. All I can say is it's a small town and all that. But, seriously. You should've known better bringing that stuff up. That's serious shit."

"Was serious shit," Cory mumbled and thought things over. He cleared his throat and shook his head as if taking a snort of glue. "Well, like you said, doesn't matter now. Yeah, I did a little of that. I was a little prick. A shit disturber. Only seventeen and looking out for myself. Only took cash and small stuff. Anything I could pawn off. Quick cash, you understand. Nothing big. And not for drugs or anything. I was smart enough to stay away from that garbage. Just spent it on games. Clothes and food and shit." He flexed an arm. "Tattoos. As stupid as I was, I tried to be smart about it. Stayed small. They catch you with the big shit and you do time. Really do time if you're a repeat offender."

"You don't do that now?" Bruno asked.

"No," he drew out. "'Course not. Well, I mean, people were dead. Things were different when the world stopped, right? It was about survival then. For real."

Bruno couldn't fault him for that. "I guess so. Same for a lot of people, then. Me included."

Cory regarded him, waiting for the backstory.

"Oh, you better believe it," Bruno said. "I foraged what I could, going from house to house. I was holed up in a mobile home for months until I hooked up with this crowd. And I was lucky when I did. Still, you learn some things. Realize you have to make do. So, eventually, I went back out into the wild on my own. Looked around. Made contact here and there. Not with everyone, mind you. You can spot the savages easy enough. It was like they were hoarding *Road Warrior* costumes in their closet or some shit."

"I heard that," Cory agreed.

"Then there were the straight-up whack-jobs. The nail bags. Every bit as dangerous. Maybe even more."

"Met a few myself."

"Man oh man." Bruno took a deep breath, lost in thought. "So how much time you do?" he finally asked.

The brow above the sunglasses furrowed. "Time?"

"Yeah, time. When you got caught."

"Who says I got caught?" Cory asked with a smile.

A second later, Bruno smiled back.

*

A few minutes later, after regrouping with Cory and Bruno, Collie decreed that the motel was secure.

"We'll stay here," she announced. "Follow me."

She led them through the motel lobby, which was mostly intact. A short hall led them past the main office and a janitorial room stocked full of supplies. Pictures hung on the wall—color prints of nearby lakes, smiling tourists, and early photos of the town. Gus glanced at a few before Collie led them all into a sizeable gym, which was behind the motel units.

"Whoa," Bruno whispered.

Natural light flowed into the room through a bank of windows along the left wall. A dozen treadmills were lined up before the window, which looked out onto a parking lot. A separate entrance was located near the reception desk, where a stack of dusty towels sat upon a front desk.

"Nice," Cory added.

"They got everything," Collie said. "Free weights. Machines. Stretching mats. Treadmills over there."

Gus wasn't overly impressed. He wasn't into exercising.

"This way," Collie said, and she led them to another door.

"What is it?" Bruno asked. "They got a pool?"

"Nope. Better."

"Better than a pool?"

Collie nodded. "The Mercers were diversified, God love them." She stopped and regarded the guys behind her. "Take a look at this."

She swung the door open.

Gus groaned.

The Mercers, goddamn them, had a dojo next to their gym.

"Kosugi Kenpo," Collie said. A thick checkerboard of red and blue training mats, arranged in a square, covered the floor. Open lockers adorned the nearest wall, and all manner of sparring gear—headgear, gloves, chest protectors and shin pads—were discarded there. About six kicking pads were positioned at the far end, resembling oversized joysticks.

"We don't have much light left," Collie said, "so I figured we settle in and go for a roll. Get some training in. Practice what you know."

Cory was nodding.

Bruno was nodding.

Gus was cringing.

"I know that face," Collie scolded. "This is for the best. You need to know how to defend yourself."

"Yeah."

"I'm serious. If you were alone—"

Gus raised his hand, remembering her spiel from before. Around mid-August, Collie, Vick, and Amy had decided to teach introductory martial arts on the island. Mostly self-defense moves that, true to their name, needed a sparring partner to work. They had no proper training mats to speak of, so their dojo was the front lawn of an abandoned house. Collie had ordered Gus to take part, and for the first thirty minutes, they practiced one of the basics.

Learning to fall.

They practiced spreading out their arms before their backs crashed into the ground, over and over until their asses were too sore to continue. Already on in years, Gus didn't appreciate the drill. He only fell a few times before he'd had enough.

Then came the first of the self-defense moves.

The thumb lock.

He actually didn't mind that one, admired how such little effort could completely immobilize an attacker. Other joint locks followed, crippling twist ties of flesh that trapped an attacker's hands or limbs, whereupon the follow-up blow was usually the edge of a hand or a fist to the balls. A lot of the follow-up moves ended with a fist to the balls. There were so many fists to the balls, in fact, Gus wondered aloud what was with all the fists to the balls. It seemed like a crash course in dirty fighting, dispensing entirely with the notion of the honorable martial artist.

Amy had provided an explanation for all the fists to the balls. On the streets, she'd said, there was no such thing as honor. Not if you wanted to live.

Made sense, as cliché as it sounded.

So, Gus essentially—*reluctantly*—learned how to fuck people up… mostly by punching them in the balls.

Collie stepped up to the edge of the shiny training mat, offered a curt bow, and stepped onto the pliable surface.

"Oh yeah. This is perfect. Perfect. Get your asses over here. All of you.

And don't forget to bow before you step into the training area."

The three men hesitated. Bruno even checked on what the others were going to do.

"Collie," Gus started to explain. "It's been a long day."

"Get on this mat, gentlemen. We're going to do hip tosses. You'll barely feel the landing on this thing."

To drive the point home, Collie stamped her boot into the mat.

Gus winced. Cory and Bruno didn't move so quick, either.

"Either you step onto the mat," Collie started, "or I come over there and judo-toss your asses onto the mat. Five, four, three—"

Gus bowed and stepped onto the mat.

The boys were a second behind him.

"Excellent," Collie said with approval. "Now, pair up, we'll go over what you know. Starting with thumb locks…"

4

After the short training session, the four settled in for the evening. Collie secured the perimeter with a makeshift alarm system, setting up several tripwires consisting of glass bottles, aluminum cans and a roll of fishing line.

When she set up the last tripwire, she straightened and inspected her work laid out around the area like one-half of an octagon.

"That'll do, pig," she said, hands on her hips. "That'll do."

"You don't think anyone will see that?" Gus asked behind her, indicating her traps.

"Not in the dead of night."

He examined the tripwires, the trucks, and the distance to the two units they chose for the night. "That all we gonna do?"

"'Course not, silly," Collie said. "How do you feel about keeping watch for the night? Just a shift."

"Yeah, I can do that."

"Good. We'll all take a shift. Just a precaution, you understand. Methinks this place is done like dinner."

"Truly done."

"But we don't lower our guard, all the same," Collie said. "Just in case. The town might be tits up, but the world isn't. Honestly, we'll see them before they see us."

Gus nodded.

"You're easy to get along with," Collie said.

"You're the professional. What you say is good with me."

"Well, I'm all ears if you have any other ideas."

"How about getting something to eat?"

They settled into two motel units that had a single connecting door. Bruno

31

and Cory had brought in the supplies too valuable to be left in the trucks, and then laid out supper on the motel room's dresser top. The group had supplies and rations enough for a week-long journey, not that they would need that much. Collie, however, decided to pack away as much as they could just in case. One never knew who or what they would encounter on the road.

The men laid out bottles of preserved meats and vegetables along with a loaf of bread and a jar of sliced beets. Just as Gus's stomach rumbled a message of *hurry up,* Cory cobbled together a set of magnificent sandwiches with gobs of butter and sandwich spread. Gus had to admit, considering the day and age, they still ate pretty damn well. And *clean.* Scott had hooked up with a group of people who did things the old-fashioned way. Everything was either grown, hunted, or fished. Even more surprising, what they ate tasted *good.* Real good. Art, the short order cook, was endeavoring to do greater things with what he had. The guy had even conceived the first pizza on the island, much to the surprise of all. It wasn't a meat lover's special or anything, but it had deer salami and pepperoni, garlic, goat cheese (which wasn't bad in the least), tomato sauce, onion, red and green peppers, and mushrooms. Everything except the deer was produced from local gardens, and Art informed them that if it wasn't on the pizza, it either wasn't in season or they were all out.

After a day of digging graves and driving through some pretty depressing countryside, the sandwiches laid out before them looked like a banquet. As good as the food was, Gus actually looked forward to the jar of beets. They possessed an earthy taste but were sweetened with natural sugars. He quickly grew to like it. Even crave it. Juice included.

They ate by candlelight, drank water from jugs, and talked in between bites, while Collie, with one hand on her hi-tech German assault rifle, parked herself by the window. The silence pressing down from the outside made their eating seem very loud indeed, and they found themselves talking in low tones despite the emptiness of the world.

"So, Collie," Cory asked after supper. "You say you got down to Ottawa once or twice?"

Holding her rifle close to her chest, Collie pressed one shoulder to the wall and peeked out at the parking lot. "Before or during meatbag season?"

"During."

"Yeah, we got down there. Checked on things."

"How was it?"

Bruno looked across the table at Gus, wondering if the questions were sensitive. Gus didn't rightly know himself.

"Messy," she answered simply. "Very messy. I was part of a team sent down that way. We were tasked with finding a dozen operators who'd been dispatched to the city about five or six months prior. To recon the area. We found them—what was left of them—inside a courthouse. Now, this courthouse was built in the early 1800s. I mean, big brother to a brick shithouse. Stone walls. Bars on windows. A small fortress, really. With modern-day upgrades. Anyway, despite all that, the place had been overrun by dead fuckers. We couldn't count the bodies, there were so many. *Too* many. It was the Moe version of the Alamo. We thought that the place was surrounded by corpses. Nope. Turns out there was a moat surrounding the place. An honest-to-God moat. All around the entire outer wall. The missing operators had filled it with the dead. Filled it to the brim. And the unliving had walked across it. They crawled up the walls, where they were shot dead for the final time. And there they piled up. There were… ramps of them. Spilling over into the courtyard and filling that up as well—all the way up to the second-floor windows, where there weren't any iron bars. There were plenty of leftovers walking around when we got there, so we engaged when we had to, to get clear of them. On our way back from that clusterfuck we got mixed up in a running gun battle with a pack of road crazies. Maybe one or two hundred psychotics in all, and every one of them very much interested in where we got our weapons. They chased us into Canada's Wonderland, where we decided to end it. Only me and Wallace walked away from that one."

A grim smile spread across her features. "We widened some assholes that day. Anyway, from that time on, we stayed away from cities. Learned our lesson. We kept to the smaller towns and such. It was safer. No trips into Toronto, either. The radiation would turn you green seconds before you melted down to the ankles."

That quieted the men. Bruno and Cory shifted uncomfortably.

Gus cleared his throat. "You guys know if toilet paper goes bad?"

Heads swung in his direction.

"What?" Cory asked.

"Just wondering. Because I noticed earlier that there's about three rolls of two-ply next to the crapper in there. The motel staff sure as shit didn't put them there, so I was just wondering."

Collie's grim smile dimmed to a smirk.

"I don't rightly know," Cory said. "I mean, it's only toilet paper."

"If it's wrapped up, it should be fine," Bruno added.

"Is there a date on it?" Cory asked.

"No date," Gus said. "I checked. Just two-ply stamped on the side."

"Is it wet or damp or anything?" Bruno asked.

"Nope. Totally dry."

The pair mulled over the question.

"Can't see a problem then," Bruno said. "It's only toilet paper."

"Only toilet paper," Gus scoffed, unimpressed. "You remember that when you're washing your shitty ass rags. Or whatever the hell you decide to clean your chuckwagon with. And I'll bet you twenty bucks that whatever you do use, it won't be your porn mags."

"Hey now," Bruno said, suddenly serious. "Those are *Gentlemen's Magazines*."

"You've been calling them nudie books."

"Which is my—my nickname for them. That's all. Truth is, it's an art collection. Contemporary adult art. But art all the same. And very collectible."

"Oh, it's collectible, all right," Gus pressed. "You bring any of that adult art along with you?" Bruno shifted in his chair and glanced uncomfortably in Collie's direction.

"Don't look at her," Gus said. "She doesn't care."

"I don't," Collie added without taking her eyes off the parking lot. "Hell, I'm wondering if you found any copies of *Playgirl*."

Bruno's beard twitched. "I have not."

"Figures."

"I think they were mostly online before everything went to hell," Cory said, and got hit with the looks. "What? I'm just saying. My wife was into that."

"For the articles, right?" Bruno asked.

"No, for the cock. My Nancy was all about the cock."

Collie chuckled. "Didn't take long for this conversation to slide into the shitter."

"No, it did not," Gus smiled. "And on that note, I think I'll take a walk. Maybe look around for some more bum wad."

He got up from the table.

"You're going out there?" Collie asked.

"Yeah."

"It's nighttime, man," Cory added.

"It's still early," Gus countered. "I'll take a flashlight if it makes you feel better." He checked on his sidearm and nodded at Cory. "Thanks for supper. That was good."

"Very good," Bruno added.

Gus fumbled through his knapsack and pulled out a flashlight, the self-generating kind that only needed a couple of squeezes around the shaft to produce a beam.

"Where you thinking about going?" Collie asked.

"Just down the street. Maybe the grocery store there. Only far enough to get the blood flowing."

Collie studied him closely, her gaze lingering just long enough for him to get one of those vibes.

Over the past six months, Gus had managed to keep his feelings for Collie in check. He liked to think his gestures spoke more than words, letting her know how much she meant to him. She was a leader and a soldier (or an operator, as she sometimes corrected him), but she was also surprisingly sweet and caring, even when she was teaching him how to break arms, as morbid as that sounded. Add in that sense of humor of hers, and Gus was done. Finished.

And, every now and again, they shared a moment, just like now, and he sensed things were moving in a very good direction. And the vibes he felt were getting stronger with every passing day.

"Well," she said. "If you need anything, just start shooting."

Gus smiled. "You know it."

Cory searched his backpack and pulled out a cribbage board and a pack of cards.

"Now you're talking," Bruno said and cleared the table.

Gus let himself out, exchanging winks with Collie as he did so. That little exchange got his heart fluttering. He gently closed the door behind him.

The temperature had dropped from perhaps ten degrees to a bitter five. Gus fluffed up the furry collar of his jacket and looked for the stars. Nothing but a ceiling of gray clouds. So be it. He needed to get back into survivor mode. Needed to remember the little things from before, to knock the rust off the gears. The body under the bed had shaken him. He supposed it was because he'd been recovering on the island for so long, distant from all the horrors on the mainland. Discovering the corpse under the bed reminded him that every town was a graveyard. Every room a potential morgue.

A deep silence greeted him, and he held his peace just long enough to appreciate that awesome stillness. The wind had even dropped out, and Collie, Bruno, and Cory were doing their best to stay quiet.

Gus rolled his shoulders, pulled his jacket tighter, and snorted back a lungful of air and all the autumn smells that came with it. He headed towards the grocery store, thinking about Collie. She was touching him more often. A hand on the shoulder every now and again. A quick squeeze of his hand at the supper table. Or when he made a funny. Two weeks ago, she startled the hell out of him by tugging on his beard and suggesting he shave.

Just the other day, her hand found his underneath the table, and it stayed there.

And that was part of the reason he needed to get outside. Out on the road, like they were, at a motel of all places, the anticipation about sleeping arrangements was matching the hornets trapped in his left boot.

"Nice night," he whispered to himself, glad that it wasn't raining. "Nice night."

He stopped and realized he was standing right in front of the grocery store.

The sign for *Mollymart East* was a dead gray in the night. A few tattered flyers announcing specials hung in the windows. The main doors were partially open, clogged with a beaver's dam of brush and dead leaves, and the windows were surprisingly intact, considering so many supermarkets had been looted.

His nerves weren't feeling so jittery, and the motel didn't seem that far away.

"Fuck it," Gus whispered. *For old times' sake.* He stuck his head in the main entrance, smelling nothing but dried paper. Some wrappers and packaging cluttered the floor, but the aisles were as dark and ominous as deep-sea trenches. The produce section had been emptied long ago.

The opening was just wide enough for him to squeeze through sideways. Gus stopped just inside and switched on his flashlight. The aisles flickered within an arctic cone of light. Out of habit, he reached for his Glock.

Gus cleared his throat. "Hello?"

And waited.

As expected, no one answered. Nothing came running at him.

He scanned the tops of the empty shelves, eyeing the stark beguiling glow of the painted metal. Exposed ductwork snaked throughout the ceiling. Cardboard and shredded wrapping littered the floor. Crimpled plastic wrap glittered like ice. The place had been picked clean, even by Gus's standards, probably by the locals. In the beginning, at least. With the town so close to the highway, lots of traveling folks no doubt stopped in for a quick looting. They probably sighted the town and took whatever they could find.

"Hello?" he repeated, just a little louder.

No response.

With a conscious effort, he kept his trigger finger just above the Glock's guard, not wanting to blow his knee off.

"Okay, so, uh… we're just passing through, okay?" he said, drawing comfort from the sound. "So, don't mind us. Don't mind me. So…yeah. Listen. I've got a gun, okay? And I know how to use it. So don't shoot me. I mean, don't shoot *at* me. I'm not alone, and if you *do* shoot, the others will find you. But, I mean… look. I don't *want* you to shoot, okay? And I'm not going to shoot anyone. I just wanna talk. See if we can, I dunno, help each other out. Y'know?"

Gus slowly swept his light over the shelves and empty aisles.

"All right. I'm coming in. Just taking a walk, really. If anyone's in here, just know that. Okay? Okay. I'm coming in. Taking that first step… now."

Gus did exactly that, and to his relief, no one tried to shoot him. No one tried to jump him, either, or grab his balls. Those were positive points.

He moved into the barren produce section, his boots softly crushing dried paper and cardboard. The ductwork overhead resembled the entwined underbellies of great serpents. Nothing dropped onto him from above. Nothing sprang at him from the tops of the shelves. The cold light of his flashlight swept left and right, revealing the ravaged emptiness of the grocery store.

"Goddamn," Gus whispered, impressed by the level of bone-picking thoroughness of the looting. A series of open coffins appeared in the beam of light. The flashlight suddenly dimmed, so Gus gave it a few squeezes, revving the internal motor. He cringed at the sound. All his talk about coming inside and shit and here he was, looking like he was jerking off in the dark.

The beam strengthened and flared across a series of open chest freezers resembling coffins. He turned around, inspecting more empty units, until he located the swinging doors at the back of the store.

That brought back memories.

"In for a dollar," he whispered.

He pushed through the doors, forging ahead. More aisles, more squished mush that might've been cardboard or paper, all mucked together by a jam of unrecognizable material, creating a rats' nest. There were stairs to his left, the layout familiar, so he climbed them, his foot nagging at him to stop.

"Yeah," he said.

His foot reminded him of the long walk back to motel.

"Fuck off," he whispered, knowing full well it *was* a long walk, especially when one leg seemed to end in an electrified squeezebox.

"Thank you, Jesus," he said upon reaching the top floor. The flashlight's beam scrolled across an employee's lounge consisting of a small table, a coffee maker, and a sofa that smelled faintly of pee. There was an open door just ahead, and Gus figured what the hell. He went to the portal and gently eased it open, cringing at the squeal of its hinges.

A large L-shaped desk dominated the room, facing the door. A smashed laptop lay discarded in a corner, behind a flowerpot kicked over and spilling soil. Two chairs before the desk were pushed aside. But it was the huge window overlooking the floor that drew Gus's attention.

"Oh my," he said weakly, and switched off his flashlight. He waited for his eyes to adjust. In time, the darkness revealed the huge store in all its shadowy splendor. The sight of that shopper-friendly labyrinth tugged a few memories loose, and for a few jarring seconds, *Mollymart's* interior was lit with sharp fluorescent lighting, the shelves full of fresh groceries to buy and eat, with people pushing carts through the aisles.

What shocked Gus the most were the voices in his head, of his old painting crew, as they watched Benny head for the exits, for a late-night meeting with the lovely Ms. Miller.

"Why's he walking that way?" Toby asked.

"Looks like he's gotta take a dump," Gord added.

"That sweet smelling devil," Toby remarked. *"God bless him."*

"God bless him," Gus sighed and smiled. He couldn't rightly remember how they'd died—didn't want to really, but he remembered how they'd lived, and that tightened his throat.

"God bless him," he repeated before reluctantly glancing around the office. A part of him was tempted to look under the desk, just to see if there was a fridge under there. He didn't, however. He gave his flashlight a few squeezes, took one final look out over the main shopping floor, and headed back to the stairs.

A soft noise distracted him when he reached the last step—the barest rustling of paper, like Christmas presents being shifted around. Gus stopped and listened, his damaged hand resting on his holstered gun.

"Hello?" he asked. Nothing replied.

A part of him strongly advised to return to Collie and the others and report the noise. Another part of him informed him that standing there with his hand on his gun wasn't helping either, and that he should check on his balls before investigating. There were no more zombies in the world, just a handful of people, the vacant leftovers of civilization.

Gus switched on the flashlight, nervously giving it a few more squeezes. He unholstered his gun and crossed his wrists like he'd seen in the movies, aiming both Glock and flashlight where he needed. With his gun hand supported by his left, he advanced down the corridor, between a tangle of empty shelves and garbage covering the floor. What looked like a dried-up puddle of used toilet paper covered one section. The sight of that grossed him out enough to reconsider going any further. He wondered just how urgent one had to be to drop drawers and squat in the rear of a grocery store. Gus sized up the tainted floorspace. Not wanting to find another way around, and certainly not pleased about it, he edged around that spent landmine of nastiness. Every careful step reminded him of walking through half-melted fudge, where his boots sank half an inch. The noise that he'd heard earlier didn't repeat itself, though he felt he was closing in on the source. His foot was really nagging him now, and every step felt like a gnashing of electrical circuits brought on by failing bionics. The discomfort distracted him, kept him from focusing on whatever the hell lay ahead. Something waited for him at the end of this trail. He could sense it, as God was his witness. A presence, hiding far and away from the light, waiting for the right time to strike.

Gus held his breath as he reached the end of the corridor and turned the corner, whipping the flashlight around. Round eyes blazed back an instant before a fox, flicking his big bushy tail, turned and fled through a gap in the shelving. That great tapered bush grazed the edges before disappearing, and Gus's heartrate spiked as he stood there, paralyzed from the ankles up.

When the fox was no longer visible, Gus realized he'd rightly refrained from firing his weapon. That was a good thing. Nice to know he had some degree of control.

"Just a fox," he whispered and wiped his forehead. "Just a fuckin' fox."

He flashed the light toward where the animal had escaped and located a depression in the aisle, under the lowest shelf. A little den with tufts of fur and feathers. Gus tracked the animal's path to a back door, opened just enough for one fleeing animal. An empty parking lot lay beyond the escape route, and Gus chuckled at the sight. When he settled down, he decided he'd had enough exploring for one night.

Good to know that wild animals were in the area. Animals that ran when people got too close.

Gus thought that was a good sign.

5

"Have fun?" Collie asked when Gus shuffled into the motel unit.

"Just ducky."

She smiled and returned her attention to the parking lot, holding back the curtain just enough to peek.

Gus closed the door and lumbered over to the bed. Three candles positioned throughout the room provided the only light. A hint of vanilla hung in the air.

"That… incense?" he asked.

"Candles are vanilla scented."

"Oh. Nice."

"A little too girly for me, but whatever. I'm more apple cinnamon. I'm all about the spice."

Gus parked himself on the bed, causing the springs to protest under his weight. The sound summoned a frown, a follow-up bounce to further test the mattress, and when that met his approval he shrugged and stripped off his jacket.

"Saw a fox," he muttered as he pulled off a boot.

"Yeah?" Collie asked.

Gus nodded.

"Wow."

"In the supermarket. Underneath a shelf."

"You didn't shoot it."

"No," he scoffed with a soft glare. "'Course not. It wasn't doing anything. I heard a noise and went to investigate. My flashlight lit up its eyes. Scared the shit outta me. Probably scared the shit outta the fox."

"You're not as fluffy."

"Guess not," Gus sighed. He chucked the jacket onto a chair and considered the bed again. The silence in the room thrummed like an exposed power cable.

"Going to bed?" Collie asked, not breaking away from the window.

"Thinking about it."

"Go ahead. I'll take first watch. You relax and sleep for a bit."

"You sure?"

"Sure I'm sure. I'll wake you when it's time to switch."

"What about Bruno and Cory?"

"They'll get their shifts in." Collie tugged on the remaining nub of her nose. "They're only next door. When you finally crash, wake one of them to take over. The way Cory snores, it might be best to get him up first. Let Bruno get some sleep."

"We might hear that."

"The snoring? Probably. But hey, if that's all we hear, then we're good."

Gus thought about that. "Doesn't seem like there's too much out there, Collie."

She nodded. "I'm only keeping watch out of habit, to tell the truth. But it's clear to me there's nothing going on out there. Lots of places like this between Ontario and Quebec. People move on to safer places, or places they think are safer."

"Like where?"

Collie grew silent for a moment. "Anywhere away from the shit. Mostly out of towns. Into the hills. Remember that motel? Where that gang kept those people pinned up? With the one guy over the pit filled with the Moe heads?"

"Jimbo."

"Yeah, that's right. Jimbo."

Poor old Jimbo, Gus reflected, remembering the beaten and abused man who'd been saved from being eaten alive, only to suffer through an even grislier ending at the hands of the killer called Sick. Just the thought of it stabbed Gus to the core. There was shitty luck, and then there was Jimbo's.

"Wallace and I came across more than a few places like that," Collie said. "Boarded up and fortified. Some had a few survivors. Some didn't. Some went back with us to Pine Cove. Others didn't."

"What happened to the ones who stayed?"

Collie shrugged. "Not my business. To tell the truth. I only find them and present my argument. If they don't like it, I leave."

"That ever come back at you?"

"You mean, like, bite us in the ass?"

"Yeah."

"Sometimes," Collie admitted quietly.

Gus's hand smoothed over the quilt covering the bed, appreciating its softness. It smelled wonderfully musty but was clean—or as clean as any bed not slept in for a few years.

"You miss him?" Gus asked and inwardly cringed, hating himself and wondering where the hell *that* question came from. He set his jaw and braced for the answer.

"Wallace, you mean?" she asked back.

"Yeah."

Collie kept on staring out the window. "Yeah. I do. Every day."

The words hit Gus hard, rendering him speechless. He knew he had to do *something*, so he nodded, reminding himself he'd asked for it.

"But…" she paused. "It's not so bad these days."

Gus stopped breathing. "Why's that?"

She turned from the window and looked at him. "Because I have you, you dummy."

She said it softly, but there was a layer of bedrock underneath, which she immediately clarified. "And I meant that affectionately. I would've said 'you fuckin dummy' if I meant it any other way."

Gus smiled despite himself. "Yeah, I guess you would've."

"Besides," Collie said. "Who else would have me? I'm no princess. And I got my share of baggage."

"I'd have you," he said in a low voice, his heart thumping, realizing he'd just rolled a mighty big meatball way out there.

Collie smiled at him. "I bet you would, you savage."

They shared a long moment then, until Gus shifted and a bed spring twanged.

"You relax," she said quietly. "I'll keep watch for a little while longer."

"You…, ah, gonna sleep over there tonight?"

She didn't answer right away. "No, I'll sleep with you when I get tired."

Gus's back straightened.

"I said *sleep*," she warned. "Sleep. That's all. Nothing else."

"Got it. Nothing else. I can do that."

"Good. Cause I ain't camping out on this carpet. Who knows what fluids this shit's soaked up 'til now."

Gus pulled back the quilt on the bed. He got in and settled back, hoisting the blankets and sheets to his chest. He didn't bother taking off his shirt. There was a slight chill in the room that had seeped into the mattress. That would change shortly.

"Give a holler if you need anything."

Collie had already returned her attention to the window. "I will."

Gus closed his eyes.

He woke up much later, the room plunged in darkness. All was very, very quiet, except for Collie's soft breathing, her head pressed against his right shoulder. Her arm lay across his belly, and her leg was pressed firmly against his. Her hair, cut short and to the point, was only a few inches from his face. Collie slept, and Gus didn't make a move, for fear of waking her. So there he stayed, marveling at the operator's softness, and treasuring every passing second.

6

In the morning, the group drank well water from the cooler and ate a cold breakfast of bread with generous dollops of homemade strawberry jam. The motel didn't have running water, so they did what they could with the limited facilities. Toothpaste had long since become a thing of memory, and anything they cracked open now was chalky and dry. They discarded their waste in the cracked motel toilets, and although the toilets didn't flush, the local ass napkins worked just fine.

When they were ready, they hit the road.

The group drove along a scenic, lonely strip of the 104, with wide rivers and open fields sweeping past them, while the clouds above scattered and the day brightened. Some of the abandoned cars along the highway had pulled over to the far shoulder, as if their drivers were simply getting out for a stretch. The heads of white birch appeared over the hilltops skirting the road on either side, their leaves ready to fall at the next good gust.

"Do you ever miss it?" Gus asked Collie at one point.

"What?"

"Everything. You know. Doing things. Day-to-day life."

"Oh, that shit?" she asked. "Along with the fights, the pollution, the people, and the assholes? Stray cats shittin' in the flower beds? Then there's the traffic, the restaurants, and the take-out food. The arts, the plays. The music. The television shows. Oh, God the *internet!* Can't forget the internet. The cars. The bikes. The *movies.* The outdoor concerts in the summertime and the hockey games in the winter. The wonders of modern medicine, aviation and architecture, and the charm of... I dunno, just staying inside on a cold day and turning on the heat just by pushing a fucking button. Or walking into a grocery store and buying a tub of Heavenly Hash. You want to know if I miss any of that?"

Gus was smiling. "Yeah."

"Big time. Don't you?"

"Yeah."

"I have to say, though, sure as hell is quieter these days."

"You said it."

"The peace of it all…" Collie mused.

"It's something."

"It is."

"But…" she said and tapped on the dashboard. "We got music. Looks like over a thousand tunes. That's road trip bliss right there. Anytime we want 'em. Just say the word."

Gus did not say the word, however. And Collie, getting the message, eased back into driving.

"What do you think of the boys?" she asked after a time.

"Cory and Bruno?" Gus stared ahead. "I think I mentioned I met Bruno a while back. Crazy bastard. I mean in a good way… but crazy. There I was, getting ready to head back out on the road, right? To try and hunt down Maggie and the kids, when Bruno magically appears on the front lawn. You understand, at the time, he wasn't Bruno to me. He was just a fucking yahoo wearing the same winter cap he swiped off Dr. Seuss. Standing right there on the front lawn, smiling like… I dunno. Smiling like he's got Jesus Christ the sniper perched on a rooftop behind him somewhere, aiming an honest-to-God elephant gun at my crotch. I mean, it was surprising, y'know? And all the while, I'm thinking this ain't right. There's something off here, in that either you got some serious back-up somewhere, or everything you're wearing is fucking bulletproof. Or, maybe, you got head-stomped and you just don't give a shit anymore."

Gus shrugged.

"Anyway. We talk. And all he wants to do is trade and he keeps bringing up how he wants to trade nudie books. I ended up leaving some Kraft dinner for him. I think I left him some noodles, too. So there. I gave him food. He got food outta me, Collie. Fuckin' food. He went from being this weird-ass road squirrel to getting food outta me. That's how… *subtle* he is. How goddamn friendly he is. 'Charming' comes to mind. No, wait… *disarming*. I swear. If I had a fucking Big Mac, I would've given it to him. Not half—the whole burger. I still wonder how he did that. And I mean, I felt *good* about doing that. He gave me a lead on Maggie and the kids, but still… honestly, I could've threatened the guy—*hurt* the guy and got that outta him. So, yeah,

I'm glad he volunteered to come along. If we come across a pack of killer nuts…" Gus chopped the air before him. "Send him in. That guy just might have them humming *Kum-ba-yah* before it's all over."

"That kind of diplomacy is an art," Collie pointed out.

"But that's not diplomacy. That's Jedi mind-fuckery right there. Of the highest order. Don't get me wrong, I like the guy. Hell, I'm *mystified* by him. But I'm happy he's around."

"And Cory?"

Gus shook his head. "Not so sure about that one."

"Go on."

"Feel weird talking about him."

"You did fine with Bruno."

"That's different. I like Bruno, even though I think he's crazy."

"You don't like Cory?"

Gus became silent for a few seconds. "Not that. I'm just not sure about him. He's a scrapper. I heard that from Vick. The kinda guy you want on your side, but at the same time you're not sure he'd have your back. Bruno found him holed up in a hotel on the south shore. The guy had been alone for a couple of years. Had a couple of rooms full of supplies, one of which Cory had turned into his own personal bar. Hard drinker. I don't know. I've never talked to him one-on-one, but he seems fine enough. He reminds me… of me. A little."

"Fine assessments of both men," Collie said. "I agree. Bruno is solid but Cory is something of a question mark. He's a survivor, no doubt, but is he a team player? So far, so good. Bruno did vouch for him, however."

"There's that, I guess," Gus supposed. "What do you think of him?"

"He's a question mark, but right now he's *our* question mark, and we don't have a lot of people to choose from to do this. Who are willing to do this. Your buddy Scott there? He was wise to stay back. Not that Amy would let him go, you understand. Those two are one of the community's original couples, and frankly, they have to keep popping out kids. I wasn't going to break up any families for this field trip."

Gus studied Collie's profile.

She sensed the scrutiny and a little smile brightened her face. "We gotta refuel before we go into Amherst," she said, checking the gauge. "And Moncton. Don't want to take the chance inside the city."

"We could go around," Gus suggested.

"We could, but it would burn corn. We need speed. Only got enough juice to get to Whitecap and back with no sideshows. And that covers heading into the States. Faster that way. We'll cut across New Brunswick, go through Maine and Vermont, and come up behind Ottawa. Go around the city, and then its straight on until dawn."

"We're going around Ottawa?"

"Roger that."

"Why not drive through?"

"Because… the thought of Ottawa sort of grosses me out."

Gus cocked an eyebrow. "What?"

"Look, there's a skull on the side of the road."

"Fuck the skull. What about Ottawa?"

Collie shrugged. "Remember the courthouse? All those corpses? It was unreal. Greatest concentration of people is in cities, and right now they're like open graves. Every side street, every alleyway is rotten with the stink of carrion. Out in the wild, in the small towns, it's different. Things break down faster. Decompose right down to the bone, and hopefully that will be the end of it. Get grown over. That'll happen in the cities but… it'll take longer. The decomposing biomass will be deeper. Thicker. And everywhere. Like that playpen—the one in the motel with all the heads. Except on a citywide scale. I figure by now most bodies should be dried up like leather, but frankly, I'm not sure, and I'd just as soon not investigate. Let Mom Nature work her magic until its all nothing but bones and dust. We'll take a peek in two or three years."

Gus looked back out the windshield. "Whitecap's good for me."

Collie nodded *see?*

Most of the signs along the highway had been smashed off, leaving a series of dismembered wooden posts. Gus knew Amherst wasn't too far away, however. Soon they were passing exit lanes into town and crossing overpasses above rooftops.

"Gonna pull in here," Collie announced.

A car dealership came into view, and just past that was a four-story hotel. All manner of unused cars, trucks, and SUVs filled the dealership lot. Collie put on her indicator and slowed.

"Going off-road," she said. "Grab your salt and pepper."

Gus braced for the rugged terrain just before his ass cheeks lifted from the leather. The truck rumbled down over a small embankment, where they jumped and bounced in their seats. At the base of the descent, an unexpected drop rattled his teeth. The entire chassis hit so hard, so bone-jarringly *solid,* that Gus expected to see parts dropping off the truck. The ride smoothed out, however, and Collie steered for a gap in the line of vehicles. She drove through with a foot to spare on either side and swung to the left. Bruno and Cory followed, their own ride bouncing along as if their tires were made of super springy balls.

"Yee-ha, baby," Collie deadpanned. "You all right over there?"

"Think I rolled over my nuts," Gus winced.

"You'll get over it."

"I'm talking about my balls here."

"I heard. And frankly, I'm glad they're hanging off you and not me. What I'm saying is walk it off."

He gave her a look. "Are you giving me a hard time?"

"Nope." A smile appeared underneath her sunglasses. "Just putting things into perspective is all. When I start calling you 'civvie' is when you'll know you pissed me off."

They drove through the dealership lot and exited onto a road, motored another three hundred feet or so before stopping behind the hotel, out of sight from the highway. The building's broad side faced them, scarred and abandoned and coated in a noticeable film of filth. The main entrance had been smashed out entirely, as if pummeled by a sledgehammer, creating a welcome mat of crystals.

Gus sized up the place. "We stopping here for the night?"

"Too much daylight left," Collie said, and got out.

Gus got out on the other side, inspecting the brown paneling of the motel. He stretched his legs while Cory and Bruno parked behind them. Collie flipped open the box cover of the truck bed, where they stored several containers full of ethanol.

A truck door slammed shut. "We're not heading into town there?" Bruno asked. He placed his hands on his lower back and grimaced.

"Nope," Gus said.

"Why's that?"

"She wants to stay away from the cities. Says they're too full of shit. And by that I mean decomposing people."

Ohhh Bruno quietly mouthed in understanding.

Cory exited the driver's seat and lumbered off to the rear of his truck, intending to refuel as well.

"Gus, keep an eye on things, will ya?" Collie said, then turned to Bruno. "You too, matey. Arrr."

"Hey," Bruno said. "Whatever puts a smile on your face."

Gus inspected the motel's exterior for any structural damage, then turned to Bruno. "How you two doing?"

"Good," Bruno said. "Sore ass, mostly. But we're getting along."

"He talks a lot," Cory said from the other side. "Mostly shit."

"I do not," Bruno remarked with mild annoyance. "He's kidding. We're like an old married couple."

Cory shook his head. "You were talking about how if this was a sci-fi movie, we'd be wearing red shirts."

"Well, we would." Bruno shrugged at Gus. "But that's all just shooting the shit."

"You said," Cory continued, "that if we were going to be taken off the road, I'd be shot first. Right through the windshield."

"Storytime. Fiction. I was bored."

"Right between the fuckin' eyes. That's what you said. My face would be blown out the back of my head. A gob of strawberry jam in the back seat."

"Haha," Bruno muttered. "Ahhh. He's a kidder. You're a kidder, Cory."

Cory smirked and concentrated on refueling.

"Gotta say something to entertain myself," Bruno confided to Gus. "I mean, the countryside is deserted. On one hand it's pretty damn horrific the way everything up and went, and on the other, after an hour or so on the road, it gets boring. Same shit everywhere. Gotta talk about something. Otherwise, the mind wanders. You and Collie talk, don't you?"

"Yeah, we talk," Gus said.

"What about?"

"Things we miss about civilization."

"Bet you mentioned drive-throughs."

"Don't think we did, actually…" Gus said, and stopped talking.

There, across the way, standing under the shade of a forest and just inside a belt of tall grass, was a dog. A big dog. Not a German shepherd but close, with brown fur that practically blended in with its surroundings. The animal studied them, at attention. Gus knew the breed, but the sight of the dog momentarily robbed him of his memory.

"That's a retriever," Bruno said, adjusting his sunglasses.

"Retriever," Gus repeated. "That's right. Holy shit."

"What's that?" Collie asked.

Gus pointed. "There's a dog over there. Just the one. Poor little bastard."

"Probably someone's pet," Bruno said.

Gus figured the same thing. Back in the day, there were plenty of unwanted animals taken out of town and permanently dropped off somewhere in deep country. Dogs, cats, rabbits, snakes even. All released into the great outdoors. The thought saddened him, but he knew a survivor when he saw it, and the dog giving them the eye was the canine version of a prepper.

"Can we take him?" Bruno asked. "Hell, I'd love to have a dog."

"No room in the trucks," Collie pointed out.

"Awww."

Gus wasn't so disappointed. When he was down in the Valley, picking through the thousands of houses in undead suburbia, he'd come across his share of expired animals. Not reanimated, although he did stumble across the remains of pets that were trapped inside their homes with their ravenous owners. Some of those owners had eventually broken out of their homes in search of more good eating. Gus remembered discovering a bird cage in one home's living room, covered in a pillow's worth of bloody feathers. At first, he'd thought a cat devoured the birds, but the little-old-man creature that lurked in the bathroom canceled that idea. The memory of being attacked by a zombie with feathers stuck to its jowls had been suppressed by medicinal shots of rum… until now.

Gus's mouth went dry.

"We can at least feed him something," Bruno said. "Some of the deer."

"No," Gus said. "Wait."

Bruno looked at him. "No?"

"No. That dog ain't hungry. He's just checking us out. Probably wondering if we're going to eat it."

Bruno's expression soured at the thought. "Looks tame to me."

"You think everyone is tame," Gus said.

The two men went right on watching the dog.

"Saw a TV show once," Gus started, "about house pets, and how they would be the unspoken victims if something happened to their owners in an apocalypse. If they were inside the house with their owners, well, you can imagine what happened. One of two things. Take a guess at what the first thing was. Now, with the second thing, maybe their owners weren't around when everything went down the shitter. But they were still left alone inside a house with a closed door. Pets can't get out. Pets can't get at any food in the cupboards. If it's a dog or a cat, it might have water from the toilet bowl, but in the end, the poor creature will die anyway of starvation. Trapped in its home. Some are lucky, though. They get out through a doggie door. Or an open window. Thing is, once they go outside, well, they're still in a world of shit. After the outbreak, people were trying to kill and eat anything edible. People were trying to eat *people*, which to those animals was probably just as disturbing. So they ran. Well, the ones with the long legs ran. The ones with the short legs… they didn't get very far."

"Jesus," Bruno muttered.

"Evolution right there," Gus said, scratching at his belly. "Puts me in a bad mood just thinking of it. The smaller breeds with the stubby little legs? They get killed off pretty quick because they can't run, not as fast as the bigger ones. They survive. That pooch right there? That's one that got out. That's a four-legged Robinson Crusoe. Funny thing. I never did see many animals alive down in Annapolis. Not even when I was house-picking."

He stopped there, remembering that he did come across one species in abundance.

"He might come over if we toss him something to eat," Bruno said.

Gus shook his head. "You're too much of a diplomat."

"Animals are great for therapy. Post-traumatic shock therapy and all that."

The man had a point.

Gus studied the dog, watched it watch them. The animal didn't move for a very long time, and that was kind of eerie. Gus's eyes strayed to the trees behind the dog. Grass. Weeds. Everywhere. Nature was slowly but surely pushing back, reclaiming the world.

Just along the edge of the pavement, where the grass sprouted in a thick curtain, a pair of twigs caught Gus's eye. Except they weren't twigs, not after closer inspection. They were bony fingers, the drooping phalanges crooked and lifeless, as if the owner of those fingers had exhausted himself pulling his own corpse from a grave.

"You see something?" Bruno asked, and Gus knew that Collie's eyes were on him, wondering just what he was up to. He wasn't sure himself, but he crossed the pavement anyway.

A hand, connected to a skeletal forearm, not quite picked clean. Then… a torso.

Gus stopped at the pavement's end, bent over, and parted the grass, uncovering the ravaged and weather-stripped remains of a person. A skull— locked in a scream—stared in the direction of the hotel. Its left arm was missing.

Then Gus saw the rest of the corpse, hidden within the thick vegetation. Dread clutched at his innards and caressed the back of his neck. Behind him, a boot heel clicked on pavement. Someone muttered something about gas. Fluid sloshed heavily in a container, but he didn't pay attention to any of that.

The other skeletons had his complete attention.

Dismembered and strewn along in clumps, the bones were every bit as dusted and discolored as the hotel behind him. There was no pattern to where they fell, as if Death himself were polishing off a bucket of fried chicken and chucking the bones out the window, letting them fall where they may. Some of the skulls were screaming, some were grinning, but all of them faced him. None of the heads, as far as he could tell, had any bullet holes or any other sort of head trauma.

The dog had not moved; instead, it watched Gus with its ears perked. It dared him to come closer.

"No thanks," Gus whispered, and backed away. The feeling was evidently mutual as the dog turned and trotted off into the forest. The animal quickly faded into the foliage.

Bruno was beside him then, studying the bone collection.

"Zombies?" he asked.

Gus shook his head. "Maybe. Maybe just… people. I dunno."

He walked back to the truck, thinking about graves. Open graves.

And the things crawling free of them.

7

After refueling their trucks, Collie gathered the men into a circle.

"All right, boys," she said, glancing at Bruno and Cory. "Next is Amherst. We'll have to slow things down, though. The highway will be thick with dead material."

"Dead material?" a puzzled Bruno asked.

"Cars," Collie provided. "Trucks. Motorcycles. Delivery vans. Transports. Hell, I wouldn't be surprised to see a goddamn baby buggy somewhere out there. An honest-to-Christ jug fuck of rubber tires, loose springs, and airbags. Might be impassable in places. I'll worry about that. Just stay three cars back off my bumper, okay? And I say three, in case I have to stomp on the brakes and reverse my tin ass lickety-fuckin' fast. And keep your weapons ready just in case. We good?"

Bruno lifted a hand.

"Melinda?" Collie asked.

Bruno made a face at that. He glanced at Gus for backup.

Gus refused to make eye contact.

"Jug fuck?" Bruno finally asked.

"What's that now?" Collie asked back.

"What's a jug fuck?"

"You can't guess at the meaning?"

Bruno blinked and didn't say a word.

"I think it means a shit storm," Gus put in quietly.

Collie approved with a nod before turning on Bruno. "Any more army piddley shit lingo you need definitions for?"

Bruno shook his head.

"So we're good?" she asked.

The men nodded.

"Outstanding," Collie said softly. "Roger Dildo. See you on the other side."

As they climbed aboard their trucks, Gus glanced over at the operator and asked, "You expecting anything?"

"Prepare for the worst and all that shit," she replied and started up the engine.

The two trucks cruised through the Amherst city limits. Large buildings rose in the distance, stamping shadows across wide plots of unused farmland. As expected, there were plenty of vehicles on the highway, some dented or scuffed, others wrecked completely. Gruesome knots of glass and metal where vehicles had smashed heads. Metal clipped metal underneath the two trucks, and one frightening clatter made Gus brace for impact, before an exhaust pipe rattled out from underneath.

"Relax," Collie told him. "It's not ours."

A crunch of demolished cars blocked the highway, forcing Collie to slow down and find a route off-road. Gus held on as the truck listed to his side. He saw skeletons. Complete sets littered the shoulders of the road—stretched out or simply flattened. Some intact, some not. Collie ignored them as she maneuvered through and banked hard onto a less cluttered road. Nothing stopped them this time. Stores with bright, tattered signs lined the streets, the windows smashed, glass spilling onto pavement. Parking lots of shopping meccas resembled aging battlefields. A high school came into view with a huge section of its structure collapsed, as if an explosion might've been responsible. Nothing raised its head to see where the trucks were going.

No one charged the vehicles.

And, most importantly, no one took a shot at them.

Thirty minutes later, they had rolled through not only Amherst, but neighboring Sackville as well.

"Well, all right," Collie announced, hugely satisfied with the lack of resistance.

Gus checked his side mirror. Sackville remained a quiet gray place as it shrank in the distance, occasionally blotted out by Cory and Bruno's truck following close behind.

"That went pretty good," he said.

"It did."

"I was clenching the whole time," he remarked.

"Just keep watch back there is all."

"Why's that?"

"Well, you never know," Collie said. "That's how we got into a fight with those Norse fuckheads. *Norsemen.* The fuck were they snorting when they came up with that name? Anyway, we were driving through the burbs, minding our business, when suddenly a dozen rigs appeared in our rear-view mirror. It was like we boot-fucked a beehive and left it in the dirt. They were riled up something fierce."

Gus leaned forward, watching his mirror with greater attention. "Looks clear. For now, anyway."

"Let's hope it stays that way."

Around a quarter after one, the group stopped to refuel some fifteen klicks away from Moncton. A road sign informed them that the exit was only seven kilometers away. The wide grassy median dividing the six-lane highway had become a collection of cars that had veered off the road. A transport trailer had stopped on the shoulder, leaning dangerously to the right. Gus kept watch as the others poured ethanol into the gas tanks. He stood a few paces at the front of the pickup, gazing at the horizon.

"Jesus," Cory hissed. "Ethanol truly sucks ass, don't it?"

"Great for the environment," Collie said brightly.

"Yeah, but it seems like we're constantly gassing up every other hour."

"It does have pretty shitty mileage," Bruno added.

"Yeah, well, maybe we'll luck out and find an engineer," Collie said. "One who specializes in improving shitty mileage."

Gus quietly chuckled at that. That was his girl. At least he hoped she would be his girl one day. He ignored the thought by examining the treeline.

"Gus," Collie said after a few minutes

"Yeah?"

"You drive."

"You expecting trouble?"

"No more than usual."

That was enough for Gus. He was getting bored riding shotgun. He started up the rig as Collie climbed aboard. She pulled one of her pistols free and inspected the weapon's condition.

"You sure you're not expecting trouble?" Gus asked.

Collie smiled. "Moncton's a bigger city. Bigger population. Bigger chance of us attracting unwanted attention."

Gus heard that.

Collie studied his profile. "You're taking orders really well, you know."

"*Phht.* Like I'm not going to. Far as I'm concerned, this is a military thing.

And you're military. I'm just a civvie. I'm fuckin' *glad* you're in charge."

That sentiment amused the operator.

A minute later, they crossed an overpass. The adjoining exit ramps and roads reminded Gus of a steel spider that had died on its back, with its legs folded in on itself. A dead parade of unmoving vehicles jammed the ramps, bumper-to-bumper, with some of the impatient ones bashed onto shoulders. Moon roofs were opened, windows were lowered, and the wasted occupants barely visible. Grass surrounded it all, creating a tilting flood plain of yellow and green. All under a cloudy sky.

"Take your time," Collie said, craning her neck one way and then the other. "You're doing fine. Nice and easy."

"Too much shit on the highway to go any faster," Gus said, thankful that the overpass lanes weren't so clogged.

"Just take your time," the operator said, peering down beneath the overpass. "See those exits?"

"Yeah."

"Notice anything?"

"Besides all the cars?"

"That's right. All those cars. Roads are completely blocked. No one can use those lanes to come up behind us. Not unless they want to bash their way through the guardrails."

"Places up ahead," Gus said, pointing to a collection of buildings on either side of the highway.

A minute later, they rolled through Moncton's outer limits, consisting mostly of truck stops, gas stations, drive-throughs, and abandoned chip trucks. Roadside water amusement parks with bone-dry half-pipes. Motels and multi-level hotels. In between these structures were roads snaking down into shallow valleys, offering fleeting glimpses of empty streets and long-dead neighborhoods of the inner city. Massive shopping complexes came into view, their fronts pointed towards an army of unmoving cars. Lawns, like so many others, had grown to jungle heights.

"The world up and died, Gus," Collie remarked with just the barest note of remorse, surveying that desolate roadside show. "She up and died."

"If we're lucky," Gus said.

That turned the operator's head, but only for a few seconds before she zeroed in on a structure on the right.

"Something wrong?" he asked.

"Maybe. Just keep on driving, but be ready to stomp on the gas when I say." Collie held her Sig between her knees.

"What is it?" he asked.

"That hotel."

The building resembled a ski chalet from the Swiss Alps, reminding Gus of Mortimer's mansion. Painted white with a striking blue trim, the building had a distinct shape and gentle roof, with a number of pointed dormers on all sides. Several cars were parked outside a fire exit, all lined up and facing the road. The lawn was overgrown, but freshly beaten pathways led from the parking lot to the highway. That must have been what perked up Collie's nose. Someone had recently driven off the lot and onto the strip, leaving tiger stripes on the pavement.

That worried Gus.

The hotel windows were nothing more than black squares, but there were enough of them overlooking the road. The more Gus looked at the place, the more he thought of old forts positioned atop hills overlooking rivers.

"See anyone?" he asked, driving along three wide lanes that were surprisingly uncluttered of vehicles.

"No."

"Think someone's in there?"

"We'll know in a few seconds."

The hotel loomed as Gus's heartrate increased with the growing tension. Any moment, he expected crazies to burst out of the fire escape and rush for their vehicles. There would be a chase. Maybe a firefight. The victor might have to deal with prisoners, and the notion of being captured didn't sit well in Gus's mind. He wasn't going to be anyone's prisoner ever again.

The hotel drifted by and disappeared behind them, but Collie kept her attention on the site in her side mirror.

Gus's knuckles tightened on the steering wheel. He squirmed, stopped, and adjusted himself again. Seconds ticked by, and the distance between them and the hotel grew.

"We clear?" Gus asked.

Collie held up a hand, asking for a few seconds more, then, "I think so. I think we're good. No shots fired. No one going for the cars."

"Thank you, Jesus."

"All jacked up, are you?"

"Yeah. A little."

"Sorry," Collie said. "My fault. Those tire tracks in the grass spooked me."

"Should we be worried about that?"

She shook her head. "I think we're good."

Gus nodded and kept on driving, but he didn't feel any better. He rubbed a hand over his forehead and felt sweat there.

"Don't you worry, babe," Collie told him. "Believe you me, on this road, we're the scary ones."

8

TransCanada Highway 101. Twenty-three kilometers west of Matheson,
Ontario.

"And hurry the fuck up or I swear to sunny Christ I'll blast your shit brains
across the asphalt."

The threat caused the 'meat puppet' to freeze on the spot, tire jack in hand.
The poor bastard raised his other hand slowly, as if to ward off the shotgun
pointed at his head. O'Leary would do it, he'd blast this fucker's head clean
all over the road on impulse alone. The self-professed surgeon had a very low
tolerance for dawdling and would enjoy shooting a few meat puppets. Just to
light a fire under the ball sacks of the rest.

"Goddammit O'Leary," the Jipman barked.

"What?"

"You froze him."

"Well, fuck it. I can unfreeze him."

"Yeah, how you gonna do that? By shooting him? Or maybe shooting one
of the others?"

"Thinkin' about it."

"How many others do we have?" the Jipman demanded.

A pause, during which the meat puppet squeezed his eyes shut and waited
for the inevitable blast that would take his life. His breathing had already
increased, as did the locomotive thumping of his heart. If O'Leary didn't
shoot him, he just might drop dead of a heart attack anyway. He wondered
which would hurt more.

"How many others do we have?" the Jipman repeated.

A deadly silence, then O'Leary replied. "You tryin' to be smart?"

"Nooo, just tryin' to get a point across. So how many?"

An uncertain pause. "What? With us?"

"Yeah, with us."

"The fuck you care?" O'Leary snapped.

"Don't be like that, dude. Just don't."

"Yeah? Or what? You thinkin' about doin' something?"

Rocks along the road's shoulders dug into the meat puppet's knees. His arms were starting to tremble, betraying his growing aches. The sun was out and smiling, hard enough to make one sweat in October's late glory, and the meat puppet was already stewing in his own filthy juices. At no time did the puppet think about using the tire jack as a weapon. That thought did not enter the puppet's head.

O'Leary's retort noticeably cooled the Jipman's attitude. "Just sayin' is all. Just sayin'. Don't you get any thoughts in your head."

"Like what?" O'Leary spat. "Like maybe shootin' you right here? Huh? Like just blastin' you off the road and leaving you like a spilled chocolate shake? Huh? Like a hundred and fifty pounds of bad meat? Thoughts like that?"

"Ease off, you fuckin' savage," the man called Top Gun warned. The meat puppet didn't know what Top Gun's real name was. All he knew was O'Leary would shoot Top Gun as quickly as any of them.

"He started it," O'Leary huffed, sounding very close to going full nuclear.

"He did not start it," Top Gun said calmly. "*You* started it. You seem to always start it these days. What's going on in that caveman skull of yours, huh? You're getting more and more unpleasant to work with every fucking day."

"Don't like stupid questions, is all," O'Leary said, but his tone had dialed back a bit.

"It's like this," Top Gun explained. "How many meat puppets did we have when we first started out here?"

"Five."

"How many we got now?"

"Three."

"And why is that?"

"'Cause I shot the others. But that was—"

Top Gun held up a hand. "What did you just say?"

O'Leary didn't answer.

"You said something just then."

"No, I didn't."

Top Gun waited, not impressed. "Repeat it, please."

O'Leary sighed in what sounded like embarrassment. "'Cause I shot the others."

"'Cause you shot the others."

"But that was because—"

"Ah!" Top Gun interrupted again, as if he were dead-lifting a tractor tire. "You shot the others. *You.* You pulled the trigger. You blew their heads off. All because they didn't do something fast enough or didn't answer fast enough. Now you're about to fuckin' execute a *third* meat puppet. I can't let you do that, son. Just because, if you do, you severely limit our workforce, and I'm not gonna change a fuckin' tire because of you. Not me. And not the Jipman."

"Fuck no," the Jipman said, nervous.

No one spoke then, and in the tense stillness that followed, the puppet's arms ached even more. He thought about putting them down, but didn't, mostly because O'Leary was standing right behind him. The surgeon was back there, his presence as palpable as a blazing furnace.

"Get back to work," O'Leary commanded the meat puppet. The meat puppet obeyed.

The conversation continued behind him, however.

"Glad that's over with," Top Gun said. "You did a wise thing, O'Leary. A very wise thing. You gotta have more patience in times like these."

"I think you two are ganging up on me," O'Leary rumbled.

"We're not—" Top Gun faltered before taking a breath. "Goddammit, you fucking moron, think for a second. Stop thinking with that boom stick of yours and use your other brain."

"The hell's all the shouting about," a fourth voice asked from a short distance. Jake. 'Jolly Jake', as the others called him. The meat puppet remembered the name. Reminded him of buccaneers.

"Fuckin' O'Leary," Top Gun answered. "He's getting a little overeager about shootin' people."

"What?"

"They're gangin' up on me," O'Leary protested, the anger returning. "Both of them."

"I'm not ganging up on you," the Jipman complained.

"Look," Top Gun stressed. "All I'm sayin' is… take it easy with the threats, all right? Just take it easy. We only got three meat puppets left. That's three. We don't want to use the merch in the trailer, right? I mean, that's all fresh. So, we gotta use what we got, and all we got left because of you are three slabs of meat," Top Gun carried on. "That's it. That's all. Look, in an effort of preserving the peace, go ahead and shoot the meat. I don't give a shit anymore. But I'm *not* going to change that goddamn tire. You understand me? I am not. And Jipman ain't gonna change that tire, either. Old Jolly over there got a fucked-up leg, so you know he's not gonna do it. So that leaves you. Understand?"

Peace then, of an uncertain kind. The meat puppet remained poised in front of the tire, tensed and waiting.

"You know something?" O'Leary spat. "Fuck it."

He fired.

Top Gun jumped at the sound.

The blast removed the top part of the unfortunate meat puppet's head and slapped a tattered rag of scalp and bone and brain matter against the very truck he was poised to work on. He fell over as if shoved from behind. Top Gun and the Jipman were speechless, partially in shock, and partially wondering if they should just shoot O'Leary right there. Top Gun had said it before—in private. The surgeon was a little past being desensitized to these impulsive acts of violence. Top Gun used to think O'Leary simply didn't care about what he did. Now, however, Top Gun suspected O'Leary was enjoying himself. Very much.

"Gotta break a few fuckin' eggs, right?" O'Leary swore, spittle flying from his bearded chops. "Gotta break a few to make the others work, right? Right?"

The Jipman nodded, and that took the attention off him. "Sure, dude. Sure."

Top Gun sighed, his shock bleeding away. It was only then when he heard the screams coming from the six-by-twelve cargo trailer hitched to the rear of his Raptor. O'Leary heard it, too, and while the man wasn't big, his unsettling anger and eagerness to kill made him a much bigger problem than Top Gun cared to admit.

"See what you did?" Top Gun said and turned to the trailer. He slapped the trailer wall, near a series of airholes punched into the side. Fingers poking out retreated when Top Gun hit the wall a second time, and a few wide eyes quickly withdrew into the trailer's dark recess, for fear of being poked.

Top Gun was beginning to think it was time to lessen the gang by one. Just to be on the safe side. He knew he'd sleep better at night. Hell, if he really wanted to sleep better at night, he'd just leave the whole unsavory business. It wasn't for him, anyway.

A child moaned from within the trailer and that annoyed O'Leary. He primed the shotgun and walked up to the airholes. "Shut the fuck up in there! Shut the fuck up or I'll put a round of shot in there right fucking *now*. Maybe two blasts and fuck the mess. Just fuck it. I'll wash out the whole trailer with a garden hose next time we stop. Hear me?"

The moaning ceased, as if someone had clamped a hand over the kid's mouth. O'Leary jammed his shotgun against one of the holes anyway.

The Jipman exchanged glances with Top Gun, and both men fluttered with indecision.

The meat puppets were one thing.

The *cargo* was another.

And just as Top Gun braced for more carnage, laughter erupted from the lead pickup truck.

Jolly Jake, apparently, had found humor in the proceedings.

"The fuck you laughing at?" O'Leary demanded, eyes wide and back-lit by a stick of crazy burning far too bright.

"You, dude, you," Jake laughed. An elbow jutting out of the driver's window was all that could be seen of the man, until he stuck half his head outside for a second. Only a second, as if daring O'Leary to take a shot at him. "You're hilarious. 'You kill him and you'll have to change the tire. I'm not gonna change that tire. I'm just sayin', you shoot him and you'll have to change the tire' and *fuck it*! BLAM! That shit *tinkled* it was so fuckin'cold."

Jolly Jake laughed again. Laughed so hard he even put a hand to the pickup's horn, the sound goosing the air and causing the Jipman to flinch.

"*Cold*, O'Leary!" Jake yelled. "Drop dead cold! What was your field of specialty again?"

O'Leary stopped and stared at the lead truck, the distraction disarming the tension. "Ruh," he said, as if trying to remember. "…Rhinoplasty," he finally managed, looking a little uncertain, and more than just a touch breathless.

"Rhinoplasty!" Another hearty chortle. "Goddamn. You sure as hell took care of that slab's nose."

The surgeon smiled. "Sure did. Damn straight, I did." And he released a soft chuckle.

"Well," Jake said. "You gonna change that tire, now?"

"Yeah. Sure."

And to Top Gun's and the Jipman's mutual dismay, O'Leary handed off his shotgun to the Jipman, giving him a look of *you gonna help or what?* No sooner did the Jipman take the weapon when O'Leary got to his knees and went to work on the flat.

"Fuck me gently," Top Gun muttered at the unexpected scene of roadside assistance. He waved off the Jipman, urging him to cool down. The Jipman indicated that he would, but he clearly wasn't happy about it. Shaking his head, Top Gun turned and walked away, believing the dangerous moment had passed for the time being. He kicked up pebbles scattered along the blacktop as he approached the lead truck in their two-truck caravan and faced Jolly Jake.

Jake was a long-haired hippy freak, with icy eyes and a mouth containing only half a load of teeth. His hair had been tied off in a foot-long tail with an elastic, of which he had about half a dozen spares around his right wrist. Jake was also a merchant of highjacked meat and bones. A pusher of prime, forcefully appropriated ass. And he was the captain of the little miserable band that Top Gun—once a high school gym teacher—found himself an increasingly unwilling part of.

"How do you do that?" Top Gun asked Jake, keeping O'Leary in sight as the brutish man struggled with the tire.

"Do what?"

"Talk him down like that."

"It's all in the laugh," Jake said with that spotty smile. "Laughter's the best medicine, right? Takes the sting outta everything, don't it?"

"Guess so," Top Gun said with a relieved shake of his head. Then he leaned in. "He's getting worse, Jake."

The Jolly one smiled. "Relax, Gun my son. Stay cool. I mean, really, we're all a little too close to the chicken barbeque, right? O'Leary's under some pressure is all. Let him have his fun—or in this case, let him blow off some steam. But, sweet Christ almighty, never challenge him. That's the road to some serious Tom-fuckery. Especially with him. And, if all else fails, just remember… ask what his old job was."

"He worked in a used bookshop," Top Gun whispered.

"See," Jake scolded with a frown. "You're fucking up again. In *his* mind, O'Leary was a cosmetic surgeon. A damned good one. Just don't ask him to do any work on you is all."

Top Gun couldn't help but smile nervously at that.

"Seriously," Jake carried on, lowering his voice and eyeing O'Leary. "What the hell, right? What does it matter what he thinks his old job used to be? Or his new one? Let him be Fire Chief Jim if it keeps him under control. A fucking astronaut if he pleases. Just remember to play along with the whole idea, but not, like, in a condescending way, right? But in a good way. It's an off-button, okay? For times like these."

"He was about to—"

"I know what he was about to do, which is why I started laughing here. And look. Suddenly everything is rum and roses. You get it now? Off-button. Just remember that. You gotten learn how to handle the freaks better. It ain't hard. All they want is attention, really. A little acknowledgement. That's all."

Top Gun supposed that was all, but his balls were still drawn up all tight and tingly.

"Look," Jake said, studying his companion's face. "He'll ride with me from here on end. That savage is too damn valuable to lose. Oh, make no mistake, one of us will end up shooting the poor bastard in the back of the head one morning, either before or after breakfast beers, but let's hold off on that for as long as we can. Whatever you might think of him, the bottom line is he's valuable. He terrifies the cargo. Terrifies them. Terrifies the meat puppets, too. You can't... teach that shit. You can't. You either got it or you don't. And he's. Got. It."

Top Gun exhaled a note of *Oh he's got something all right.*

"Listen," Jake continued. "Don't you worry. You and the Jipman can drive on behind us. Play some tunes. Play 'em loud if you want. Fuck it, dude. Just *fffff*uck it. We got the goods, and this time tomorrow is payday. So fuck it. Okay? Hear me? You good?"

By "payday", Jake meant supplies of food and gas in exchange for the cargo.

Top Gun felt uneasy just thinking about that, but what he said was, "Yeah. I'm good."

"Smooth. *Hey O'Leary!*"

Top Gun flinched as the surgeon's—the delusional surgeon's—head snapped up.

"You get that done, then come on back here. You're ridin' up front with me, you crazy rabid bear fucker you. Hope you like *Deep Purple.*"

"Fuckin' love *Deep Purple!*" O'Leary's eyes lit up, and for a brief moment he resembled a big old shaggy collie who'd just heard the rattling of treats in a can.

The sight amazed Top Gun.

"Well, get that shit done, son!" Jake yelled out.

An enthusiastic O'Leary got back to work.

Jolly Jake fired off an expression of *See?* at Top Gun before winking at him.

Top Gun saw, and frankly, it both amazed and scared the living shit outta him.

9

The two-truck motorcade stopped ten kilometers outside of Timmins, at the last Blue Star EV charging station this side of the TCH. Half of the building's roof had charred and collapsed, as if God himself had decided to pop a propane pimple with disastrous consequences. The main office, attached convenience store, and restaurant remained intact, however, although the smashed windows and wide-open doors indicated it had long since been gutted by looters. There were three main charging areas out front, all lined up like a regular parking lot, where each individual zone had a single charging station positioned at the end. On a lot that might service a total of fifty or more cars, there were only three mid-sized vehicles occupying the recharging zones. The chargers were white and blue, with yellow lightning streaking through a blue sun on their bulky sides. They reminded Top Gun of old-fashioned parking meters but with a few extra kilograms of armor slapped on top.

When Jake and his crew designated the place as their rendezvous spot, Top Gun had himself a waltz through the adjoining facilities, because one never knew what looters might have missed the first dozen times through. Sadly, however, the whole facility had been picked clean.

Not even a road map.

Someone had tossed all the metal racks into a corner behind the counter, creating a nightmarish Jungle Jim of sorts. Broken glass, squashed plastic bottles, and an assortment of flattened juice and milk cartons littered the floor near the coolers. There had been a faint smell of piss around there, as well. The place certainly had had its share of visitors after the fall of civilization, but as of last week it had been deserted.

O'Leary got out of Jake's truck. He wore a Kevlar vest, which needed some stitching on one side, and a dinged-up riot helmet. The armor encased the self-proclaimed nose surgeon in a bulky, intimidating outer shell. He adjusted the helmet aggressively, as if pissed off he couldn't jam a finger into his ear. Once that was done, he bent over and crept towards the open doors of the station.

"Jesus," Top Gun said. "He must've put that on while in the truck."

"Bet that was an experience," the Jipman said on the passenger side.

"Bet it was."

The two men sat in the second truck and stared.

"Jake don't give a fuck," the Jipman finally said. "Probably suggested it himself."

"Probably." Top Gun eyed the highways running east and west and the derelicts dotting the lanes. There were abandoned vehicles everywhere, but they usually were more of a pain in the ass around bigger cities, where the sheer volume forced a driver to reduce his speed to a crawl. Or simply turn back and find another route.

"I tell ya," the Jipman said, staring off in the direction O'Leary had gone. "That guy's on a fuse."

"I know," Top Gun said.

"A short fuse."

"I know."

"One of us will haveta put him down."

"Probably."

"I could do it," the Jipman offered. "Just pop him when he gets back. When we all sit down to eat. No trouble. I just need the go-ahead."

"Jake won't like it," Top Gun said, squinting at the aging afternoon. "He says we need him, even though the guy's crazy. He has a point."

"We only need him for shock and awe. That's it."

"That's *exactly* it," Top Gun agreed. "You gotta admit, when O'Leary gets it in his head to go through a door, he goes through a door. Can't find help like that anymore."

"Suppose not," the Jipman said, but he clearly wasn't convinced.

The conversation got quiet then, and Top Gun turned off the engine to preserve fuel. The silence thrummed in his ears, and he lowered his window. A breeze passed through the cab, cold to the face but refreshing. Someone thumped in the cargo trailer from behind, as if they'd fallen over, and Top Gun glanced at the padlocked doors. No one was going to try and escape.

O'Leary came back into sight and waved them in.

"All clear," Top Gun said.

"No one's been here for ages," the Jipman declared.

"Rather be safe than sorry."

Under an overcast sky, they left the pickup, their sidearms holstered on their thighs. Top Gun stretched with a soft groan and focused on a clump of trees across the highway. The Jipman did the same on the passenger side. Both men wore jeans and t-shirts held in place with some tactical webbing.

Upon sharing a look, the Jipman started walking toward the rear. "Gonna check on the cargo," he said.

Top Gun let him go.

Jake stood beside his ride. The leader stretched as if he were unlocking his entire spine. He croaked happily and ran his fingers through his greasy hair. The guy loved his hair and couldn't go five minutes without touching it, as if he had stringy gold sprouting from his scalp. Once finished, Jake sauntered along the truck, limping just a little and rubbing his belly. He slapped the cargo trailer's length before breaking into a full-on drum solo, grinning the whole way, until he got to the end. He stopped at the rear doors, studied the upper frame, and disarmed the booby trap located there. Five seconds later he unlocked the trailer and opened the container.

Even with the air holes and the freezing ventilation of the highway, a gym-stink of unwashed skin and shitty-ass clothing reached out and rudely invaded Top Gun's mouth and nose, stealing his breath by the fistful. That olfactory jack-slap to the face stopped the man cold, left him wishing for a gas mask. Or a firehose.

"Get out, you shitty-assed fuckers, get out," Jake merrily told them, but his hand was on his Sig Saur in a *don't test me* sorta way.

Shadows stirred in the depths of the cargo trailer. Chains rattled along the floor. Two pitiful figures staggered into the daylight. Grease-smudged hockey masks covered their faces, the plastic kind a kid might wear on Halloween. They wore clothing that might've been washed in rancid animal fat. Their hands and ankles were shackled, a single chain connecting them to one another. They lurched to a stop some three paces outside the trailer and steadied themselves like a pair of drunks trying hard to appear sober. Jake used to call them 'meat', or 'slabs of meat', before finally adopting the current favorite 'meat puppets'.

"Sit," Jake ordered.

The two men lowered themselves to the ground, settling down on their hands and knees.

"Christ almighty," Jake chuckled and pinched his nose. "We're gonna haveta get you some new clothes. Maybe something for winter, too. You like that idea? Maybe some sweaters?"

The two meat puppets nodded energetically.

"Well, maybe that's what we'll do. Do a little early Christmas shopping. Sweaters and some woolly socks. That sound good?"

More enthusiastic nods.

"You up for some Christmas shopping there, Top G?" Jake asked a little too loud for Top Gun's liking.

Top Gun frowned. The meat puppets made him uneasy. He didn't like Jake accepting and taking them for this side-quest. But, like before, he kept his mouth shut.

He feared he wasn't going to keep it shut for much longer.

"No?" Jake asked. "Shit. We *gotta* keep Christmas in mind. That's the happiest day of the year. Presents for all the good boy meat sticks and good girl meat sticks. That's my new favorite name for you sonsabitches. Hey, how's the cargo looking, Jipman?"

From the rear, the Jipman waved an affirmative. "You wanna let them out for a walk?" he asked.

"Mmm… yeah, let them out for a bit." Jake said, studying the puppets on their knees.

"One took a shit near the door."

A look of horror appeared on the Jolly one's face. "*What?*"

"Yeah. Smelled it when I got back here."

Top gun sniffed and got nothing. The breeze was taking it away from him.

"They shit in the back?" Jake demanded, clearly offended.

"One of them did."

"Well, goddammit. That's just rude. You'd think they would hold it in."

"O'Leary blasting the head off the slab might've had something to do with that," Top Gun suggested, and only because O'Leary was currently gravitating to the restaurant section of the recharging station.

"What? Jake asked. "Scared them *that* bad? Christ. If they're like that now, what are they gonna be like after a few days with the Leather?"

Top Gun didn't know. Didn't want to know, really.

"Well, shit," Jake said, hitching his hands on his hips. "I'm tempted to let them just fucking wallow in that. I don't appreciate shit like that. Fucking rude. Shitting in the trailer. You hear that, boys?"

The two slabs nodded again.

"Someone dropped some corn fudge in the trailer. Take a guess as to who's gonna clean that up barehanded?"

The two meat slabs nodded but didn't comment, as if they'd been gagged. Truth was, they *were* gagged, their mouths clogged with plastic balls and kept in place with strips of black studded leather. Oddly enough, Jake had no issue with using ball gags on the meat, but he didn't like the look of the things. Thank the Lord for their hockey masks, which covered up all that unpleasantness.

"Fuck it," Jake declared, changing his mind. "They couldn't hold it in, they can damn well stew in it. And I'll tell you another thing—their walking privileges have just been suspended. Let 'em stretch their legs in the trailer and try not to touch their own shit."

"When's the Leather coming around again?" Top Gun asked, wanting to change the subject.

"Dunno exactly," Jake said. "Sometime tomorrow. Hopefully in the morning. The Leather's weird though," he continued, turning toward the distant treeline. "He might be around here now. And just watching us."

That unnerved Top Gun. "Really?"

"Oh yeah. He's fucked up like that. Even though we got the merch." Jake spun around and raised his voice. "You hear that? If you're out there, we got your merch!"

"Jesus, Jake, keep it down," Top Gun winced.

Jake's smile reappeared. "Fuck it, Gun my son. Fuck it. What are we worried about? No one around. And if they were, we got the mad dog shotgun surgeon with us. That right?"

"You got it, Jake," O'Leary said, weapon slung over a shoulder as he walked back to the truck.

"You say tomorrow morning?" the Jipman asked from the rear.

"Hopefully tomorrow morning," Jake said.

"What direction is he coming from, you think?"

"Fuck if I know. So many back roads around here. Why?"

"That him, you think?"

The question got the whole group's complete attention. There was no mistaking what they saw. There, about a kilometer back, on the crest of the open highway, was a pickup truck—the windshield and roof dull underneath the overcast sky.

"Well, now," Jake said, snarling good naturedly at the vehicle. "That's a good question."

The pickup wasn't getting any closer. It was just out there, poised on the absolute edge of their vision, as if sensing it had been detected.

Top Gun eyed the machine with a questioning grimace. The thing bothered him. He reached for his holstered Beretta and slipped the weapon free.

"Where are the spyglasses?" Jake asked.

"In the truck," O'Leary replied.

"Get them."

"I think it's a car," the Jipman said. "The Leather drive a car?"

"The Leather drives a *truck*," Jake reported, holding out a hand and waiting on O'Leary. "The Leather needs a truck. Can't stuff the merch in the backseat of a Honda Civic."

Top Gun supposed not, not when the merch was prone to laying fudge pipe when frightened. "I don't think it's the Leather, Jake," he finally said.

"I'm pretty sure it's not the Leather," Jake agreed. He immediately put the binoculars to his eyes once O'Leary handed them over. "Don't think the Leather would try sneaking up on us, either."

"Didn't you just say they might be watching us?" Top Gun asked.

"I was only fuckin' around then. You gotta have more trust, TG. More trust. We have a business arrangement here."

"What do you see?" the Jipman asked, half-turned to his companions.

Jake didn't answer. He fiddled with the magnification and grew agitated. "Goddammit," he finally swore. "Who fucked around with these things?"

O'Leary glared a warning in Top Gun's direction.

"One of the doors just opened, I think," the Jipman said. He disappeared behind the bulk of the trailer. Top Gun did the same, his paranoia alive and thrumming.

"You hear me?" the Jipman asked, coming into view on the other side, just beyond the box bed and the trailer hitch.

"I heard," Jake said, no longer quite so jolly. "Hold on a second, goddammit. All right. Yeah. It's a truck. Two doors are open. There's the driver. Getting out."

Top Gun saw a stick figure emerge, visible from the chest up, and partially hidden by the door.

"The fuck is that?" Jake said aloud, adjusting his binoculars again. "All right, all right. Hold on. Okay. I see him. One guy. Wearing—"

There was a weird spurt and a crinkle of exploding glass, and Jolly Jake flew backwards, his arms flopping as if he were fending off a swarm of mosquitoes. That happened for all of a split second. The curt metallic shriek that followed prompted Top Gun to race for cover, his gun out and poised at his ear. He looked back and saw Jake—ten twitching toes up—and a grisly stew of head cheese spattered across the black top. Black flies were already making halos around the dead man. The binoculars lay just outside of the corpse's reach, one lens shattered, the fragments shiny in the daylight.

"*Holy shit!*" O'Leary screamed. "*Holy shit!*"

"Get down!" Top Gun yelled, and O'Leary, suddenly not so insane anymore, did exactly as he was told. He disappeared behind the front of Jake's ride.

"Sweet fuck almighty, Top," the Jipman said from the other side of the cargo trailer. "Jake's dead."

"Yeah."

"You see who did it?"

"No," Top Gun replied, his heart and temples pumping in the disquieting silence following the kill shot.

The Jipman had pressed himself up against the trailer, in between the truck's tailgate. He swung his head around and carefully tried to locate the attackers. "Fuckers must have a sniper rifle."

"You think?" Top Gun snapped off. "Keep your head down."

"Who do you think it is?"

"Jesus Christ's love handles, I don't *know*. Now shut the fuck up and keep your eyes open." Frustrated, Top Gun stayed low and scanned the road, right up to that crest and the truck beyond. The driver was gone, at least from his sight.

"They're coming for the cargo!" O'Leary blurted.

Probably, Top Gun thought. Theirs was a budding market, and no doubt there would be rival companies seeking a slice of the action. Ones that didn't mind killing off and robbing the competition. Top Gun no longer cared. They could *have* it.

"That's the Leather and he's coming for the cargo!" O'Leary continued, his words slowly becoming a rant. "He's coming for the cargo. He's coming for the cargo and the meat and he don't wanna pay for any of it. Decided he's just gonna kill us and take it! Just gonna *kill us and take it! That Leather-coated piece of cocksucking shit! WELL FUCK THAT NOISE! I AIN'T LETTIN' HIM!*"

There was a growl then, of pure uncorked rage and adrenaline. A lethal combination capable of transforming a psychotic gluebag like O'Leary into a batshit crazy superfreak. And O'Leary was working himself through a positively frightening metamorphosis. He panted back there, a loud, gibbering, frothing growl. Loud enough that Top Gun believed today was the day he'd have to put a bullet through the man's skull. If he was able. Thing was, he might *need* the fucking lunatic. Might need his extra firepower until they determined who their attackers were.

Well, shit! Top Gun's scrambling mind fired off. He'd just been dumped into perhaps one of the most dreadful situations he could imagine—caught between a sniper and a short-circuiting wingnut.

BOOM!

The explosion spun Top Gun around. He took aim at the truck behind him. One of the two meat puppets had toppled over; his head looked like it had been fed into a lawnmower.

Thing was, the sniper out there had no shot of the puppets. The angle and cover of the two pickups didn't allow one.

The guy doing the shooting was none other than O'Leary himself.

"Christ almighty," the Jipman was saying, but the words were barely audible over the frantic whimpering of the other meat slab, and the *schlacking* of a fresh shell being racked and readied.

BOOM!

A spray of black matter and another fleshy thud. Top Gun clapped a hand over his scalp. "Quit that shit, y'fuckin nipplehead! Those are *rentals* you're shootin'!"

"*HE AIN'T GETTIN' THEM!*" O'Leary screamed, hard enough to potentially burst his brain.

If only I was so lucky, Top Gun thought, his gun held to his ear.

"There's only one shooter," the Jipman yelled. "O'Leary, *wait!*"

"That's the *Leather* out there!" O'Leary shouted back, steaming red and full-on savage, caught in the middle of refilling his lungs. "Don't wanna pay for the merch. The Leather's like a fuckin' cockroach! *A fuckin' cockroach!* And *where there's one—!*"

The Jipman's exploding head distracted Top Gun then, and he flinched in horror as his companion's torso pitched forward and dropped out of sight. The Jipman must have given the mystery shooter a big enough target to fire upon.

Which the unseen marksman had done, to spectacular effect.

O'Leary screamed, arms flailing as he stood between Jake's trailer and the front of Top Gun's truck.

"They got the Jipman," Top Gun exclaimed in a panic. He immediately clamped down on that shit, knowing that if he freaked out, he'd be dead in seconds.

"They got—" Top Gun began just before O'Leary (as he and the newly deceased Jipman so often speculated would happen) finally, *mentally* detonated.

Perhaps it was the shock of seeing Jake go down in a decidedly inglorious fashion. Maybe it was the ease at which the Jipman had the top of his own skull surgically removed by a bullet. Top Gun figured it was a perfect, instant crazy-cake mixture of everything O'Leary needed to explode.

The shotgun surgeon screamed hard enough to blow out his vocal cords. Hard enough that Top Gun pointed his gun in that direction when he knew he should be paying attention to the sniper picking them off. O'Leary screamed again, a death metal peal of unintelligible gibberish, and charged out from between the two vehicles. Red-faced and eyes wide in a ghastly, howling caricature of a Japanese Tengu mask, O'Leary blasted into the open like an armored sumo fired from a cannon.

And was immediately blown backwards, as if he'd caught an enemy battleship shell square in the chest.

At least, that's what it looked like to Top Gun.

O'Leary's screaming melded with that familiar metallic buzz for all of a split second, before he landed flat on his spine—some ten feet back from where he was hit.

Jesus Christ! Top Gun swore and got low. He struggled to think. Screams clawed at his brain, and it took him a moment to realize it was not coming from his head but from the gagged prisoners chained inside the trailer.

Top Gun fumed. He debated if he should make peace with the sniper for killing O'Leary, attempt revenge for killing the rest of his crew, or just unhook the lead trailer and get the sweet nut fudge out of Dodge.

It took him a whole second to think that one through.

And the answer surprised him.

Someone had gotten the jump on them, but Top Gun wasn't done just yet. Matter of fact, when he got right down to it, he was getting mighty pissed. As weird as it sounded, despite his earlier misgivings about the whole operation, Jolly Jake, the Jipman, and even batfuck crazy O'Leary were *still* his crew.

And Top Gun wanted a little vengeance.

He crowded the trailer hitch, careful to keep his ass behind cover, and glanced to where the poor old Jipman lay dead and leaking. Top Gun's partner in crime had well and truly passed on, but the Jipman's gun was nearby. A Berretta. Not so far out of reach. Top Gun was tempted to try and reach it, but he soon decided an extra sidearm wasn't going to win this fight.

He had something else in mind.

Dealing with the hammering in his chest, Top Gun's thoughts centered on what he had stashed into the back seat of his ride's crew cab. The very reason why they called him Top Gun. Though he might've been a teacher in the old world, he did have training, once being a part of the Canadian Infantry. Top Gun kept his head low as he pressed up against the rear bumper.

He took a deep breath.

Top Gun raced out from around the truck and threw open the driver's side rear door. A formidable rifle lay on the floor. He grabbed it, clapping an elbow off the edge of the door. A hot buzzsaw of pain licked his arm all the way to his fingers. Groaning, taking in the carbonated sting that enveloped everything below his left bicep, Top Gun heaved himself back onto the pavement.

Just as a bullet rudely punched through the window of the open door, missing his head by a split second.

A breathless Top Gun scurried underneath the truck, shimmying along on his belly. He pulled the rifle in with him, despite the angry sizzle paralyzing his left arm.

Step one down. He struggled to orient himself. A second later, he clawed his way underneath the crusty chassis, towards Jake's truck.

Someone yelled, the meaning lost on him. Then O'Leary answered, risen from the dead, roaring a stream of hot filth that scorched the very air.

"I'll kill you, you piece of shit dog fucks!"

The scream from the pretending nose surgeon caused Top Gun to jerk his head up, right into the metallic guts of the pickup. The connection was brilliant, the effect immediate. He dropped to the ground again while grabbing at his head, the smoldering nerve pain of his left arm pressed against his ear.

"Goddamn salt flap, sonsacocksmoking bitches!" O'Leary released in a voice frayed and threatening to blow itself out. He rolled over onto his belly, drew his legs up enough that his ass pointed to the heavens, and shuddered from the waist up. Top Gun watched from underneath the truck, and cringed.

"Get down, you stupid fuck!" he shouted.

O'Leary did not get down. With one hand pressed against his bulletproofed chest, he somehow got to his feet while still gripping his shotgun. Adjusting his helmet as if he'd just been gorged by a bull, O'Leary was too furious to do anything more than rant and rave.

And fire his shotgun.

One-handed, into the air, which stunned Top Gun for all of a second.

Before a bullet expertly perforated the tempered glass of the man's face shield in a splash of bright jam. That shot knocked O'Leary back onto his ass a good five feet, splayed out as if nailed to the ground and waiting for the fire ants.

Even as a potential distraction, O'Leary had failed to deliver.

Fucking numpty, Top Gun fumed, getting some feeling back into his arm. He checked on O'Leary, confirmed that the man was indeed expired, and considered his next move. He wondered if the killers were advancing. A second later, he resumed crawling towards the front and didn't stop until he was out from underneath his truck. With his ass on the pavement and his spine against the grill, Top Gun readied his own long-distance cannon with practiced familiarity. He extended the bipod, checked the magazine, and took another breath before priming the Australian-made AUG-20 long-range assault rifle—a superior upgrade from the older, less reliable models. He then considered the open ground to his left, where a meat puppet corpse lay in a blood pool. Jolly Jack was just a few feet beyond that, which caught Top Gun's eye, and got him thinking.

He would only have a second, if that.

Top Gun lunged toward the corpse, landing hard, metal and bone scrubbing pavement. He skinned out his unprotected elbow on the coarse surface and felt a moment's terror when his right foot slipped and blew out behind him. But then he collapsed upon Jolly Jake and rolled over his dead leader. He got onto his chest and gave the corpse a quick pat down.

No keys.

Top Gun hoped to God that Jake had left them in his truck, because he wasn't crawling back to his own ride. Without another thought, the part-time soldier slapped the AUG-20 down on Jake's sunken ribcage. He screwed his face into the sights and scanned the distant crest.

Pickup truck.

Open door. On both sides.

No shooter, however. None that he could see.

A man stuck his head out from behind the door, moving around, staying low but being sloppy about it. No doubt thinking the dirty work had been done. Or that he was well out of range. The guy had a thick beard and wore a winter cap. Sunglasses shielded his eyes.

Top Gun centered the reticle upon the target's face, intending to give back some pain. He forced himself to exhale and the bearded bastard ducked just as Top Gun squeezed the trigger.

Missed.

But the unmistakable blast and scream of the bullet had alerted the target. The guy dropped from sight. Furious, Top Gun panned right. There were no targets besides the obvious, so he made do with that. He fired, squeezing the trigger three times, the rifle softly bucking against his shoulder. Spidery holes appeared in the vehicle's windshield with misty pops. The fourth shot punched the road's shoulder, spraying crushed stone.

Baring his teeth, Top Gun adjusted his aim. The truck's tires weren't visible, but the engine block was.

So he placed six shots into the grill, the impacts sparkling.

"Take that, you piece of shit," he snarled. "Take that."

Satisfied, Top Gun yanked back his weapon and staggered into a run, thinking of escape. Jake's ride was there, ready and waiting. He hurried to the driver's side, whipped open the door, and scrambled aboard, shoving his weapon muzzle-first into the passenger side. Slamming the door, Top Gun located the key fob and jammed his thumb into the ignition button.

The pickup's engine flared to life with a biodiesel roar.

"You want the cargo, bitches?" Top Gun asked, his voice laced with venom. "Then take 'em."

No merch was worth his life.

With that, he put the truck into gear and stomped on the gas. Cargo trailer still attached, Jolly Jake's pickup surged forward, charging for the town of Timmins with a steel-belted scream of rubber.

10

"Jesus *Christ*," Gus winced as he dove for cover after the first shell plugged the windshield. A destructive pattering followed, as more bullets blasted the truck's face, popping glass and metal.

Then nothing.

Until a speck of a figure sprinted in the distance, keeping close to the pickup and trailer. Seconds later, the engine flared to life and the truck bolted towards the city.

"He's getting away!" Gus shouted. "Collie, he's getting away!"

"Roger that," Collie replied. She'd set up shop some twenty feet away from the pickup. She lay on her chest, aiming a high-tech rifle, one of the few pillaged from the battleground that had been Whitecap. Her sunglasses were pushed up on her forehead, and when she looked away from her scope, she pulled them back over her eyes.

"No shot," she said. She sighed when she saw the damage done to the pickup. "Well. Goddamn Jimmy Jesus."

Gus rose to his knees. "We going after them?"

Collie sized up the distance. "No."

"No?"

She shook her head.

Gus stood, his knees cracking as he did so. Steam drifted from the perforated engine block, and the sight prompted him to massage the back of his neck.

"Bastard shot our truck," he muttered, at a loss for anything more.

Collie hurried to the driver's side, tossing Gus the rifle as she passed him. The action surprised him, but he caught the weapon all the same.

"Nothing," Collie said, leaning into the cab and attempting to start the motor. "Not a fucking gig. Well, shit. I mean, the engine's *made* of metal."

She reached down and popped the hood.

Gus looked off in the distance, watching the fleeing pickup and trailer fade into the distance. The sound of an approaching vehicle distracted him. Bruno and Cory stopped their truck beside him. Bruno lowered his window and grimaced at the sight of the crippled ride.

"Dead truck?" he asked.

"Dead truck," Gus replied.

"Well, that sucks beaver hole."

That nasty bit of expletive goodness stopped Gus for all of a heartbeat, but then he joined Collie at their mangled vehicle. The bullets had ripped through the thinner metals of the motor. Smoke wafted from different points. The bullet holes inside the cavity resembled hot splashes of chrome. Connecting rods were dented and twisted. Severed wires dangled. The battery had taken a round straight through the heart. Fluid from multiple tubes dribbled onto the pavement, and the smell of burning rubber and acid was strong enough to back Gus up a step.

"Anyone got any duct tape?" he asked in a defeated tone.

"Later," Collie said, focusing on the abandoned pickup and cargo trailer left on the highway. "After we check on that trailer."

Gus looked at the far-off truck.

"Let's ride, amigos," she shouted, then opened the rear door of Bruno's cab.

"What about our gear?" Gus asked, going for the other side.

"We'll come back for it after we check that thing out."

Timmins stood tall in the distance, an angular patch of brooding towers and apartment boxes stamped against the skyline. Gus didn't like the look of the city. Didn't like the feeling of dread percolating in his guts. That feeling had started that very morning, when he was squatting over a hole dug in the ground with a little garden shovel. They'd gone off-road to avoid all the abandoned cars on the highway, and stopped at a clearing in the forest. It was around then when the shouting rudely interrupted Gus's morning constitutional. The following gunshot got his bowels moving again, however, with explosive urgency. The far-off laughter that followed had creeped him out. If a skeleton could laugh, it probably sounded like that.

Thinking back, Gus realized that the last three days had been easy. Too damn easy, in fact. Sure, they'd had a few tense times—rolling through the smaller cities, crossing over the St. Lawrence, and skirting around Ottawa came to mind—but, ultimately, nothing had happened. They'd driven on through a dead landscape, through a world slowly being reclaimed by a greedy Mother Nature.

"Okay," Collie said, sitting on the other side of two hockey bags of supplies. He could only see her profile—and the upper section of her assault rifle. "Right here, Cor'."

Cory braked hard and stopped the truck alongside the trailer. He parked the machine with a hard shove of the stick.

"All of you stay aboard," Collie ordered. "Get ready to leave fast if we have to."

"You expecting trouble?" Bruno asked.

"I'm always expecting trouble," she said and got out.

"God knows we're finding it," Gus muttered and got out on the other side.

And landed boots first in the gore spattering the pavement.

"Well fuck," he groaned in distaste, eyeing the bloody mess.

"What?" Collie asked.

"I'm standing in fucking blood over here."

She didn't answer; instead she approached the deserted truck with her drawn sidearm. She didn't take her rifle, and Gus knew it was because of her left arm, where she'd been shot through the bicep a few months back, during the firefight at Whitecap. Even though the wound had healed, the arm hadn't regained its full strength, despite Maggie's physical therapy sessions. As a result, Collie could only carry and use her rifle for short periods of time.

She had no problem with her pistol, however.

Sig Saur aimed and ready, Collie approached the truck.

Gus hung back, having learned the hard way that she was bossy in tense situations. She'd reminded them repeatedly that she had a shitload of experience in these kinds of operations, but Gus suspected the operator was being extra protective of her civvie crew. Not that it offended him.

But it did make him feel about as useful as a dick stitched to an elbow.

Collie neared the driver's window. She checked the interior, deemed it clear, and switched to the rear seat. Once satisfied, she moved to the trailer.

Collie scanned the long container, then peered underneath the carriage. She ran a hand along the exterior, stopped at the rear doors, then locked eyes on Gus. Before she could speak, she was interrupted by a rustling from inside the trailer.

Gus's eyes narrowed. "The hell was that?"

"There's people inside this thing," Collie said. "Saw them through the air holes.'"

"Air holes?"

"Yeah. Air holes. But not too many. Can't have the meat too uppity, right?" Collie shook her head. "Just stay back for a second."

The sound of a power window lowering filled Gus's ears.

"Hey Collie, there's people inside that thing!" Bruno exclaimed.

The operator sighed at the egregious breach of silence. "Yeah, I know."

"What's going on?" Gus asked.

"We're gonna find out." She winked at him.

Gus had to admit, he felt some funky goodness when she did that. He followed her around the truck and nearly stepped on a corpse with the splayed-out hair of a hard rocker. Collie stepped over another dead man and patted down his sides. She reached inside the carcass's pocket and pulled out a set of keys.

Voices reached Gus's ears—muted somehow, as if gagged, like those poor bastards lying on the pavement with the hockey masks. One mask had been twisted aside, revealing half a face mashed into the asphalt, and what looked like a cord of leather lashed around his head. Gus looked away, feeling it was far too early in the day for such pictures.

"You gonna get them out?" Bruno asked from his passenger window.

"Yes, I'm gonna get them out," Collie answered. "Just stay where you are for a minute, okay?"

Bruno nodded, but Gus wasn't sure he believed him.

Collie focused on the trailer doors. "Relax in there," she called. "We're gonna get you out."

The grunting intensified, and if Gus wasn't mistaken, the grunting didn't seem too keen on the idea.

Collie noticed it as well. She stepped back, her weapon lowered. She motioned Gus to come closer, and when he did, she handed him the keys.

"Open it up," she said. She stepped back and took aim at the doors.

Gus rattled the chains locked around the two doors.

That plugged screaming went up several notches. The padlock in his hand, Gus shot Collie a questioning look.

"I don't know," she answered. "Hold on a second."

She went to the trailer sidewall and peeked into an air hole.

"Jesus Christ," Bruno hissed. "You guys smell that?"

"I smell that," Gus said and covered his mouth, knowing human waste when he smelled it.

"They're bouncing all over the place in there," Collie reported. "They're real excited about something. Can't see everything."

"Jesus. Sounds like a dozen weightlifters in there blowing out their ass rings," Gus said.

Collie winced at that.

Gus released the unlocked padlock, and the resulting clatter generated a second group scream from within the trailer. He flinched at the suppressed squeals of terror and backed up a step, trading looks with Collie. If the people inside were energetic before, they were going insane now. The trailer rocked on its chassis from an unseen barrage of physical contact, as if bodies were launching themselves at the walls. All that frantic motion seemed to lift the stink originating from the trailer and flap it in Gus's direction.

"I gotta feeling I'm gonna see something I don't wanna," he said.

"Probably," Collie agreed.

"Cleared to open this thing?"

"Wait." She stepped in close to the trailer. "Relax in there, okay? We're going to let you out."

An excited outburst answered her, and it did not sound happy.

"Something's wrong," Gus muttered.

"Sure is," Bruno said from the truck. "They're trapped in a trailer of their own shit and God only knows what else. They heard gunfire, and they don't know who we are, or what we're gonna do to them."

"Yeah, there's that, but..." Gus rubbed his head. "There's something more here."

Sensing the same, Collie holstered her weapon and inspected the trailer doors, even as the rocking trailer threatened to fall off its own chassis.

"Wogs," she said under her breath and examined the upper section of the frame. She leaned in and ran her fingers along the closure. A frown creased her features. When she reached the center of the door, she stopped. Her eyes went wide.

"Well, now," she whispered. "Aren't you the potential party shaker..."

"Find something?" Gus asked. "Collie?"

"Uh-huh?"

"You find something?"

"I did, dear."

Gus knew when he was being fucked with, so he shut up. Until she extracted her boot knife, whereupon he gave her all the room she needed. Collie checked her footing and climbed onto the rear step of the trailer.

"Gus?" she asked.

"Yes dear?"

That stopped her. "Don't you put a smile on my face. Not now."

"Sorry."

"Do me a favor? Tell the folks inside this meat locker to keep still for a few seconds. Okay?"

Orders received, Gus approached the sidewall, noting how shadows flittered beyond the air holes. The stink of the trailer swelled, becoming so bad, so wickedly foul, that he dreaded opening his mouth. "Hey! *Hey!*" he shouted. He cringed, absorbing that unspeakable cloud and feeling his tongue curl. "Keep it down in there. Okay? Keep it down. Relax, for Christ's sake. I mean… oh god*damn*… You guys assfuck a skunk in there or what?"

That settled matters down considerably. The trailer's rocking subsided to a tentative wavering, as if there were a dozen people standing far too close to a bomb.

That last thought froze Gus on the spot. "Ah… Collie?"

"Yeah?" she asked, as she worked her knife into the door crack.

Gus cleared his throat. "Are we in danger here?"

"You want the truth?"

That stopped him. "Uh…Sure. Why not?"

And at that exact moment, she squeezed her eyes shut, grimaced, and gently plucked at something unseen in the door.

Gus froze.

Collie opened her eyes, saw that all was well, and smiled. She pulled her knife free.

"Nope," she exhaled.

Gus looked back at Bruno, whose expression morphed from worry to shit-chugging relief.

A short time later, Collie stopped searching. "All right," she announced to those inside. "I checked out the doors here… and found what I suspect might've been a trip wire for an explosive device. Is that correct?"

Energetic grunts answered her.

Gus felt his balls lift a notch.

"Okay then," Collie continued. "You'll be happy to know I've disabled the trip wire. At least I think I've disabled it. To the best of your knowledge, and scream if you know this, is there any other trap?"

The trailer became silent.

"All right then," she said. She motioned for Gus to open the doors.

He picked up the padlock.

Collie immediately retreated about a dozen steps.

Gus questioned her with a look, to which she shrugged. He scowled and inserted the key and hesitated.

Fuck it, Gus thought, and turned the key.

11

If the smell was bad outside the trailer, the stink that wafted free of that opened box was a malevolent, life-stealing wave, redolent of diseased graves and oozing, gangrenous wounds. That colorless swell enveloped Gus, and he involuntarily turned away and covered his face.

"Oh," was all he could manage.

That breath-snatching foulness struck Collie as well, and she visibly faltered as it rolled over her. Once the fresh air cleared that pent up bubble of filth, the operator steadied herself and approached the trailer.

Knowing he was going to have nightmares, Gus straightened and peered inside the trailer confines.

Dried excrement littered the corners of the trailer, particularly near the doors. There were five people in there, their hands behind their backs and hunched over by the low ceiling. They wore jeans, sweaters, and thick shirts, but no coats, and no shoes, wearing either socks or just barefoot. All five of them wore ball gags, the leather straps tight about their heads. All five were also chained about the ankles.

"You're all right," Collie gently informed them. "Just hold on for a minute more."

Two men, two women, and a young girl, perhaps ten. All were filthy, as if they'd been dunked in a septic tank. Black smudges stained their faces, and they stared at their rescuers with wide, hopeful eyes, perhaps wondering if they'd just been saved or captured by someone much worse.

Gus swallowed thickly, muted by the sight. The little girl in particular seized his attention. She looked underfed and thirty pounds lighter because of it, with her brown hair long and filthy and sticking to her head in a flat sheen.

The sight broke his heart.

"Gus?" Collie asked.

"Yeah?" he whispered.

"Watch the roads. In case that bastard decides to come back with friends."

A part of him, the angry part, hoped that bastard would indeed come back.

Collie carefully leaned into the trailer, looked up, and inspected the inner lip of the opening. "Well, well," she said. "Look what we have here."

She reached up and fiddled with something. A piece of metal wire clattered to the floor, which she ignored. She eventually lowered her hands and held them out to Gus.

"Black pearls," she said.

Gus studied the two black objects, both the size of golf balls. "What are they?"

"Grenades. Metal pins here, see?"

"Like Christmas ornaments."

"Yeah. Except these will do much more than just sparkle."

"Yeah?"

"Oh yeah," Collie assured him. She picked up the fallen piece of metal and studied it. She then opened up a jacket pocket and deposited the sliver and the grenades inside.

"That safe?" Gus asked. "Like that, I mean?"

"Don't ask." She looked at the prisoners. "Can you guys walk?"

Three out of five nodded.

"Okay, walk towards me then. Take it easy now."

They did, the chains restricting them to shambling forward like the dead things that once ruled the world. They squinted in the daylight, and Collie, despite that crippling smell, helped each one to the pavement. Overcoming his horror, Gus lent a hand, gripping arms and easing each prisoner to the ground. Once they were out, he couldn't help but stare at their wretched condition. Mittens of duct tape bound their hands and wrists. The smudges upon their cheeks and around their eyes were really bruises, black and purple and vicious. Blood caked the nostrils of one woman. The clothes they were wearing needed to be torched and replaced.

One of the men stumbled to his knees and bent over with a whimper. That sound alone unlocked the emotions of the other captives. Red eyes— the ones not swollen shut——watered up and moistened battered cheeks.

"You're okay," Collie repeated as she moved among them. "You're okay. Don't worry. I'm gonna get you loose, don't worry."

The fob Collie had taken from the dead hard rocker included keys for the chains. Once the shackles were off, Collie pulled out her knife and freed the little girl first.

"Gus, get some water, will you?"

Collie's request activated him, and, still in a daze, he walked to the back of the truck and retrieved five jugs of water. Collie helped the survivors with their ball gags, working on the more stubborn straps. One guy came close to puking when she removed his gag.

As soon as they had those wicked devices removed, the five stretched and massaged their jaws.

Gus held out the water jugs until each of the survivors had one.

"Thank you," croaked a man with one remarkable shiner, his voice raspy from either screaming or dehydration or both.

"Don't drink that too fast," Collie advised. "Just take a mouthful."

The man with the shiner did just that. His hands shook until Collie helped steady them. One of the women dropped her jug and broke down crying.

Gus wavered and looked at Collie.

"All right," she said, studying the wretched group. "You're out of there. Take a few minutes. Drink some water. When did you folks eat last? Are you hungry?"

"Not hungry," said the one lady who remained composed the longest, though she sounded physically and mentally wasted. "They fed us. Thirsty, though."

The guy with the black eye spotted the dead men lying on the pavement. His mouth became a tight line. "There's one more," he said.

"We know," Gus told him.

"He got away?"

"Yeah. He did."

"Are you going after him?"

Gus looked at Collie. "Are we?"

"No."

That bit of information caused the man to slump in exhausted disappointment. "We should leave then," he finally said. "They talked about others."

"Others?" Collie asked.

"Yeah. We were—" he stopped to swallow, his throat bobbing, "—were going to be sold to someone. Called the Leather. For… for all sorts of shit."

"Sell you?" Gus asked.

"Yeah. Sell us. He called us merch. Merchandise. Cargo. That's why we stopped here, I think. I think…" He looked around, grimacing. "I think this was the meeting place."

Gus and Collie traded looks. Gus then zeroed in on distant Timmins, and that straight runway leading towards the city. There was no sound of engines, however. Nothing to indicate any approaching danger.

"Maybe we should get going?" an uneasy Bruno suggested. "Just to be on the safe side."

The operator, however, didn't appear to have heard. Gus knew what was going through her head. The same thought was going through his own noggin.

That one missing bastard was unfinished business.

"Yeah," Collie finally said. "Get them aboard."

"Aboard what?" Gus asked. "We only got the one ride. Unless we take this," he said, indicating the truck and trailer. "Already hitched. And get the fuck outta here."

He could tell Collie wasn't keen on asking the group to get back into that cage.

"What about the one who got away?" he asked.

"Gotta let him go. But hey, we nailed three of them, right? And got these people out. So that's all good."

"S'pose so."

"All right," Collie said, regarding the group of survivors. "I've got good news for you and some not so good."

"You want us back in the trailer," said the one woman who had kept her composure.

"What's your name?"

"Eva."

"Eva, I need you and everyone else to get back into the trailer."

Eva stared.

"We don't have any other way of transporting you," Collie explained. "Our second truck is dead. And if you stay here, you risk being captured again. Especially if the one who got away comes back with friends."

Eva's shoulders drooped. "All right."

And though none of the freed survivors were pleased, they climbed back into that filthy box one more time.

"Here," Collie said and handed over the padlock. "We're not locking you in. Hold on for a few minutes more. Okay? Going to close the doors here."

She nodded at Gus.

A palpable vibe of fear and uncertainty emanated from the little group, one that Gus didn't want to aggravate. He closed the doors all the same and promised himself he'd be the one to open them. One look from Collie showed she wasn't too happy about shutting them back in their cage either.

"We'll take the lead," Collie said to Bruno and Cory. "If you guys see anyone coming back from the city, flash your headlights, okay?"

"Where we going?" Bruno asked.

"No idea." Collie looked at Gus. "You ready?"

"Yeah."

"Let's boot."

They hurried to the Raptor and climbed aboard.

"Jesus, this thing smells like ass," Gus said, sour-faced.

"Total ass," Collie agreed. "A lot of that going on today."

"Now you know why I'm such a nut about toilet paper."

"I never questioned the toilet paper thing. One of these days, I'll tell you about what I had to do while on a seventy-two-hour *S and E* sometime."

"*S and E?*"

"Search-and-evade."

That did sound interesting.

"I got a surprise for you," Gus said. "Check the back seat."

She looked over her shoulder and saw what he had noticed in the rear-view mirror. A couple of sheathed medieval swords set upon racks in the rear window. There was a gun belt as well. Beneath it all was a landslide of clothing probably more dirty than clean, and a collection of coolers. The truck's key fob rested in the tray next to Gus's knee. He had no trouble firing up the machine.

"Fuck me," Collie muttered. "I hate putting them back in the box."

"Yeah, I know," Gus said and swung the rig around. "Not much we can do."

She didn't answer, focusing on her side mirror.

"Damnit," Gus ejected as he righted the truck. "Collie, we have to get our shit out of the truck. We got gas cans back there."

"And food. And our other gear. Yeah. Do it."

The world sped past them in an eight-cylinder huff of hybrid power, only to quickly decelerate when Gus pulled up beside their dead vehicle. They both jumped out.

"Keep watch," Gus shouted at Bruno and Cory. "We got shit to unload."

Bruno got out as well, and in the next five minutes, they transferred everything of value from the pickup to the cargo trailer.

"Water's there," Gus told the people they'd rescued, pointing to the jugs. "There's grub, too, if you want it."

The sight of all those worried yet hopeful expressions nailed him through the heart, distracting him from the nerve pain lighting up his damaged foot. He hoofed it back to the cab, keeping an eye on the city on the horizon. Still nothing. He had a nagging feeling, though, that he was going to see something he wasn't going to be happy about.

"Okay," he said as he got in and slammed the door. "All done. You snapped in?"

"All ready," Collie answered. "Hit them jets."

The two trucks accelerated and raced away from the scene.

Behind them, the city remained indifferent.

<h1 style="text-align:center">12</h1>

Top Gun drove through the clogged streets of Timmins, constantly checking his side mirror to see if he was being pursued. He wasn't, much to his surprise, so he eased off the gas. He couldn't drive too fast anyway; there was simply too much unmoving traffic filling the roads. So he slowed down and threaded his way through an overgrown subdivision called Greenwood Place. The empty cargo trailer obediently followed his every turn, but goddamn didn't it feel like an anchor hanging off his ass. He intended to pull over the first chance he got and unhook that beast from his bumper.

Timmins had once been a green city, an eye-pleasing union of plant and urban planning. At least it had been. Houses and garages scrolled by, mail boxes, even a playground, along with once-landscaped thickets of greenery that, in the absence of their municipal landscapers, had grown to full-on jungle. Dead leaves and twigs covered the road, creating a crispy carpet of decaying foliage.

Top Gun intended to follow the TransCanada 101 all the way to the 17. He had enough biodiesel to get to Manitoba, but after that, he wasn't sure what his options were. God help him, O'Leary didn't seem so bad now that the whole crew had been wiped out. Without his crew, he was just one hired gun on the open highways, in an eroding wilderness that was being quietly carved up. And it just so happened, his most recent contract was with the one dominant player responsible for most of the cutting.

The Leather.

That troubled him. Greatly.

And, like summoning some mythical urban monster, no sooner did he think the name when a string of trucks filled the road ahead, navigating their way through a four-way intersection. A shiny convoy of black pickups and vans hauling trailers that blocked the only way out of the city.

Effectively fucking up Top Gun's escape plan.

He hit the brakes.

Well shit, he thought. He surveyed the convoy and realized the forsaken cars and trucks had him hemmed in. He couldn't back up fast enough, not with the trailer in tow. There was a motel and an open parking lot just ahead, which would have been the best place to turn his rig around. Trouble was, there were about five trucks between him and that open space.

And the trucks weren't slowing down. Just the opposite. They sped along as if smelling fear. Or meat.

Top Gun had an idea of where they were going. Just his luck they were early. With a defeated sigh, he put his machine in park and took his hands off the wheel in a gesture of surrender.

Men stood in the box beds of the approaching rigs, their faces hidden behind black leather masks. Top Gun knew why, and despair flared within his chest, as frightening as a plastic bag being pulled tight over one's head.

The trucks pulled around him in the street, completing a noose. Two of those rigs hauled cargo trailers, much like the one Top Gun hauled. One truck stopped directly before Top Gun, not five feet from his grill. Through the rest of the small army, he glimpsed an honest-to-God fuel tanker.

Engines revved. Figures watched him from their cabs. Some of those masked individuals wore goggles, as if the masks weren't frightening enough.

Fuck it, Jolly Jake whispered from the grave. *Just fuck it.*

"Easy for you," Top Gun whispered back, counting the number of heads watching him. He eyed the nearest masked driver of the Leather. One of the Leather, anyway. Top Gun never got a name for the imposing road clan other than the Leather. Not that it mattered. They were definitely more disturbing when they referred to themselves as a collective. Perhaps that was the intention.

An ominous figure emerged from one of the pickups. Three more got out behind him. All of them wore black—sweaters or t-shirts, and matching coats. Some of the coats were full-length dusters, though some ended at the hips. All three men sported padded shoulders and masks.

Boots clicked on the pavement as the foursome drew closer. Top Gun kept his hands up and visible. No one else moved, at least not the ones he could see. They all watched him, however. And for a few seconds, Top Gun felt like a prize trophy in the middle of a safari.

A shadow fell over him. The tall, intimidating representative for the

Leather leaned into Top Gun's window.

"Hi," Top Gun greeted in a wary tone, noticing the individual's wide shoulders.

The Leather did not reply. The Leather wore a mask fashioned in the guise of a vulture. Top Gun wasn't sure if the material was indeed leather, or plastic, foam, or rubber, but the guy had blackened the skin around his eyes right up to the lids.

A weird vibe nudged Top Gun's head the other way, towards the passenger side, where another representative of the Leather stood, aiming a loaded crossbow at his face. That mask looked like a glossy special from a kinky sex shop, with visible stitches running from the temples all the way to the back.

"Ah… remember me?" Top Gun asked, turning back and not daring a smile. He had a feeling if he did smile, if he showed any teeth whatsoever, a dart the size of a Roman *Pilum* would be fired into his ear.

The Vulture mask didn't answer.

"We had a deal, remember? Five of us? Find some new meat and bring them back to you." Top Gun hesitantly pointed over his shoulder. "We were supposed to meet back there. At that recharging station. Ah, change of plans. We had a problem. A couple of problems, really."

The Vulture continued to watch him, his eyes narrowed in either suspicion or dislike. Or perhaps both.

That made Top Gun even more nervous. "Anyway," he said, licking his lips. "Long story short. I'm the only one alive. Just me. We were attacked at the recharging station. Jake and the Jipman. And muffin shit O'Leary. All got killed. Anyway. Ah, more bad news. Those meat puppets you lent us? Ah, yeah, they all died too. Same way. Same shooters."

Sure, Top Gun was fudging the details, but he didn't think Jake would mind, and there was a chance it would save his own ass.

The Leather didn't respond.

"We found some new meat," Top Gun continued, feeling it prudent to fill that ominous silence. "One was a little girl, even. But…sorry. There was too much heat. In five seconds I was the only one left. Everyone else was bleeding out on the asphalt. It was… insane, how quick everything went down. One second Jake and I were talkin' and the next…"

The Vulture didn't move, didn't blink, and for a moment, Top Gun wondered if he were talking to a person or a physical manifestation of some vengeful Egyptian god. It was unnerving.

A truck door opened and another Leather got out, decked out in a long duster that reached the ankles. The figure was narrow of shoulder, but when he straightened, his head easily rose above the vehicle's roof. His mask was colored bronze, with black rivets instead of stitches, while his mouth was a series of painted slits that smiled from cheek to cheek. The Bronze stepped away from the door, further showing off that slender frame, and the black duds covering him from neck to boot. The Bronze leaned to one side, his pose asking a question.

"So, yeah." Top Gun remembered the Vulture at his window. "Yeah. I had to leave my crew back there. Gave up a truck and the supplies aboard it. Had to. To distract them, right? So I could get away. I managed to get a few shots off. No kills. Just nailed their truck. Strand them out there. But I didn't press my luck. Best to get out of there in one piece, find you guys, and report in, y'know?"

The Vulture showed no sign of knowing. In fact, the Vulture showed no indication of understanding or even having listened. After a few seconds, the mask directed its attention to the Bronze towering over the pickup. With the barest of limps, the Bronze went to the rear of the vehicle. That imposing scarecrow rooted around in the pickup box. Metal scraped metal, like a meat hook scraping the bottom of a steel barrel.

The sound was a little more startling than Top Gun cared to admit.

That was when the Vulture slowly, *purposely*, reached out and gripped Top Gun's face.

Like a soot-mottled spider, the Vulture's hand fastened to Top Gun's mouth and chin and turned his head toward that unsettling mask. Top Gun's breath shot out his nose. The Vulture's grip was strong. The black eyes within the mask narrowed.

"A little girl?" the Vulture said in a voice neither deep nor high-pitched, but damn near gender neutral.

Through squished lips, Top Gun got out, "Yes."

"And you lost… her?"

"Yes." Top Gun blinked. "Sorry."

The Vulture did not relinquish his grip. "That disappoints us."

"I'm sorry."

Top Gun's anxiety spiked when the Bronze pulled an axe from the pickup box. It wasn't just some tool for chopping wood. It was an honest-to-God executioner's tool appropriated from some medieval castle. A wicked blade hung from a long shaft, the steel blemished and curved and well-worn.

Top Gun's breath caught in his chest. He wondered what that freak was going to do with such a head-splitter.

The Bronze held the weapon in one hand but did not come any closer, as if waiting to be summoned. The Leather with the crossbow stood unwavering at the passenger window.

"We will show *you*," the Vulture continued, still holding the man's face, "what it means to disappoint us."

Upon some silent command, the Bronze approached.

Top Gun's periphery picked up other figures moving in, already free of their vehicles. They closed in as quietly as wraiths, surrounding his truck. The Vulture released him just as more masked men opened Top Gun's door. Hands pulled him out and forced him to the ground. They swarmed over him in an oily, multi-limbed carpet. He didn't struggle, didn't dare make a sound, for fear of tempting a fate worse than death.

The Leather pulled back, securing Top Gun's limbs and head, stretching him out like a man caught in a disturbing web of hands and arms.

The Bronze loomed overhead. The tall figure not only held the executioner's axe, but a length of material dangled from his other hand.

Top Gun whimpered.

The Bronze held a ball gag.

13

"So where we goin'?" Gus asked, fingers tight on the steering wheel, his eyes locked on the road.

"Well," Collie answered, looking away from the side mirror. "Any place not here and preferably off-road. We want distance between us and the city. We need to find somewhere to hunker down for the night, hear their story, and go from there."

"Go from there?" Gus asked dubiously.

"That's right. See who they are. Where they're from. Who knows? They could've been taken from some little cabin on a hill somewhere."

"Didn't you and Wallace scout this whole area?"

Collie smiled. "We couldn't check off everywhere. Ontario's a big place. Quebec's bigger. Searching for people is an ongoing process. People move around. People hide. Crazy things happen in between."

The road sped by as Gus processed the information. "So, we stop somewhere and…"

"And start asking questions."

"All right. Where?"

They were on a straight strip consisting of only two lanes. Tangles of vegetation threatened the road on either side, stopping at the edges of crumbling pavement. Tall patches of forest passed by, smoothing out into great swaths of meadowland. A small bridge spanned a river and the truck bumped over it. A few houses popped up along the way, but they were too visible, too close to the highway. There was no real place to hide.

"Keep driving," Collie said. "One thing about the boonies—there's a shit-ton of back roads. All we need to do is find one." She glanced into her mirror. "Looks good back there."

Gus hoped it stayed that way.

They drove through the town of Matheson, which resembled most of the other quiet little towns that had been plowed over by chaos. Gus followed the gentle curve of Highway 11, turned south, and scanned the forests for a suitable place to hide. Plenty of dirt roads linked up with the main drag, leading off into the sometimes open wild before disappearing into distant woodlands or hill country.

"What about there?" he asked and braked, slowing down for a gravel road on the right. It cut through a wall of birch and fir and disappeared some thirty feet or more from the pavement.

"Looks fine to me."

"We go? Cause if we go and that road ends in a dead-end, we're potentially fucked for getting back out."

"Guess we'll find out."

Gus flicked on his indicator to give Bruno and Cory the heads up. He turned off the highway, the tires lurching as they left the pavement.

The road wasn't a good one; the surface of the moon was probably smoother. Several times he checked on the trailer, fully expecting to see the five survivors tumbling out the back of the thing. He slowed to a crawl, and that didn't improve the ride. In a way, it was worse. The slow-motion rise over the rocky terrain and the inevitable crash into potholes became a stomach-turning repetition.

"I'm gonna puke," Gus muttered as the truck took another sickening dip.

"Glad you said it first."

"You too?"

"Oh, I'm clenching over here."

Gus didn't like the sound of that. In his side mirror, Cory and Bruno followed, bouncing along. Their windshield was dark from the overhead foliage, but the grill gleamed through the dust.

"Jesus Christ," Gus muttered, unimpressed. "You see the dust clouds back there?"

"It'll settle down," Collie said, bracing herself. "It's worse for the folks in the trailer."

"Yeah. Suppose it is."

A shallow stream crossed the road and Gus slowed to a rolling stop. The pickup still thumped through the waterway, despite his best intentions.

"Goddamn," Gus managed. "Must've been a rough winter."

A marker consisting of a few black tires with bald surfaces was stacked in a clump of wild grass. The road narrowed and curved left and right. The forest crowded the caravan on either side, reaching out and brushing the vehicles with long strokes. Branches were plied back and released with whipping force.

"This is gonna fuck up the paint on this thing," Gus said.

The road grew even narrower, but the truck pushed through. The trailer bumped behind them, and he hoped the thing didn't unhitch. He kept his speed at twenty kilometers an hour, but that did little to lessen the sensation of being shelled by artillery.

"This is going nowhere," he said.

"All roads go somewhere," Collie countered.

"Yeah, but this one is going *nowhere*. And we're going to find ourselves at the very end of it very soon."

They rocked and rolled over a few jagged teeth erupting from the ground. They cleared great shards of rock but felt none too good about it, for they knew they'd probably have to come back and brave them again. Deeper they went, twisting one way then the other, rising over small hills and descending into shadowy dips.

"This thing is going fucking nowhere," Collie muttered, one hand clutching the overhead grip.

"Look," Gus said.

Ahead, the forest opened up, just enough for them to notice. They eased around a bend and beheld a bungalow perched atop a low hill. Several opaque panels coated the structure's roof, causing it to gleam in the daylight. A very wild looking garden of considerable size surrounded the home and lined the slope. Weeds invaded rows of untended crops. Apple and pear trees grew on the north end, much of their fruit piled in rotten heaps around the base of each trunk. A shed came into view, situated on the left, and a stack of what appeared to be red clay pots rested against the wall. An orange tractor was parked near a ramshackle corral, its gate left open.

"Well, well," Gus said. "Some place after all. About time, too."

"Looks like a little off-the-grid bomb shelter," Collie added.

"Lot of those around."

Gus stopped the rig and leaned forward, sizing up the house and surrounding garden. "Bet this was all owned by some long-haired hippy freaks, living off the land and all that. All about growing their own food. See the roof?"

"Yeah. Solar paneling. Very shiny."

"All over. Even the shed."

"Someone was thinking."

"Probably more like fuck the power companies," Gus said and reached for the door. "Wait here."

"I'll go," she countered, her sunglasses already in place. Collie got out and gently closed the door. She walked for a few paces, stopped, and scanned the layout. Then, with one hand on her sidearm, she hiked toward the house. There was a dusty SUV up there, its white nose peeking around the corner. Gus spotted it when he leaned to the left. He scratched at a cheek, pulled on his whiskers, and thought about the folks in the trailer. Damn if he wouldn't be shittin' himself back there, wondering what was going on. Especially after what they'd all been through. That didn't sit well on his conscience.

He opened his door and got out.

Cory and Bruno watched him from their rig, stopped ten feet from the trailer. Gus walked toward the trailer doors and, after a moment's hesitation, knocked.

"Hey," he announced. "It's me. One of the people who, ah, saved you."

No response.

"So, anyway, I'm gonna open the door here. Give you some fresh air. That's all."

Without waiting for an answer, Gus opened the door. Daylight fell across the filthy black floor. He peered inside and stopped to take a breath. Despite his best intentions, he was unable to cope with the smell, which was still a plank to the head.

"Oh…" Gus bit down on his first impulse of *Christ and titties* and took a moment to reconnect with his thoughts. The five inside pressed themselves against the rear of the trailer, clearly wondering what his intentions were.

"Just keeping the door open, okay?" Gus took two steps back, then a third. "Just hold on a few minutes more. My… friend is checking out a place. To see if it's safe for us."

"Where are we?" Eva asked in that detached tone of voice.

"South of Matheson. On an old road."

She didn't ask anything else.

In the growing silence, Gus wasn't rightly sure about what to say or do. He settled on the jugs and coolers taken from their dead truck, which were untouched. "You didn't try any of that? I mean, the water's just water, but there's some homemade bread in there, along with preserves and butter. Everything's home-grown. Even some salted meats in there which are pretty good, I must say."

The guy with the wicked black eye looked at Eva.

"Who are you?" Eva finally asked.

"I'm Gus. Hi."

Eva didn't return the greeting. "Where are you from?"

"East Coast."

"Just the four of you?"

Gus hesitated on that one, suddenly wary. "Yeah. Just the four of us."

"That's... risky."

"Yeah? Why's that?"

"There are crazies all over the place. Some more organized than others."

"Yeah, we know. Where are you guys from?"

Eva didn't answer right away.

"That's fine," Gus said. "I understand. Dangerous times and all. Don't worry about us. We're good people. We're just worried about you folks."

"Why would you be worried about us?" Eva asked pointedly.

"Because... you know. We don't know who you are," Gus answered honestly, a touch of sadness in his tone. "Hard to know who you can trust these days, right? Sometimes it takes a while."

Eva didn't answer, but the guy with the shiner nodded with understanding.

"How you doing there?" Gus directed at the girl.

She didn't answer.

"What's her name?" Gus asked the guy with the shiner.

"Don't know. She... she was here before us."

"How'd that happen anyway?"

"We were looking for someone," the guy with the shiner answered. "The four of us. One of our people got lost and we went out to look for him. Camped out overnight and when we woke up... those men you shot? They were waiting for us."

"In the kitchen," the other woman whispered.

"And the living room," said the other man.

"Yeah," the guy with the shiner said. "After that, things got bloody."

"What's your name?"

"Davis."

Gus nodded. "All right, so there were four of you. And you don't know who the girl is?"

"We were gagged. Couldn't talk anyway."

Gus supposed so. He lowered himself until he caught the little's girl's attention. "You got a name there?"

She stared back.

"Nancy?" he tried to no avail. "Lisa? Monica? Lulu?"

Lulu, he thought in disdain. *Fuck off, brain, if that's the best you can do.* He regarded the others. "So she was already here? In the trailer?"

Davis nodded. "Yeah. She wasn't too happy about it. Stayed there in the middle, away from the rest of us."

"What's your name?" Eva asked the girl without much enthusiasm. She didn't even get a look.

"That's what she settles into," Davis explained. "That look right there. Not on the verge of freaking out, like before. Just… watching."

Shock, Gus realized, remembering Collie's assessment. The adults had recovered faster, it seemed. Maybe it took children a little longer.

"All right," Gus sighed. He stood, trying hard not to stare at the little one. The girl was filthy. Her long hair hung in tangled cords, partially hiding the right side of her face. She wore socks, but they were in tatters, her toes and black heels showing through. She wore baggy jeans and an oversized sweater that had once been white, but there were so many smudges in the material, Gus shuddered to think what she'd been rolling in.

"All right," he repeated and took a step back, unable to take the smell any longer. "Oh my Lord, how the hell can you people *not* smell that? I mean… sorry. I'm sorry."

Feeling the heat in his cheeks, Gus removed himself from the rear of the trailer. He stepped onto a gravelly shoulder, where the grass reached mid-thigh. "Just get out and move around if you want," he said.

None of them wore shoes or boots, so he figured they wouldn't run off. And if they did, they wouldn't get far. There wasn't anywhere to go. Thing was, none of them budged at the invitation.

Collie appeared then, coming out of the house on the hill. She waved them toward her.

"Okay, you guys," Gus said. "We're going up there. Hold on."

He didn't bother closing the trailer doors again, believing nothing short of burning the thing would remove the smell.

14

Two bodies occupied the main bedroom, their heads close together and facing each other, as if whispering secrets or performing some Inuit throat song. They lay together on a queen-sized mattress, with sheets decorated with prints of pink roses. Black matter stained the headboards in an explosive decal. Everything had dried, but Collie still made it a point to cover up the couple (married, she guessed, from the wedding bands) and to close the bedroom door behind. Both bodies had decomposed into tatters, the skin dried out into cheap leather. The husband had a shotgun in his lap, tucked under the chin and thumb on the trigger. The result was a charred crown of skull and skin, and a black spot of gore that was going to take more than one scrubbing to clean. Before he died, he arranged the arm of his dead wife around his shoulders.

Or so Collie described.

Gus didn't bother looking. Didn't want to think about the backstory of the couple.

Collie directed the five survivors into the living room, where there was a surprisingly comfortable wraparound sofa set and twin recliners. Whoever the dead people had been, they'd had cash, and had spent most of it on their furniture. Once the survivors had been given some time to relax and process the events of the day, Collie ordered Cory to grab a mop and scrub out the trailer. Water still flowed from the kitchen tap, amazingly enough, which she attributed to an underground well and a still-functioning pump.

Even the lights worked.

"Think it's safe to use those?" Gus asked quietly. "If we're here for the night?"

"Oh, we're here for the night," Collie said. "Best to stay out of sight and decide where we go from here. After we process these folks."

Gus, Collie, and Bruno gathered in the kitchen, located only a few steps away from the living room. On the whole, Eva and the others seemed to be awakening to the idea that they weren't prisoners anymore, and that they were, for the moment, in a much safer place. Gus leaned against a stainless-steel fridge. He glanced at Eva and company lounging on that luxurious sofa set, and that picture granted him a few seconds' worth of contentment.

Then he returned to Collie. "You mean question them."

"You got it."

Gus mentioned his conversation with Eva and the man with the shiner back at the trailer.

"They got lost, huh?" Collie repeated. "All right. Good. I'll keep that in mind when I start in."

"Where you gonna do all this?"

"There's a den in there. Just before the bedrooms. I'll take them in one at a time. Gotta say, this place is nice. Three bedrooms up here and an extra one down below, along with a big old rec room. Three bathrooms complete with TP."

"TP," Gus smiled.

"Thought you'd like that," Collie said, then became all business. "Okay, I'll get working here, but there's something I want you to do…"

*

"All right," Gus said to Cory. "How's that look to you?"

Collie's makeshift alarm system with the bottles and cans lay across the road, right at the treeline marking the perimeter. The string would be invisible at night, and certainly give them plenty of warning if someone attempted to creep up on them.

"Looks okay," Cory said. "I'm just not sure we need them. We should hear anything coming up that road long before we see them."

"I said the same thing to Collie. She wanted to have this just in case someone decided to get out and walk."

Cory nodded at that.

"All right," Gus said. "We're done here. Let's move those rigs behind the house. Get them out of sight. Then we can see how those interviews are going."

Two hours later, daylight was gone.

Gus sat at the kitchen table with Cory, while Bruno conversed with the survivors in the living room. A sparse light provided by a single lamp on a coffee table lit the room. The curtains had been pulled across to hide that little glow of civilization. The quiet reminded Gus of his childhood, when winter storms knocked out the power and drove his family to the basement. There they would gather around a warm woodstove and talk about whatever, waiting out the night until power was either restored or it was time for bed.

Collie questioned Eva last. The other woman's name was Allie, and the man without the shiner was named Clifford. Gus still didn't know who the girl was. She remained content to sit by herself in a recliner, staring at the ceiling with hooded eyes. She had glanced over when he came back into the house, but nothing since.

Bruno eventually sat down near her, and the man's long winter hat caught her interest. He sensed something amiss and turned to see the little one staring at him. Not one to shy away from conversation, Bruno stared back for a few seconds before realizing that he would need to bring out the big guns. He picked up a backpack and reached for a jar of homemade raspberry jam.

"Something on my face?" he asked the girl.

She kept on staring, her expression blank.

"Something here?" he asked and touched his nose.

No response.

Bruno dabbed his finger into the jam and touched his cheek. "Here?" he asked, leaving a ruby print.

The little girl frowned.

"How about here?" he asked, dotting his chin.

The frown became a smile that broke through the dirt and filth covering her face. Her teeth were strong and good looking, but in need of a cleaning.

"Oh-ho, that's the problem," Bruno said, and scrubbed at his whiskers. "All gone?"

The girl's smile dimmed just a bit, but he had her attention.

"What's your name?" Bruno asked, studying her.

No answer, just that same kid-at-the-edge-of-a-wharf expression, hoping—waiting to catch sight of a whale.

"I'm Bruno," he said and cleaned his cheek a little more thoroughly. He tasted the jam and brightened. "Oh, that's good stuff. Real good. The folks back home made this. Want some?"

Indifferent to the offer, she glanced away.

"Here," he said, and held out the jar.

She didn't even look.

"No? That's too bad. It's real good."

And it was, but the girl clearly wasn't interested.

"What's your name?" he asked again.

That sank it. The pleasant little happy face disappeared. Bruno watched it go and didn't like what appeared.

The opening of a door distracted him, however.

It distracted Gus as well, and he turned to see Eva appear in the hallway, her features ghostlike. Collie followed.

"Well, everyone, thank you for your patience," the operator said. "Very much appreciated. Guys, I think we've found a new group of friends."

"That so?" Gus asked

"Very much so. There are just two things we have to do."

That quieted him, and he picked up on the looks traded between Cory and Bruno.

"We have to get them home," Collie said, "and talk with their leader."

Gus leaned back. "Sounds good. We can leave in the morning."

"Yeah," Collie drew out. "About that. Eva and I were talking. She has a request, to further show our own good intentions. Remember that guy who got lost? His name's Carson. He's the one who went out to look for parts in Matheson and never came back. Been gone for a few days, when Eva decided to organize a search party. They went to the same town and searched for Carson but couldn't find him. Right so far, Eva?"

"That's right," she replied in a subdued voice.

"And that's when they found themselves ankle-deep in the shitter with those lunatics I shot earlier."

Gus wasn't exactly sure where all this was going, but he suspected he wasn't going to like it.

"So," Collie said, "she asked if we could look for him. Find him and bring him back. After we bring her and the others back to their home base."

"Look for him where?" Gus asked.

"We can try Timmins, since that's the direction those crazies were headed."

"Head out again?" Cory asked.

"Yeah. A little side mission."

That quieted the three men.

Gus met Collie's eyes. He knew there was something more going on for her to deviate from Whitecap.

"He's a mechanic," Collie said, answering his unspoken question. "And a budding electrician. Grew up around cars and trucks and branched off from there. Apparently, he's responsible for their little power grid, am I right?"

"You're right," Eva replied.

"So he has one of those important skill sets we need to get back on track. Eva and Davis and the others have each made it clear that their little community of about two dozen people are keen about having access to a doctor. Even trade, perhaps. But they want to find out what happened to Carson first. And whether or not he's alive."

Gus looked over at them. "A mechanic?"

"And electrician," Davis added. "A jack-of-all-trades. Everything we have going is pretty much because of him. We owe him a lot. Some of us owe him our lives. We certainly owe him a search party. Find out what happened to him. We were it."

"And we got our asses kicked," Clifford mumbled, his hand dabbing his bruises.

"Pretty much," Allie added.

"Can we talk about this in private?" Gus asked Collie.

"Sure."

"I just need clarification."

"Will you excuse us, folks?"

Collie and the three men exited to the den. Bruno stopped at the door to keep an eye on the living room.

"So, what about our plan?" Gus whispered.

Collie shrugged. "It'll have to wait. We can spare a day or two to find out what happened to this guy. We still need to secure Whitecap but… in my mind, this is an acceptable side mission. They've established a community and have gotten to this point by common sense, living off the land and whatever's left over. Sound familiar? I got the same story from each of them. They're just regular folks getting by, but this Carson guy is the beacon. The sheriff. The guiding fucking light. If we find him, we'll get brownie points. Did I mention they produce their own ethanol? That should mix just fine with our corn. Plus, we might gain the confidence of a genuine automotive technician and all-round do-it-yourself person."

"I think them having access to a doctor is more important than the mechanic," Cory pointed out.

"Agreed," Collie allowed. "Aces over kings. But a little help with their missing person won't hurt us. It'll only prove we're good people. Eva and the others have made it clear they want him found. They owe him. Apparently, he's the one who rounded them up. Organized them. Kept them safe."

"What if he's missing because of the same savages that caught Eva and her crew?" Gus asked.

"Possible. If so, they're down by three. Eva already said their captors were taking them to someone called the Leather. That they were stopped at a meeting place—where we nailed the bastards. That was a short way from Timmins. Carson might've been picked up in Matheson and taken back to the same designated spot. In any case, it's a place to start looking. So, what do you say? You in?"

"And if we're not?" Cory asked.

"Mighty cold of you, since our second priority is to locate and establish relations with other survivors. If we continue north on our secret mission, without attempting any further help, that could go against us."

"That won't happen because we have a doctor," Cory said.

"We do," Collie noted.

"And we freed them from those dipshits," Gus pointed out.

"We did that."

They quieted down, each mulling over the consequences of this new plan.

"A mechanic, huh?" Gus finally asked.

Collie nodded.

"The sheriff?" Cory asked.

"Uh-huh."

"The guiding fucking light," Bruno muttered softly.

"And they want him back…" Collie finished.

Gus sighed.

*

A little after midnight, a hand shook Gus. He woke with a snort and beheld the wraith sitting next to him on the single bed.

"Morning, Moonbeam," Collie whispered.

"Morning Sunshine."

She smiled. "Your shift."

"Already?"

"Three hours later. Sleep good?"

"Give me a few minutes," he groaned softly and checked the red numerals of the clock. "Twelve-twenty. Yuck. Didn't think I'd nod off."

"Yeah," Collie said. "A lot's happened in the last twenty-four hours."

"How's everything out there?"

"Good. Quiet. Everyone's sleeping as far as I can tell. Cory and Bruno are in the living room. You know Cory farts in his sleep?"

"I… did not."

"Well, he does. Not manly ones either. Little mousey things that frigging last forever. Like air leaking out of a balloon, y'know? Although there was one or two that fluttered at the end."

Gus had nothing to say to that.

"I could understand if it was coming out of the girl. Those are little girl rips. But not big hairy butcherman Cory."

"Baker."

"Right. I forgot. Anyway, he's firing off some wet whistlers."

"What about Bruno?"

"Don't get me started. Bruno talks in his sleep. Not all the time, mind you, but just enough to let you know he's there. He started not twenty minutes ago. The way he was going, sounded like he was having a town meeting with himself."

"Doesn't surprise me in the least," Gus said.

Collie shook her head. "Distracting is what it is. Wouldn't be so bad if I could understand whatever the hell he's saying, but it's all under his breath. Comes out like gibberish. Just loud enough that you can hear him. Like a couple of kids whispering under a porch and dad's standing on one of the steps. In-depth conversations, though. I can tell."

'I bet."

"Between Cory and Bruno, it's like a midnight Morse code out there. One's going dot- dot-dot while the other one's letting off dashes."

She quietly chuckled at that, and Gus smiled at the sound.

A comfortable peace surrounded them then. Gus lay there, studying her shadowed face, charmed by an even greater sense of how lovely she was, despite the battle history etched upon her features. He hesitantly reached out and placed a hand on her knee, and that soft contact woke him up even more. To his surprise, she didn't protest. She certainly didn't break his arm.

Eventually her hand covered his.

"Come on," she whispered with a pat. "Time for your shift."

"Do I gotta?"

"'Fraid so."

Gus propped himself up and leaned in close to her face. Their shoulders touched. Her scent gave him pause, a slight musk not unpleasant at all. Collie didn't draw back; instead, she studied him in turn. Their faces circled each other like dark moons dangerously close, drawing even closer, considering, wondering. Gus's hand slid to her very warm thigh in an exploratory caress. Collie didn't protest, her face so near that her lips were only a lick away. He leaned in and lurched to a stop when she unexpectedly pulled back, ever so slightly—but enough to break whatever spell had befallen them.

"Sorry," she whispered in that awkward silence. "Time to work."

Gus drew back. "Yeah. You're right. Sorry."

"Don't worry. I'll be here when you're finished."

He took a few seconds to process that. "You'll be asleep."

"So sleep with me."

That got his attention. "Okay. That… sounds good."

"Yeah, that would perk you up."

Their smiles returned.

No longer sleepy, Gus swung his legs out over the bed and stood. He'd napped on top of the covers, leaving them wrinkled. He sniffed, rubbed his bald head, and eyed the dark doorway. Collie was already taking his place.

"Nice and warm," she whispered, lying on her back and placing a hand behind her neck. "I like this already. Always did prefer a warm bed."

They studied each other.

"Collie?" he asked, keeping his voice low.

"Uh-oh."

"What?"

"I didn't like the way you said my name just then."

"Ha. Yeah."

"What's on your mind?"

He was seriously out of practice in such matters, which resulted in him not replying right away. *All in*, he decided, yet faltered again, not quite knowing how to put his feelings into words. "Are we… okay?" he finally managed.

Collie wasn't hindered. "We'll find out in the morning, when we get on the road."

"No… I mean are we… okay? You and, uh, me."

Her head turned ever so slightly on the pillow, towards him, deepening the shadow upon her face. "We're okay. Let's just… take things slow. That okay with you? I'll let you know. When."

"Sure."

They stayed like that for a few heartbeats more, just studying each other in the dark. Until Gus remembered he had a shift to do.

He left for the living room.

15

The morning was cool, bright, and cloudless. Thankfully the cabin had running water and soap, so the group of survivors were able to clean off the filth they had been covered in for so long. Once the group had finished eating, they gathered outside and inspected the condition of the SUV. The little girl stood close to Bruno, who reached out and gave her shoulder a comforting squeeze.

After Collie filled the SUV's tank with fuel, Gus crossed his fingers and tried the ignition.

The engine turned over.

"Eva," Gus said, leaning out of the rig. "Collie and I were talking. Would you mind traveling with us? The others can take the SUV."

"Afraid we'll run on you?"

Gus smiled. "Yeah. Sorry. But… they get to drive by themselves."

Eva smiled back, the first bit of emotion she'd shown since being freed. "Don't worry. We talked about you last night, and we decided you're good people."

"Oh. Well, that's good to know. Thanks."

"I'll ride with you."

"Thanks again."

"Gus?" Collie said. "I want you to ride with Bruno this morning. Cory can come with us."

That caught Gus off guard. "Is this about me saying you drool in your sleep?"

"Might be. We did snore in each other's face for about three hours last night."

"We did," he said fondly. "Sure. Okay, I'm with Bruno."

"We'll take the lead. Bruno, you and Gus are in the rear."

"Right," the lanky man said. "Like a vanguard."

"That's the front," she corrected.

"Right. My mistake. We're rearguard."

"All right," Collie said. "You guys get my fishing line?"

"Done," Gus said, sensing a joke in there about how nice and shiny her cans were, but he wouldn't crack it in front of the little one.

"Then let's get out of here," Collie said.

They turned for their vehicles, but the girl refused to go with the group in the SUV.

Gus saw her pouting. "What's wrong?"

Bruno shrugged. "She doesn't want to go with them."

"No?" He regarded the young lady. "Who do you want to go with?"

She reached out and gripped Bruno's sleeve.

"Well, that was easy," Gus said.

"Yeah, I guess so." Bruno muttered, not entirely pleased.

"Aw, she won't take up much space."

"Suppose not," Bruno said, his expression lightening as Gus left for the pickup. The girl still held onto his arm. He opened the rear door and made some space for her.

"Buckle up," he instructed as she hopped into the back. "Seatbelts save lives."

She looked up at Bruno, as if deliberating a question, but it never came. Realizing she wasn't going to speak, he closed her door and climbed aboard.

Gus was already behind the steering wheel. "Never thought I'd be babysitting," he said.

"We're babysitting?" Bruno asked.

"Yep." Gus started up the engine.

Bruno looked into the back seat for a few seconds. The girl was mashed into the confusion of duffle bags and containers there. One well-placed coat would hide her completely.

He looked back to the windshield. "Ah well. She's quiet enough."

The engine rumbled, eager to get moving. Gus glanced in the rear-view mirror, checking on their backseat passenger.

She met his stare and held it.

Gus frowned just before he put the machine in gear. Collie and company took the lead, followed by the SUV, and Gus with the captured pickup and trailer full of supplies. The vehicles rumbled around the property and moved along the road, leaving the house framed in their mirrors.

"So how come Collie switched you and Cory up?" Bruno asked.

"No idea."

"Huh. Well. He's not a bad guy. And I base that on spending three days on the road with him. You get to know things about a guy."

"Good enough for me," Gus said as they rattled along.

A short time later, the little caravan turned back onto the main road and drove north.

"Man," Bruno said with relief. "Glad that's over. That is one bad road. You okay back there?"

The little girl looked at him and didn't say a word.

"I'll take that as a 'yes'."

"Hey, you find out her name?" Gus asked.

"No, she won't talk."

"Did you try guessing it?"

"No, we didn't. Why?"

Gus shrugged, staying some five car lengths back from the SUV. "I dunno. Maybe that might unlock something. Jar a memory loose."

"Think so?" Bruno asked.

"Worth a shot. Unless we give her a name. And use that until she tells us what her real name is. I don't want to keep calling her 'the kid'."

Bruno glanced back at the girl. "You hear that? I'm gonna give you a name, okay?"

"Just a temporary one," Gus added. "Until you tell us your real one."

"How about Louise?" Bruno asked.

"Louise?" Gus repeated. "Bit old-fashioned, ain't it?"

"I had an aunt named Louise."

"Aunt Louise? You serious?"

"What's wrong with Aunt Louise? There's nothing wrong with Aunt Louise."

"I'm sure there wasn't. Look, I'm not makin' fun or anything."

"I think you just did."

"Well, I wasn't."

"Better not be," Bruno warned good naturedly. "Aunt Louise was the best. The *best*. That woman treated me like gold. Loved Aunt Louise."

"Maybe she should decide," Gus said.

Bruno consulted their backseat passenger again. "How about it? Louise okay? You good with that?"

The little girl stared.

"I don't think she cares for it," Gus said. "How about Lisa?"

"Lisa?"

"Yeah, Lisa."

Bruno turned around. "How about Lisa, then?"

No reaction.

"That's out," he said.

"Lisa's nice," Gus said. "Little more modern."

"How about… Jessica?"

"Not Jessica," Gus said.

"Why not?"

"Knew a Jessica once. She was… not nice."

"Isabella?"

Gus frowned. "You into classic literature or something?"

"Jeez, it's just a name."

"Call her Paris."

"Paris?" Bruno asked with a note of disdain. "You give me a hard time about Jessica and Isabella—"

"—And Aunt Louise."

"And Aunt Louise, and then you come up with Paris?"

"What's wrong with Paris?"

"You wanna be called Paris?" Bruno asked the girl.

And to his surprise, the hint of a smile appeared on her round face.

"She likes Paris?" Gus asked, picking up on the vibe.

"She's almost smiling back there."

The little girl surprised them both then by tightening up her lips and grunting, "Mm."

The two men traded looks.

"What was that?" Bruno asked. "What was that sound? You said *mm*. Like '*mm*maybe'?"

"More like her name starts with an 'M'," Gus said.

"That it?" Bruno continued to probe. "Your name starts with an 'M'? Like Molly? Melody?"

She didn't take to either of those.

Bruno looked at Gus. "What other 'M' names are out there?"

"Fuck if I know."

"*Hey*, watch that."

"Sorry. Slipped out. I'm sorry. Forgot she was there."

That floored Bruno. "What do you mean you forgot she was there? She's right there. How could you forget her?"

Gus ran a hand over his beard. "I'm not around children too much." He then remembered Becky and Chad, and hoped Bruno didn't pick up on the lie.

Bruno didn't. He turned back to the girl. "Martha? Is that it?"

She shook her head.

"Oh wow. She just shook her head."

That prompted Gus to glance back at her. "Mindy?"

"Mm… mmm…" she kept on, trying to unlock whatever psychological knot prevented her from speaking.

"Monica?" Bruno asked.

"That's a good one," Gus approved.

"I thought so, but it's not it." Bruno studied her. "None of these helping? Marie? Maria? Milly?"

Gus scowled.

"I'm running out of 'M' names here," Bruno said. "Mary? *Oh!* Mallory?"

The little girl sighed. She reset herself, and, again, produced, "Mm. *Mmm.*"

That got Gus's attention. "That last one sounded angry."

And it did. Heat rose to the child's cheeks as she struggled to produce words through lips that might've been sewn shut. One last mighty *Mmmm* petered out into a whimper, whereupon she flopped back into the gear surrounding her, mentally spent and looking more than a little pissed off.

"Don't you worry," Bruno reassured her. "Don't you worry one bit. You take your time. We'll call you 'Monica' for now, okay? That's a good name. And when you're ready, you let us know what your real name is."

Another sad '*mm*' and the little girl—Monica—quieted down.

The three vehicles rolled through Matheson without incident and proceeded north on Highway 11. The forest on either side was scraggly and unhealthy, which made Gus think about a bug infestation of some sort… which led to memories of fire.

Two hours later, after passing only a couple of abandoned vehicles, a dirt road that might've led to a campground of sorts appeared on the right. Collie took the turn in a wave of dust, and the others followed. Gus wasn't keen on going off-road again. Not five seconds before he left the highway, he glimpsed two pointed nubs of wood sticking up from a mound of crushed stone, just barely visible. It took him another couple of seconds to realize what he'd just seen.

"That was a sign back there," he said. "Or what was left of one. You see that?"

"Missed it," Bruno answered.

"Well, it was there. Chopped down right at the ankles, mind you. Bet plenty of folks go right by it without another look."

"I didn't even get a first look."

"That's right," Gus said. "Can't check something out if it doesn't get your attention. That's the first line of defense right there."

Bruno scanned the gravel shoulders for hints of civilization but saw nothing. Light filtered through the patchy forest, but after ten minutes in, the trees and undergrowth began to thicken.

"The hell we goin'?" Gus wondered aloud.

"Can't be a town," Bruno reasoned. "Not a big one, anyway."

"Maybe a campground?" Gus suggested. "Can't think of anything else being out this way."

The road curved to the north, and the rigs ahead rocked over the uneven length, summoning thick clouds of dust. The forest thinned out dramatically, revealing a plain of short, wild grass. Tall pillars of fir spotted the land, spaced out at irregular intervals, but the grass got Gus's attention. Someone had cut down the growth and piled it up in neat stacks behind the trees.

Holy shit, he mouthed.

Lurking behind it all was the shimmering blue surface of a lake, growing larger with every passing second. Overturned canoes and row boats came into sight, all resting along a white shoreline.

"Oh my," Bruno said softly.

The single lane they were on snaked through a park, complete with blackened barbeque pits and picnic tables.

"Campground," Gus smiled. "Called it first."

"You win… absolutely nothing!" Bruno exclaimed before finishing with a whispery cheer, sounding very much like a small audience. Charmed, Monica joined him, her round features lighting up.

Gus interpreted this as a positive sign. He hoped Monica would soon break free of whatever was troubling her.

The two men saw a wired fence protecting rows of tilled earth just beyond the trees and the grass. A shovel was propped up against a post. All the idyllic setting needed was a few cows or goats. Gus was about to slow down for a better peek when Bruno pointed ahead.

In the middle of the lake was an island.

At a glance it resembled a crown of dense evergreens, some hundred feet or more offshore. Rooftops and other structures peeked through the treetops there, and when the men neared the shoreline, they noticed a wooden truss bridge connecting the mainland to the little refuge. It was an old bridge, perhaps a heritage piece from the 1920s, complete with cedar slat shingles.

"Oh my, oh my," Gus whispered, very much impressed.

Then he saw what waited for them at the bridge's entrance.

Sharpened fence pickets jutted from the ground at an angle, pointing outwards and ready to impale anyone reckless enough to charge the fortification. The road they were on continued straight through that barrier of fat spears, right up to what resembled a medieval gatehouse. Sheets of iron reinforced the closed gate, while battlements ringed the top, some twenty feet high. Figures stood behind those battlements, underneath a flat, weather-proof roof. Only their heads and upper bodies were visible.

"Oh, it's like a… like a…" Bruno faltered, not knowing the exact name of the structure.

"Like that thing in front of castles," Gus said. "A gatehouse, *Arrr.*"

Bruno gave him a curious glance.

"*Arrr?*" Gus repeated with uncertainty. He abandoned the joke, focused on the road, and pulled in behind the stopping SUV. There was movement at his shoulder—Monica leaned forward between the seats, to see better. She spared Gus only a second before returning her attention to the gatehouse.

Ahead, Eva got out of Collie's truck and approached the entrance. She exchanged words with the guards there, and some of those figures behind the battlements began to move. Gus watched with interest as, seconds later, those stout looking gates were pushed open. Two guards emerged, dressed for autumn, and they cleared the road for passage.

Eva returned to the pickup, and the three-vehicle parade rolled forward. Collie's truck disappeared inside the fortified bridge.

"We're going in," Gus said, shifting the stick and easing ahead. "Just like going into a tunnel."

Monica remained quiet, but she was pulling on the seats with little-kid excitement. Gus drove by the two gatekeepers—two unshaven men who gave their truck a wary glance. Gus nodded at them, trying to look friendly without coming across as an idiot. The front tires hit the planks in a rattle and creak of trusses. The three of them were plunged into shadow a second later. They all hunkered down, just so they could see the ribbed sections of the roof overhead. Narrow sun beams stabbed through in places, providing all the light to see that glorious rustic interior. A door on the left passed by, perhaps leading to a stairway that went to the roof.

"Oh, this is cool," Bruno whispered, a huge smile splitting his face. "You seeing this, Monica?"

Monica promptly nodded, her little hands gripping the cushions.

"How old you think this thing is?" Bruno asked Gus.

"No idea, but old. New Brunswick has dozens of these things." He checked his side. "Not much clearance, though. I got about two feet on my side."

"That's what I got here."

"The whole floor is covered in planks," Gus noted.

Ahead, daylight entered the bridge as a second set of gates were pulled open.

"Nice," Gus said.

"All they need is a place to grow crops," Bruno said.

"Those were the fields on the way in. All fenced off with chicken wire."

"Not a bad setup. Not bad at all."

Collie's rig rolled free of the bridge. The SUV followed.

"Almost through," Bruno exclaimed like a kid on a carnival ride.

Monica braced for a drop.

The truck emerged with a thump onto a gravel road. Cottages rose up on either side, meters back from the water and well concealed behind grandiose trees and wild foliage. A huge sign with the faded image of a cartoon wolf greeted them. The character was winking and giving visitors an enthusiastic thumbs up while poised over big carved letters: *"Camp Red Wolf Welcomes You!"*

"Camp Red Wolf," Gus whispered, unable to contain his smile. "Well, aren't you the cheese."

"A summer camp," Bruno said. "They're holed up in a summer camp."

"Not just any summer camp," Gus pointed out. "It's Camp Red Wolf. Best damn summer camp north of Wonderland."

"Really?"

"No idea. I made that up."

They drove into a wide clearing, where school buses presumably would have stopped in faded yellow zones to offload summer guests—although Gus wondered if a bus could fit through that tunnel of a bridge. A series of squat billboards was situated on the eastern edge of the island. Several crushed stone pathways led off into the woods, towards large structures partially hidden by flora. Flowerbeds flourished along the trails and buildings. A small hillside of green grass was ready for anyone wanting to spread out a blanket and sit, as well as a lengthy shoreline hedged by waist-high bluffs. There were tall A-frames and dormitories, as well as several one- and two-story cottages that might've housed the camp staff. Just to the left, at the end of another trail, was what looked to be a sizeable outdoor gathering area, where several granite blocks had been placed in a semi-circle facing the water.

The compound was surrounded and divided into sections by well-planned and carefully maintained curtains of fir, oak, and other vegetation.

Gus stopped behind the SUV, and the moment he did, Bruno leaned forward and pointed. "Ohhh, look at that."

A water slide in the distance. A plastic intestinal tract built on a gut-punch of a slant and colored jungle-green. The thing looked like so much fun, Gus even had thoughts of trying it out.

Monica bounced with excitement.

"Settle down," Bruno said with a smile. "I'll bring you over there myself. I promise. Especially if you start talking."

"Now I know where all the rich kids spent their summers," Gus said.

"Oh man," Bruno marveled. "This place has it all."

They climbed out of the SUV and immediately felt at ease. The air was pleasant, warm, and comfortable. Fresh. About a dozen inhabitants emerged from front doors or hurried along walkways, converging on the parking area to get a look at the newcomers. Eva was already out of the pickup and embracing an older woman with long silver hair and spectacles. Davis and the others got out and the inhabitants gave them a warm greeting. That warmth turned to alarm when they saw the bruises. Several turned their attention to Collie's group, their eyes now narrowed with suspicion. Gus could very nearly hear their thoughts. *What happened? Who did this? Are you okay?*

Gus tuned it all out, focusing on a few menfolk armed with shotguns of the combat variety. Weapons designed to punch holes in people while knocking them back a dozen feet. He noted more than a few handguns as well, kept in shoulder and thigh holsters. Some of the women carried sheathed knives in addition to their firearms. One bearded guy wore a cowhide vest with a wide straw sombrero, and Gus noted the collection of sidearms he had on him. Two under the arms, two on his hips, and one on the left side of his chest.

The gunslinger eyed Gus in return, none too friendly.

"They saved us," Eva finished explaining, waving a hand at the new arrivals. "If it weren't for them… I don't know what would have happened. We probably would never have seen you again."

The suspicious glares softened into guarded curiosity, but that was a lot better than outright hostility in Gus's mind. He summoned what he hoped was a friendly smile, keeping his mouth closed for fear of unnerving the folks.

"No Carson?" a man asked, tall and skinny and wearing a ball cap. His hair hung in a braid at the back. He had a long chin whisker that resembled tufts of cotton, but his upper lip was shaven.

"We were captured," Eva explained. "Like I said. By a group of savages." She regarded both groups and decided introductions were in order.

"This is Collie, Gus, Bruno, and Cory. I don't know who the little girl is."

"We're calling her Monica," Bruno said. "Until she lets us know otherwise."

"This is Ben Garrett," Eva said, introducing the tall guy with the mangy cotton beard. "And over here is Sarah Burton, Rich Trinidad, Jeremy Walton, and Jane Wong. Alfred Laredo—"

Sarah Burton was the older woman with long silver hair, who could've been the lead screamer in a '70s rock band. Rich Trinidad was the grim gunslinger who might've had his face scrubbed by a ball of barbed wired. As for the others, about a dozen more, Gus forgot the names almost as soon as he heard them. They were a wiry group, all fit and lean. There were others, standing away from the little reunion, casually armed and keeping close watch on the newcomers. Gus didn't blame them for being careful, but it didn't make him feel any better.

Two dozen at least, he figured, even spotting a couple of teenagers in the mix. A little pocket of humanity dug in and doing whatever it took to get by.

Ben Garrett finally managed a smile. He nodded at the newcomers before focusing on Collie, who stood with the sun glinting off her shades and her thumbs hooked into her belt.

"You're a soldier?" he asked.

"How can you tell?"

"The fatigues."

"These old things?" she asked. "Hell, anyone could have a set of PJs. Plenty of them around if you know where to look."

"You're not a soldier?"

"Oh, I am. I'd give you references but… they're all dead."

That was met with silence.

"Thank you so much," Garrett eventually said. "For bringing them back. We thought… well, we didn't know what to think. Except maybe it might be wise to not leave camp for a while."

"You're welcome," the operator said. "Quite the setup you have here."

"This? Well, yes, I suppose it is. I'm the head administrator here... or I was, back before everything went to hell. When the dust started to clear, I figured this was the place to be. And you? Where are you folks from?"

"Back east," Collie said. "Nova Scotia. Like you, we survived the worst of things and found a safe place to call home. Now we're searching for others."

"Searching for others?" Garrett asked. "Really? You've come a long way to be looking for people."

"There aren't too many people left. Not the kind we're looking for."

"And what kind of people would that be?" Sarah Burton bluntly asked.

"People to start over with," Eva answered. "We've already had a talk. They seem decent enough to me."

"And to me," Davis added.

"Well, they brought you back," Garrett noted. "That certainly counts for something. No Carson, however?"

Collie shook her head. "Sorry. We'd very much like to find him, though, if what Eva tells me is true. He's quite useful to have around."

The camp islanders tensed just a little, as if some great secret had just been revealed. Carson was important. Even valued.

"He is," Garrett said neutrally. "Very useful."

"I'm curious," Collie said. "Why would you let such a useful person go out on his own? You have to know what it's like out there."

"Because," Sarah Burton said with some heat. "He's a cranky, self-centered asshat who can be a goddamn pain in—"

"Sarah," Eva said, warning the woman to button it.

Bruno looked at Monica and frowned, encouraging her to forget such language.

"Well," Collie said. "I've already covered this with your people. Eva in particular. We're willing to head back out and find out what happened to your mechanic."

"Yeah, right," Sarah started up again. "For a price, I bet."

"That's right. Nothing comes free these days."

"I bet."

"But it's a manageable fee," Collie continued, unfazed by the snark. "We're running a little low on fuel. Eva says you make your own ethanol?"

Some uncomfortable shuffling then, and a few more looks.

"Jesus, Eva," someone remarked.

"Relax," she told the islanders. "Just hear Collie out."

"Yeah, just hear her out for a minute," Davis said. "It's not that bad."

So they did.

"Like I said," Collie continued. "We're looking for people. Good people to exchange food, services, and skills with. Our little community has about a population of about four or five dozen. Mostly people with regular trades, trying to do things the old way, to survive with the pieces left over. We don't have a mechanic. We do, however… have a doctor."

That got their attention.

"As a sign of good faith," Collie said, deciding not to point out that they'd already shown plenty of good faith in freeing Eva and the others, "we'll go back out there and look for Carson. For whatever fuel you can spare. If we find him, we'll bring him back. Talk some more. We have a doctor, and, if you're willing to parlay, at the very least we can see to it that anyone needing medical attention gets it. What do you think?"

"A doctor?" Jane Wong asked.

Collie nodded. "ER doctor, in fact. Honest to God. Worth her weight in gold. She saved my life already."

That changed the vibes radiating off the group, from one of polite guardedness to keen interest. Gus knew they were in business. Even the scarred gunslinger called Trinidad seemed to be considering the offer in a different light.

"Or," Collie went on, "you guys can decide who goes out again. From your own crew. You got a few faces here who look like they could chew their way out of a prison cell."

"Oh, we can protect ourselves," Sarah Burton said, pushing her glasses back up onto her nose. "Make no mistake, honey."

Collie didn't respond to that.

"What Sarah means," Garrett interjected, "is we certainly do have people who can take care of themselves, but I don't want to risk losing anyone else if I can help it. If you're willing to find Carson and bring him back, we can discuss other matters further. See what we come up with. You trust them, Eva?"

"Enough to bring them here. Enough to ask you to listen to what she has to say."

"Well," Garrett said after a moment's thought. "We can certainly do that. We're not savages."

He looked over at Sarah, who appeared to be seriously thinking things over. She eventually nodded, but reluctantly.

Garrett cleared his throat. "We'll need to keep one of yours with us. Until you return."

"Sure," Collie said. "Take him."

That wiped the smile off Bruno's face, and his pirate's stocking cap wilted just a little.

Garrett saw the man's unease, took a moment to process it, and chuckled. "Why don't we talk about this over something to eat?"

Collie approved. "Sounds good. Lead the way."

And Gus knew then, as God was his witness, that they could trust these people. He sensed no scheming intent, no evil plans, just a lost group so much like themselves doing what they could to ensure their own safety and survival.

Garrett extended a hand, pointing to a gravel pathway, when the ringing of a bell stopped him in his tracks.

And the sound of approaching engines turned him towards the bridge.

16

The sound of engines grew closer.

And the lookout person ringing the bell was seriously getting into their work.

"Places, everyone!" Garrett yelled, hurrying to the bridge.

Gus glanced at Collie, who hesitated only a second before running for her truck. She pulled open the door and extracted her assault rifle. With a wave to Gus, she jogged to a grassy mound that faced the far shoreline. He raced after her and together they landed on their chests in grass and weeds. Collie readied her weapon.

"Christ almighty," Gus muttered, watching the road to the island. "What the hell is that?"

Collie pushed her sunglasses up onto her forehead and screwed her eye into her weapon's targeting scope. She grimaced. "That, my friend, is war."

That worried the unholy squirts out of Gus. He eyed her profile before glancing behind them, spotting Cory and Bruno crouching at his heels. Cory crawled toward them elbows-to-grass to get a better look. Bruno was on his knees, halfway between dropping to his chest and curious as to what was coming. Little Monica was there as well, holding onto Bruno's shoulder like a cat dunked into a vat of ice water.

About a half-dozen islanders dropped down on either side of them, spaced out along the waist-high shoreline, Eva among them. An assortment of shotguns and handguns gleamed in the tall grass.

"We didn't bring them, Eva," Collie said, still peering through her scope.

"I know. But you're here now."

"We'll help if we can."

"I know that, too."

Relief flared through Gus, knowing at least one islander wasn't blaming them for anything yet. Dark outlines moving through the trees on the lake's far side seized his attention. More shapes followed the first. A sinister parade of ill-kept vehicles was rolling towards them, spewing black coils of smoke.

"Collie," he said.

"I see it."

"Mm—*mmmm*," Monica moaned in desperation.

"I know, honey," Bruno told her. "You just stay close to me."

The approaching vehicles grew louder, punctuated by the peppy streaks of motion that could only be motorcycles. The parade came into better view. A black stream of vehicles as noxious and polluted as an undersea oil spillage filled the road, speeding towards the bridge. A collection of revving engines that buzz-sawed through the sleepy peace of the afternoon, no longer concerned with stealth. Trucks. Cars. Motorcycles.

Then an engine came into sight, one that had no right being on the road in this day and age.

The raw horsepower of a monster-sized transport blasted the air, drowning out the motorcycles. The growls of all those engines coalesced into one harsh, mechanical concert—a heavy metal motor show, charging the island with tsunami might.

"It's a fucking biker gang," Gus said, his spine suddenly cold. "Biker, car, and *trucker* gang."

"Looks that way," Collie said, watching the column through her scope. "There's a lot of them."

"I know."

"Holy *shit*, there's a lot of them," Bruno exclaimed softly, no longer concerned with censoring his words.

"What do we do?" Gus asked.

"We wait," Collie said, poised and ready for the dirtiest and bloodiest business transactions. "For now."

He glanced at the operator. Her assault rifle never seemed smaller, however.

Monica continued with her worrying *mm—mmm* grunts, as if trying to force words through glued lips.

The motorized army turned towards the bridge, trailing a serpentine tail obscured by the treeline. There didn't seem to be an end to them, and the churning smoke concealed their numbers just enough. Gus spotted a second transport truck farther down the line, and that knotted up his stomach. Then he remembered those few defenders posted at the entrance. A part of him shouted at them to get out of there, that the island was already gone.

That last thought chilled him.

Since they were on an island with only one way in and out, they had no place to escape. They were trapped unless Eva and Garrett had a couple of boats stashed away somewhere.

An oily surf of wheels, metal, and windshields pulled up before the bridge's entrance, well back from the spear wall. The island's one fortification seemed as impregnable as cotton gauze against the force spreading out along the opposite shore. There, the invaders gathered and strained, idled and thickened, growing into a great wall gleaming with chrome. The pump and revving of engines growled louder as more machines pulled up and lurched to a stop. Mephitic plumes of exhaust wafted through their ranks.

One vehicle caught Gus's attention.

A school bus. A school bus painted black.

"They're doing something," Gus said, leaning over to Collie. "They're doing something over there."

Collie pointed.

Within the bridge's fortifications, several islanders scurried—the same islanders that had allowed Gus and company to drive through the gates. About five of them moved about, taking aim at the force amassed at their doorstep.

One thought kept repeating itself over and over again in Gus's head. *So many. So damn many.*

"How deep's that water?" he asked, raising his voice.

"Twenty feet plus," Eva replied. "Deeper in other places. The sandbar is shallow near the shore, but it drops off about twenty or thirty feet out. Those rigs got no other way across except the bridge."

That didn't make Gus feel any better. "Collie?"

"Yeah?"

"I think we should be leaving."

"You heard her," Collie said. "That bridge is the only way across. Unless you want to swim."

Gus's answering grimace was all *fuck me gently.*

The army of trucks, cars, and motorcycles trembled as if restrained by a weakening leash. They pumped accelerators and produced smoke. A single figure emerged from between the vehicles. Clad entirely in black and wearing a mask, the figure strode ahead with a swagger that was one part drunk and three parts attitude. He carried a pole. A second character followed the first, similarly dressed but carrying something different, an item that was a dirty shade of white.

The first masked man stopped in front of the island's makeshift spear fence and craned his neck, studying the defenses. He cocked his head with drawn contempt. Then, perhaps aware of the time, he lifted his pole overhead.

The masked man held the pose for seconds.

Knowing he had the stage, the masked man spiked the length of wood into the road's soft shoulder. He worked it deep. Once planted, he stepped back and eyed the bridge's defenders.

Then he turned and strode back to the rumbling line of automobiles.

The second figure walked up to the pole and fixed a white bulb to its tip. When he completed his task, he also withdrew.

"Oh my God," Collie said, just above the commotion.

"What?" Gus asked.

"You see that thing?"

"No, why?"

Collie handed him the rifle. Gus took the weapon and peered through the scope. Cars, trucks, smoke. Shadowy drivers and hunched shapes gathered around the trunks. He shifted the scope.

And spotted the grim sign left behind.

A dog's skull, polished to a shine, the disturbing jaws hanging at a sharp angle.

"Oh, that's fucked up," Gus muttered.

"Royally fucked up," Collie added and took back the weapon. "Eva?"

"Yeah?"

"Tell Garrett shit's about to happen."

She would not get the chance.

Somewhere behind that mass of vehicles, a barrage of oddly colored pillows was being launched at the island. They rose into the sky, shifting, wavering, even sparkling, like oversized teardrops the color of ginger ale. Perhaps a dozen or more missiles, spread wide and growing wider by the second.

"*Stay down!*" Collie shouted.

The sight of those tumbling bags paralyzed Gus. There was nowhere to run. No *time* to run. And no escape from what was coming. The blast radius of those bombs would envelop just about the whole of the parking area, and probably decimate everything within.

So Gus cringed, and did nothing except wait for the inevitable.

Until the first of those explosive devices burst not ten feet away from where they all kissed grass—soaking Gus and everyone nearby. Water splashed over him. He recoiled from the contact, shocked that he was still in one piece, inspecting the dark stains that doused him. Screams and gasps tore from the islanders as, all over the camp, those clear bladders fell and burst apart, spraying everything nearby in shocking spatters.

Plastic bags. They were only clear plastic bags, filled with—

"Water," Gus said, still surprised that they were alive. "It's only—"

Then the smell hit him.

A rancid, decomposing stench that wrinkled his bearded face and left him rattling his head.

"Oh, god… *damn,*" he blurted, recoiling in nauseated awe. He pinched his nose, trying to escape that horrible smell. Dark stains soaked through his legs, already touching skin, while a line went up his side and probably marked his back as well.

"Oh, that's nasty," he winced, actually tasting the stink. Those around him were suffering as well. Eva looked as if someone had kicked her in the stomach. One islander lowered his head and retched into the grass. People were moaning in agony, some with dripping faces where the balloon broke right in front of them. Others sat up and shook their arms, frantically attempting to dry off. All over the parking area, great wet bullseyes stained the ground, and the smell stole their breaths as effectively as plastic bags being slipped over their heads.

Worst of all, there was something oddly familiar about the stink.

Collie had buried her face in the valley of her right elbow, just for a second, before coming up for air. "Urine," she gasped. "Christ almighty, that's *urine.*"

That both horrified and mystified Gus. "Urine," he sputtered, pawing at a few drops running down his temple. "*Piss?* They're throwing *piss* at us? In… plastic *bags?*

Another round of the pungent projectiles launched into the air. *Piss bags!* Gus's mind screamed, watching the rise and fall of those wobbling, shifting bladders just before they crashed down with explosive spatters.

"*Mmm—mmm*" little Monica was saying, tugging, no, *pulling* on Bruno's arm as if he were a stubborn sapling refusing to be uprooted.

One woman rubbed at her eyes, as if she'd taken a full splash to the head and was trying to scrub the foulness off. A man appeared and pulled up his shirt to clean her face. Other islanders who took cover behind trees, fences, or even the camp's billboard (which had taken a direct hit) inspected themselves as if they'd been doused while wearing their Sunday's finest. One guy was gesticulating a *'what the fuck?'* with his open arms, when the revving of an engine—a *big* engine—flared to life on the other side of the water.

The black bus rolled towards the gatehouse, and the brave guards hunkered down in the pillbox atop the bridge. Suddenly, the defenders were falling, crumpling behind their fortifications as if shot dead. But they couldn't have been shot dead, as there were no gunshots, no killer stutter of automatic weapons, no *nothing* to be heard over the din and roar of that motorized army. And, yet, Gus saw one guy in a pillbox window flinch and drop out of sight. No one else moved, until one woman staggered through the fortification's back doorway. She collapsed against the doorframe, first sinking to a knee, then to both hands, as if searching for a fallen needle.

Feathered shafts protruded from her back.

She fluttered a hand, and that one gesture caused her to fall on the roof.

"We gotta go," Gus gasped, getting to his knees, struggling to swallow one breath, just one lungful of air that didn't smell like the rancid nut-juice squeezed from the bag of some ancient invalid. "We gotta——oh shit, Collie, we gotta get *outta* here."

Collie was rising, pulling back, equally affected by that overpowering, eye-watering stink that was as debilitating as tear gas.

"Mmm—mmm," little Monica urged. Her cheeks flushed, trying to get her message across that they had to leave *immediately.*

"Go," Gus barked and sucked in a mouthful of poisoned air. "Eva, we need to go."

"Yeah," Eva croaked. She was crouched over, horrified by the wet spots dappling her clothes as if scalded by hot water.

The motorized roar of the bus drowned out the moans of the islanders. The vehicle ran right through the spears, snapping several in splintery pops. The bus charged the bridge's entrance and then its front end disappeared from view.

Arrows, Gus's mind screamed, suddenly back online. "They're shooting arrows, Collie!"

"Crossbows!" she yelled back.

There was a short clatter of metal, followed immediately by frightening pops and the rustling of timbers. Gus couldn't see anything as a mixture of sweat, tears, and urine blurred his vision and smeared the scene. He wiped away the worst of it. Another crack and crash of metal, followed by a mechanical groan of laboring winches. There was a sad note of wood creaking to a breaking point, followed by a disturbing snap that could've been bone.

Then the most unnerving thing of all.

Damn near all the engines of the motorized army stopped running. All at once.

That halted Gus and Collie in their tracks.

"*Mmm—MMMM!*" little Monica was screaming now, as if she was about to pass a coconut. She dug in her heels and pulled on a shell-shocked Bruno.

A shriek split the air from the other side of the water. A ball-clenching peal of rage that Gus had not heard in a long, long time, but one he recognized, which turned his legs into boneless slabs of dough. But that *couldn't* be right, because they were all—

A hundred more voices joined the first screamer, or so it seemed, and then a boots-to-metal charge up an unseen, yet quivering gangway. Through fading coils of smoke, blurry figures appeared, flailing their arms and screeching notes of ravenous hunger. All the while Monica was somewhere behind Gus, behind them all, pleading that they just *listen* to her, just *listen* and *move their asses.*

A shape stumbled out of the back doorway of the gatehouse, tripped by the dead islander lying there. That stumbling figure bumbled to one side and pitched off the roof, falling some fifty feet to the water below, where the lake swallowed up the thrashing screamer in one great gulp of a splash.

Others pushed free of the gatehouse, stepping over the roadblock and running full tilt across the slanted roof. They stampeded across those cedar slates towards the island. They were heedless of the uncertain footing. They ignored the danger.

"Oh sweet Jesus," Gus panted, his eyes on the verge of popping from his face.

Monica said it best, as the sight of those charging creatures unlocked her mouth so that she could finally formulate the one word she was trying to convey all along.

"*Mindless!*" she screamed. "*MINDLESS!*"

17

The mindless charged across the rooftop, shrieking, snarling, howling. An inhuman gush of fury. Feet hammered across wooden shingles. Some of the mindless fell through rotten wood, crumpling to their knees or thighs. The rampaging figures behind them slammed into the floundering roadblocks, the impact causing the runners to plummet from the roof and into the lake, where the waters churned with limbs and torsos.

Across the water, figures emerged from their rides like wraiths pushing aside coffin lids.

Collie squeezed off a short burst, blasting the foremost of the mindless off the roof. "Move!" she yelled, breaking the paralysis of those nearby. Gus moved, but only to flank her, drawing his gun and taking a shooter's stance.

"This way," Eva yelled, getting his attention. "Everyone *to the Point.*"

But not everyone was running. Some of the islanders had taken a full blast to the face from the exploding piss bags, and they were staggering about as if mortally stricken by acid. Perhaps they were, as the few drops that had made contact with Gus's profile lit up his skin there as if being devoured by worms. That horrible sensation caused him to drop his aim and rub at the side of his face.

"Go!" Collie ordered without sparing him a glance. "*Go!* I'll slow them down."

She hefted her German-made hell-bringer of an assault weapon and took aim. She fired, her upper frame thrumming, the rifle's ejector spewing casings in a dull arc. Short, flaming beams of light erupted from the muzzle, lancing into the mindless charging across the roof. Arms were blown off. Torsos exploded in cherry-red puffs. Bodies were twisted in mid-charge and launched over the other side as if hit by a speeding car. A few heads burst, the bodies continuing a step before dropping and rolling off the edge of the roof.

The charge faltered again.

Half a dozen islanders crouched behind the gates. They held shotguns and pistols, searching for targets and well aware that their attackers were coming overhead. The man called Garrett was among the defenders, gripping a sidearm while waving at Eva to *get going*—when a crossbow bolt spurted out of his cheek, torqueing his head hard to the left.

The sight of the man toppling unlocked Gus's legs just as a shaft of light whizzed by his shoulder, missing him by a few hairs, and whistling hatred loud enough to startle. That drove him into a crouch, where he retreated a few frantic steps before dropping to his chest. A wave of bolts hissed overhead. Steel flashed in the daylight, and Gus glimpsed those deadly missiles a split second before they smacked loudly into wood and rock.

Run, his mind screamed, but he was unwilling to leave Collie.

The few islanders remaining at their barricaded posts fired blindly, hitting nothing.

Collie was on one knee and aiming at the cars across the water. She trembled as she returned fire upon the attacking enemy.

One masked shooter flew backwards as a burst tore into his chest and tossed him between the cars.

A second shooter had his head blown off before he could take better cover.

A third figure ducked behind an open car door, so Collie put a short burst through the machine's front in a vicious patter of tin. Shredded metal and steam peppered the air. Windshields were ventilated in harsh lines. A few nearby trees caught those steel-jacketed hellos, where the bullets chomped into the wood in explosive puffs of fiber and splinters. Collie strafed right, then left, and back again, controlling the recoil and her aim.

That short but meaningful contact sent the masked shadows diving for cover.

She wasn't finished, however.

"Oh, you sweet bitches," Collie whispered, searching for targets. "You have no *idea*…"

She pivoted on her knee and turned one windshield into a tracery of spider holes and sparkling ice chips. She ripped a line through another hood, the car vibrating from the impacts. Heads bobbed and ducked, but no one presented a viable target.

The mindless—the familiar undead once thought extinct—resumed their charge across the roof of the bridge. Not wanting them to think she'd forgotten about them, Collie swiveled back and unloaded. The zombies had reached the halfway point when the bullets tore into them. Bodies jerked and jigged before tumbling off the roof. Two heads exploded in a meaty drizzle. One figure was blown backwards in a spray of dark matter and fell out of sight, twisting like a livid eel. Collie blew the leg off one completely before altering her fire and taking out huge chunks from a clump of torsos, blasting the undead from the roof entirely.

The charge again faltered, the air misted with pieces of flying meat and ink. The mindless stalled, fumbling about the newly dead cluttering the path. Some tripped and fell, screaming into the water. A few actually recognized the direction of the gunfire, just before 5.56 mm rounds ripped across their upper chests and faces. One screamer took a full burst across the chops, which blew out the back of his skull. A second later, Collie shifted and scalped another with a single bullet.

She ceased firing, her empty magazine falling clear of her weapon. She turned to run just as the bus withdrew in a frightening rattle of wood and metal. A dust cloud billowed out from the entrance.

Gus crouched behind the operator and watched as the bus backed up. He didn't think that was a good sign. Shadows lining the opposite bank crept back behind their cars, sensing the lull in the return fire. There they stayed low and gathered strength.

"Follow me," Collie ordered and ran past him.

Gus did just that.

The last thing he saw before taking off was the mindless who'd fallen into the lake… clawing their way to shore.

Collie withdrew some twenty meters before ducking behind the corner of a small green cottage. Gus stopped beside her, pushing her back a step, and slammed his upper body against the clapboard wall.

"Stay low and out of sight," she told him.

"I know," Gus grated. "I've been shot at before."

Collie replaced her magazine with a slap and a good luck tickle.

Gus peeked around the corner, scanning the bridge. Cars and trucks were now in reverse, spinning jets of dirt into the air. The far shore was a mess of dead rides and exhaust, but shapes moved within that mess. Of the islanders, they were either dead or nowhere in sight.

"Collie?"

"Yeah?"

"I think we're the only ones left."

Collie pulled him back and took the corner. She stuck out half a head and glanced about. A second later she withdrew and pointed to a trail cutting between a pair of cottages and disappearing into the forest. There, one man waited and waved, urging them to follow.

"That Davis?" Collie asked.

Gus checked. "Yeah. Looks like him."

"So much for defending the homeland," Collie said and stopped right there.

Motors were revving up again.

"I gotta take care of that bridge," she said.

"How?"

As an answer, she opened the flap of her breast pocket.

Gus winced at the sight of the golf-ball-sized grenade.

Another bout of collapsing metal echoed over the lake's surface, followed by a short shriek of hinges and an earth-shaking clang, as if an enormous manhole cover had crashed onto the ground. A surge of engines then, and a gravelly spewing of crushed stone followed.

Gus stood next to Collie and peeked around the corner.

One of the mindless, dripping water, stood in the very spot he and Collie had just vacated upon the grassy ridge. The zombie spotted him immediately and charged, water-logged clothing flapping as it ran.

Gus took a two-handed aim and squeezed off three shots before one bullet blew apart the thing's head, not twenty strides from the cottage.

He was about to speak when Collie yanked him back.

A squall of crossbow bolts slammed into the cottage, hard enough to rattle wood. One bolt punched through the thin clapboard with a shiver. Several more blew past the corner, needling the very spot where Gus had been standing a second earlier. More missiles sped onwards, ending their killer flights in other cottage walls, trees, and bouncing off rocks.

The sound of one engine alone rose and overpowered the motorized chaos beyond.

"This way," Collie said. "Watch your ass and watch my back."

Gus would do just that.

They hurried around the back of the cottage, ignoring the frantic waves from Davis. They stopped at the other corner of the home, where they had a better view of the bridge's closed gates on the island side.

That mighty engine flared again, and a speeding mass entered the tunnel with a jarring crackle and crunch of wood. The vehicle raced along the interior like a speeding torpedo, the sound amplified by the enclosed space.

"They're going to ram the gate," Collie said behind her lowered rifle.

No sooner had she spoken when a pickup with an attached snow plow smashed through the closed barrier. The gates blew outward, folding up and over the machine's hood in a spray of wood. Planks crumpled and were swished away like freed propellers. Slabs of debris fell from the rampaging truck as the driver fought for control. Lengths of wood bounced off the roof and flipped out of the box bed. The machine halted in the clearing with a spray of dirt, drawing up broadside in a swirl of dust.

The truck huffed and smoldered, the front blade scratched and mean-looking, but far from finished.

Until Collie lobbed the grenade under the machine.

The blast launched the truck skyward about ten feet, lighting up the day in a frightening conflagration that both lifted and engulfed the frame in a fiery fist. The rig slammed back to earth with a two-ton crunch of metal, the husk charred and burning. Tires blew out with ear-crackling bangs.

Collie bared her teeth.

"We go now?" Gus asked, ready to run five minutes ago.

"Fuck no," she said, propping her rifle alongside the house. She dug out the other grenade. "One more of these bitches will take care of that bridge."

A zombie clambered up over the little cliff facing the lake, dripping water and savage because of it. Gus sighted the thing and fired four shots before one round tore away the left side of its head in a brutal smear of color.

"Collie, those fuckers are coming ashore."

"Yeah?" she said and cocked back her arm. "Ever tell you I kill at dunk tanks?"

Not waiting for a reply, Collie stepped out around the corner and threw her second grenade as if it were a baseball being sent home from right field. The explosive bauble didn't fly down the throat of the bridge, however, but rather bounced a few feet short before wobbling inside and greeting a second oncoming vehicle—just as its headlights flared to life.

The blast blew apart the bridge mouth, sending fragments and shingles both sideways and skyward in a storm cloud of destruction. Flame flashed and waved merrily for a searing split second. Gus glimpsed the car's grill go straight up before the sides of the bridge puffed outward. One shard of debris, a lightning bolt of metal or wood—he didn't know which—actually *impaled* a zombie through the head as it was rising up over the nearby embankment.

Then the resulting dust obscured everything.

"Happy birthday," Collie said, a little breathless. "Now we go."

18

All had been going well, right up until the islanders started firing back. Firing back with automatic weapons, no less, at which point the sound and fury of such a surprise cranked the head of the Vulture toward the prisoner called Carson. Trucks and cars surrounded the captured man, who was currently strapped to a forklift, his bare feet kept in place by duct tape. Vast amounts wrapped his forehead and naked torso as well. The Leather had, in fact, used a complete roll on the mechanic.

A red ball gag filled Carson's mouth, preventing him from talking. The exposed rubber was slick and dewy, and every now and again, snot streamers fired out from the man's nose as he released a breath. Carson didn't look well since being captured. He'd certainly lost color after they extracted information from him, information that detailed the location of the island village, the men and women living there, their professions, and their defenses.

Including the number of weapons.

At no time did Carson say anything about automatic rifles. Or grenades.

That…angered the Vulture.

The grim executioner wearing the bronze leather mask straightened. The Bronze caught the stern look from the Vulture, and he hefted a hammer.

Carson's eyes bulged. His cheeks puffed as he struggled for breath. Whimpers laced the air. The Bronze stepped in close, where Carson's bare feet were taped to the forks. The toes had remained exposed for better access. Three of the little piggies on his left foot had been smashed into red pulp and now resembled flattened grapes. The mechanic had started talking after only one of his toes received the hammer, but the Vulture deemed the others necessary, as punishment.

Carson grunted and spewed more snot. He managed to thrash a little, but he was so bound by duct tape, the struggle amounted to nothing more than muted twitches.

The Vulture wondered what else the mechanic had forgotten to tell him.

Kneeling at the leader's right knee, a half-naked meat puppet cleared his throat. The Vulture ignored the meat, and the nearby Leather brought the enslaved individual to heel by pulling hard on his leash. The meat puppet croaked, unable to breathe, and settled down.

That minor interruption quelled, the Vulture held up a hand, staying the Bronze's hammer just a little longer. The leader then regarded the bridge's entrance.

The bus reversed in a surge of horsepower, pulling back the makeshift ramp on its roof, the very ramp that had allowed the Leather to bypass so many walls in the past. Two pickups replaced the bus, reversing until they were mere feet away from the weakened gates. Figures scrambled between the two vehicles, hooking chains and quickly getting clear. A hand chopped the air, and the trucks spun dirt before yanking the gates off its hinges.

The way to the island lay wide open.

The rammer was given the signal to go, and the truck equipped with the snow plow entered the tunnel.

The legions of the Leather, armed with heavy crossbows, unleashed a wave of bolts at the island. The sight of that deadly sprinkle distracted the Vulture from Carson.

The rammer smashed through the gates on the other side. The truck skidded to a stop in full view—seconds before the vehicle exploded and left the earth riding a geyser of flame. Blazing chunks of wreckage rained down, some smashing into the mindless flailing around in the water. That spectacle shocked several of the Leather, freezing them where they stood.

The Vulture, however, bristled with anger.

Three shots rang out, informing the leader that some of the enemy still lived.

The Vulture motioned for three cars to enter the tunnel. He then signaled his lessers to prepare to advance. A hundred fighters reloaded their crossbows, while a hundred more readied axes, clubs, and spears. The ammunition of the old world had long since dried up, so the Leather had adopted more primitive but just as effective weapons, preferring the medieval might of points and edged steel. They didn't mind revving engines of their machines, however, considering them the war chariots of a new age.

The Age of Leather.

The cars disappeared into the tunnel depths, and the Vulture raised his hand, ready to unleash the army at his back. Carson had told them lies, as incredible as it was. The Vulture would personally attend to his punishment.

The far end of the bridge exploded in the same spectacular fashion as the rammer. The unexpected blast surprised them all once again, including the Vulture, who had dropped into a crouch. He straightened and stared at the smoking wreckage, taking in the ribbons of flame and dense coils of smoke. The lead vehicle had been destroyed. Perhaps even all three.

Leather-clad figures soon entered the bridge's interior, hands shielding their faces. They entered the smoking aperture, coughing, yet forging ahead.

A minute later, word came back.

The bridge, while damaged, was still intact. Cars could not pass, but the Leather could cross on foot.

That pleased the Vulture, who sensed a greater game afoot. The islanders, those remaining, were readying themselves for another attack. Or worse, attempting to flee. The Vulture suspected he'd been lied to once again.

Organizing his thoughts, the leader was distracted by the unruly meat slab who had the gall to stand and tear off his mouth gag.

"That's the same shooter—" the meat gasped before the Leather holding onto the leash pulled hard, transforming the words into a pain-filled grunt. Red-faced and grimacing, the meat dropped to his knees.

Three lessers wielding pipes and bats moved in to deliver punishment.

The Vulture stopped them with a hand.

"*Guh,*" the meat panted, once again permitted the privilege of breathing. He clawed at the leash, granting himself a little more slack.

The Vulture waited.

"That shooter—that sniper…" the meat slab managed. "I bet… I bet he's the same guy. Who shot up my crew. Those grenade blasts? Bet there's only two. If it's the same guy, he took them from our trailer. Back at the recharging station. Along with the merch. The trailer had a booby trap. Two grenades. I know. Rigged it myself. I'll bet… I'll bet my life it's the same fuck puppy who chased me off. Same crew, even. Only two grenades on that rig, though. And he used them just now. Bet they got nothing left. Except the rifle."

The Vulture waited.

"Same person," the meat puppet once known as Top Gun grunted while holding his throat. He steadied himself and considered the Leather surrounding him. "Just wanted to—to tell you. That's all. That should count for something."

The Vulture absorbed the information. It did indeed count for something. He signaled the Leather to pounce on the prisoner. They brutalized the puppet until he collapsed. Continued brutalizing him into silence.

The Vulture ignored the violence at his back. He looked to the rear, sighted one lesser, and issued commands by hand. The lesser signaled back.

The bus pulled to one side of the bridge, allowing passage onto the island.

The air filled with a loud rumble and squeal of a semi-truck. One of two in this war party. The huge machine reversed and angled its load toward the bridge. Several of the Leather marched alongside the approaching trailer doors.

Doors that were chained shut.

<h1 style="text-align:center">19</h1>

Collie and Gus pounded over a wide path of crushed stone. They raced deeper into the island's sub-temperate zone, which resembled a dense rainforest. Fir trees crowded them in, their long branches resembling fish bones. Those boughs quickly hid the shoreline. Velvet green drizzled the larger rocks between the trees, while spicy fir and fresh earth scented the air, except Gus couldn't smell any of that.

"Jesus Christ," he barked, his face puckered in disgust. "I smell like sick donkey piss."

"Maybe it is donkey piss," Collie replied while running and patting down her tactical webbing. "Well shit."

"What?"

"Only two magazines left. That includes the fresh one I slapped home."

Gus didn't like the sound of that. He knew she had only brought five magazines, since their original plan was to restock at Whitecap. The remainder for her rifle was in their pickup, abandoned back at the bridge.

"I got four spares for mine," he huffed.

"The way you shoot, you'll need them."

Gus scowled. That one hurt.

Mayhem scorched the air back toward the bridge, the combined voices of hundreds of zombies howling at the sun.

"We don't have much time," Collie said.

The two saw Davis up ahead. He was standing by a directional signpost sprouting a dozen arrows in different directions. "This way," he said, waving them through as he skipped into a full run.

"Where's this 'Point'?" Gus asked between sharp breaths, hoping to God he didn't develop a stitch in his side. Or leg cramps.

Davis pointed. "Up ahead. They killed Garrett."

"And everyone else back there," Gus said.

"Why are they doing this?"

"Talk later," Collie advised the islander. "How far to go?"

"Ten-minute run," Davis said. "If you can do it."

"Ten minutes?" Gus blurted, suddenly very much aware of the hot buzzing in his foot.

"Yeah, ten minutes."

"Where are your cars?"

"Back there," Davis panted as he ran. "But Sarah and Rich had a pickup and a car parked on the other side of the cottages. In case something like this happened. They drove on with the others. I stayed back to get you. In case you got lost."

The wild screaming of hundreds cut through the surrounding forest, urging Gus to run faster. Davis and Collie glanced over their shoulders, but Gus did not. He knew what was back there. Just ahead, in the shade of a singular maple, a white boulder with a pink happy face spray-painted upon it came into view. There, the path split off into three directions.

Davis took the right. Gus and Collie kept pace, their feet pounding over crushed stone.

The shrieking grew behind them, sounding even more intense in Gus's ears. The thickening uproar raised the hairs on his neck. They were exposed. Way too exposed, and he felt far too rusty to evade an army of deadheads. The dense forest made it difficult to see the path behind them. Gus really didn't want to see, but like anyone trying to outrun a flash flood, it was counterintuitive *not* to look.

And that ravenous wailing motivated him to red-line it, tapping into whatever speed his nearly fifty-year old carcass could muster.

Davis and Collie had a good ten-step lead on him—and Collie was carrying the rifle.

"*Run!*" she yelled back at him.

Red-faced and feeling like a boiler about to explode, Gus chugged along, instinct telling him to glance once again over his shoulder. Nothing. No one. But goddamn he could hear them just fine. Just through the trees. And they were closing in from damn near everywhere behind him.

"Where we going?" Collie asked between breaths.

"Other side of the island," Davis said. "Secret escape route."

"A road?"

"Not quite."

Not quite? Gus wanted to bark, but he didn't. Couldn't. He was trying to keep up while saving a little gas for the inevitable sprint for the finish.

"Then what is it?" Collie asked. "And don't say boats."

"I won't," Davis answered.

The forest thinned out, revealing a pathway leading to a large dormitory. An open field gradually came into view, where a playground complete with a set of monkey bars, ropes, and slides waited to be used. The crushed stone underfoot became a trail of dried mud. They pushed up over a series of sun-baked mounds that killed Gus's calves and got him gasping. Sweat left him in sparkling sheets. It wasn't fair. He'd lost all that weight, all of it, and he was still on the verge of dropping dead. All the while, his foot crackled with its familiar pins and needles.

"Move, Gus!" Collie shouted.

"Moving," he got out. "I'm moving."

A single voice released a stream of insane gibberish, startling him badly. With a quick double take, Gus glimpsed a body crashing through the underbrush. One arm reached up before the torso disappeared from sight entirely, as if swallowed up by a sinkhole.

That was it for him. He forgot about his burning foot and squeezed out a little more speed.

He then glimpsed more ghostly outlines running through the bushes.

"Run!" Davis yelled.

"We almost there?" Collie shouted.

But Davis wouldn't answer.

The mindless cut through the undergrowth—pushing, fighting through as if the forest was some great dastardly webbing. Thick branches clotheslined a pair of zombies, their feet leaving the ground as if caught in a windstorm. Some tripped and fell, toppling others behind them. Despite the natural barrier of the surrounding woods, the undead stampeded forward, heedless of the boughs whipping at their faces, and slowly catching up to the three fleeing runners.

Collie glanced back at their pursuers, and unless she was exercising on the sly, Gus didn't think she was operating at the best of her physical ability. And he certainly wasn't sure if she could fire that automatic cannon while on the run.

Then it hit him.

Davis was running along a snaking, curving path that darted in and out of clumps of trees and half-hidden cabins. The mindless, ironically enough, were charging in a straight line. And gaining.

As if sensing that thought, Davis suddenly yelled, "This way!"

He turned left, leaped over a hedge, and bounded towards a large building looming beyond the brush. A signpost flashed by, pointing to the dining hall.

The place didn't look secure at all. Two floors, connected on the outside by a grand set of stairs, that led to an outdoor deck where hot sunlight pooled in the summertime. The walls consisted of nothing but a series of squared cookhouse windows from one corner to the next. Several handcrafted picnic tables and concrete barbeque pits dotted the lawn around the building, eagerly waiting for campers to return.

"Shortcut!" Davis wheezed and ran past the tables, right up to the main doors. He pulled them open and left them that way for Collie, who was two strides behind him. She halted on the threshold, her frame heaving from the run.

She glanced back to check on Gus, and he noticed the unchecked shock upon her winded face.

He looked over his shoulder.

And wished he hadn't.

Mindless.

Zombies, Moes, deadheads, gimps, and meatbags—names that were all fine and dandy descriptors, but *mindless* truly described the pursuing mob bursting through the evergreen thickets. Ragged and torn clothing covered their infected hides, and some didn't have anything on at all. They charged the dining hall in fleshy gushes, resembling jets of skin-colored water punching through a failing dam. Meaty lines of fury, their faces lit up with gluttonous hatred, their hooked fingers swiping at the air. The lead runners reached the outer edges of the picnic tables with ease and jumped over them, but they didn't descend as gracefully. Some crashed in a painful twist of limbs. Faces clapped wood. One outstretched arm hit the deck all together wrong and a red spear of shattered bone popped free of the skin surrounding it.

Collie started shooting.

Light tore into the foremost runners. A chest ripped open in a great explosion of red and white. A head got half sheared away while the body underneath continued to run for a split second. An arm blew off, savagely spinning the creature around before Collie took his skull off with one shot.

The rest, however, continued to charge.

And in the face of that fearless onslaught, Gus ran for his life.

He plunged through the doorway and crashed into a structural post. Collie withdrew, allowing Davis to slam shut the outer doors. The camper then immediately twisted the locks at the base and at the top.

Outside, the infected wave of bodies rushed the building.

"This way," Davis gasped. He rushed through an aisle between two great sections of tables and chairs. Gus labored after him, glimpsing the interior. Vending machines flashed by, grand totem poles of lacquered wood, and a huge stage at the far end. A banner hung over the platform which read, *"Camp Red Wolf Welcomes you!"*

The mindless crashed into the door with an explosive bulge of wood and windows—but the frame held. Arms thrust through the glass in spurts of blood and falling shards. A couple of heads slammed into the surface, rattling the barrier. More mindless heaved up behind those initial few, squashing them against the windows and main doors in a steam press of meat and momentum. Hands slapped glass, smashing through the barrier like cheap cymbals.

And over their screaming heads and jostling shoulders, more mindless were rushing forward.

Collie backed up a few steps and unleashed a full killing spray across the windows. Sunlight bounced off the flying shards of glass. Heads burst apart in technicolor spurts. Whole torsos slunk from sight as if slurped down by the earth.

"Come on!" Davis yelled, from the other side of the dining hall.

Collie ceased firing and ejected the spent magazine. "Just thinning them out."

Not that the mindless cared.

She turned, leaving behind a writhing wave of clawing hands and contorted faces.

The sight reminded Gus of the early days.

Zombies climbed through the shattered windows. Some of them hooked themselves on the glass teeth, opening their guts in shocking clumps that spilled forth.

Davis held Gus's shoulder and pushed him through another set of doors. "Watch them from the other side of the lake, if you want," he said.

Collie exited the building just as Davis slammed the doors shut. "Can't lock these," he gasped, his face shining with sweat. "We're almost there."

"Didn't you say that a few minutes back?" Gus demanded, very much out of breath. He lumbered into a run regardless, through a near-identical setup of tables and chairs. His left foot felt like it was bearing down on an electric buzzer with every step. Collie was behind him, straining with her own exertion.

"I said that," Collie corrected him. "Never did. Get an. Answer. And we. Sure as fuck. Better not be heading to. A pier."

"No pier," Davis managed as they put distance between them and the dining hall, bolting through a fine gazebo and a well-maintained garden. "Docks are that way."

He flailed in a direction far to the right of where they were going.

"So where—" Gus started, but Davis, shockingly spry for a man who looked to have the living shit kicked out of him, ran on ahead.

Leaving Gus and Collie trailing behind.

Noise of the mindless smashing through the dining hall receded, but to the left, more of the zombies scrambled into view.

Davis cut off the path and hopped over a hedge, heading back into the woods. Gus and Collie followed, except Gus belly flopped flat onto his face and groaned into the grass.

By the time Collie flipped him over and hauled him to his feet, Davis had threaded his way up and over an incline, a dark outline traveling through a shade that got Gus thinking about thatched beach umbrellas. He and Collie raced after the islander, over hard-packed dirt generously sprinkled with green and orange needles and other forest debris. Gus hurried at his best speed, which was failing fast. The hill leeched his strength and injected fire into his calves. Sweat stung his eyes and fell in a steady patter.

He made it to the top of the hill, however, just behind Collie, who didn't let him lag too far behind. They reached the crest, where Gus lurched to a stop and gawked at Davis. The man was as lithe as a deer, descending the hilltop and darting between thick trunks. The islander sprinted toward a pristine white beach, the sand shimmering in the midday sun. The smell of fresh water cut across Gus's face, and between the evenly spaced trees, waves sparkled.

Davis cut left.

"Come on," Collie ordered, leaving boot prints as she started down the hill. Gus filled his lungs and hurried after her, letting his momentum do most of the work. Davis bounded along a wet track of shoreline, his frame winking in and out among the last few trees. He waved and pointed toward the open lake.

Gus saw them.

"You gotta be fucking kidding," he croaked.

There, strung out in a curious zigzag in the middle of the water, were about a dozen islanders. They had already made it more than three-quarters of the way to the far shoreline, their figures clearly visible against the huge backdrop of woodland on the other side. There were no posts, no guide ropes, and nothing to indicate a path from Gus's vantage point, but of course that couldn't be right. Still, the summer camp islanders hurried along. Little Monica included, still clinging onto Bruno, easily identified by his pirate cap.

A few of those faces turned and spotted Davis racing along the beach.

"This way," Collie urged Gus, and she bounded after the islander with renewed energy.

Legs damn near dead, chest close to bursting, and eyes bugging, Gus practically ran into a tree and placed a bearded cheek to its trunk. He gawked at the operator as she cut through that darkened landscape, traversing an angle meant to catch up with the fleeing islanders.

The voices of the mindless reached him.

Sucking down another tankful of air, Gus detached himself from the tree and floundered after Collie. He ducked under a low branch and almost fell flat on his chest, but after frantically pinwheeling his arms and screaming *"JESUS!"*, he somehow managed to remain vertical. Every footfall stung. Every breath stretched and squeezed his ribs like a withered accordion. The smell of water gave him an extra shot of juice, and those scintillating waves were blinding. In short time, he charged onto the beach and nearly toppled, boots kicking up sand.

Collie's improvised path had brought them closer, however. Just ten feet away, the beach became a black mass of rocks that sloped underneath the water.

Davis stood in the lake, some fifteen feet offshore, waves lapping at his ankles. He urged them to hurry. The other islanders had nearly reached the other side.

"Stay inside the markers," Davis ordered as loud as he dared and pointed underfoot. "And watch your step. It gets slippery."

Collie was already wading into the lake, her camos soaking to the knee.

Gus staggered to the rocks, swayed upon them like a drunken Atlas, and couldn't spare the wind to swear. And he really wanted to swear, to just light up the air around him with a few choice firecrackers of shit-bagged dismay. He couldn't, however; he was that spent. He was a kettle that had evaporated all his water, while the smoldering fire under his ass threatened to melt him whole.

The lake would kill him. This he knew inherently.

Then he saw the rocks.

Two strings of beach rocks resembling gigantic pearls slipped underneath the water, marking a trail just a little thinner than a sidewalk that vanished in the waves.

Collie was already strides ahead upon the narrow trail. She halted and half-turned, enough to shoot him a look of *move your ass*.

Orders received, Gus sloshed into the lake and stepped onto the flat mantel of rock underfoot. He stayed on course, still amazed at the hidden walkway. *No more than two or three feet across*, he figured. Considering the size of the surrounding lake, it was like stepping onto a slick tightrope of slate. Outside the submerged markers, the edges dropped away and the water took on that gauzy, forbidding tint of unknown depths.

The water sloshed at Gus's ankles. At times, it rose to his knees. The day focused its glare upon the lake surface, the October sun throwing down a feverish heat. The air was cleaner, however, fresher, cutting through the stink of his piss-stained clothing. Just sucking it down rejuvenated Gus a little. He divided his attention between watching where he walked and Collie and Davis forging ahead. The path veered one way and then the other. One wrong step and a person would drop off into watery oblivion. Slogging through the lake, however, was worse than racing through the woods. The grind was harder, and Gus discovered he was moaning.

Then he heard the commotion behind him.

Collie glanced back. She then turned around completely and crouched to a knee. She brought up her rifle. The screaming intensified, prompting Gus to look behind him.

That was his undoing.

Practically exhausted, he stepped onto a rock which slid out from underfoot in a startling, split-second yank-and-tip sensation. Gus went lopsided, arms splayed as he splashed down on his back. Pressure squeezed his chest as a galaxy of bubbles exploded about his face. He twisted, steeping himself even deeper. His fingers grazed the edge of the rock mantel—the very one he walked upon only a second earlier.

Then nothing.

And that was the most frightening part of being dunked—that slow-motion sense of sinking. He released a watery *garp!* and pawed for land that was no longer there, while sheets of angelic light shimmered around him. The mantel's edge receded into the gloom the deeper he sank.

Instinct took over. Gus fluttered his arms and kicked his feet. He breast-stroked, zeroing in upon the imposing slab that was the mantel. He swam toward that murky wall, his clothing as clingy and troublesome as a strait jacket. His panic spiked. His brain demanded air but his mouth and lungs refused. He then touched rock and scrabbled for a handhold. Then toeholds. He grabbed the painted rocks, and they came free of the mantel's edge with an underwater rattle and quickly sank. Gus sank with them for six inches before he was able to worm his way back up. He latched onto the submerged ledge, on the verge of sucking down water, his lungs desperate for anything. He kicked, pressing his chest to the mantel, slapping an arm across the path. Gus lifted his face towards the shimmering surface, inches away. He clawed for a cranny, a crack, anything to hoist himself up, but found nothing. He grunted in panicked frustration, releasing a jet of bubbles before his eyes. *Air!* Bright, sparkling air was right above him, right *there*, but he couldn't get any closer. His water-logged boots pumped dreamily against the lower rock, unable to get a toehold. The goddamn mantel was as smooth as a baby's ass. With his remaining strength, he lifted himself in a last-ditch effort and rose almost enough to kiss the surface.

Before sinking back.

Arp! Gus screamed, and his lungs truly started shrieking, telling him to quit fucking around, to get his ass up on that shelf before they started taking on water in great convulsive gulps. Except Gus *couldn't* get his ass any higher. He'd blown through whatever gas he had in the tank. His brain joined the swelling mutiny of his lungs, and his mouth was a second away from opening the hatches.

The light overhead crystalized, shattering into sparkles.

Then darkened.

An arm harpooned the water and a hand fastened onto his shoulder. Collie pulled him up and Gus broke the surface with an uncontrollable gasp and sputter.

"I got you," she said, still holding onto her assault rifle. "I got you."

Gus barked a short cough and stabilized himself. His ears roared and his face dripped. His vision was a wet smear.

Collie crouched beside him, facing the campers' island.

Mindless.

The zombies charged into the lake, splashing forward like mad children. Some went to their chests and quickly sank out of sight. Some wiped out in spectacular fashion, going tits-over-ass before splashing down. A few managed to locate the secret walkway, and they stayed upon it for only a few strides before the path took an irregular turn, whereupon the mindless immediately disappeared underwater. A few hands clawed at the air, just above the surface, before sinking out of sight.

"You good?" Collie asked.

"Yeah," Gus sputtered, and he got to his feet. "Think my balls are waterlogged."

She pulled him away. They staggered along, staying inside the white lines, sloshing toward the shore. The path continued to zig and zag, and those turns saved them, as the mindless—true to their new name—paid no heed to the markers and disappeared into unknown depths. A frenzied splashing cut the air, along with the water choked cries of the zombies as they sank in deep water.

"Like… a pissed-off marine world… back there," Gus gasped.

"Save your breath," Collie said.

Davis waited for them on the shore, and when Gus released Collie and stood on his own, he realized how quiet it had become. Quiet enough for him to turn around and see what was transpiring on the water.

A light wind rustled the surface, but of the mindless, there was no sight.

The lake had sucked them down. And kept them there.

<h1 style="text-align:center">20</h1>

"This way," Davis said. He disappeared into the forest, leading them along a narrow path cloaked in a comfortable autumn shadow.

Clothes dribbling and boots squishing, Gus squeezed his beard free of water and followed. Wet and wretched and all but depleted of strength, it took everything to put one foot before the other. Every step was a wet cement spatter that threatened to pull him down. The shivers grabbed him then, adding to his misery. He staggered along, grabbing at limbs that might support him, hoping to God he didn't stumble. If he did, he'd fall flat on his soggy-ass and that would be that. There'd be no getting back up. So he wobbled and swayed through that dense patch of woodland, following a rough trail marked by axe and boot prints.

"You okay?" Collie asked.

"Huh?"

"I said you okay?"

Gus nodded.

"'Cause you look like shit."

"I'm fine," he muttered with a wet scowl. He pointed back toward the lake. "They could be… walking along the bottom. Right now."

"The MBs?" Collie asked.

"Yeah."

"We'll be long gone before they get to the surface. That right, Davis?"

"That's right."

At that exact moment, Gus's body ceased to work below the waist. He lurched to a stop and grabbed his knees, unable to go any further. "Oh Jesus. I gotta—gotta stop. Right here. I'm about to drop."

Collie let him be. Wet and winded but otherwise fine, she placed her back against a tree and gradually sank to a knee, her rifle lowered. In the shade, her sunglasses gleamed, speckled with water droplets.

Gus gasped, spat, and dripped where he stood. With a pained groan, he slowly collapsed on his ass, his knees crackling as he did so.

"Jesus," Collie grimaced. "Does that hurt?"

Red-eyed and saturated, he shook his head.

"Sounds awful."

He smiled weakly, oh-so-grateful for the few seconds of rest. He realized he'd planted his backside in a cozy bed of wildflowers. His hands were in what might've been tea leaves. He studied the vegetation briefly, wary of poison ivy and pissed-off snakes. Either one would be a fishhook in his ball sack at this point in the game. Seeing neither, however, he relaxed and laid back on his elbows, lowering himself like a broken robot.

"Just gimme a minute," he panted. "Just a minute. S'all I need."

"Don't talk," Collie told him. "Davis?"

Halfway up the hill, the islander's head perked up. "Yeah?"

"Go catch up with your people. Tell them we're two minutes behind. And if I fire a long burst, don't wait for us. Got it?"

He hesitated. "Got it. We have trucks three hills over. Three klicks from here."

"Trucks?" Collie asked.

"Three klicks?" a horrified Gus blurted.

"Yes," Davis answered. "And yes."

"Gassed up?" she asked.

"Yes, but not much of it."

"Three klicks?" Gus repeated, positively aghast and staring at his soaking boots. "Fuck me gently. Couldn't you park them *closer*?"

"The closest road is three kilometers out. We're in deep woods here."

"Oh dear Jesus," Gus moaned, his head rolling.

"Carry on," Collie said to Davis. "We'll be there."

Davis got up, brushed himself off, and started up the hill. When the islander disappeared into the forest, Gus considered the trail behind them, twisted and lost in the tangles. Somewhere beyond that foliage, there were waters lapping at a rocky shoreline. Any second, he expected one of those dead things to start wailing, announcing to the world that it had reached the other side.

Collie shifted her rifle, the movement breaking his thoughts.

"He's in better shape than me," Gus said in an exhausted voice.

"The hell you talking about?" she asked. "You realize how far you've come? You just passed basic training, buddy. You're a goddamn Spartan is what you are. A human *missile*."

Gus smirked, knowing better. Still, a part of him enjoyed that.

They stopped talking then, and in that meaningful lapse, they could hear Davis's footfalls over the hill.

"Where'd they get them, Collie?" Gus asked.

"The meatbags?"

"Yeah."

The operator offered a tight smile. "Who knows? Thing is, they got them. And... were able to stash them away somewhere. Kept them outta the fucking daylight. Or dipped them in vats of moisturizer. I don't know."

"They were runners."

"They were."

"Fresh as fucking daisies."

Collie nodded *they were that*.

"I mean..." Gus tried to make sense of it all. "Could they have... maybe... kept a head or two? Like that playpen? Remember? The one filled with only heads?"

"Snapping, biting heads," she added.

"Yeah, like that? Could some sick bastard... have an undead head tucked away? Maybe saving the virus? Just to infect people? The ones they don't like? Or have no use for. And turn them into new gimps?"

Collie thought it over. "Possible. There are some twisted puppies out there. And people are the last valuable resource around. Only water comes close. And pizza. Only need two brain cells to figure that out. Just a few things puzzling me about all that."

"The piss bags?"

"That's one of them."

Gus sniffed himself. "I still stink. That's some rancid shit. Even after the dip."

Collie checked herself as well. "Not as bad as before, but it's there. This might be trouble."

"How so?"

"I'll tell you later," she said and stood. "You ready?"

He was nowhere near ready, but he nodded all the same.

"We gotta get to those rides," she told him. "I'm not going to fucking walk all the way to Whitecap."

"We're still going?" Gus asked in surprise.

"More than ever."

"But what about Davis and Eva and company?"

"Like it or not, they come with us. I don't see a choice. And we gotta go right now, because shit's getting really quiet over there and I don't like it."

She was right. Gus climbed to his feet, his knees crackling once again. It was embarrassing. "Sorry," he muttered.

Her sunglasses clear of clinging water, Collie flashed him a smile, bright and toothy. "Don't worry about it, babe."

Then she was hiking up the hill.

Gus stood there for seconds, watching her go, and remembered to start breathing again. There was something feral in her smile that startled him, and he replayed and froze the image in his mind's eye.

Only for a second, however, before he hoofed it after her.

They caught up with Davis chugging over the second hill. He greeted them with an exhausted nod and pointed toward the crest. "The others. Just over the hill. I can hear them."

Gus couldn't hear shit, but Collie was already moving past the islander. "Come on, then. They only roughed up your face. You had scads of juice not five minutes ago."

"Everything caught up to me," Davis said.

They heard the survivors trudging through the bush before they saw them. As they closed the gap, Rich Trinidad came into view. The gunslinger walked along as a rear guard, one hand on a nine-millimeter Beretta. His sombrero lifted as he detected the approaching three, but he didn't acknowledge them.

"Rich!" Davis said and waved.

Trinidad didn't reply.

The other islanders came into view then, though partially hidden by the forest. They turned at the sound of Davis's voice.

"Anyone coming after you?" Trinidad asked.

"Not yet."

"That's going to change," Collie said.

"You figure?" Trinidad asked.

"Oh yeah," the operator said grimly. "How far to these stashed rides of yours?"

Trinidad appeared none too happy about the question, still suspicious of the newcomers.

"Still a ways to go," Davis answered for him.

The rest of the islanders were taking a break, seated along the trail. Eva was there, as well as the bespectacled Sarah. Then Gus found Cory and Bruno, with Monica close by them.

"Get everyone marching," Collie said, striding past them all and heading for the front of the column. "And watch our tails back there, Rich. This ain't over."

Gus shivered at the words. He didn't think it was over either.

*

The sight of corpses struggling upon lazy waves stopped the Vulture in his tracks. At his back was a sizeable force of the Leather, gathered along the shoreline and watching their leader. A dozen more waited upon the rocks leading to the underwater pathway. The Vulture wasn't pleased about the escape route. He was even more displeased with Carson for withholding that crucial bit of information. The mechanic was being selective with what he knew. The Vulture found that both admirable and infuriating. Even now, as dozens of the Leather swarmed over the island, searching for fresh meat, the Vulture knew nothing would be found.

Their quarry had fled. Across the lake.

Water lapped at the black rocks. White markers gleamed beneath the water.

The Vulture turned to a lesser. "Bring me Carson."

Several minutes later, a half-dozen of the Leather dumped the mechanic into the sand before the Vulture. If the man appeared pitiful before, he was even more wretched now. Carson had been removed from the forklift and marched along until his wrecked feet could take no more, whereupon he was dragged by the arms over crushed stone and forest floor. Dirt and dust covered him, and his blood ran freely from dozens of visible cuts. Tatters of duct tape clung to his skin, the ends curled and speckled.

The sinister Bronze loomed over the tortured man. His hammer had been hooked upon his waist.

"You," the Vulture said quietly, unmoved by the mechanic's injuries, "have lied to us again."

Carson whimpered and shook his head with whatever strength remained. His wet cheeks fluttered around the ball gag. One of those cheeks had been split down the middle.

The Bronze reached for his hammer while one of the nearby Leather yanked the gag free. Carson retched and bent over, only to be rudely straightened by his captors. One of his eyes was blinking badly, as if irritated. He focused upon the Vulture.

"You didn't tell us about this path," the Vulture said.

"I forgot."

That unsettling mask didn't move. "Liar," the Vulture said softly, aiming a gun finger at the man.

The Bronze jerked his hammer free of his belt.

"I forgot!" Carson yelled, his chest heaving.

"Where are they going?" the Vulture asked.

"I don't know," the mechanic pleaded. He glanced fearfully at his potential executioner.

"Yes, you do."

"I *don't*."

The Vulture clenched one hand into a fist.

The Leather fell upon Carson. The man screamed and struggled as they flattened him out upon the sand. Hands gripped his feet, arms, and steadied his head. He writhed until exhausted, and then sobbed in trapped terror.

"You have no need of your legs for your work," the Vulture quietly pointed out. "Where are they going?"

Carson squinted his good eye shut. His chest was scratched and bleeding as if he'd been pulled through a sock of barbed wire. "Go fuck yourself," he finally snapped off, tapping into an reservoir of defiance. "You bunch of goddamn parasitic cocksuckers. Go fuck yourselves. Guess what? We got a bunker over there. Poured it myself. Concrete walls a foot thick and looking down right where you come ashore on the other side. They're waiting for you right there now, ready to blow your fucking nuts off with firebombs and booby traps."

The Leather didn't react. The Bronze made no move to punish the prisoner for his outburst.

The Vulture remained impassive.

Carson's good eye flicked from one captor to another.

"That won't work," the Vulture said flatly.

"You go on across and see what won't work. The first unlucky piece of shit you send will get a bullet right between the eyes."

"No," the Vulture explained softly. "You misunderstood. We're not going to kill you. You cannot... provoke us into killing you. You cannot provoke me. We're going to keep you alive. *I'm* going to keep you alive. For a very long time. We will break you. Like we've broken others. Then you'll belong to the Leather. And the Dog Tongue."

Carson's bruised features twisted in confused horror.

"Now then," the Vulture continued. "Tell us everything about this crossing, and what's on the other side. If you forget anything, if you keep back any details, you will be disciplined. In such a way that you will never willingly deceive the Leather again. We will crush your remaining toes. Then your feet. Your ankles."

The masked leader tilted in a show of careful thought. "Your knees. And… your hips. You don't need any of that to be useful to the Leather."

A sweating, stinking Carson paled a few shades more and visibly swallowed. His head went slack upon his shoulders.

"After that, it becomes costly," the Vulture went on. "And we may put aside the hammer for other, more penetrating, tools."

At that, the Bronze flashed a scalpel. He brought the surgical tool in close to the prisoner's nose and held it there.

"Now, then," the Vulture said. "What waits for us on the other side?"

Carson talked.

When he finished, the Vulture turned to one of his lessers.

"Bring the hounds."

Minutes later, a Leather emerged from the forest handling leashes connected to the collars of three mindless. The zombies' hands were duct-taped into fossilized balls the size of grapefruits, and leather masks covered their faces, except for a hole for their noses.

The handler pulled back upon the leashes, forcing the three man-hounds to heel, which they did with excited jerks and grunts. More figures emerged from the forest.

The Vulture waved the handler forward.

The man-hounds were whipped into motion. They splashed into the water, hot on the scent of the fleeing islanders.

Dozens of the Leather followed.

21

Gus and the others marched.

They moved with exhausted urgency, stumbling, reaching out for balance, dripping sweat, eager to reach the waiting vehicles. The ground was rough. Uneven. Gus would call it a hard hike, but, in reality, it was a ball-breaker. His chest and hips ached. His calves burned as if his veins were pumping lit gasoline. He didn't think there was a dry piece of cloth on him, and if he didn't get a drink of water soon, the dehydration would drop him like a bullet to the head. Three klicks didn't sound like much, until you actually marched it, and he knew if he lived to see tomorrow, it would be with one mighty sore ass.

Garrett and Sarah Burton had the foresight to hack out a cross-country path through a rolling wilderness using axes. Just in case. They also marked the path with those same beach rocks painted white. When they depleted their supply of those, they lashed a white bar of paint across a tree.

"Sweet Jesus," Gus muttered yet again as he topped what was supposed to be the third hill, and yet, he could see nothing ahead except more goddamn forest. Dark clouds drifted overhead, and beneath that was an unbroken shag rug of backwoods as far as the eye could see. The afternoon was growing old, with only an hour or so left of daylight.

"Believe it or not," Eva said, stopping beside him. "There's a road down there." She pointed. "Goes left to right and around that hill over there. Beyond that is a highway."

"Thank Christ," Gus said. "I could drop dead right here."

Eva appeared genuinely amused by that. She didn't look anywhere near as tired as Gus. None of the islanders did. He glanced around, hoping they'd reach the vehicles before dark, and settled upon Collie. She was forging down the slope, moving gracefully enough, but every now and again she would stop and arch her back.

Taking a breath, he lumbered his way through the crowd to meet her.

When he reached the operator, he greeted her with, "You okay?"

Collie turned her sunglasses upon him. "Yeah, why?"

"You looked like you got a stick in your spokes or something."

"Ha! You wish. Just a little stiff is all. I'll be good in the morning. I haven't had to haul ass like this in a long time."

"I never had to haul ass like this."

"So you're having a good time?"

Gus answered that with a good-natured scowl. They stopped talking then and settled into the grind of placing one foot in front of the other.

At the bottom of the hill, branches had been cut to create a wide corridor. They followed that across a shallow brook, where they stopped and splashed themselves with water. Gus dropped to his knees and, seeing Sarah Burton drink from cupped hands, sucked down his share.

A yell got his attention.

It was distant, ghostly even, and didn't repeat. Water dripped from his beard as he strained to listen. Collie and Cory had also heard. The forest beyond the hills remained silent, but there was a growing sense of a secret just revealed.

"We better hurry," Rich Trinidad said with a glare. "They're coming."

Gus sensed it as well. Whoever they were, they were running while the islanders were walking.

That lit a fire under their collective asses.

Sunlight flared briefly overhead as the small group double-timed it over uneven ground. Faces glanced back, scanning for pursuers and seeing none. Gus knew they were back there. The mindless had found their way across the lake depths. Perhaps they'd sunk to the bottom and just kept on walking, until they emerged wet and dripping on the other side. It wouldn't be too hard for the creatures to find them, as the stubborn stink of old man donkey piss still hung off their clothing.

Gus knew he was on the verge of dropping any second. He thought he'd been tired before but that was a lie. That was only the borderline of a very real red zone, and his inner needle was edging closer to scarlet. When he reached the end of the meter, his internal engine would explode—just burst asunder from the pressure—and crimple into an ugly rose with dripping petals. When that happened, he'd simply collapse, face-down and ass-up, and snort dirt until whatever was chasing them caught up and—

The woods opened into a narrow clearing shaded by tall maples, where two long-bed pickups waited. One red, one black, the paint shiny and surprisingly clean. The tailgates were already lowered, and red gas cans had been stashed and secured by rope. The trucks were parked on the shoulder of a single-lane dirt road.

The sight of the vehicles gave Gus a badly needed shot of energy. Cries of relief erupted from the rest of the group as well. The islanders flung open doors and lurched inside, squeezing themselves into the plush interiors. The remainder climbed into the rear. Gus located Collie, who lay on her belly in a box bed, her rifle aimed at the treeline. Gus hopped aboard, placed his back up against the left side and flopped his legs over hers. He drew his gun and held it to his chest.

"See anything?" he gasped.

"Not yet."

The trucks started up, and Gus knew, just *knew*, the whole fucking forest was about to be crawling. The undead would leap out as the trucks pulled away, their fingers hooked and seeking to latch onto the sides. Some would be screaming, some wouldn't have the capacity to scream, but all would be ravenous. His mind's eye already glimpsed those warped faces with glazed but starving eyes.

Except nothing of the sort happened.

The black truck tore off with an eight-cylinder growl and a spray of dirt, and then bounced over the knobby landscape. Two long seconds later, the red truck followed.

The road unspooled behind them in a great earth-colored ribbon, rolling left and right then back again, sometimes straightening out before disappearing behind a curtain of branches. The truck jostled Gus, but he held onto his Glock, eyes narrowed, waiting, his finger resting against the guard. Collie was splayed out underneath him, poised and ready. He watched the road as it rolled away, the gloom pierced by occasional shots of daylight.

There was a peal of tire on asphalt, a screeching of rubber, and then the box bed jumped a foot. Gus landed hard, scraping his spine and shoulders against the box wall. The pain took a long time to ebb away. Evening sky loomed overhead, and it took him that long to realize they were on the open road, racing toward wherever.

The important thing was that they had escaped the mindless unscathed.

They were free and clear.

As if thinking the same thing, Collie rolled onto her side and placed her rifle on the flat bed. She relaxed next to the weapon and glanced over her shoulder. A relieved smirk hung off one corner of her mouth.

Gus smiled back.

The little convoy streaked along a two-lane road, the countryside buzzing by in a scream of wind. All the while, Gus watched the highway behind them, waiting to see some sign of pursuit. There was none. And as the distance widened between them and their attackers, Gus's vibe of being hunted slipped away, slowly replaced by a bone-deep weariness. Their escape had been the most physically taxing thing he'd done in… well… forever.

Day faded to evening. The clouds parted, revealing broad strokes of pink.

The metal floor rattled against his arm, which served as his pillow. Gus rocked into a doze, the truck bed alive underneath him. Dreamy sequences scrolled though his sleep-loopy mind, of screaming runners thundering across the bridge's roof. Collie firing her rifle in slow-motion. Things exploding in grainy red detail.

When the machine stopped, Gus's eyes snapped open.

"We're here," Collie whispered, softly singing the words.

He pawed at his face. "Where's that? Everything's dark."

And it was. There was no moon, and the stars were only just beginning to flicker to life. There were shapes, however, lines in the surrounding void that took on greater meaning. Houses. Or buildings. Large ones across a single street. Then a door opened somewhere behind him, cracking him into alertness.

Sarah Burton appeared alongside the truck, her face barely visible in the dark.

"We'll stop here for the night," she told them.

"Where's here?" Collie asked.

"Place called Short Bow. In between Driftwood and Smooth Rock Falls."

"And we stopped because…?"

"It's night, girl," Sarah snapped, as if the answer was obvious. "And this is was our escape plan. To loop around and go north if we were ever driven off the island."

"I like plans," Collie said calmly. "What's the rest of yours?"

"We bunk down here for the night and decide on things in the morning."

"Gotta backup place to go?" Gus asked.

Sarah faced him. "No. Matter of fact we don't. But we got this place. And some things stashed away in case we had to make use of them."

"Hope you got a bed, then," Gus said.

"Your lucky day, sailor," Sarah said and walked away, her feet clicking on pavement.

"My lucky day," Gus repeated. "You hear that?"

"Oh yeah," Collie said.

"You agree with her?"

"To a point. I do know where we are, however."

That was interesting. "Yeah?"

"Yeah. We're close to where we want to be."

"How close?"

"Thirty klicks close. As the crow flies."

"I've seen some fucked-up crows."

"In a straight line, then. Okay?"

That interested him, until he realized people were moving around the pickup. The headlights were off, but someone switched on a flashlight, revealing parking lanes laid out across a vast sheet of concrete. A mighty wall of glass appeared, set upon a brick foundation and stretched out on either side of what looked like a warehouse. An awesome display of—of all things— bedroom furniture was tastefully arranged behind the intact glass. Beds and mattresses, night tables, lamps, and matching chests of drawers were all on sale, with prices printed upon white cardboard cut-outs of exploding balloons.

Large lettering was fixed above the main entrance.

Lazy Lou's Mattress Heaven. Your One Stop For All Things Bedroom.

"Oh my," Gus said to himself, taking in the impressive storefront. "Lazy Lou. I like you already."

"Damn impressive," Collie said. "About the size of a small stadium."

Gus saw that. "Lou's been busy."

"I remember this place, actually. Drove by it a few times."

"Never went in?"

"No need to," Collie replied.

Sarah inserted a key into the main entrance door and opened it, ushering the islanders inside.

"Go on in," Sarah told them. "We'll lock up once we're all in. We'll park the trucks out back, in the loading zone. There's a rear door there."

Gus nodded, and with Collie at his side, they walked into Lazy Lou's Mattress Heaven. With a name like 'Lazy Lou', Gus really wasn't expected much.

He was wrong.

He was so *spectacularly* wrong.

Someone flicked on a second flashlight, its beam weaving through the various displays of furniture before finally settling down. That, combined with the first flashlight, revealed a showroom the size of an aircraft hangar, containing a veritable dreamscape of bedroom décor. White lanes guided shoppers through a display wonderland of bed sets, complete with tasteful comforters and luxurious satins. Night tables stood as sentries, and upon every one was a matching lamp and price tag. Mantels were covered with assorted books. Snow-white canopies were tied back with braided rope. Someone had even placed tasteful sets of nefarious tea candles throughout, highlighting the possibilities of cozy home décor even more. Not only was there a reserved showroom displaying all manner of potential room configurations, there were whole sections of individual items as well. Mattresses of all sizes. Quilts and comforters for all seasons. Pillow cases and sheets made of Egyptian cotton and possessing thread counts in the tantalizing *thousands*. Bedside furniture ranged from Kids to Adults, Art Déco to Rustic, Retro to Contemporary, and all priced to sell, individually or in complete sets.

Taking in that vast cavern of nocturnal delights, the first thought to enter Gus's mind was that Lazy Lou had a serious fucking hard-on for bedroom furnishings. A *serious* fucking hard-on.

"Goddammit Lou," Gus said under his breath.

"Nothing lazy about him," Collie added.

"No ma'am. This is unchecked insanity. The hell is this place, anyway? And it's out in the middle of nowhere."

"Lazy Lou's pretty big west of Ontario," Bruno said nearby.

"Bought my bedroom set from him," someone said.

"I think he's in BC," added another voice.

"Chain of twenty or thirty. With one in Hawaii, I think," said yet another.

"All right," Gus groaned. "He's the king of bedrooms. I'm not gonna argue the point. Obviously, he had something on the go."

"Lie awhile," a voice sang softly. "Lie awhile, and if you're gonna lie, lie in style."

Gus frowned. He didn't know Lazy Lou from an asshole in the ground, but he sure as hell knew he could come up with a more imaginative jingle than that.

"Sleep anywhere," Sarah Burton said to the group. "Maybe back from the windows. There's plenty of partitions to give you privacy if you want it, but don't go too far. Lots of pillows and blankets, comforters. Grab anything you want. Sleep and we'll have a group huddle in the morning. Talk about where to go from here."

"You posting guards?" Collie asked.

Sarah traded looks with Rich Trinidad.

"I'll watch the front," the gunslinger said. "Until I get tired. Then I'll swap out with whoever's willing."

"I'm willing," Collie said.

"Yeah, me too," Gus threw in, although he was eyeing one contemporary bed set, complete with what looked like a propane fireplace. The whole thing radiated an alpine ambience that made him think of winters and season-long hibernations.

"Good," Sarah said. "That's good. Get some sleep then. I'll get someone to watch the rear doors."

Eva had a chat with Bruno, and the man walked away with her and Monica. Cory had already found a corner of his own and was taking his shoes off. Gus continued sizing up his chosen bed, a silky, midnight black affair that would definitely have been out of his paygrade once upon a time. Yet, there he was, about to pass out on one. The notion put a smile on his hairy face. Every now and again, the apocalypse would do you a favor. Collie placed a hand upon his shoulder then, the contact electric, and led him over to that Swiss dream.

"You read my mind," he whispered.

"More like I saw you drool."

"It's a dream," Gus said, stopping at the base, and focusing solely upon the bed. "An alpine dream. I mean, I ain't ever getting over to the Alps, but if I did... I'd want my hotel room to have furniture like this."

"See the price?" She pointed.

He did a double take. "Jesus Christ. How the hell do they justify that? Swiss elves make that thing or something?"

Collie glanced around, eyeing the rest of the group. Some wandered around back corners, but most stayed well within sight. She went to one side of the bed—a sizeable queen—and perched herself on the edge.

"Oh my," she said, running a hand over the comforter.

"Nice?"

"Try it."

Gus sat down. "Oh my sweet Jesus. I can feel a smile across my ass. Right across my ass. Both cheeks."

"Keep your voice down, people are going to sleep."

Gus supposed so. If they were camping out on such comfortable islands like the one he was planted on, they'd be asleep in no time.

He swung his legs onto the bed, boots still on, and stretched out.

"Goddamn. This is coming with me. Wherever we go. I'm taking it."

"Beats sleeping on the ground."

"And shitty-assed motels."

Collie lay on her back and stared at the ceiling. Around them, the group was settling in with sighs and similar whispers of disbelief. Someone farted. A goose shot prompting a giggle that Gus knew belonged to little Monica. He realized then that he hadn't checked on her or Bruno, to see if she could say anything more than 'mindless'. And how it was she came to *call* the undead that name.

"Well," he whispered. "Thus ends a fucked-up day."

"Ended pretty damn well if you ask me," Collie whispered back.

"Not for some of those campers."

"Well, you're right there."

"You got time to talk?"

Silence then. "Sure. For a bit. Until I start snoring, anyway. What's on your mind?"

Gus turned onto his side to face her, adjusting his junk as he did so. "Just wanted to continue that conversation we started. Back in the woods there."

"Go ahead."

"Who are they, Collie?"

"The pricks with the masks? Who knows? Never saw them before. Another bunch of road crazies. Maybe looking for others. Like us."

"Not like us if they're using deadheads."

"Suppose not. I just hope they're not religious. Those bunnies give me the creeps."

"What do they want?"

Collie paused. "I don't know, Gus. Hard to say. Some people just want to survive and pick up the pieces. I know we're looking for people to carry on. To salvage what's left of the knowledge pool. The skill pool. Not to mention the gene pool. But others? Others will see an opportunity."

"To use dead things like that? To sic 'em on people like dogs?"

She frowned. "More like shock troops. Think of it. Why waste your living soldiers when you have a corps of fearless, ass-munching gluebags at your disposal? The sight of that charging you is a scary thing. People would think it was the outbreak all over. Whoever was staring that down might very well decide to drop everything and run. For their homes or their rides. If it's their homes, maybe those people get trapped in there and, well, it's up to those leather dicks to get them out. Sorta like hounds chasing the fox into a hole."

"And if those people get away?" Gus asked.

"Good question. Maybe they keep on hunting."

"Jesus."

"Yeah," Collie agreed. "Well, we got guards posted."

"But where are they getting the gimps?"

"I don't know," she admitted sadly. "Maybe… maybe they're people who refused to surrender? Or what happens to subordinates who fuck up? We've seen the dead rot away into nothing but heads, so these guys must have saved a specimen. You might very well be right about keeping a reanimated head or two around. They could sling that over a wall and wait out the craziness inside. A weaponized biohazard all over again. I tell you, the depths of insanity people can sink to? Fucking amazes me."

"Christ almighty," Gus whispered.

"We don't have enough information, yet," Collie said. "But I think we're close on that. Our purpose is pretty clear-cut these days. You survive or you don't. You rule or you follow. Any way you cut it, there's always some sick puppy around to twist things to suit their own agenda."

"But using zombies, Collie?"

"I know. It's fucked up."

A silence followed.

"One last thing," Gus eventually said.

"Sure."

"What was it you were going to say?" he asked. "Back on the trail?"

Collie faced him, her dark eyes twinkling despite the dark. "You really want to know?"

"Yeah."

"You're not going to like it."

"Tell me."

"It's just a theory, but you're really not going to like it. If I'm right, that is."

"Collie…"

"I'm trying to say it's pretty fucked up."

"*Collie.*"

"Okay," she relented. "Fair warning and all that bunk. And, remember, I have nothing to back this up, except for what I saw. We know the undead retain some of their senses, smell being perhaps the strongest. We were doused with some pretty strong shit, just before the meatbags came charging after us. I think that their handlers…"

"The leather douchebags."

"Yes," Collie smiled. "The leather douchebags. I think they figured out a way to direct the undead. The MBs came right for us, not the masked douchebags. Drawn to a scent that they can't resist."

Gus couldn't believe what he was hearing. "Holy shit."

Collie smiled again. "See. Told you."

"That *is* fucked up."

"Explains a couple of things. How the undead came running after us when there's perfectly good meat right behind them."

"Why *urine?*" Gus wanted to know. "I mean, why not blood?"

"Don't know. Maybe blood goes bad. Maybe its not about quality but *quantity.* Everybody needs to take a leak sooner or later, so there you go. Blood is a little more troublesome to collect, harder to store, but urine? Everybody's gotta take a whiz sooner or later. The only problem you got there is stockpiling the stuff. And no worries about it going bad, not if you only need it to stink, right? Probably stinks even more after a few days."

"Easier to smell," Gus added.

"Exactly."

Gus turned over and peered up toward the warehouse ceiling. He was speechless.

"Feel like sleeping now?" Collie asked.

"Not right now, but give me a few seconds."

"No problem."

Gus turned to her, and she watched him, their faces less than a foot apart. "What have we gotten ourselves into here, Collie?"

She took her time in answering. "Not sure. But we're here. We're in it. And we'll get clear of it."

Gus didn't say anything to that.

"Even if we have to break some balls to do so," Collie finished.

22

Some time after midnight, Collie returned to bed after her shift of guard duty. Gus lay underneath the comforter, the thick edges pulled up to his ears. She watched him for a bit, as his snores softly buzz-sawed the vast cavern of the showroom. After several seconds, she placed her rifle upon the floor and sat down on the side of the bed. The mattress didn't groan, but Gus's head flinched.

"That you?" he whispered, half-asleep.

"Yeah."

He dropped back onto the pillow.

Collie peeled the comforter back and slipped into the bed beside him. It was cold on her side, making the heat from his body all the more attractive.

"Busy night?" he asked.

"Nah," she said, turning towards his back. "That guy Davis is on watch."

"Black-eye Davis?"

"Yeah. That's a good name for him."

Gus shifted, burrowing deeper into the established warmth. The smell of sweat enveloped him, but she knew she smelled just as bad, so it didn't bother her. The dry heat radiating from him, however, was another matter entirely. Unable to resist, Collie moved closer and slid an arm over his ribs, spooning him, pressing herself up against his frame as if she were hugging a furnace.

That woke Gus up just a little more, and he turned his head in a question.

"Just getting comfortable," she murmured. "You're so nice and warm."

"Wish you didn't do that."

"Do what?"

"That."

"You mean spooning? Didn't think you would mind."

"I don't, but you're waking up my dick."

"Gotta feeling it doesn't take much to wake him up," Collie whispered. She pressed her chest into his back, hooked a leg over his, and held on even tighter. "He better settle down if he knows what's good for him."

They lay in bed that way, front-to-back, tighter than a wet knot.

"Collie?"

"Mm?"

"I, ah… have a problem."

"Still got a chubby?"

"Actually, I do. Half a chub, anyway. But, something else."

"Yeah, what?"

He released a long sigh. "Just so you know… I find myself… thinking about you a lot."

That quieted her, and she frowned ever so slightly in the dark.

"A lot?"

"Yeah."

She had to be careful about the next bit, not quite sure how he was going to react. "Well, that's good. I think about you, too. A lot."

"You do?"

"Yeah."

Nothing then, for a few seconds, then Gus tried to turn over, but Collie wouldn't let him.

"Not right now," she said, pressing her head against the nape of his neck. "Let's just sleep on this, okay? Why do you keep bringing this shit up when I'm ready to drop and cut some zees?"

"Sorry."

"That's all right," she said, relaxing. "I'll punish you in the morning."

"That sounds nice."

"Thought you'd like that."

So they slept.

*

"Black-eye" Davis sat in an office chair facing the store's front windows. He was positioned some twenty meters back, behind a full bedroom display, with his arms resting on a hutch, his chin parked in the folds of his arms, and the rest of him out of sight. He had a clear view of Lazy Lou's front doors and the forbidding parking lot outside—not that there was much to see beyond the glass. It had been only thirty minutes or so since he replaced Collie, but he was still exhausted from the past few days and regretted his decision to volunteer for the job. Still, he needed to do his part. Understood that they all had to do their part. Rich had completed his shift, the local sheriff that he was, but even he needed to rest at some point. Collie as well.

On that note, Davis rubbed his head, feeling the thickening grease coating his hair, before prodding his swollen eye with a knuckle. Christ almighty they'd worked him over. His body was covered in a collage of bruises. His captors had only given him one shot to the face, but they made it count. He could barely see out of the thing, and it watered for some unknown reason. Just up and started weeping whenever the mood took it, as if stuck in a mire of self-pity. Davis's other eye was fine, however, working a little double-time to pick up the slack. Mentioning his eye might've gotten him out of guard duty, but he wouldn't feel right about that. He just needed some time to relax, that was all. Like everyone, he supposed.

He sniffed, catching the faint pissy smell lingering off his ass, and marveling at its power. A bath was in his future. Next body of water he spied he was going in, even if he had to jump from a moving truck to do so. He focused on the windows again, looking past the lines and pointed corners of the bedroom sets, past the clear panes of glass, and the empty void beyond that. Davis had to admit, if it wasn't for the occasional snores and grunts of the group spread out in the warehouse, he'd be feeling very much creeped out. For security, Trinidad had given him one of his many guns, the make unknown to him. It was a gun and that was enough for Davis, and it rested not five inches away from his right hand.

His eye started to ache. It did that every now and again. A dull, knife-edge ache that pulsed at the very back, all the way into his brain. As if someone had stuck a butter knife in there, left it, and flicked the goddamn thing whenever they felt like it. Just twanged it, like it was a balloon hanging off a door handle. Davis hoped that as the swelling went down, the discomfort would go away, but he wasn't sure. He'd feel better if and when he could see the doctor Collie had mentioned. That would put his mind at ease, and he hoped things would work out so that he *would* have access to some honest-to-God medical attention. A real-life doctor. The idea seemed incredible in this day and age. Getting quality care from a trained professional and not having to look shit up in a book or guessing what wild herb did what would be a tremendous relief. Davis shook his head and smiled, remembering a time when he and his friend Barry argued over whether some mushrooms they'd discovered on the summer island were edible. They decided to test them for safety's sake, and ended up being quite stoned for the better part of the day.

Funky times.

Davis's mirth faded when he realized Barry hadn't shown up after the onslaught earlier in the day. He'd been left behind on the island, probably dead… or worse.

The night sky would brighten in the next couple of hours, and the world beyond the glass would slink back into existence. Davis couldn't believe how damn dark things got on a cloudy night, when there were no streetlamps or fires or *anything*. It was all so surreal, and more than just a touch eerie, which made him grateful he wasn't on any of those medicinal mushrooms they'd found on the island. He wouldn't mind a bottle of gin, however. Gin could armor a person to the bone.

He gazed at the glass and surrounding framework of the storefront. Something caught his attention, just to the left of the locked doors. Collie said to wake them if he saw anything. Rich had said the same but he wasn't a soldier, just a gun nut trying to be the law. Davis wasn't sure, however, if he was seeing something or just uneasy. He peered at that section of the glass, wondering what exactly had hooked his good eye.

Nothing was there, however.

"Well, dammit," Davis whispered, listening to those peaceful snores in the background. He wavered, thinking on the next course of action, before picking up the gun. It was heavy in his hand, but he held it at arm's length, by his thigh.

"Dammit, dammit," he muttered. There was one main walkway splitting the front of the showroom in two, which led directly to the main doors. Davis crouched low, bent over at the waist, and quietly threaded his way through the assorted bedroom sets, using the furniture to conceal his approach.

He stopped halfway and squinted at the troubling spot in the glass. His danger sense was tingling, but damn if he wasn't sure what the hell he was looking at. With a quick check on what lay before him, Davis edged closer, stopping just behind a high chest of drawers.

Was something moving *out there?* He couldn't be sure, as it was as fine as a black thread floating atop an oil patch. An inky blot that teased him to come closer. Davis tapped the sidearm against his thigh, its weight comforting.

A whistle filled the still night air, and the frightening surge of an engine that just had its gas pedal stomped to the floor. Except Davis didn't realize it was an engine until the headlights flared to life, the spellbinding glare freezing him in place.

Just as the front of the store exploded inwards with a clap of brick and glass and a gust of debris.

Davis leaped away and bounced off a mattress, where he tumbled onto the carpeted floor. His gun went off when he landed, sending a bullet through his right temple like a black thunderbolt that ended all thought.

*

That burst of shattering glass yanked Gus awake, and the crackle of fabricated wood fiber, metal, and ceramics ripping apart almost made him shit the bed. Cold air flooded the showroom, carrying a gritty puff of dust. People screamed. Collie was already out of the bed and arming herself, while Gus propped himself up at arm's length, paralyzed by the smoking, hateful glare of headlights peeking out from behind a roadblock of smashed bedroom furniture.

"Move!" Collie yelled at him, hoisting her weapon to her shoulder.

Gus did, but he saw past the wreckage of the truck, saw the leather-clad figures storming through the breech, invading Lazy Lou's showroom.

"Gus!" Collie shouted.

That unlocked him, and he kicked himself free of the comforter. Thankfully, he still had his boots on, and he met Collie behind the bed's hutch, where she was already retreating deeper into the thicker patches of bedroom furnishings.

"This way," Sarah Burton shouted, running through the showroom. Gus followed, still trying to comprehend what was happening. The screams behind him were fading now, but he could still hear a clatter of bodies banging into unseen end tables and flipping over low dressers. An invisible corner of an easy chair clipped Gus's hip with all the force of a hammer. The momentum spun him sideways, where he landed on a bed. He rolled off and landed hard on his feet. He hobbled into a run, fixing on the islanders fleeing into the dark, scampering towards the rear of the building. One of the campers went down amongst the bed sets, as if a rug had been pulled out from underneath her. Monica squealed, and he thought he glimpsed both Bruno and Cory hustling her through the showroom maze. Collie fired off a short burst, lighting up the dark and pulling Gus's attention toward her. She was threading her own retreat, skipping around low obstacles while hindering their pursuers.

In the jagged broken hole that was the main entrance, shapes invaded the interior and ducked out of sight, blending in almost perfectly with the dark surroundings.

Oh shit, Gus thought and, at that exact moment, clacked both knees on a block of solid wood. The impact was mind-freezing. Gus landed in a clump, his battered knees unsteady and hurting, both joints signaling that they'd been rudely hyperextended. He rolled and flexed, dealing with that wobbly wheel sensation while landing an arm across the very thing that had taken his legs out from under him.

"Goddamn *night table*!" he swore, wanting to shoot the miserable block of wood.

"*Move!*" Collie shouted from behind.

Gus limped as fast as he could.

Collie appeared beside him, keeping pace. "You okay?"

"Almost broke my knees off."

"Keep moving. This way."

She grabbed his left shoulder and pulled him along, dodging pieces of furniture and whole mattresses as they materialized out of the dark. Harsh puffs of air sped by them, some ending with solid whacks.

Crossbows.

They reached a wall where Rich Trinidad waited with a gun in each hand. "Go that way. Follow the corridor. I'm right behind you."

Collie took the lead and Gus shambled after her. His legs still ached but were firmer, and the hall wasn't cluttered like the showroom floor.

Rich Trinidad started firing behind them, the gunshots like fat firecrackers going off in Gus's ears.

Ahead, lights flared brightly, illuminating a huge storage area, just beyond an open doorway at the end of the hall. *Headlights*, Gus realized, flashing against a loading bay door.

Collie guided him into a sizeable loading area, where plastic-covered furniture shone wetly in the peripheral glare of the headlights. Huge rectangles of cardboard the size of garbage bins packaged and protected surplus furniture. The various blocks were stacked in towers against the walls on either side, resembling ancient ruins. Rising above it all were massive shelving units filled to capacity, creating a dusty pattern of straight beams and uneven blocks all the way to the ceiling.

Two pickups waited on the main floor. The islanders piled inside the idling machines, their heads and shoulders bouncing around the interior. Gus caught a lungful of exhaust, and that got his mind off his knees. The islanders had parked the vehicles inside Lou's warehouse, but the sight of that paneled wall of the loading zone filled him with confusion. They might've had the time to manually crank the door open enough to get the trucks inside, but he doubted the crazies would wait for them to do it again.

Collie pushed Gus towards the nearest truck bed, and he rolled inside the box. She hauled herself in after him, flipping onto her chest and aiming for the doorway they'd just come through. Rich Trinidad was there, firing at unseen targets. Gus lifted his head, looked around, and was instantly mesmerized by the red warning light swirling atop a forklift. The machine rumbled towards the bay door, the forks already lowered. They slid into the lower end with a screech of steel. Hydraulics chuffed and wheezed and forced themselves upward with a clanking protest.

Collie pulled Gus back inside and flattened him to the floor. "Keep your head down."

Gus stared at her.

"If the fuckers chasing us know what they're doing, they'll have someone covering the rear."

His mouth dropped open at that thought. A second later, the lead truck shot out of the bay. There was a jarring slap of metal and a pop and jingle of strained bolts coming free. The last panel on the loading bay door flapped heavily over the pickup's roof with a squeal of hinges. The truck banked hard to the right, tires squealing, and Collie rolled across the box bed floor and crashed into Gus. The truck then slammed into a wall, shaking the pair to their bones, before powering through in a screech-song of tires and burning rubber.

The escaping truck lurched forward with all the force of an unloading ballista.

Dozens of impacts lit up both sides of the box bed, but the vehicle picked up speed. As they sped away, Gus looked back at Lazy Lou's warehouse. Low clouds hid the night sky, but about four pickups were parked across the rear of the loading area, barring the way. One pair, once parked nose-to-ass, now had a sizeable gap between them where the islanders' truck had bashed through, leaving the two vehicles there resembling leftovers in a demolition derby.

A second set of headlights—the other truck filled with islanders—gunned for that gap.

Collie pushed away from Gus. On her belly, she took aim and fired. Controlled bursts punched into the machines forming the roadblock, and they shivered with every bullet. Collie shifted, taking care not to hit the islanders' truck as it plunged through the wrecked gap and raced into the night.

"Thank you, Jesus," Gus muttered, watching as the second vehicle caught up with them.

They raced north, and at present speed, he figured they should have no problem escaping their pursuers.

A second later, he heard a dismal fluttering, and his balls froze as if dipped in liquid nitrogen.

"Don't fucking tell me," Collie said, cocking her head.

Gus propped himself up, the cold night air whipping past his face. Their ride gradually took on a disturbing shimmy. He held on, disbelieving their luck.

The driver braked and pulled off onto the shoulder.

"Goddammit," Gus said, leaning over the side.

Flat tire. Both of them on his side. Then he saw the crossbow bolts.

"No way," he muttered.

The islanders were already getting out of the stopped rig. Cory jumped out from the passenger side and stepped back, inspecting the damage. He got closer and hunkered down, his face screwing up in distaste.

"What is it?" Gus asked.

"Nails," Cory reported. "Goddamn nails. Looks like we rolled over one of them spike strips. The kind the cops would use to stop speeders."

"Improvised spike strip," Collie declared. "Crude, but it worked. Fucked up all four tires. Everybody *out!*"

She slapped Gus across an ass cheek to get him moving. The other pickup waited alongside, filled with familiar faces.

"What about the truck?" Gus asked.

"Can't wait," Collie said. "Pile into the back and hold on to something."

She tossed her rifle into the box and went for the driver's side. "Out," she ordered upon opening the door. "I'm driving from here on end. Get out or get in the back, but do it fast."

"Wait," Gus said, suddenly holding his nose.

She smelled it. As did they all.

The first truck had rammed its way through the roadblock but ruined its tires in doing so. The second truck, while untouched by the nail strips, suffered a different fate.

A disgusted Collie looked over the box wall and sighed. She used her rifle to reach inside and hook the plastic bladder that had ruptured upon impact. She held up the dripping husk for all to see.

"Not the piss bags again," Gus groaned.

"Piss bags or not," she said, flicking the offensive matter away, "this is our only ride out of here."

Far behind them, but not far enough, headlights appeared. Several sets.

That got the group's feet shuffling. No one wanted to get into the box.

"If you can fit in, hang on," Collie said, leaving them for the driver's seat. Gus hopped for the passenger side, beating out Cory before he could protest.

"Where are we going?" Sarah Burton asked from the back seat, mushed against the window. Little Monica was crammed in there as well, holding tight to a worried Bruno. Gus took a second look at the man, disturbed by how dark and sunken his eyes were.

"What?" Bruno asked.

"Nothing," Gus replied, deciding to keep his thoughts to himself.

Collie hit the gas, throwing Gus back into the front seat. "Buckle up, honeydew," she said, squaring her shoulders and holding the steering wheel at arm's length. "We're going for lightspeed if I can get it."

"Where the hell are we going?" Sarah Burton demanded, grasping the head rest.

Collie kept her eyes on the road. "North. We're very close to where we want to be."

"Where's that?"

"Secret government bunker."

That silenced the islander.

Collie glanced at the fuel gauge. "We got a full tank here. That should get us to Whitecap. Maybe. Did we lose anyone back there?"

The interior grew silent.

*

With a dozen Leather at his back, the Vulture stopped upon the threshold of the loading bay and stared out into the predawn night. The mask revealed nothing of the frustration coming to a boil, but the guards surrounding the leader dared not whisper a word. The Vulture took a moment to study the wrecked trucks and the gap punched between them. He saw the improvised spike strip—or what was left of it. The trap had been laid out by the Leather watching the rear door. There was a chance one or both trucks had their tires punctured. If so, the Vulture would find them.

And punish them for their continued impudence.

Engines chuffed and growled to life around the warehouse, moving to the rear where the Leather boarded their rides.

A commotion at his back turned the Vulture around. There, being shoved into the loading bay, were the survivors they'd captured. Bruised and bloodied, but intact. Three were forced to the concrete floor. Machetes tapped necks, keeping the prisoners in place.

One of the lessers approached the Vulture. He paid his respects and the leader bade the man to talk.

"One is an office administrator. One is a bank teller. The other is an assistant manager for a hotel."

None of that impressed the Vulture. "Where's the girl?"

The lesser shook his head.

The Vulture turned his head back to the night sky.

The lesser waited.

"Convert them," the Vulture commanded.

The lesser slowly bowed, keeping his eyes on the leader the whole time.

We're going after them right away, the Vulture repeated in his mind, fuming at how this small group of nothing flesh managed to once again deny him his prize. They were going somewhere, and the Leather would follow them to the end. When that happened, the Vulture intended to make his displeasure very much known.

And to take the prize for the Dog Tongue.

From the shadows, two of the Leather brought forth a box into the loading bay.

A short time later, the sound of the motorized armada flared to life, drowning out the prisoners' screams of terror.

23

The pickup sped northward under dawn's spreading light.

The mood inside had gone from frightened awareness to one of misery. Gus knew the feeling. The loss of a few more islanders had depressed the survivors. Their absence affected Gus as well. He didn't know one of the missing, but he knew Davis, and Clifford—the other banged-up guy they'd freed from the trailer not so long ago. And he certainly knew Eva, quiet and composed and now feared captured. Not knowing what had happened to them bothered Gus, almost enough to tempt him to go back and attempt a rescue. Collie squashed that idea, reasoning there was no way a handful of them could possibly take on the small army of masked crazies, crazies who commanded an army of undead. Not when Whitecap beckoned. As long as they stayed ahead of their pursuers, Collie was certain that she could lose them in the maze of roads surrounding the mountain.

So they drove, passing through the little town of Cochrane on Highway 574. At one point, Collie pulled over and got Gus to take a turn at the wheel. So he did, grateful for something to occupy his mind. He nervously checked his rear-view mirror every five seconds, fully expecting to see a blazing display of headlights. Nothing of the sort happened, however.

A hot wire of light crisped the horizon ahead. The forest on either side of the road grew thicker, more distinct. Collie sat in the passenger seat, her sunglasses lowered, her expression neutral. The clouds broke apart, and the sun that peeked over the hills was a thing of beauty.

"Right there," Collie said, harsh daylight coloring her face. She pointed. "Slow down."

Gus did, spotting the turnoff onto a dirt road up ahead. He braked and stopped a few feet away, checking his mirrors as he did so. A sign that read

"Private Property" had fallen over in the middle of the dirt road. Dried mud and dust covered the metallic sign, as well as the prints of tire treads. Along the shoulders of the road, however, was something even more ominous. Deep industrial-sized tire prints stamped the earth, creating a stitch-work of great ruts and potholes filled with water. A ruined assortment of saplings and dead brush resembling snapped bones lay in the wake of those prints.

"What came through here?" Sarah Burton asked from the back seat.

"A big ol' truck," Gus replied. "Biggest one you ever saw."

That quieted her for a moment. "A *truck* made those tracks?"

"You'll see," he said. Gus exchanged looks with Collie.

"That rig barely fit the road," Collie noted. "Like a tank driving over a footpath."

The operator got out of the truck without comment. She strode over to the sign as if to verify, and then rounded the front of the truck to the driver's side.

"I'll take over," she said, opening Gus's door. "No one following us."

"But they will," he said.

Collie smiled. "They'll try."

"We there yet?" Bruno asked, careful not to disturb little Monica cuddled in his arm.

"Not yet," Collie said, getting behind the wheel. "Give another two hours or so."

"That far?"

"That far." She checked the fuel gauge. Gus knew what she was seeing.

"We got a quarter of a tank left," she said.

"Yeah," he agreed.

"It's gonna be close."

"How close?"

Collie fixed him with a neutral look before driving off the highway. "Pay attention now," she said and pointed. "You remember the way?"

"Who, me?" he asked. "Hell no. I was stoned for most of the ride here. And I wasn't driving on the way out."

"Well, don't worry," she assured him. "I got this."

Gus hoped so. He glanced out the window and studied the deserted highway behind them. As they advanced, the highway disappeared behind a screen of trees. Gravel and rocks popped under the tires, and potholes made the ride a jumpy one. He settled back, bracing for the deeper drops.

The forest thickened into a spotty blend of orange and yellow held up by columns of wrinkled brown. They drove deep into those backwoods, and more than once the road forked off to destinations unknown. Collie kept the truck moving forward without hesitation. Gus tried to remember each turn, tried to commit a landmark to memory, but soon gave up and left the driving to her. He cracked a window, allowing fresh and surprisingly warm air to flood the interior.

Soon the trees parted, framing a set of mountains in the distance.

"That's it?" Gus asked.

"Not quite."

"We're getting closer, though, right?" Bruno asked.

"No," Collie said as they bounced past a *No Trespassing* sign. "Not even close. This whole network was designed to confuse Joe Blow from getting anywhere near the base. There were hidden guard posts about halfway in, where security started taking a special interest in anyone ignoring the signs. You know about the Men in Black?"

"Yeah," Bruno said.

"Well, we had *agents in camos* stationed all along this road. Enough to scare the bejesus out of the nosier types. If you got this far and didn't have the right plastic with you, you were greeted by some very intimidating individuals who wanted to know why."

A nervous Bruno glanced out his window.

"'Course, that was back in the day," Collie said. "Now, not so much."

They scaled a small hill, the road bordered with smashed trees, the splintered branches left upon the shoulders. The whole road was like that, hinting at the passage of a massive piece of machinery.

"Christ almighty," Gus said. "That thing just fucks up landscapes as it goes along."

"Easy to see why they had it."

"What're you talking about?" Sarah Burton asked.

"You'll see," Gus said, then to Collie. "How's the gas?"

She shook her head. "Remember when I said it was gonna be close?"

"Yeah?"

"Well, I might've been wrong."

That worried Gus. He wasn't looking forward to another hike in the woods, road or no road. His legs hadn't recovered from the day before. Hoping to God above that the truck made it all the way, he sat back and watched the wilderness roll by. One thing for certain, they wouldn't get lost, not when the mighty Komatsu truck from days gone by had left its mark upon the world.

An hour and change later, the pickup began to gasp and sputter.

Gus sat up and glanced over at Collie. She stopped the truck and met his worried stare.

"Don't tell me we walk from here on," Gus asked.

She answered with a sad smile and cracked open her door. "Everyone out," she ordered. "From here on, we walk."

Fuck, Gus silently mouthed.

"What?" Sarah Burton asked from the rear seat, shoving her glasses up on her nose with a single finger. "What does that mean? I mean, how far do we have to walk?"

She got out of the truck with the others and faced Collie on the other side.

"Another hour," the operator reported, retrieving her rifle. "Sorry, I had no say in where the place was built."

Cory stood beside Bruno, and little Monica was between both men, nervously watching the exchange. The others formed up in front of the dead truck. Allie was there, the quiet woman they'd freed not so long ago, as well as Jane Wong and Jeremy Walton. Rich Trinidad was there as well, which, at a quick count, placed the total number of survivors at an even ten.

"It'll go faster if we start walking right now," Collie said. "Gather up whatever you got left."

"There's nothing left," Sarah Burton said.

"Nothing?"

"We unloaded everything back at Lazy Lou's," Sarah answered. "Wasn't much to begin with. Just some dried meats and preserves. Stuff that would last a few months if we had needed them. Thing was, we didn't really expect to *have* to need it."

"Not at this stage," Jane Wong added in a quiet voice.

Collie studied them each in turn. "This way," she said. She started marching, holding her rifle two-handed. "Wish I had a shoulder strap for this bastard," she muttered under her breath.

The group followed her.

Gus lagged a bit, watching the road but not able to see very far back.

"You comin'?" Rich Trinidad asked, walking backwards.

Gus took one last look before picking up the pace.

*

The Vulture sat in the formidable cab of the biofuel-burning Mack truck. His elbow lay upon the windowsill, his fingers tapping out a slow cadence of

180

impatience, one that would irritate anyone listening. The driver, another masked individual, simply lowered his head and awaited orders. Chrome spikes lined his knuckles, which only tightened upon the steering wheel.

The Vulture wondered where their quarry thought they were going. He had reasoned that the bedroom store had been a gathering place for survivors, in the event the island was attacked, but he didn't know where they would go after that. However, it was clear they were heading somewhere, somewhere with a purpose, rather than fleeing into the Canadian wild. Perhaps another place Carson had chosen not to reveal, despite the Leather's best attempts at persuasion. He might have to interrogate the mechanic again, but he wondered how much damage Carson could take before he became completely useless.

In any case, this area was littered with dirt roads that snaked off into the wild, most adorned with *No Trespassing* signs and the like. The road itself wasn't a wide one, but wide enough to fit the Mack truck. Distinct prints stretched beyond the gravel, flattening the earth on either side, as if a pair of transport trucks or even bulldozers had gone over them multiple times, side-by-side. These prints continued along the roads the Leather ignored, crushing and leaving a terrible stamp upon the countryside. The Vulture doubted that bulldozers had been used, but something had done that to the earth. Something remarkably heavy.

The Vulture's eyes shifted to his side mirror. Framed there was a long train of vehicles, including fuel tankers. Individuals clad in shining leather rode those machines. Some were visible behind the windshields, while others stood in the box beds of pickup trucks, leering over the roofs like polished gargoyles.

They were mechanized titans. Fuel-injected warlords. And, in this new world, they were the last remaining road clan of any notable power, laying claim to whatever spoils remained.

The Vulture's eyes drifted from the mirror to the huge skull bolted down on the Mack truck's hood. The skull shivered from the mighty machine's idling. Not thirty feet away from the chrome teeth of the machine was a pickup truck. Two of the Leather stood in its box bed as sunlight flashed off the welded majesty of assorted plates and pipes. One of the Leather glanced back at their leader's ride, waiting for a signal, while the second Leather watched over a cage hitched to the rear of the pickup. Leather reins stretched tightly down over the top of the cage's bars, lashed to individual harnesses worn by a clutch of emaciated man-hounds. The mindless were stick-thin and dressed in rags more filth than fiber. The heads of those feral creatures whipped about as they strained against their bonds, trying to break free, eager to chase down the meat tainted with the scent. They were wretched things, masked, with hair sticking out from necklines that hung past their shoulders.

The Vulture often wondered just how far the man-hounds could track their prey when the scent of urine was applied. He believed they had an even stronger sense of smell than dogs, which could smell a female in heat up to four kilometers away. These creatures had proven to be much more powerful trackers, even when the scent they used had almost lost its strength. The distance from a relatively fresh scent was even easier for them to track. So when the road split off in a direction that seemed counter-intuitive to those menacing tire tracks, the pickup pulling the cage slowed to a stop. The man-hounds would either gravitate to whatever side the scent pulled them, or they would remain stationary.

Sort of like a much meatier set of divining rods.

And, right now, that frightful pack wanted very much to get moving in one direction, towards a side road stamped by those troubling tracks.

Where it would all lead, the Vulture had no idea.

Tucking that thought away, he stuck his hand out the window and chopped at the air.

The pickup truck turned onto the side road and crept forward until the man-hounds shifted to that side of the cage. Their heads bobbed as they took in the rancid stink trail.

The Vulture gave his driver the signal to follow.

And no more than fifteen minutes later, they discovered the abandoned escape vehicle belonging to their quarry.

*

"I'm gonna need a new pair of boots after all this," Gus muttered.

"We got boots at the base," Collie informed him. "Any size you want, as long as you're not too picky about the style. All made in China."

"Got sneakers?"

"'Course we got sneakers. Clothes, too. Right down to your tighty whities and pinchy panties. But nothing too fancy there, so don't expect much."

Gus wiped his sweaty hands on his jeans. "When this is all over, I'm going to get into shape. I don't care what it takes. Hiking. Your self-defense shit. Don't care."

"Duly noted."

Those deep tire prints lining either side of the dirt road drew his eyes once again. "Never realized how damn big that thing was."

"Well," Collie said, sparing the tracks a glance. "We were being shot at, if you remember."

"Maybe we should take the thing back to the coast."

Collie's mouth hitched into a half-smile. "Yeah, right. That thing would eat us out of house and home."

"Yeah, I suppose so."

The road curved, a long gradual bend that was hidden by forest. Gus looked back at the others, straining to keep pace with Collie. Rich Trinidad, holding rear guard, met his stare with a menacing glower. Gus turned back to Collie.

"That Rich guy is a fierce one."

"One in every group," Collie said. She nodded ahead. "Look."

The dirt road straightened into a long stretch of pavement, and the forest cleared around them.

The land had been cleared some fifty meters or so, leading up to a fixed perimeter, where a stout building had been constructed. A checkpoint, distinctly military, with broad concrete partitions, heavy-duty chain-link fences, and decorative razor wire that stretched out on either side. Abundant warning signs gave precise instructions on how to proceed. Pillboxes flanked the main building, equipped with what looked like drooping machine guns. The big kind. The .50 caliber kind. Armored cameras the size of mailboxes were mounted on the building's roof, monitoring incoming and departing traffic. There were red and green queue zones for vehicles—a pair of two-lane roads that bordered either side of the building. The lift bar with a red STOP sign remained lowered on the right side, but the left was in tatters—smashed lift bar, twisted wire fence, crushed concrete partition.

Which was where the Komatsu truck presumably had entered.

"She didn't fit," Gus observed quietly.

"Apparently not," Collie agreed. "But they still got the big girl's ass through." She turned to face the rest of the group. "Stay behind me. Don't wander off the path and don't go into the woods to take a leak, unless you see a crater and a clear path to get to it."

"Why's that?" Sarah Burton asked.

"That means someone already stepped on the mine."

That silenced the lot of them and made them visibly uneasy. They gravitated towards the middle of the pavement and the broken white lines painting it. The wire fences stretched out on either side, eventually disappearing from view. Unchallenged, the little group walked through the queue zones, peeking inside the open door of the checkpoint building. It resembled a small office, one that the janitorial staff hadn't visited in a few years.

Collie stopped at the open door and inspected the interior.

"Any guns in there?" Gus asked.

She shook her head. "Picked clean. Too bad they didn't do any other cleaning."

There were other buildings inside the perimeter's fortifications, low structures built of brick and steel, with grime-caked windows and open doorways. A few scraps of cardboard littered the edges of concrete and the pavement beyond, where the road continued.

"Bunkhouses?" Gus asked.

"Barracks. Waiting stations. For the quick reaction teams."

Gus guessed at what that meant. "Any guns in there?"

"You're not happy with yours?"

"Just wondering."

"You can check, but I'm guessing no. Shovel's group probably took everything. All the good stuff is in there."

She pointed toward the complex's interior buildings, which resembled a small alpine town. Rising beyond all that was Whitecap.

Impassive. Awesome. And indifferent. Wearing a tattered cloak of forest around its shoulders.

The dark tunnel mouth resembled an unpleasant maw, where a pale tongue of a blacktop unfurled in a long ramp, ending in a tangle of destruction that brought back memories for Gus. It was difficult to locate a spot on the complex grounds that *wasn't* littered with debris. Motorhomes had had their faces bashed in, their fiberglass asses crushed. Trailers had been upended and left for ruin. Smashed vehicles littered the compound, many of which had exploded and were now in multiple piles. Garbage bins had been overturned as if picked up by giants, shaken empty, and thrown to the earth. Broken glass covered the white concrete in wide sprays and glittered under the sun. Brass shell casings gleamed in fragmented streams.

Just below Whitecap's mountain entrance was the unmoving iron husk that was the dead Komatsu truck.

The vehicle was still upright, parked at the end of that shocking path of ruin. All four tires were intact. The considerable length of metal that was the flatbed lay on its side, bent at a subtle crook across the behemoth's face.

And in that deep reflection of battles fought and finished, in that serene mountain silence, Sarah Burton said it first.

Perhaps even said it best.

"…The fuck happened here…?"

24

"This way," Collie said, herding the little group across that junkyard landscape. They tromped over concrete and glass, their sneakers and boots crinkling upon far-reaching streaks of debris.

"Watch your footing," she warned, but even Gus had trouble minding that one. The newcomers' attention strayed, taking in their surroundings and the leftovers of a small war. Cars and trucks half-flattened by the Komatsu truck. Sofas and chairs hanging out of RVs. Glass framework bent into angular puzzles and left for garbage. A wall of shredded sandbags. There was even a trail of twisted pipework and fittings that ended in a kitchen sink, lying half a football field away from the nearest destroyed motorhome. More than one high-tech rifle was discarded on that plain of rubble, the most notable of which had a bent barrel.

"Those gas tankers have anything in them?" Rich Trinidad asked from the rear.

"Maybe, but I doubt the octane levels are there," Collie said.

Gus studied the great white plain and all the shit covering it—destruction he left during their escape from Whitecap.

Whitecap's maw loomed closer, while a white cloud as fine as silk stretched out across the mountain's heights. There were other rock formations behind that towering peak, but Whitecap was the tallest. The most imposing.

With every step toward Whitecap's entrance, the massacred machinery and debris cleared a little more. Beyond the sandbag line, however, the group could make out hundreds of desiccated bodies splayed out over a wide area. Gus heard Bruno telling Monica not to look. The crows had feasted. Sand spilled from the destroyed wall, covering a few of the corpses, but not nearly enough. There were hundreds, although after the long winter, you really couldn't tell where one body ended and another began. Rotten eye sockets stared. Skulls bared teeth. Bony torsos wearing rags stretched out as if catching some sun.

Collie sped towards the ramp, picking up the pace.

"You gotta use the can or something?" Gus asked.

She didn't answer; instead, she picked up the pace even more until she reached the base of the paved slope. Decayed remains covered this area, too, shredded and torn apart by Shovel's minigun. The sight of all those dead husks caused her to turn around. She surveyed the mass destruction surrounding the camp, adjusting her shades as she did so.

"You really did a number on this place, buddy," she said.

"You were with me," Gus reminded her.

"You were driving."

That shut him up.

Collie turned to the rest of the group. "All right. Watch your footing from here on out. It looks all clear to me, but just be careful."

They weren't looking at her. Not really. They were looking at the ramp.

"Oh my gentle Jesus," the one called Allie quietly remarked, and Gus couldn't remember her saying a word until that moment.

"We have to go up there?" Sarah Burton asked.

"If you want to see the bunker, you do."

"*That's* a bunker?"

"Way back in there."

"How far?" Rich Trinidad asked.

"It's a hike," Collie informed him. "Another klick and a half."

There were eyerolls at that, as well as a few tired sighs.

The incline was difficult for the group; their calves screamed. Sweat soaked their clothing. Halfway up, Gus's eyes started to wander toward the imposing mountainside and all the greenery growing off its face. He remembered reading an article about how the brain always sought patterns, faces, in inanimate objects. If Whitecap had a face, then its eyes were closed, and the mountain had puked upon itself, poisoned from within by something yet unknown. And they were marching up its filth-covered tongue, which was coated with a dried-up froth of corpses.

The sight caused Gus to shiver.

"You know something?" Collie said. "I thought I'd recognize more people. Nope."

"Collie," Gus said, "you think it's safe in here?"

"Fuck if I know."

That floored him, and it showed.

The lower part of her face broke into a smile. "Having second thoughts?"

"Yeah, I am."

"Honestly, I'm ninety-nine percent certain it's safe," she admitted. "Which is pretty solid to me. I wouldn't be bringing us here if I thought we'd be at risk. And with all that's happened in the last couple of days, well, you can't hang around outside. Not in the open, and not down there."

She jabbed a thumb at the mess behind her.

"Don't worry," she said. "You aren't going any farther than the next checkpoint. I'll do the rest, by which I mean I'll check on the weapons and munitions."

"And if all that's good?"

"We pack up what we can." She locked eyes with him. "And if those assholes are tracking us, we get ready for a fight. Maybe even make a stand right here."

No sooner had the words left her mouth, Gus looked back the way they'd travelled, over the concrete battlefield, all the way back to the first military checkpoint. He stopped marching, which caused Collie to stop.

"What?" she asked.

Gus held up a hand, and the rest of the group halted.

"Something up?" Bruno asked.

Gus motioned for silence, which prompted the rest of them to turn around.

Then, like a whisper teasing one's ear, he caught it again.

That distant, unmistakable purr of a motor. A very big motor.

"Well, *shit*," Gus muttered. He turned to Collie. "You hear that?"

"Yeah, I think I do." She waved at the rest of them. "Best to hurry along, people. We might not have much time."

The group started moving again, casting fearful looks in the direction of that first checkpoint. Gus hurried at his top speed, energized by the latest booster shot of fear. He wondered if his nerves were fraying out. Or even his heart.

They raced for the entrance, straining, panting, and eventually reached the cavern mouth. Collie aimed her rifle and peered through the scope. The tunnel was rounded, with smooth chalky walls made of concrete. A collection of cables ran along the roof, resembling the veins of one's wrist. Two huge, circular ceiling lamps hung high, perhaps thirty feet apart. Both were unlit, and if there were any more beyond, they were hidden in a deep, intimidating blackness, where daylight failed to reach. A smaller security camera was perched before the first lamp and aimed at the cavern mouth.

Collie immediately located a panel that, at a glance, might've held firehoses. She smashed out the glass with the butt of her rifle and forcefully cleared the frame of any leftover shards. To Gus's surprise, there *was* a firehose in there, as well as what appeared to be a breathing mask and a matching red fire extinguisher and axe. Collie pulled out three rechargeable flashlights, the kind recharged by squeezing the grip. She powered one up and flicked a switch, producing a white cone of light. She immediately handed the flashlight over to Gus.

"Pass that and this one along," she ordered. "You keep the last one and aim it over my shoulder. Everyone else get in a line. Hands on shoulders."

Gus did as he was told and powered up his own flashlight.

"All ready?" Collie asked.

"Yeah."

She started ahead, leading a frail string of humanity away from the light of day.

*

The lead truck stopped at the first checkpoint, with the caged man-hounds pressed against the bars and pawing at the air, so gripped they were by that infected sewage-piss stain that tantalized their senses. If he ever had the chance to put a lab together, the Vulture would have to sit down and analyze just what it was in the urine that attracted the creatures. That scientific dalliance would have to wait, however, as the military structures ahead drew his eye. The rest of the Leather pulled up around the main checkpoint building and jumped out of their vehicles. They entered the guard house and rooted around. The Vulture waited aboard his transport, studying the destroyed base that lay beyond the chain fences and concrete barriers.

His eyes centered on the mountain in the distance.

It was the crown jewel in a range of four smaller peaks, all stretching out behind the first mountain's mass. The first of a series of green and gray cones stamped against the sky. Trees and other vegetation grew out of the beast's back, all the way up, thinning out into a barren peak.

He zeroed in on the mountain's upset mouth at the base.

The caged mindless strained against their bonds. They weren't concerned about the nearby buildings. Where he was sitting, the Vulture could see that the hounds were aiming their noses straight ahead.

Towards that dark and mysterious opening at the base of the mountain.

Then he spotted the Komatsu truck.

The Vulture froze, his eyes narrowing in disbelief. The fortifications. The distinctly military dwellings. The trimmings of razor wire and strategically placed mailboxes that were surveillance cameras. The glittering broken glass and the unmistakable gleam of brass, and the reams of crushed vehicles and mobile homes. The end of the world *location* of it all, far and away from prying, *protesting*, civilian eyes.

The Vulture's driver noticed the tense posture of his leader and immediately wondered if he had anything to do with it.

Without warning, the Vulture stuck his head out the passenger window. "Go!" he shouted at his lessers. The Leather that had stormed the checkpoint stopped and listened, their upper bodies visible through the windows. Masked heads turned in his direction.

"Go now!" The Vulture pointed, infuriated by his minions' confusion. "*There*! To the mountain! They've found a *bunker!*"

25

Rock dust coated the cavern floor, thick enough that Gus and company left a trail of footprints in their wake. As daylight receded and the dark enveloped them, the flashlights flickered to life. Gus swung his around, taking in the cement blocks that lined the walls and ceiling.

"Keep that light pointed ahead," Collie warned him.

"Sorry. Got distracted."

She didn't reply, and he vowed to do better.

The beam bleached the tunnel floor, revealing concrete covered in dust and grit. They were well beyond the cavern's mouth, perhaps closing in on the one-hundred-meter mark. Flashlight beams scanned the area, revealing featureless walls and nothing else. A soft breeze pushed past Gus's face, however, and he wondered if someone had left open a back door somewhere. Then there was the silence, a noticeable absence of any noise except for their own heavy breathing and the occasional scuffing against the floor. Some heels clicked, and the sounds carried long and far enough to cause Gus's unease to spike yet again.

"Home sweet home," Collie whispered. "Look there."

Ahead, the flashlight swept over a slanted pile of debris that buried the far-left lane. Broken rock, jagged concrete slabs, plastic pipes, and girders filled half the tunnel. The mess was piled up at a steep angle, to where the structure's integrity had failed. Gus lifted his light to better see the cross-section of pipework, both plastic and steel, as well as severed fiberoptic cables. Wire dangled in strings and contrary clumps. The resulting dome of raw stone appeared all the colder and harsher in the white glare of the flashlight.

"The hell caused that?" someone asked quietly.

No one had an answer, and Collie kept moving. Gus angled his light ahead, but he looked back to the entrance and was surprised to see it half gone.

"Did a bomb go off in here?" Sarah Burton asked.

"Unknown," Collie admitted. "But definitely an explosion. Multiple explosions."

"Any idea why?"

"No," the operator said flatly. "But I imagine we'll find out."

When Gus looked back again, the entrance was gone. The flashlights uncovered more destruction as they slunk over makeshift struts and broken sections of chain-link fence that might've once kept the walls and ceiling from collapsing. Dry decay wafted throughout, and the temperature rose noticeably. The debris filling the tunnel was much denser now—rock fragments, fencing, destroyed machinery.

Collie stopped so sharply that Gus bumped into her from behind.

"Sorry," he whispered, and he saw what had stopped her in her tracks.

Bodies.

Once *undead* bodies, as their heads had either been partially destroyed or blown off entirely.

There was no mistaking the heap of blue-gray cadaver flesh and bone spread out across the floor. Some of the torsos had meaty holes punched through them or bitemarks the size of a shark's jaws, while the remaining musculature surrounding the wounds was dried out and sunken. Unseeing faces stared at the ceiling, while some ogled the living. A few of the dead were practically naked, which seemed odd, but others wore varying Whitecap uniforms—military, technician jumpers, lab coats—all of which was dried stiff with blood and viscera, glued to each other in a congealed tar that, thankfully, no longer had an odor.

Someone dry-heaved near the back.

"Watch your footing," Collie told them, drifting to the left.

Gus swung the light over to her and stopped when the beam centered on the dusty ass-end of a backhoe. The engine of the great machine was turned into the wall, where a chunk of fallen rock and metal prevented it from going any further. The group stayed away from the machine, stepping in puddles of crooked, lifeless arms to avoid running into it. At times, dead fingers touched their ankles. They threaded their way past the backhoe, where a dead snake collection of chains connected it to what appeared to be the rear of an armored truck. The truck's back doors were pried open and the interior bare.

More corpses lay unmoving around the vehicle. Beyond that were slabs of debris stacked in a crude stairway. The slabs rose to a hole near the ceiling perhaps half the size of a car lane.

One body's legs were pinched off midthigh by a giant slab of concrete.

"Holy shit," Sarah Burton released with morbid delight. "Almost like the tunnel bit down on the guy."

Gus turned around to comment, but his voice caught in his throat when he spotted Monica shielding her eyes with the sleeve of Bruno's coat. None of this was new to him. But to a kid no more than ten, if that, the tunnel was the clingy stuff of nightmares.

The screech of a speeding vehicle from behind distracted him.

"The hell is that?" Sarah Burton asked, peering into the dark.

"That's trouble," Collie replied and rushed up the stairway of concrete slabs. Gus fumbled after her. She stooped to clear the low ceiling and waved the others up and over. Bruno raced past with Monica, while Cory was right behind them.

"Go, go, go," Collie said. "Gus, you take them ahead. I'm pretty sure the way's clear. The meatbags had to come from somewhere."

"I'm staying here with you."

Collie fixed him with a look. She was about to say something when the white glare of headlights filled the tunnel.

Collie pulled Gus down behind the rubble. She hefted her rifle and positioned it on a high point, amongst chunks of debris. Gus pulled his Glock out and aimed at the approaching vehicles.

"Sarah?" Collie called out.

"Yeah?"

"Take everyone ahead. We'll cover you here. Slow them down. Give you time to reach the bunker's second checkpoint. We call it the box."

"What about you two?"

Collie turned away from her rifle. "We'll be along so get going. You got a klick to go. Get to the box. Past that is a garage. Huge area where the bunker's vehicles are parked. Find the EV section. Those are the electric cars. Get one and get back here. Pick us up. We'll be on the move by then—probably being chased."

"And if you aren't on the move?" she asked.

"Then you lock down the box and you're on your own. Go down to level five. Look for a small storeroom filled with dry foods. There's a door with 'EVR' stamped on it. Crack that open and go."

"Go?" she asked. "Go *where?*"

"Out," Collie said. "It'll take you under the mountain. After that, Bruno knows the way home."

With that, she took up a shooter's position behind the rubble, facing the advancing motorcade. Bruno and Cory hesitated, along with one or two of the islanders. Sarah Burton was already hoofing it into the dark.

Gus shooed Bruno away, and once they started moving, he watched their beams of light flicker about for a few seconds.

"Switch off that flashlight," Collie said, adjusting her rifle with a metallic click.

Gus did so, hunkering down not two feet away from the operator. The opening at the top of the rubble heap was about six feet across with shards and jagged edges on either side. Gus and Collie had good cover with clear sight of the tunnel.

The approaching headlights grew stronger.

"Okay," she said quietly, cheek pressed against her weapon. "Get ready, 'cause we're gonna stop a shit tsunami."

Some fifty meters ahead, the advancing vehicles slowed to a halt. Brakes squealed. Headlights fully revealed the extent of the cave-in, as well as that gruesome welcome mat of decomposing bodies, the abandoned backhoe, and the armored truck. Multiple vehicles filled the tunnel, the glare as fierce as magnified starlight. The tunnel debris and the piles of the dead prevented them from coming any closer.

"This is good," Gus said, taking a deep breath. "Real good. We can hold them off for days."

Collie smiled, her eye pressed to the assault rifle's scope.

"Ah, how long do we stay, exactly?" Gus asked.

"As long as it takes."

Just then, the unmistakable sound of doors opening perked their ears, followed by boots pounding upon concrete.

"Get ready," she said quietly, fingers flexing on the rifle.

In the tunnel beyond, dark things swarmed.

*

The tunnel had narrowed into just a single lane, filled with all manner of morbid surprises. While the entrance into the mountain had accommodated their forces, the Vulture soon realized the only way forward would be on foot. Before entering, the mindless' handlers had released them from their cages and tied them to the lead truck's front bumper. Tires slowly rolled forward over fallen pebbles, rocks, and wire fencing, until the truck, guided along by the pack of man-hounds, halted. That caused a ripple effect down the line. A lesser jumped out of the passenger side and waved at those behind, motioning for them to back up a few meters. Rigs reversed, and they spread themselves out.

When they all came to a stop, an impatient Vulture opened his door, got out, and sucked in the exhaust-laden air. He tripped on a small section of fallen pipe. He regained his balance and scowled at the sight before him—a backhoe, apparently reversed into the wall in a hasty retreat, blocking much of their path. The dead things covering the road no doubt had a hand in that, or so the Vulture assumed. Rubble buried two of the three lanes, slimming the passage ahead into a tight bottleneck.

The Vulture eyed the dormant ogre of industrial might. Like the enormous Komastsu truck outside, which the Vulture dearly wanted to investigate closer as well, the backhoe could be salvaged, repaired if necessary, and later utilized.

After they had captured the remainder of Carson's islanders.

And the girl.

Especially the girl.

The Vulture raised a hand and signaled his minions to check on the condition of the machine. Engines idled as doors opened and figures emerged, leather-clad wraiths holding a positively medieval assortment of weapons. They hurried past the Vulture, converging upon the bulk of the backhoe. The quickest one climbed the short ladder to the operator's cab and examined the controls with interest.

The Vulture waited.

In the glare of headlights, the minion gave a thumbs up. A second minion relayed to the Vulture that the machinery was all intact, it just needed a new battery and more fuel.

Both of which the Leather possessed.

Without warning, the first minion's shoulder exploded in a single crack of gunfire, and the man fell onto his companions at the base of the backhoe. Panic ripped through them. The Vulture instinctively crouched behind his door before rushing to the rear of the pickup.

Another shot then, and a second Leather bounced off the steel hide of the backhoe, a bloody gout erupting from his ruined chest.

A third Leather had his head snapped back before dropping, long dead before the echo of the shot petered out.

The others bolted for cover, crawling under the backhoe itself or sprinting for the trucks.

More gunfire. Single shots, each within a second of the last.

A black-clad minion flew backwards as if yanked from behind, landing among the corpses covering the blacktop.

Another figure twirled about, his hands going to his fountaining throat. He died slower than the others, falling to his knees before lowering himself onto a thin mattress of decomposing bodies.

Bullets ripped into the front of a nearby truck, and the headlights winked out.

The Leather scrambled over themselves as they sought protective cover. Cries of warning reverberated throughout the cavern, guttural messages and grunts. Once the lessers were clear, the crossbowmen dropped to their knees and returned fire. Steel-head bolts flew straight into the tunnel, their fletchings slicing the air. The missiles cracked off rock and metal, while a few disappeared through the opening at the top of a mound of fallen rock and concrete.

The Vulture studied that gap, where jagged teeth rose on either side.

He thought he saw movement there.

Scowling behind his mask, the Vulture marshaled his minions.

*

Collie fired.

Selectively. Repeatedly.

And each flash of her muzzle drove Gus to the ground and kept him there. He gripped his Glock, holding it two-handed as hard edges poked and prodded him. Collie fired twice more before dropping back. Truck headlights seeped through some of the more porous parts of the debris they crouched behind.

"Get 'em all?" Gus asked.

"You're funny," she said and considered her weapon. "Got about twenty rounds left. After that, sidearm."

"And when that runs out?"

"I'll take yours. Not like you're using it."

Gus scowled at that.

A series of cracks and whistles rang out above them, and flashing slivers split the air overhead, whizzing into the darkness beyond.

"Crossbows," Collie whispered. "Primitive sonsabitches. We'll hold them here." She edged back towards a 'V' formation in the ruins. "As long as we can. Long enough for everyone to make it to the box. Then we run."

Gus's scowl deepened.

"That's it, honey," she said. "We run. It's nothing but a straight line from here. And if Bruno or Cory can't get an EV to start, or the damn things are all fried or God knows what, then you and I, my friend, are on the royal cusp of being Fubar."

He didn't like the sound of that, either.

"Nervous?" she asked.

"A little."

"Not a lot?"

"Yeah, okay, a lot."

"Never been in a gunfight before?"

"Sure. Lots of times," he wavered.

"But…" she prodded.

"I was usually drunk. Or usually shooting gimps. They're different. Usually."

Collie peered over the ridge. "Being modest. I've seen you in action."

A roar of engines drew her back to the battlefield.

"Oh my," she whispered, peeking at what lay ahead.

*

Under the direction of the Vulture, the Leather mobilized for war.

Once they loosed their bolts, the shooters took cover and reloaded. During their early scavenging years, the Leather made use of whatever they could find on the battlefields where the dead and the living had squared off—Kevlar vests, riot helmets, armor-plated knuckles. These bits and pieces of armor they pulled onto themselves.

Then came the weapons.

Fire axes. Spiked bats. Lengths of steel pipe. Long knives. Crossbows. Makeshift spears. Some carried honest-to-God broadswords strapped to waists. Others hefted chains that could be whipped about. Shields hung off arms—huge metal barriers with extra handles bolted on the inner part.

They weren't super soldiers with high-tech weaponry. They didn't belong to any particular law enforcement body with formal training. What the Leather had, however, was experience, earned during those early years as modern-day hunters and gatherers. They were conquerors of the aftermath, possessing two key attributes that made them both deadly and frightening at the same time.

One was their singular hive mentality.

The other was their willingness to inflict pain upon others.

Amongst the flurry of getting battle-ready, the Bronze moved among the lesser like a grim sergeant-at-arms. The tall scarecrow inspected the minions, and when they were ready, he signaled the Vulture.

The Vulture chopped at the air, and the first truck reversed in a huff of steam. Its headlights had been destroyed, but that wasn't the reason for its retreat. The vehicle halted alongside a second pickup, creating a barrier of sorts. There, the Vulture brooded behind a box bed, watching that mound from which the gunfire originated. Headlights from some of the other vehicles still shone ahead, whitening the debris and casting bizarre shadows. The Vulture suspected that whoever was firing from behind that concrete hump was alone. And that the shooter was buying time for Carson's islanders to retreat somewhere safe.

The Vulture would not allow that to happen.

26

The shouting of perhaps a hundred voices blasted past Gus and Collie.

Collie rose to one knee and targeted a wall of shields charging around an armored pickup truck. She aimed at the shield closest to the backhoe.

Three quick shots punched into its flat surface, twisting the owner to one side, enough to present a target. Except, before she could get off a kill shot, the crossbow crew snapped off an answering wave of bolts. Two sliced past her head, missing her by a sliver as she dropped behind cover.

"They're coming," Collie said, keeping her head below the crest.

Gus lifted his Glock. He straightened and fired at the first thing he saw. His shots slammed into metal but failed to slow the human train charging them. The masked freaks stomped over the grim welcome mat of corpses, reached the slope, and chugged up the concrete steps. The edge of the shield came down hard on the top slab, spraying dust and chips.

But then the shield lifted.

Whereupon Collie blew out the owner's feet.

Standing below the shield's rim, she had no trouble placing two quick shots into those boots. The shield carrier dropped to his knees, his scream rising above that collective howl. Two others floundered behind him, creating long shadows upon the wall. The train's forward momentum frazzled, but not before one of them flung a spear at Collie's head, missing her by inches.

Gus shot the masked men from the other side, catching them in the chest and shoulders. The impact flung them back, twisted them around, and blasted them back into the others. The first man tumbled past Gus and Collie with a clatter, as if he were holding onto a refrigerator door. He landed facedown and the operator quickly put a bullet into the base of the guy's neck.

Gus continued firing, hammering that stalled mass of arms and weapons.

They were so close, so packed together, he couldn't miss.

Damn thing was, they just didn't seem to be dying.

A second shield pushed its way into sight, channeled by another stream of masked men, bent over and screaming like a murderous rugby scrum. They lumbered past the first line of assailants and pushed up the hill.

Gus fired twice, his shots hitting low and tipping a shield forward, enough that the edge caught on another's body. Two figures behind the shield fell, leaving the men behind them unprotected as they went down. Gus unloaded his Glock, catching one in the helmet and knocking him flat. Collie also fired into the besiegers, further disrupting the charge. She then dropped back, flinging the rifle away before pulling out her Sig Saur.

Gus tried to maintain his cover while still shooting, the flashes of gunfire lighting up the attacker's masks. One blast burst apart a neck, and the man flopped to the ground.

But that was just one lucky shot.

Gus continued shooting. He hit torsos, shoulders, even twanged a round off a helmet. Collie joined in from the other side, catching fallen attackers from an angle. Men screamed. Some of those on the ground tried crawling out of harm's way. One fell against the front of the armored truck just below Collie's perch and crawled underneath the front bumper.

Gus directed his fire at the masked figures between the trucks, driving them to the ground. Then his gun clicked empty, and a crossbow bolt buzzed by, almost shaving him to the jawbone. That near connection startled the shit out of him, and he dropped behind the mound.

Across the way, with a man facedown and dead between them, was Collie with her handgun. She cocked her head at him in a *how about that shit!* kinda way. They stayed there for seconds, waiting for more. When none came, Collie reached out and patted down the back of the nearby corpse.

The screaming on the other side had died away into pain-stricken moans.

"Wearing a vest," Collie muttered, studying the body between them. "That's not fair."

"I think they were all wearing something."

Collie glanced toward the tunnel behind them.

"Think they're there yet?" Gus asked.

She shook her head. She then peeked over the top of the rubble and dropped back. "Looks like they're licking each other's asses."

A bolt sizzled overhead, bouncing off a wall before hitting pavement. Engines revved to life then, and the smell of exhaust singed Gus's nostrils.

"Letting us know they're still there," she said.

"You think they'll charge again?"

"Oh yeah."

Gus sighed and reloaded. He then peeked out through the rocks and sized up the armada. The tunnel was alive with trucks and masked characters keeping low between them.

Collie rose just enough to clear her gun and let off three rounds. A headlight exploded in a short frazzle of sparks, and the light dousing them dimmed. She rose and blew out other headlights before dropping back.

"Letting them know *we're* still here," she said.

"How long do we keep this up?"

"Until we see lights that-a-way," she said, pointing at the tunnel behind them.

Gus rubbed the sweat off his brow, examined his hand, and wiped it on his pants. He looked into the tunnel. The sight of that immeasurable void sucked the confidence out of him.

They returned their attention to the army before them.

Minutes passed.

A heavy, frantic panting growing louder whipped his head around.

Three masked figures rushed up the slope, their bared teeth flashing, their hands ending in what appeared to be bowling balls. Collie half rose, gun blazing, and took the head off the first zombie in a flash of tracer fire and disintegrating teeth. There was a scramble then—Gus shot the second and third attacker in pure fright-fueled reflex. The second gimp landed flat on its chest, its arms splayed as if sliding across home plate. Collie straightened her arm and shot the thing point-blank in the ear, the blast bursting rotten brain matter through the other side.

In that split section of execution, the third zombie leaped past them both, and Gus tracked it with his Glock, unloading rounds before the mindless crashed into the lower end of the slope behind them.

Collie emptied her magazine into the mob following the three zombies. She hit several masked men, driving the rest to cover. She dropped behind the mound and quickly reloaded, peering back every so often.

Something caught her eye. A single figure stood alongside a parked pickup truck. In the shards of light and shadow from the remaining headlights, the bastard had his arm cocked back, holding what looked like a bouncing condom. Its tip filled with about eight ounces of God only knew what.

Collie knew what it was.

She rose high enough to clear the crest and put a bullet through that evil bladder, bursting it in an instant. The piece of shit holding the balloon recoiled as if he'd had his hand lopped off, and then quickly dove for cover. Collie did the same, not wanting to catch a crossbow bolt.

"Yeah," she muttered. "You rethink that one."

"The fuck was that?"

"Nothing," she replied. "They were trying to distract us. Gonna throw another piss bag at us."

"But we just shot their Moes."

"I gotta feeling they have more."

From the other side, men and women yelled out while machines revved once again.

"Fuck," Gus let out in disgust. "These guys got nothing better to do than to wear Halloween shit and piss in baggies?"

*

The last exchange flustered the Vulture. The shooter was good. Too good, as evident not only by the routing of the two charges, but one well-placed shot that destroyed a bladder. He'd lost three of his mindless and several lessers, including most of his meat puppets.

That pissed the Vulture off.

Nearby, the Leather sloshed water over the pavement where the bladder had landed, diluting it so that the mindless would go for the freshest, the *purest* scent.

The individual who'd been splashed stripped and set fire to his garments.

The Vulture ignored all that, focusing on the shooters ahead. There were at least two just beyond that pile of rubble, and he suspected one was the same shooter they'd encountered back at the island. The shooter had a rifle. A military rifle. And there was at least one handgun as well. He didn't know how much ammunition they had left, but, apparently, they had quite a bit.

The Vulture only had one such weapon, but no one to properly use it.

That thought stopped him.

"Bring me the new meat," he said to a nearby Leather. "The one who called himself Top Gun."

27

The remaining headlights winked out. Behind the rubble, the tunnel was black once again.

"Eyes open," Collie whispered.

"Not so worried about them anymore," Gus whispered back.

"Yeah? Why's that?"

For several seconds, he studied the last zombie he shot, sizing up the corpse not a step away from his feet.

"You gonna let me know what's on your mind or what?" Collie asked, distracted by his silence.

Gus shook his head, yet clearly bothered by something. "Well, I *thought* they were zombies."

"They are zombies."

"Not so sure they are."

"The fuck you mean you're not sure? *I'm* sure. Killed two of them myself."

"You sure you shot a couple of undead?"

"Hell, yeah, I'm sure. There and there."

She pointed with her sidearm, indicating the recent kills.

"Yeah, well, I'm not so sure that one there was a zombie."

"Why?" Collie demanded.

Gus took a breath. "I didn't shoot the head."

That got her attention. She immediately inspected the dead thing captivating Gus's attention. "You sure?" she asked.

"Yeah, I'm sure."

That got her thinking. "Watch them. And give me your flashlight."

He handed it over.

"They doing anything out there?" Collie asked.

"They're just keeping low. One of them tossed some water over the piss bag you blew out. Saw some heads peeking out around the trucks. Couple of them with crossbows."

"They're putting water on the piss splashes?"

"Something, anyway," Gus said. "And I smell something burning."

That gave Collie pause for a moment. "I'd give my right nut to have one of those grenades now," she muttered. "One of them lobbed underneath a gas tank would be a sunny day in Northern Ontario, I shit you not. Now look here."

Staying low, she edged toward the unmoving corpse, aiming her Sig at its head all the while. Grimacing, she reached out and rolled the skull one way, then the other.

"Wearing a mask," she muttered. She angled the flashlight downward, so that their attackers would not detect it. "Switching on."

A fist-sized point of light appeared on the ground, near one of the fallen deadheads. Scowling, Collie reached down and grabbed its leather mask. She lifted it and twisted it by the chin.

"Anything?" Gus asked.

Collie shook her head. "Not a goddamn scratch. You hit it in the chest there. No problem seeing those blasts. Two holes."

"I got off about four shots," Gus said.

"Yeah, well, you hit it twice. And no head shot." She dropped that meatball with a thump. "So they slipped in a live one," she reasoned.

"Slipped in a live one? You listening to yourself?"

"I am, and maybe you should be."

"If he was alive, he was crazy."

"Plenty of those around."

Gus scratched at his beard. "That means the other ones were alive."

Collie scowled again. "That's not right."

"A head shot will kill the living as well as the dead," Gus pointed out. "All I'm saying… that one *there* clearly died from two shots to the chest. Not a head shot. So that means he was alive. The other ones had to be alive, too, right? Because I don't think the dead would work with a living one. I mean, look at the *blood* for Christ's sake."

Collie's scowl deepened. Then, after a thoughtful few seconds. "Check on those fuckheads out there."

Gus did, ensuring that the little horde of crazies wasn't sneaking up on them. While he did, Collie removed the mask from the dead man's head. She hissed in distaste while she worked. The unmasked head *reeked*, as if someone had personally shat a hot party streamer inside the mask before pulling it over the thing's face.

"Oh dear Jesus," Collie said.

"That thing stinks," Gus agreed.

"No, well, yeah, that, but… oh God *damn*."

Gus waited.

She gripped the head and twisted it, violently, pulling it so that Gus could see. She hunched down and, using the mask as a cloth, gripped the unsettling swamp grass that was the thing's hair. As she lifted the head further off the ground, the nearby light illuminated its face.

Gus didn't say a word. He'd seen more than enough dead people to recognize the one Collie had a grip on was indeed a genuine Moe. A man, with black sunken eyes, of which only one was present. The other was merely an oversized cigarette burn of a cavity. There were holes in both its cheeks, as if the things had accidently—or intentionally—chewed through the meat there. The skin color was a pale blue, even under the flashlight's glare.

But then he noticed it, and what he saw drew him closer.

"What?" Collie said, also studying the face.

"Around the mouth," Gus pointed out. "Those black things that are usually there. Like barnacles."

Collie got in closer. "There are none."

They shared a look then, one of mutual shellshock, where the implications didn't quite sink in.

"Check the others," Gus said. A headache was hammering nails into his brain, a result of being stressed, tired, and confused.

Behind the pickups and beyond, the masked crazies were watching and making their own plans. He just wasn't sure what.

"Look at this," Collie said.

"Holy shit," he whispered.

28

"Guh," Top Gun spat. Threads of fat silk stretched from his lips as the ball gag was removed. He wiped his face and breathed, unobstructed, through his mouth for a change. "Christ those things taste like dead dog balls. Not that I know what dead dog balls taste—"

One of the four Leather surrounding Top Gun slapped him across his face. Top Gun took it, took the hint, and shut up. The Bronze was one of the foursome that hauled his ass to the forefront, and the Bronze had a hammer hanging off his waist.

Top Gun was on his knees and didn't look up, because the Bronze's hammer was right there at eye level. He hadn't seen the Bronze use the tool, but he had heard the tall executioner use it, repeatedly, on one poor bastard.

Trucks began pulling back toward the entrance to the tunnel, where it broadened into three lanes. Top Gun watched with casual curiosity, until a dark figure appeared before him. Top Gun raised his gaze toward the fabricated face of the Vulture.

"You," the Vulture said. "You can shoot a rifle."

Even though he'd been a slave to the Leather for only a couple of days, Top Gun had learned quickly not to keep any of them waiting—especially the Vulture. "I can," he answered after only a second's hesitation.

The Vulture snapped his fingers, and a lesser appeared holding Top Gun's sinister AUG-20.

Top Gun blinked at the weapon.

Nearby, the Bronze extracted his hammer with slow, deliberate care. He hefted it very close to Top Gun's bruised cheek.

"I want you to shoot some people," the Vulture instructed. "From a distance. They are preventing us from advancing into this tunnel. Do you understand?"

Top Gun didn't ask why the Leather couldn't find one of their own to fire the weapon. Instead, he swallowed and said, "I understand."

Another Leather held out a small ammo case. Top Gun knew it well.

"Kill them," the Vulture said. There was no promise of better treatment. No words of being kept alive. But on some unspoken signal, the Leather surrounding him seemed to edge closer, their meaning clear.

Top Gun didn't hesitate. "Sure," he said.

<h1 style="text-align:center">29</h1>

The two mindless were as bare around the lower jaw as if they had shaven with a straight razor before they died. None of the characteristic skin tags that identified zombies were present. After a thorough inspection, Collie met Gus's quizzical expression. Collie even reached down and stretched the cheeks of both, one way and then the other, to ensure they weren't missing anything.

"The fuck does it mean?" Gus wanted to know.

Collie met his pleading eyes. "No clue."

"Are they zombies?"

"I'm pretty sure they're zombies."

"But they can die just by being shot in the body. Doesn't have to be the head."

Collie lifted her head as if shifting into a higher gear of thought. "We don't know that. You shot only one and it died. To prove that, we'd have to shoot more of them. And not in the head."

The revving of engines distracted them both. Collie switched off the flashlight.

Gus crawled to his perch and checked on the pack of psychos. Collie did the same from the other side. Exhaust billowed in the light and shadow. The pickups were pulling back, but not far. The two nearest trucks drew back about thirty feet, just clear of the corpses littering the pavement. The rest of the vehicles retreated farther back toward the tunnel entrance.

"What are they doing?" Gus asked anxiously.

Collie didn't answer right away. "Something," she finally let out. "Keep your head down. And if you peek, don't pop up in the same place twice."

"Right."

Gus listened to the rigs moving behind the rubble.

"How long would it take for them to get to that box thingy you were talking about?" he asked.

Collie thought about it. "Given that they're tired, running on empty, I'd say close to ten minutes. If they start to lag, tack on five more. Give or take another five to get inside—if they *can* get inside—but I'm certain they can. Then another five minutes to locate the EVs and fire them up."

"What if they're dead?"

"They're not dead. This whole place draws power from its own grid. Geothermal, man. If there's no activity in the base, it's programmed to go into sleep mode. Those rigs would still get a charge. Except..."

Collie faltered.

"Except what?"

"Battery life."

"Battery life?"

"Yeah. I'm not sure exactly how long the batteries in those rigs can keep functioning before... burning out."

Gus lowered his chin onto his chest.

"But if they are good," she resumed, "then they can hit sixty klicks an hour. Someone would be back here in a minute for us."

"Okay, so, how long have we been here?"

"Since they left? Maybe twenty-five."

"Maybe?"

"Maybe twenty."

Gus wasn't sure himself. He juggled balls that weren't there. "So they should be back soon, right?"

"...Maybe."

He considered the long dark tunnel leading to Whitecap, waiting for headlights to appear. "The fuck's keeping them then?"

"They'll be back. Question is if we'll be alive when they get here."

Commotion from the leather-clad freaks drew Gus's attention, so he crawled back to his perch, careful to get behind a different cluster of debris. The crazies were still moving things around.

"They're up to something," he said.

"My guess..." Collie began. "They're pulling back from where I shot that piss bag."

"That was a good shot."

"That's your tax dollars working right there."

"Nice to know I'm getting something back."

"Honey, you got the best."

"What do you think they're doing?" Gus asked, not knowing if he would like the answer.

Collie thought about it. "Those two rigs are serving as a blinder to block our line of sight. This pile of shit we're hiding behind—I'm guessing that the armored truck was here, and when the backhoe rooted it free, the ceiling fell in. Part of it. Enough to unfuck the passage for Whitecap's undead personnel to march up and over it. I'm guessing those leather fuckheads will want to open it up a little more. Maybe pull back that backhoe. Then the truck. Then try another rush."

"But we're still here."

"Yeah. And we rodeo-fucked them last time. Chances are, we won't get them like that again."

Collie smiled at him. "But that doesn't mean we'll stop trying."

30

There were only two rounds left in the AUG-20. Top Gun figured someone had a grand old time popping off a few shots at road signs or some similar shit before realizing the ammunition was a finite resource. Still, he loaded the remaining bullets by forefinger and thumb into the magazine. If he'd had a full mag, he would have popped off as many Leather dickheads as he could before trying to escape.

As it was, he really couldn't do a damn thing. Not with four of the insane fuckwits hanging right off his ass. They weren't literally hanging off his ass, but they were close enough that if he tried anything besides shooting the shitbags holding up the raffle, they would smash the living pudding out of him.

He was roughly five truck lengths behind the lead pickups—the same vehicles that had their headlights punched out by full metal jackets. He perched the AUG-20 across one corner of the box bed, with a clear line of sight at that hole in the rubble. The truck was stable enough for a shot, but with only two rounds, he'd have to be point-on accurate. The Bronze was standing right behind him, like some dusted-off drillmaster from a 1970s terror squad. The Bronze gripped the hammer in his right hand, well within striking range of Top Gun's skull. Considering all the horrible fates the Leather could inflict upon him, Top Gun figured if he *did* get his head bashed in, he'd be lucky.

He also figured he just didn't have that kind of luck.

Regardless, his sonnavabitch chuggernut of a captor had given him a job to do. One job. And, incidentally, one he could do with a fair chance of success. Shooting a target in a dark tunnel, less than a hockey rink away, through a mess of concrete and fallen rock and shit.

That… Top Gun could do.

There was nowhere to extend the bipod on the AUG-20, so he simply shouldered the weapon, placed it across the box of the truck, stared down the scope, and let the reticle do the walking. The single green dot crept over a broken hedge of rubble, swept slowly from left to right. Top Gun focused on his breathing, searching for any telltale sign of life just over that pile of debris. The Vulture said there should only be two shooters back there, and that was fine. All Top Gun needed was a glimpse of hair. The top of a head. Part of a face. Given any of that, he could make the shot a kilometer out. This close, however, he could do laser surgery.

"I'm ready," he said in a low tone.

Several trucks were parked in the tunnel, all of them drawn to one side, where the backhoe and armored truck provided some measure of protection from gunfire. One of the Leather's trucks was backing up very slowly, guided by a half-dozen lessers, and maybe even a functioning camera or two. There were no warning beeps as the rig backed up. No warning lights.

The rear doors were chained.

The Vulture had explained the plan to Top Gun.

Shoot anyone he could see.

But Top Gun knew that crooked cock-nose had something else planned. A contingency plan in case the rodents holding up the show refused to lift their faces for the camera. That plan involved those godawful bladders. And the mindless they packed away in a twenty-wheel transport trailer.

A small unit of Leather formed up just behind Top Gun, the surviving leftovers of that initial charge. One of them carried two of those sickening bladders, hanging from his hands like a pair of glistening sausages.

Top Gun noticed that the grunt had no boots on.

In fact, the grunt crouched low, almost invisible in the dark, as he disappeared underneath the backhoe.

Top Gun flexed his fingers before gently caressing the curve of the AUG-20's feather trigger.

31

"You hear something?" Gus whispered.

"No," Collie whispered back.

He hesitated, his ears perked like satellite dishes, but could not discern anything outside of the low growl of motors. However, something had drawn his attention. He lifted his head, just enough to peek over the rubble. Collie watched him, not exactly at ease by what he was doing.

Nothing moved among the freshly killed carrion littering the slope and beyond. Past the armored truck and backhoe, the Leather's trucks were still in place, but Gus could see dark heads weaving about. The thought of sending a bullet or two in their direction might buy them a little more time. He was just about to suggest that very thing, when the lightest flutter from somewhere in front of him got his attention.

Gus drew back in reflex, not quite understanding what he was looking at in the dark.

When the piss bag exploded right across his face.

32

Top Gun had a shot.

Matter of fact, he had a great shot, of a set of narrowed eyes and a hairless head that resembled the ass end of an egg. The shot was even improving, and Top Gun waited for just a little more face, before he put a shell right between those squinty eyes.

His finger tensed on the trigger—when the target's face was suddenly blotted out.

Top Gun looked up from the scope in confusion before quickly taking up aim once again.

And just off-center of the reticle, just to the left of the killer dot, a full torso came into view.

*

A black bag whipped across Gus's face and exploded with all the pus-filled energy of an oversized pimple caught between two fingernails. He staggered back, clawing the thing from his face as a stomach-curdling stink filled the air.

A few droplets hit Collie, and she instantly realized what had happened.

As Gus staggered backwards, she rose and rushed across that empty space, exposing herself from the sternum up. The stink was stunning, a putrid, gaseous nebula that was borderline debilitating. She pushed through that toxic haze and grabbed Gus by his shoulder, yanking him down and out of sight. They landed hard, with him sputtering and spitting.

"In my mouth," he grunted, groaned, and scrubbed his bare hands over his face. Collie tried pulling them away, but he resisted. "Even my *eyes.*"

"Use your sleeves," Collie told him, glancing in the direction of their pursuers, seeing none.

Gus used his right sleeve, let out a frustrated "*fuck*" before switching to his left. That seemed to work better.

"Right across the chops," Collie said.

"*Eeeyeah*," Gus confirmed through clenched teeth.

In truth, he had taken the piss bag clear across the *face*, where the ends of the thing had clapped his ears a split second before its shifting, warping mass burst upon contact. His scalp and face dripped. His beard and neckline were soaked. The sensation was horrible. His face burned and crawled, as if maggots were feasting upon his skin.

"Oh, you stink," Collie hissed.

He nodded, eyes squeezed shut, as if permanently blinded. He blinked hard and attempted to focus.

Collie returned to the mound. She took a breath and rose on one knee, letting loose a barrage of pistol fire, lighting up the dark. She then briefly checked to see if anyone was coming and then hurried back to Gus.

"Can you run?" she asked.

"Yeah."

"Come on, then."

"Bruno and Cory are back?"

But Collie didn't answer. She hefted him to his feet and, glancing over her shoulder, pulled him toward her.

"Everything's blurry," Gus muttered, pawing at his face.

"I know."

"Can't see *shit*."

They ran, an off-balanced gait that didn't improve. Collie looked over her shoulder—no pursuers… yet.

"We could've held them back," Gus cringed.

"Not with you like this."

"Face feels like there's shit growing out of it."

Collie chose not to comment as she glanced back toward the tunnel entrance again.

"Wait," Gus said. "Look."

Collie turned her attention back to the access tunnel that led deeper into Whitecap.

And saw the growing glare of headlights.

33

The egg-shaped head was out of sight before Top Gun could take a bead on it, and at least two of his sphincters clenched at the missed opportunity. He remained in position, waiting for the target to reappear.

It did.

About ten seconds later, two feet from the initial spot.

And it cut loose with gunfire.

Great booming shots of fire shrieked past Top Gun, forcing the Leather around him to duck for cover. A few rounds smacked into hoods and windshields while others ricocheted off concrete.

Then nothing.

Top Gun hunkered down behind the tailgate. A hand touched his shoulder.

The Bronze.

The forbidding executioner was hunched over like the rest of them. It turned its masked features toward Top Gun, close enough this time that he saw the gleam of cold black within the eye slits.

Unsure of what to do, Top Gun blinked, waited for the commotion around him to settle down, and wisely kept his mouth shut.

Footsteps then, a dull pounding of soles on pavement and other organic matter.

The Bronze looked away from Top Gun.

The Leather who had thrown the bladder was pointing frantically towards the tunnel opening.

"They're running!" he exclaimed.

A second later, dozens of the Leather broke into a run. They rushed by the Bronze, who was receiving orders from the Vulture.

Upon finishing, the Vulture hurried to the forefront.

The Bronze and the other three Leather guarding Top Gun pulled the man up by his arms and hauled him forward by his throat leash. As a unit, they hurried after the others. The Vulture had arrived at the mouth and was overseeing his leather-clad minions as they climbed up the slope and peered into the dark beyond.

Faint at first, the Vulture recognized a set of headlights approaching from within the tunnel, partially obscured by the silhouettes of two fleeing figures.

The Vulture motioned for Top Gun. The lessers brought him forward and dumped him onto the edge of the concrete slabs. The Vulture pointed toward the two escaping shadows.

"Stop them," he ordered in a strained voice.

Top Gun set up his rifle.

34

Almost a hundred meters out, Collie and Gus stopped running, and Cory pulled up alongside in what appeared to be a huge golf cart without the overhead canopy.

"You guys okay?" he asked, his face concerned. He looked at Gus and immediately crinkled his nose. "Jesus, you shit yourself or something?"

"Yeah," Gus replied, still attempting to clear his eyes. "Or something."

Collie pushed Gus towards the back of the vehicle. The cart's doors were only waist-high, leaving the EV very open, much like a convertible. Polished railing ringed the passenger seats. Collie upended Gus into the backseat, where he tumbled hard to the floor.

Collie grabbed his ankles and shoved his legs clear.

"They coming?" Cory asked.

"Probably." She climbed into the rear, perching herself in the tiny cargo hold in the rear.

"All right," she said, grabbing the railing. "I'm in. Go."

*

Top Gun saw the figures clamber into the little buggy. He saw one upend another, heaving the unlucky bastard into the back seat. A set of boots stuck up in the air. Those he ignored, choosing to track the vehicle's turn and focusing on the first target acquired.

Top Gun ignored the Leather standing around him. He guided the green reticle over his target and kept it there. He hissed softly, releasing his breath.

And fired.

*

Hunching over the steering wheel, Cory turned the rig around. He put his foot down on the accelerator just as a metallic scream buzzed by him, and a bullet hole as fine as a spider's web punctured the EV's windshield on the passenger side.

From where he was, splayed out on the EV's floor, a blurry-eyed Gus watched as Collie landed in a crouch in the rear trunk area. She leaned forward as if gripping a rail… when her back exploded in a startling burst of black matter. A warm wetness spattered Gus's face and hands. There was no warning, just a lethal combination of speed (brought on by Cory stomping on the pedal) and forward inertia.

Then she was gone, tumbling forward, out of the cart and onto the hard pavement.

With a pain-filled squawk, Gus hauled himself up as Cory swerved right and left, trying to make the EV as hard a target as possible. The rocking slammed Gus into the seats and floor, battering him before he finally got to his knees. He pulled himself up and immediately looked back.

Speeding away from them was the ghostly eye of the distant tunnel entrance.

Collie was nowhere in sight.

"*Cah…*" he huffed, his voice cracking and his eyes watering. He blinked hard, pawed at what was left over, and hunkered down, gripping onto the railing.

No Collie.

Not a trace.

But there was plenty of her blood sprayed across the trunk, and her Sig Saur right in the middle of it all.

"She's gone?" Cory yelled out.

But Gus didn't answer him, transfixed by that terrible void, and the glaring light near the end of it all.

All the while, the EV sped down the throat of Whitecap.

35

A short time later, shadows crowded around the dead soldier. The Leather assumed she was a soldier by her uniform, just as easily as they saw she was dead by the baseball-sized hole through her chest.

One of the Leather stooped and flipped the dead woman over, allowing the Vulture to step in and inspect the kill. Shock filled the soldier's staring eyes as blood dribbled from that grisly crater, airing out the right side of her ribcage. A mild trace of scent hung about her carcass. The Vulture frowned.

"Get her out of the way," he rumbled with venom, in case the mindless would be distracted by her. That would not do. That would be a waste of time.

Flicking fingers to get the lesser moving, the Vulture turned and stared down the tunnel. Several of his minions flanked him, stretched across a clear three-lane strip of pavement.

He peered into the dark, where the fleeing vehicle had escaped. A vehicle that was practically soundless. Without a word, he strode back towards the light, where his minions were already preparing to reanimate the backhoe.

In his wake, two of the Leather dragged the dead soldier off the path by her ankles. They quickly hauled her over to a gutter, which separated the wall from the pavement. There they dropped her and, for good measure, shoved her back against the wall with a few well-placed boots.

Boots that left bloody prints as they walked away.

*

The dark receded, the tunnel walls now a glossy larva white. Black ribs rose to the ceiling, connecting to spines of gray piping. Rings of light hung from that constructed backbone, flashing overhead at precise intervals as if trying to calm Gus's grief-stricken mind.

Collie crouching.

Then her back exploding in a black flare. That sight was going to haunt him for a long time. A very long time. The desire to be done with it all filled him, and he wanted nothing more than to curl up on the bottom of the EV's floor and hope that Cory drove it over a cliff. He couldn't go on. Not now. Not without her. She was the direction he needed, the driving force he very much depended on, and the lady that, gradually, over time, had captured his heart. As cliché as it sounded.

The ceiling lights flared overhead like calming sunspots.

Then they slowed.

Gus covered his eyes. He didn't care. Didn't care when Whitecap's spinal cord of lights and pipework disappeared into a stainless-steel maw crenellated with blunted tusks. The EV braked hard and the world shifted, rolling him into the rear of the driver's seat, where he saw the brass gleam of a lost Loonie on the carpeted floor, right below the cushion springs.

"Where's Collie?" Bruno asked, distracting Gus.

"She's gone," Cory answered, the EV bouncing as he got out of the vehicle.

"Gone?"

"Yeah."

Silence then, but someone said "shit" in a stunned tone.

"What's the plan?" one of them asked. Maybe the one called Jeremy Walton.

"Level five," Sarah Burton said with a dazed sigh. "She said get to level five. So that's where we go."

More silence.

Followed by hands grabbing Gus and lugging him out of the rear seat. He stood in a drunken stupor, not resisting.

"Oh man, he stinks," Jane Wong said.

Yeah, well, life stinks, Gus thought blackly. Life was just a black crusted shithole and he was a dingleberry hanging off it. All he wanted now was to be done with it.

"All right, we go," Sarah Burton said. "Gus, we're leaving."

Leaving.

He didn't take his eyes off his stained boots. *Leaving* sounded just fine to him.

"Maybe I'll leave, too," he said and looked up for the first time.

The lighting system wasn't completely on, and more than three-quarters of them were dark, powerless plates. The ones that were on, however, produced cones of pallid light. The islanders were in a hangar—no, a *garage*, of massive proportions, where reflective white lines split apart into parking zones. Cars and trucks filled some of those spaces, gleaming underneath that sparse light. Way off near the back, where the light barely touched, were what might've been a pair of backhoes. Extensive pipework and clusters of huge panel boxes adorned the walls. Some of those boxes were fire stations. A set of enormous doors—perhaps steel or titanium—marked the entrance. Their edges were lined with rectangular blocks, designed to interlock in a precise seam when closed.

Beyond the doors was the tunnel they had just traveled through.

The lights began to wink out at that moment, right up to the doors, creating a void in its wake.

"Hey!"

Gus turned around. Bruno was there, pirate-cap Bruno, looking more scared than pissed-off but putting on a face, because little Monica was standing not a foot behind him, red-eyed and jittery as if she were just coming to her senses after a serious fright.

That sight brought Gus back to his senses, and he faced Bruno. "Yeah?"

"You okay?"

"No. Not really."

"You know how to get to level five?"

"Not really, no."

That quieted everyone.

"Well, that's just great," Jeremy Walton muttered.

"Level five is around here somewhere," Sarah Burton snapped. "We get to a staircase and figure it out from there."

Gus's attention drifted to what looked like a space-age chamber against the far-right wall. It was the length of two school buses with a single glass window that stretched at least half that. All manner of chairs and consoles filled the area inside, and Gus spied something that lifted his spirits.

A gunrack. Partially filled. With accompanying lockers.

"Did you figure out the doors?" Cory asked, nodding at the impressive entrance.

"No," Sarah reported. "It needed a security code. I punched in a few keys but no. Those doors are staying open. Which means we gotta get moving. Now."

"They'll be here soon," Cory said.

"How many, Gus?" Bruno asked.

Gus focused on him again. "What?"

"How many are there?"

"A lot," Gus replied in a lifeless tone. "All of them. The tunnel was filled. Lips and assholes. We…"

His throat clutched at the thought of Collie again. He cleared his pipes. "We slowed them down. Shot a few, even. But there's more. Plenty more."

That silenced them.

"The cars work," Sarah Burton offered, indicating a bank of parked battery-charged vehicles. There were more than enough to transport the group. "We take those and get going. Right now."

After a flurry of assenting nods and grunts, the group turned to leave. Bruno and Cory had gone five steps when Monica stopped them, pulling on Bruno's sleeve. She pointed.

Gus remained standing next to the EV he rode in on.

"Hey," Bruno said. "You thinking of making a last stand or something?"

"Sorta."

"Well, forget it," he said with a disapproving scowl. "C'mon, man. She'd kick your—" he glanced at Monica, wavered, then said, "Collie would kick your ass if you tried that shit."

"Yeah, she would," Gus agreed. "Guaranteed. Which is why I'm not doing that. But I'm not coming with you guys, either."

That stopped the rest of the pack.

As an answer, Gus reached up and squeezed his beard, wringing it free of the rotten liquid. Droplets speckled the floor. "You all smell it," he said. "I took one of those piss bags right across the chops. I'm… *spattered* with the shit. And you know what that means. They still got some Moes left. I don't know how many, but I know if I go with you, they'll track us down. They'll track *you* down. So… I'm staying here."

He rolled his eyes, indicating the garage. "Somewhere around here, anyway. Whichever way you go, I'll go in the other direction. Give you more time."

"Hell with that," Cory said. "Just strip right here."

"It's not only on my clothes. It's on me," Gus explained. "My face, my beard. I'm covered. Look. You go on, now. Don't worry about me. I'll find you when I'm able. You two—," he nodded at Bruno and Cory, "—take them back to the island. I'll get back eventually. No more than a couple of weeks."

If you can, their expressions said.

Bruno stared, torn between arguing the point or staying or some other shit Gus couldn't understand. A second later, however, the man extended his hand.

"No handshakes," Gus said, warding off the gesture. "I got this shit on my hands. I don't think the mindless need much to find you."

Bruno dropped his arm. "If you… ah… stick around here. Any amount of time," he began in a creaky voice. "And come across any nudie books…"

Gus smiled. "You got it. You bet."

That seemed to satisfy him. Bruno turned and faced the others. "All right. We're wasting the man's time."

The islanders moved. Sarah Burton nodded at Gus before hauling herself aboard an EV. Cory was already behind the wheel.

"Watch yourself, Gus," he said. "Good luck."

They finished piling into the two vehicles and started the rigs. Rich Trinidad hung back, sizing up Gus as he, in turn, sized up the gunslinger.

"Want one of these?" Rich asked. He held up a very futuristic gun in one hand. It was sleek, black, and shorter than most rifles.

The sight of the weapon got Gus's attention. "Yeah," he said. "I do."

"Over there. In that long-assed booth there. We didn't take them all. We were going to, but we decided to wait. Until you got back…"

Gus glanced at the booth along the far wall. "Thanks," he said. "I'll do that."

"Don't take all day, now."

"I won't."

Rich Trinidad considered the EV and people waiting for him. He backed up and boarded the vehicle. His cowhide vest gleamed underneath the sparse light, and he tipped his sombrero in Gus's direction.

Jane Wong sped off first. Cory followed, while his passengers, Bruno, Monica, and Rich Trinidad, kept their eyes on Gus.

Jane Wong signaled right.

"We're going down," Sarah Burton shouted, her voice carrying in the garage.

Shit, Gus cringed, glancing over his shoulder to see if anyone was coming up the tunnel. When he looked back, Sarah and Jane were already gone, and Cory was about to make his turn.

Monica waved.

Gus lifted his hand, but the little girl disappeared around the turn before he could wave back.

36

The EVs were completely silent as they whizzed around the corner, out of Gus's sight.

He stood there, in that overwhelming garage, and hung his head. Oddly enough, no thoughts went through his mind. Not a goddamn one. He was drawing a blank, and in his grief, the idea pushed through that perhaps he should start thinking. Start remembering.

You thinking of making a last stand? Bruno asked him.

Sorta.

"Well, forget that. Collie would kick your ass if you tried that shit."

He chuckled. Collie would indeed kick his ass if he tried that shit.

But damn he was tempted. So very, very tempted. And, even though, ultimately, he hadn't really decided which way he was going to go, he was going to do one thing, before all else.

He released a long sigh. "Just so you know…" he whispered into that haunting silence of the garage. "I think about you. A lot. A whole lot."

And then he was back. Back at Lazy Lou's showroom, on that wonderful piece of mattress heaven, face-to-face with Collie. His words quieted her, and she frowned ever so slightly in the dark.

"A lot?" she asked him.

"Yeah."

"Well, that's good. I think about you, too. A lot."

And Gus believed, truly believed, that his happiness at that moment in time, rivaled the brightness of the sun.

"Yeah," he whispered again. He looked towards the yawning chasm of darkness that was the tunnel.

"Yeah," he said with a little more heat, a little more resolve.

"Well, that's good," Collie agreed. *"I think about you, too. A lot. Still got a chubby?"*

Gus barked a laugh and wiped the side of his miserable, ass-stinking face. He shook his head and stared, stared at the dark tunnel. Whitecap's throat. And he was standing, he supposed, not quite around the back teeth area, but close enough.

The gunrack caught his eye, then.

From where he stood, he could see three of them. Three of those high-powered death-dealing bang sticks.

"Got half a chub, babe," he said as he walked over to the open door of the booth. "At *least* half a chub."

The booth was indeed some sort of checkpoint, streamlined and clean enough that it might've been quarantined. All the interior lights were switched on, which made him wonder why this room was still powered but not the rest of the place. *Government bunker*, he figured. Probably had a janitorial equivalent of an AI or the sort, programmed to go into sleep mode. Or limited sleep mode. There was a keypad to the right of the door, but he left it untouched. All he needed was to punch in a number or two and have the door slam shut in his face.

Gus stepped into the room, perhaps just a little wider than a bus. He went over to the gunrack and softly whistled at the sophistication of the firearms. BELGIUM MADE was stamped into the stock, along with the serial number 'ST1X9990T'.

"Stix," Gus whispered. "*Boom* sticks," he added as a smile spread across his face. "That's a goddamn good omen if I ever saw one."

He took one of the weapons, marveling at how light it was. The gun was awkward against his shoulder at first, as the barrel and stock were much shorter than he was used to. Once he braced it, however, he understood how it was supposed to fit his shoulder and his hand. Along the top of the weapon, a clear plastic casing contained what appeared to be a fucking leg's worth of stacked ammunition.

"Jesus," Gus whispered. He started counting the rounds and gave up after he got to forty, telling himself he had a shit-ton of ammunition. If and when he ran out, the gun would let him know.

Beneath the rack was an open cupboard. Five more identical magazines lay upon the top shelf, leftover ammunition the islanders had left for him and Collie. They were just over a foot long, and he realized the ammunition itself probably weighed more than the actual gun.

He placed the spare mags on a desk.

"All right," he huffed. "Armed and fuckin' dangerous."

And so very alone.

Gus stewed in that depressing moment, but not for long. His fucked-up foot distracted him, buzzing like an outboard motor stuck in neutral.

"Enough of that shit," he rumbled as he hefted the weapon.

He peered through its sights, noting the blue targeting dot in the center. Open lockers stood against the wall just past the computers, in the back where there weren't any windows looking into the garage. A light switched on as he stepped in front of one locker, illuminating the contents of the cubbyhole. Combat gear. Gus scowled at the padded vests, knee pads, elbow pads, and riot shields. He tapped the ST1X's muzzle on one shield. Not glass. Not plastic either, but some other material he was unfamiliar with. There were metal shields as well, but after lifting each one, he let them be, deeming them too heavy. He'd need both hands for the ST1X.

His eyes drifted back to the body armor.

It wasn't turnout gear from a fire station, and thus, didn't offer full-body protection, but it would work for now. He struggled into the armor, thanking Christ above for Velcro straps and plastic buckles. The chest piece was bulky, ribbed, with an excess of flaps and pockets. The armor was light, however, which he greatly appreciated, and once he had it on, he paused and glanced around the place for a mirror.

Of which there was not one.

Gus pulled on the elbow and knee pads. He left the boots but grabbed a helmet and pulled out a black balaclava stuffed inside. The wool mask went on, as did the helmet in a comfortably snug fit. A black visor protected his eyes, while an extensive bar shielded his cheeks and jaw.

Feeling positively badass, Gus paused when he realized he could smell his own foul breath, as well as the nut-juice in his beard.

"Fuck me," he muttered, taking in that stink.

He reached up under the face bar and pinched both the chin strap and the balaclava, to get some fresh air in there. He looked around for gloves but failed to locate any. There was some tactical webbing, but he was at a loss as to how to put it on.

"That's that," he grumbled. He stepped over to the spare magazines, picked up one, and realized he had nowhere to put the damn thing.

"Don't laugh, Collie," he whispered. "I'm doing what I can. You should see me with paint gear."

On impulse, he leaned over the desk and peered out the window, eyeing that yawning black chasm that was the outer tunnel. Nothing came forth. It was blissfully quiet. He examined one of the computer terminals, one of which was already powered up. It showed a red screen curtly asking for an authorization code.

Gus left it and walked back out into the garage.

He spotted a black luxury liner of a limousine parked in front of a bank of elevator doors at the far wall. He had to walk a few steps to really get a good look at the car, but there was no mistaking it. The thought of *'what the hell was a limo doing in a secret government bunker?'* didn't last for long. No doubt it belonged to the Prime Minister. The EV Cory had picked him and Collie up in was nearby, and still functional. A quick inspection of the basic controls and Gus figured he could drive the thing.

He returned to the main booth and leaned against the corner in thought. He settled in and gazed at the dark tunnel beyond. It was almost peaceful, except for the shitty smell all around him. With a sigh, he cradled the ST1X in one arm, pointing it at the ceiling.

They would be coming sooner or later.

He'd be waiting for them when they did.

37

Gus jerked into focus when an explosion rolled along the length of the tunnel's throat, followed by a haunting, metallic peal of failing steel. There was a second, deep-throated groan of what might've been a submarine's hull being squeezed to breaking point, then a startling clap of an immense collapsing weight, not unlike a beer can being crushed next to a microphone.

Then silence.

Gus scanned the tunnel, his automatic weapon (at least he thought it was automatic) ready and braced against his shoulder. His anxiety level had gone from zero to ten in an instant. Nothing moved within the dark, but he knew they were out there.

Getting closer.

He waited, still positioned at the booth's corner, wavering on whether he should stay and make like he was brave, or run for higher ground. The plan was to buy enough time for Bruno, Cory, Monica, and the rest of them to get away, to find that secret door and get out of Whitecap. But what if they couldn't? What if that exit wouldn't open for them? He vaguely remembered Collie once talking about being unable to enter the bunker from the outside, because those access points were secured and locked from the inside. But what if whatever had initially blasted the ceiling out and blocked the main tunnel had also rendered that escape route useless?

"There's a way out," he whispered, trying to alleviate those thoughts. "Right, Collie? That's right. Why else would you send them to level five? They can get out. Sure they can. I just hope they can find it."

With an uneasy swallow, he leaned against the corner and kneeled. He wished for infrared goggles or some other fancy soldier shit to help him see in the dark. He bet there was something like that in the complex behind him, which was weird as you would think they'd have it near the entrance. That lack of foresight annoyed him. At least he had a gun with ammunition. Considerable ammunition. All he needed now were targets. If things got hairy, he had two options—retreat into the guard booth, or jump into the EV and drive for the coast.

Figuratively speaking, of course.

A minute passed. Then two. Nothing moved in the tunnel.

Ammunition, he thought while eyeing the dark. He faltered and checked his weapon. He'd already flicked off the safety, so that wasn't bothering him, but he sensed something amiss. Plenty of ammunition was inside the booth, and he could quickly reload if he…

Gus stopped and studied the weapon in the frail overhead light. A chill lanced through him.

How the hell did you reload *the goddamn thing?*

Did the magazine pop out or eject straight up or… what?

"Shit," he whispered, not seeing any kind of switch that did just that. "Well… *shit.*"

Then he heard it.

A low wail, like a gush of water from a broken dam, except it was a rabid flood of voices, rising and falling. A harsh, tuneless screaming that weakened his knees the very second he identified it. Gus should have been used to that sound by now. The truth was, however, he'd usually been drunk—*imperviously* drunk—and rendered one-hundred percent mentally bulletproof against the horrors of the day.

He had no such protection this time.

With the maddening roar now filtering out of the tunnel and into the garage, Gus rose and went back inside the security booth. He took the two other ST1X battle rifles off the rack and carried all three back to the corner. Once there, he leaned the extra weapons against the wall, within easy reach. They were all loaded, and he figured it would be easier to grab a fresh firearm than reload a spent one.

That was his thinking, anyway.

And God above, how the mindless *screamed.* A singalong of enraged gibberish, tormented and plague-ridden, and yet absolutely *yearning* to either spread their disease or just straight-up kill. And not just kill, but tear the living apart.

Gus listened to the approaching squall of insanity. For a full minute, he vacillated between shooting them all or running away. There were a lot of mindless charging toward him. A regular rampaging mob of thrashers. Sweat dribbled into Gus's eye and he squinted it away. The stink still plaguing him was borderline, stomach-turning rancid. His bad foot was livid, droning on like two bees fucking in a thin blanket.

His fingers flexed upon the gun's grip under the barrel.

Nothing appeared out of the dark.

Even more interesting, the motion-automated lights remained off—the same lights that he and Cory had triggered when they drove through the tunnel.

His ears perked as he caught a new sound, one that accompanied the mindless screaming. An underlying beat to the screeching, flaming disintegration of vocal cords, as if an entire town was attempting to gargle through one massive coordinated act of fire-eating. Gus didn't know what that new sound was, but it came across like barrels rolling across a floor.

Then it hit him.

Boots.

That straightened his spine.

Hundreds of boots, sneakers, bare feet, whatever the fuck.

And all of them running toward him. *Smelling* him. Knowing he was just ahead at the end of a long and tenebrous passageway.

"Collie," Gus whispered, scanning that impenetrable screen of tar just beyond the box, feeling his throat click as he swallowed. "Listen.... This might've been a bad idea."

He glanced back at the EV, its headlights pointed towards the deeper parts of the garage. *Shit.* He should've scouted out the rest of the garage, made certain he knew where *he* was going, and what he was doing. But he didn't. At the time, he was ready to die, ready to go down underneath a mass of twisting, writhing limbs and biting mouths. Firing or swinging or just plain swearing all the while.

With every passing second, he realized just how *wrong* he was.

Again, he glanced at the EV. Ten steps and he'd be there. Ten seconds and he'd be driving off, picking up speed, and trying to outdistance what was coming. The nagging intensity of his foot was cut off by the energy thrumming in his calves.

A spike in volume yanked his attention back to the tunnel mouth. Gus stared into that sunless space beyond the bunker. His chest ached. He braced his rifle hard enough against his shoulder to make it hurt.

He waited for the storm.

And waited.

And *wait*ed.

And then, as though a curtain had suddenly lifted, the automated tunnel lights blinked on and there they were. A monstrous collage of faces, hundreds strong, popping into sight in near-perfect unison. A fire-hydrant gush of torsos, chugging arms, and sprinting legs that all seemed to shift into an even higher gear of frenetic energy upon the horde smelling him. That livid, emaciated line of insanity charged forward, hundreds of eyes bright with rage and jaws stretched wide—and they *thundered* towards the subterranean endzone that was the wide-open bunker.

The screaming had long since peaked, yet feral shrieks of pure, wicked glee punched through the unvarying roar, spiking the air.

Against instinct, against every fiber of his worn-out body urging—*begging*—him to haul ass out of there…

Gus stepped out from the corner and fired.

38

A murderous spray of gunfire cut across the charging zombies.

Chests erupted. Heads blasted apart. Chunks blew out of necks. Shoulders shredded in a blink before the line of star fire whipped across faces and violently removed them. The air became a carbonated mist of blood as the first rank collapsed, instantly tripping up the second and third ranks.

A huge wedge formed in the middle of that tsunami of savagery then, as if God himself took a whack at it with the back of a shovel.

The wings of the mob, however, sped onward, homing in on their target.

So Gus alternated left and right and hosed them down as well.

The ST1X had no recoil. No kick. Tracer fire erupted from the muzzle in an unending Morse code of death. Spent casings shat straight down Gus's left leg in a heavy patter, rather than to the side like some of the other guns he'd fired. 'Course, this was the first time he'd gotten his hands on an automatic weapon. A *military*-grade automatic weapon.

And like a firefighter wielding a high-pressure hose, he whipped that thunder stick to the right, wiping out a dozen or so figures with it in mere seconds. Then he raked it across the floundering middle, then toward the left wing.

Gus was smiling. Hunched over with his cheek plastered against the gun, he didn't even have to aim, the mindless were so thick. The ST1X churned out an astonishing stream of light that ripped the forward ranks apart, and those that followed were immediately hosed down as well. The gun was a death rattle. A white-hot butcher's knife slicing knobs of undead butter. And all the while he was shooting, at the tail-end of his unchecked astonishment at the level of destruction he *alone* was causing, he wondered how— seriously—*how* the hell did he *not* get his meat mittens on one of these things in the *first* place? He could hold off a goddamn *army* of the undead with one of these guns. He could mow down entire hordes of the screamers. He could—

The gun ceased firing.

That single, near continuous laser-beam stream of heavy-metal demolition stopped without warning, and something clicked against Gus's cheek, startling him like a thumb jammed into his ball sack.

He lowered the weapon and saw it was empty.

Goddamn *empty!*

Sixty—maybe even a hundred rounds gone in less than *fifteen* seconds.

"The *fuck?*" Gus blurted, and realized right then and there where he was. What he was doing.

Fifty meters out, and less than half to where the blast doors shut, the mindless kept right on charging.

Gus nearly ripped his fingernails off as he grabbed onto the emptied magazine, whereupon he immediately flung the casing away. Only to realize he didn't have any fresh spares—just fresh guns.

He dropped the first ST1X battle rifle and snatched up a second one. It was already primed, so he pressed it to his shoulder and started firing. And light, praise Jesus, pure and holy light, spat forth and ripped the undead multiple new assholes north and south of the border. That destructive onslaught clotheslined the attackers, dividing them. The charge fragmented then, as those in the rear tripped or stumbled over the dead. Instead of a single solid mass, streamers of flailing, clawing, undead sprinted towards him.

Gus unloaded, whipping the gun back and forth, decimating any Moe getting too damn close.

And ran out of ammunition in ten seconds.

Christ almighty! Gus mentally swore and chucked the second weapon. How the sweet fuck was he supposed to kill zombies when—

The overhead lights lit up a full stadium's worth of undead as they blasted past the raised doors of the bunker. Very much aware of how fast they were rushing him, and very much eager to pick up the last remaining ST1X, Gus grabbed for the weapon.

His outstretched hand—his fucking *fingertips*, in fact—inadvertently *knocked* the gun a good five feet away from him. It clattered across concrete, well out of reach, and presented him with a choice. A crystal-*clear* choice.

He could either go for the weapon… and continue his bloody spraying down of the rapidly advancing mindless.

Or… he could turn and run for the nearest EV.

In the maddening din of his nearing attackers, Gus never even considered it a question.

He went for the gun.

And in his own frenzied haste, he fumbled in picking up the weapon. Through the open door of the booth, Gus glimpsed figures storming past the window therein. And if the mindless were noisy before, they were deafening now.

With a distressed whimper, he snatched up the firearm, didn't get a good grip on it, but that didn't matter. He had the gun. Now, all he needed was cover. He whirled and lunged for the nearby doorway of the security booth.

Where the frame smacked the weapon out of his hand.

That sudden freeing of the gun jerked his head around in time to see the contrary piece of plastic and metal skitter along the floor.

In his peripheral vision, outlines continued blurring past the window of the booth. He could hear their feet rattling off the floor, getting closer.

Inside the booth, Gus spotted a keypad next to the door. He slapped his palm down on a red button, right below a green one. The booth's door slid shut just as a torso appeared in the gap, just as dozens of fingers scrambled to stop the closure. The door closed anyway, momentarily muting the screams from beyond—a second before the hammering began. A furious taiko drum set where the musicians had loaded-up on performance-enhancing drugs and were swinging for distance.

Gus thumbed an additional knob and a message flashed across a small screen, notifying him that the door was locked. Sighing relief, he backed away from the rattling surface and flinched at the startling pounding on the booth's window. Dozens of mindless were there. Men. Women. Teenagers. All banging the glass surface with skin-splitting force, letting the living know they knew he was in there. The clear pane trembled under the assault, and Gus pushed himself up against a table shoved against the opposite wall. Office organizers spilled pens and paperclips onto the floor. He ignored the mess, his attention fixated on those savage, wide-eyed faces.

Some pressed their cheeks against the glass, stretching pallid skin. Others flattened their foreheads. Others faceplanted the clear surface and smashed out their remaining teeth in bursts of bloody spit. Noses squashed in red spurts. One woman reared back in superhero style and punched the glass, breaking her knuckles in a rain burst of dark matter.

But she kept on punching, heedless of the ruination of her hand.

Mindless.

No other description really applied. Or mattered.

And despite their breaking bones and bursting skin, they kept on smashing at the door.

The scent, he realized. The urine covering him drove them gluebag crazy. They could probably smell him right now, right down to his dewy dingleberries.

The mindless crowded the security booth, filling the window from left to right. There weren't as many as before and Gus thanked Christ for that. At least he thinned out the herd a bit, before he took sanctuary within the checkpoint walls, which were a lot more resilient than he'd thought. Still, the sight of the mindless mere feet away from him, behind a partition of unknown material and thickness, did not lift Gus's spirits. He wasn't free—he was in a long box, on display, witnessing dead people smash the living shit out of themselves.

That stopped him in his tracks.

Gus watched the undead outside, thinking back to his own shooting spree. Could they be killed by shooting the body as well as the head? He'd had his chance to clarify that and missed it. He couldn't see shit past the gore-stained glass. The mindless outside continued to inflict horrific injuries onto themselves, and they showed no signs of slowing down.

"It's like a fucking Black Friday sale out there," Gus said under his breath.

The glass was holding, but he didn't know for how long. Once they got through, he'd be dead. The closest thing he had to a weapon was…

He looked around the office area and spotted a large stapler next to a keyboard.

The walls rumbled as he trudged into the back of the booth. More body armor but no weapons in sight. There were still a few magazines underneath the gunrack, but no guns to use.

The booth's windows seemed to shiver under the constant bombardment of faces and appendages. He'd be safe for a while, he figured, until…

Well… *shit.*

Until the masked sonsabitches that were chasing him arrived on scene.

That Tom-fuckery, he thought, channeling his inner-Toby, *would simply* not *do.*

But there was no way out of the box. There was only one door, and that had been shut.

He sized up the walls, the floor, the *ceiling…*

The square grid of an airduct stared back at him.

Gus stood on a chair to remove the six screws securing the grate, and then he pried the thing open. Before he could climb into the duct, he had to place the chair on a table to reach.

"Seeya later, bitches," he said before straightening up inside the duct. He faced a solid wall, so he turned around and met the shriveled gaze of a dead man staring right at him. Gus screamed. His shoulders rattled off the edges as if electrified, and he almost lost his balance on the chair. The dead guy remained the same, which allowed Gus to warily compose himself. A shot of anger bubbled up inside of him, and he almost punched the corpse.

That's when the screwdriver got his attention.

Pushed to the hilt into the dead guy's brain. Through his right eye.

"Well… damn," Gus whispered, examining the shrivelled corpse, and cringing at what *had* to have been a painful death. The drumming below reminded him of his own situation, so he pulled the body out of the ventilation duct and out of the way. It was awkward, and it took a minute, and it almost distracted him from the zombies hammering at the glass.

In the end, the dead guy fell to the floor, thankfully missing the chair.

The corpse landed with a thud, with those dry yolky whites staring at the ceiling. The dead guy's mouth—caked in black—was locked in a grimace. Gus understood why. He hadn't seen it when he was pulling the dead guy out of the vent, but when the body was on the *floor*… it was obvious.

The guy's lower left leg—the meat of his calf—had several bites taken out of it. Pant leg and all.

Perhaps the mindless had gotten to him as he was hoisting himself up into the ductwork. Perhaps that first crackling bite had energized him enough to get above his attacker. And perhaps… just perhaps, the dead guy, realizing he was about to *be* a dead guy, had decided to end it on his terms.

By sticking a screwdriver into his eye. Straight through the brain.

"That is nasty," Gus whispered in horrified awe.

He pushed the chair back into position and climbed into the duct. He looked down the shaft and saw at the other end an opening glowing with soft light.

Gus recreated the rest of the dead guy's backstory. He was probably being pursued from the other end, crawled up and into the duct, got bitten, and realized, when he crawled over to this grate... he couldn't open the damn thing from the *inside* of the shaft. Couldn't unscrew the grill from his side.

"Thanks buddy," Gus said, knowing the other end had been left open.

Sensing he had very little time remaining, he hoisted himself into the duct.

The hardest part of getting in wasn't taking the screws off the grill. It wasn't pulling the grill down, either. It was pulling himself up into the narrow shaft. He finally pushed off on the seat of the chair, feeling it give under his toes and then crash to the floor.

Then he was lying in that rectangular box, his legs swinging.

Dust as thick as white frosting coated the metal. With a groan, Gus realized just how tight the system was. He also realized he wouldn't be able to pull up the grate behind him, since there was no way he was turning his ass around in such cramped quarters. Nor was he able to go far, as the ductwork had wire mesh placed inside the system, barring off portions to no doubt dissuade anyone from doing what he was about to do.

The only grate that was free and open was the one the dead guy had accessed. Gus pulled his legs up and crawled through the passage, knocking his knees and elbows along the walls. He eventually stared down into a room that needed a little more than a bottle of sanitizer and a cloth rag to clean it up. Desks were upended. Computers were trashed. Paper and other office materials had been flung in every direction as if the world's dirtiest battle royale had gone off right below him and the organizers left without cleaning up their shit.

And, right in the middle of it all... was a stepladder.

Lying on its side, leaving him with an eight-foot drop to freedom... of a sort.

Gus sighed.

With no room to maneuver, nothing to hold onto, and no cushion to stop his fall, he prepared himself for impact.

"This is gonna... *fuck*," he grimaced, not liking the next few seconds in the least. He stuck his head out and glanced around. The room itself might've been an office before an undead typhoon struck it. There were a few bookshelves but nothing else. To his right was an open door leading to a dark hallway. The faint light source turned out to be a single fluorescent bulb, tube-shaped, set into the wall above the door.

Emergency lighting, or at least some sort of energy conservation measure. Nothing moved, so Gus edged forward, got one arm through, and then plopped onto his chest and got the other arm through.

Then he was dangling from the shoulders.

Then from the sternum.

The ladder would be his not-so-friendly cushion.

Gus edged forward, reaching for the ladder—when gravity grabbed him.

He crashed headfirst and landed on his back, hyperextended at the waist. The impact stunned him, only for a few seconds, before the discomfort settled in. Still, armored as he was, no arms or legs were broken.

Gus slowly got to his feet and kicked at the ladder.

"Piece of shit," he mumbled. "Do your job next time."

He eyed the door. In the muted distance, the mindless continued to crash against the glass, wondering what he was doing. Gus examined the wall and figured a foot of concrete separated the two rooms. That was fine by him. It gave him time to find some clean clothes.

The open door beckoned.

Gus waded through the clutter and stopped upon the threshold. There was nothing around to use as a weapon—not even a broom. Nothing could be heard outside, and the way he was stinking, if there were mindless out there, they would have taken a run at him by now.

Gus peeked into the corridor.

And there was light.

The moment he stuck his head outside, pale emergency lighting flickered to life, illuminating the edges of the hallway. The walls were a rich red-panel wood, the kind one might see in a fancy elevator, with a single brass rail on either side that gleamed under the light. A padded material of some kind covered the floor. The ceiling was something else, however—it mimicked the open night sky, its surface revealing the Milky Way in all its celestial beauty. And, as Gus watched, the emergency lights continued to brighten, revealing more of the hallway and its features.

Without warning, the hall to the right dimmed, but the light to the left remained on. Gus took in that starry expanse, wondering just how deep they were underground. One thing was certain, Whitecap had power. Limited, perhaps, but it had power.

Not wanting to walk along in the dark, Gus went left, keeping a shoulder to the wall. His footfalls were softened by whatever material padded the floor, but he kept glancing back, checking for pursuers. Either for the mindless or just regular Moes.

Because they were different, he realized.

One could be killed by just headshots, while the other could be killed just like a regular person. *Why* was a mystery. One he may never solve.

As Gus made his way down the hall, he passed a wide glass door with the word "LIBRARY" etched across. He stopped and peered inside, and spotted numerous computer terminals, VR decks, and multimedia booths, as well as shelfing for a respectable collection of books. Penlights winked on and off around the librarian's desk, but the place was otherwise empty.

And the doors did not open.

There were more doors along the grand hallway, unlabeled, closed, and metal. Gus passed by a fire station, complete with a hose but missing an axe.

The hallway ended and he wandered into an exceptionally large chamber, where the red paneling ended in angular cuts of bedrock. A single mighty column of wet rock, perhaps the girth of a California redwood, stood at the center of the room. Water trickled down over the rock and dribbled into a pool that ringed the rock's base. The air was moist and pleasant, like that of a small lake in the summertime. The ancient-looking pillar of corded rock reached the ceiling, which, again, simulated a clear night sky. Gus stopped and gawked at the stars, and realized, as his eyes drifted to a rocky edge, that one section was gradually getting brighter, as if heralding the approach of the moon. Constellations spiraled into focus, the stars twinkling through a soft cloud.

That got him thinking. Remembering. A report he once watched on television. Regarding bunkers for the ultra-rich. Subterranean dwellings, particularly bunkers, might impart a touch of claustrophobia upon long-term residents, in addition to other mental illnesses he couldn't rightly remember, so creating an underground world that mirrored the one above was crucial. Convincing the mind that one *wasn't* living beneath the earth for months, even years, was essential for long-term mental wellness. Maintaining the illusion of day and night, and its regular passing, right down to the precise second of sunset and dawn, was crucial for long-term survival.

The stars above were probably some elaborate screen playing a recording…or even the actual onset of night as seen by a hidden camera posted outside and broadcasting real-time feeds. In any case, it certainly looked like Gus was standing at the base of a solitary butte, deep within a hidden slot canyon, enjoying the onset of night. Except it was entirely manufactured. Constructed. A technological mirage, designed by experts, and convincing enough that Gus almost wanted to stop, pull up a lawn chair, and just stargaze.

As he watched, the outer edge of a full moon peeked into view, beginning its arc across a cloudless night sky. As his wonder grew, he became aware of the sound of crickets chirping all around him.

Four passageways led out of that fabricated canyon. Only one of these had its emergency lights on. Gus paused, listening, and other than that soft chirping of crickets, he heard nothing. Certainly no mindless.

He decided to explore the lit hall.

The size of the installation and its attention to detail staggered him. Mesmerized him. At one point, the corridor widened into three lanes. Sky-blue walls replaced the panel wood, while artificial palm trees, beach grass, and colorful flowerbeds adorned the path. In some places, trees rose up on both sides only to be chopped off at the ceiling, but dark imaging that resembled branches thick with leaves spread outward, creating an illusionary canopy. Soon the trees grew in number, narrowing the path to just one lane. Meadows broke out throughout the wooded area, where all sorts of flowers sprouted, while in the distance, some ten feet back, a calm sea—or a wall-sized flat-screen showing a calm sea—shone under a starry night. The distant silhouettes of giant mountains soared above the horizon, while columns of rock garnished with green tops sprouted out of the seafoam below. Lawn tables and chairs were set up along the walkway, so people could sit and enjoy the imaginary view. Behind a wall of glass was a nighttime beach, facing a pool fashioned into the guise of a sea. The horizon disappeared into a lightless ink that Gus suspected would be blazing with starlight if he walked into the beach room. Or sunlight, come the morning.

He reached the sliding doors leading to that wonderous mirage but they were locked. Access denied.

Gus's face soured at that. He really needed a bath.

More mind-boggling sights came into existence the deeper he wandered into the bunker. Office parks and homes shone under the pale moonlight. Glass partitions revealed well-kept but shadowy interiors of pure escapism. There was an amusement hall, with an arcade right out of the 1980s. A pool hall with billiards tables, bars, table tennis, the works. Two small movie theaters, a mini-golf course, shooting range, gyms, and swimming pools. This underground city rivaled anything he'd seen in Annapolis. He even spotted a go-kart racetrack perhaps a kilometer long. There was even a goddamned *food court*, with a dozen different restaurants, and that blew Gus's mind more so than the go-karts.

A government bunker had a *Pizza Hut*.

Oh, that pissed him off. That pissed him off more than being denied a dip in the pool.

When the fuck were the elected officials supposed to be *working* to save the world?

None of the doors leading to the compound's attractions would open for him, as if sensing he wasn't worthy to enter. Gus meandered through it all, lost in a daze. The lights behind him switched off once he was a certain distance away, while the road ahead continued to light up every three or four steps in front of him. Gus felt he was drifting through a museum of sorts, where every modern amenity of pre-outbreak civilization was on display. There were no people, however. Not a soul in sight, and no living quarters, either. Gus figured he was on a level geared toward fun and relaxation.

All out in the middle of fucking nowhere.

Under a goddamn mountain.

Considering the size, scope, and grandeur of the place, Gus was surprised politicians even bothered with Parliament Hill. He wanted to run for office just to get into one of those underground beaches.

The thought of his people back on Tancook sobered him up. He wondered if they might be up for a little relocating. Unless he was missing something, the bunker seemed intact. Perfect, even.

Except for that little thing about the mindless. And the bastards controlling them.

Especially them.

He entered another walkway—Gus certainly didn't call it a hallway, because no hallway was built to create the illusion of a beachside boardwalk, at midnight, with sailboats floating on an ocean as calm and flat as glass. He wanted a Mai-Tai just from looking at all that Caribbean goodness.

The floor lights kept coming to life, guiding him along.

Until he got to the waterfall.

The canyon behind him had grabbed his attention, and the seaside stroll amazed him, but the sector he just entered stopped him cold in his tracks.

The first thing he noticed was a waterfall, pouring from three stories up, over a glistening rockface. Tropical greenery clung to either side and flourished all around. The relative humidity in the room went from a comfortable thirty percent to a borderline sixty. Two pagodas created an ambience of Zen within the chamber. Arched bridges crossed over narrow canals, all lit up in a serene display of misted flora.

Gus stepped onto one little bridge, because it was lit up, and saw the goldfish swimming beneath him. That was the cherry of this subterranean cathedral of serenity. He shook his head and felt like swearing, a lot, but God probably expected him to curse a blue line, so he kept his mouth shut.

Then he saw it.

Behind the waterfall.

A single archway of fragmented light, blurred by falling water. It was off the illuminated trail, but at this point, nothing surprised him.

Gus stepped off the bridge and onto a slab of rock. He carefully threaded his way through a thick garden that he probably wouldn't have been allowed to walk on, but there was no other way unless he plunked down in the water. And he wasn't about to piss off the goldfish swimming in the canals.

The lights behind the waterfall flickered, and when he reached them, the most astonishing thing happened.

The archway blazed through the water in a fluid white rush and the rock wall within parted without a sound. A small elevator waited there, with that familiar redwood paneling and shiny brass railing.

Gus hesitantly stepped inside, enduring a brief shower.

The doors closed behind him.

And the trail lights leading up to the doors winked out, as if the golden walkway he'd been following had never existed in the first place.

40

The elevator doors opened.

One incandescent ceiling lightbulb flickered to life, forming a pale cone of light just outside of the elevator shaft. Beyond, Gus could see several computer terminals, each with a battalion of monitors stacked two high and three wide. These workstations ringed a central command console, where a naval officer's chair was perched upon a raised dais. A second source of light caught Gus's attention, a solitary glow that slowly drew him out of the elevator. There, some twenty paces away, was a secondary ring of computer terminals with accompanying monitors.

The light came from a small lamp, set to one side, well within that second ring of workstations.

Gus stepped into the high-tech grotto, scrutinizing the deep shadows of the chamber. Processors whispered evil nothings in the background.

Not a soul in sight.

At least, no one Gus could see.

The elevator doors closed behind him.

"Don't be… don't be alarmed," a voice said, causing Gus to jump.

The voice came from the second ring of computers. The little lamp flickered, as if someone briefly blocked its light by passing in front of it.

"I'm sorry," the voice said. "I… I wasn't able to communicate with you. There's been damage to the system, isolating me up here. Communication isn't my forte."

A giggle then, low and hoarse and strained.

Gus didn't move. He was still well armored, but weaponless.

"I… I won't hurt you," the voice said. "I think that should be clear. You wouldn't…" another unnerving giggle. "You wouldn't be here… if not for me."

"You were lighting up the hallways?" Gus asked.

"Ah… yes. To a point. In the main sectors the emergency lighting is automatic. To conserve power. We still… have considerable stores of it, but… why waste it? These days, power is like clean water. Clean air. Come closer. I won't bite."

But the words finished in a scratchy, throat-blasted giggle that rattled Gus's nerves.

"Please," the voice said.

The lights emanating from the monitors switched off, but the table lamp remained on. There was a motorized whirring, and half a figure—the shadowy head and shoulders of a man—rolled into view from behind the stacked computer screens.

"I'm here," the dark outline said. "Come closer."

Gus wavered. "You're not going to try anything?"

"I will not. You…" he chortled again. "You have my word."

"That don't mean much these days."

"Please. Remember. You're here because… I wanted you to be here."

Gus supposed that was true. "Where's here?"

"Security… command. The… the watchtower—the inner keep… of the king… the kingdom."

Gus took a cautious step forward, staying close to the wall. He eyed the edges of the room, watchful for others potentially hiding in the dark. All the while, the seated figure remained still.

Gus's boot kicked something, freezing him in place. He looked down and saw the outline of a plastic container the size of a pack of cigarettes on the floor. It was too dark to see anything else.

"Oh…" the giggle again. "The floor might be… might be filthy. Keep your boots on."

The giggle spiked in a wheezy piping that damn near made Gus look for a keyboard or a chair to swing, just in case.

"You're awfully fucking merry over there," he said.

"I'm sorry," the figure said, and genuinely sounded like he was. "It's a nervous reaction. If you've seen the things I've seen, you'd be… you'd be a little nervous, too."

"You're not crazy, are you?"

A solemn reckoning, then. "I don't think so."

Which, in Gus's mind, gave him a fifty-fifty chance that the man was fucking insane.

"Come closer," the figure urged.

Gus took another two steps before his foot crunched on another plastic container. Then another.

"You don't houseclean up here?" he asked.

"I'm sorry. Really. I… I didn't expect anyone. Really. Not ever. I thought… I thought I'd be alone here for the rest of my life… so… you understand. Things just got thrown around."

Gus kicked a clutter of plastics, and what he kicked rattled off more unseen garbage. He took another step and looked down. A carpet of discarded plastics covered the floor, thick enough to crowd the ankles of his boots.

The giggle again from the shadowy figure. "I'm sorry. The… the janitors haven't made their rounds in… in some time."

"Guess not," Gus said, and without thinking, he bent over and picked up one of the containers. Oddly enough, they all seemed to be the same size. He brought the item in close.

Deodorant stick.

An empty deodorant stick. Right down to the inner plastic.

"Well, at least you don't stink," Gus said under his breath. He casually dropped the used container.

"No, I don't stink. Well. Not much anyway. You get used to… to the smell. I suppose."

Gus moved closer to the man. He took a quick look at the computer screens, all showing video feed from surveillance cameras around Whitecap. Storefronts. Living quarters. Hallways. A screen switched feeds and displayed the empty beach that he'd just passed, but from the inside looking out. Sitting next to a keyboard in a bloom of ripped packaging was a case of deodorant sticks. Four of them, unopened.

Gus looked to the mystery figure seated in front of him. The man was in a wheelchair, some fifteen feet back or so, his features indiscernible in the dim light. What Gus did see, however, made him uneasy.

He'd seen this before.

Gus became aware of a smell, of unwashed flesh and unscrubbed crevices.

"Don't worry," the man said. "Don't… worry. As I said, I won't hurt you."

The silhouette shivered then, around the jawline. The speaker's skin was dark, again just barely visible, but the eyes, the right more so than the left, were wide open and blinking. All the while, the man's chin quivered as if he'd just taken a dip in arctic waters.

"Don't stare," he said, catching Gus's scrutiny, and he smiled, quelling that alarming trembling of the mouth. "Don't. It's not… it's not polite."

He ended that with another chuckle, one that he cut off, as if realizing the sound might very well be unnerving to his guest.

Which it was.

"Just stay right there," the seated man said. "Where you are. That's… that's close enough. For the moment."

The smile was a permanent thing, Gus soon realized, only diminished with a concentrated effort. The shivering of the lower jaw was just as continuous, as was the smell of the man's unattended ass crack.

"My name… is Joshua… Rogan." The head twitched then, but Gus forced himself to pay that no mind. "I was… I *am*…a research assistant working in… biology. With the medical corps stationed at Whitecap."

Gus nodded a greeting.

"I…" Rogan giggled again but quickly gained control over the involuntary action. "I… watched you come in. Watched you all… come in."

Gus straightened. "Watched us all come in. You do anything to the people with me? Because if you did…"

Rogan raised one arm in an odd jerk, as if a marionette was manipulating the limb.

"They're on the lower fifth," he said. "Looking for the hidden evacuation route."

"How do you know that?"

The edges of that shadowed face hitched in a smile, the lower jaw still shivering. "Been watching them, too. Watching everyone. Months of nothing and, suddenly, everything's on TV."

Rogan cackled then, and he allowed that ghastly laughter to fill the room.

"Been watching you, in particular. You're very brave. Or suicidal."

Gus didn't respond to that, but he did shuffle his feet, stirring up all that plastic underfoot.

"You've brought the barbarian hordes," Rogan said. "… to the gates. Of the kingdom. I never thought I'd see people again. Never, never. Let alone…."

He lifted an arm, pointing a finger. Gus looked over his shoulder, at the computer screens.

The mindless. Plowing through a corridor. Pawing at doors, at walls. Arms waved madly, shaking broken hands and fingers, destroying, *polluting* the charm of each sector in the compound. They slammed the screens of woodland wonders. They knocked over trees and trampled through greenery. They smashed into the wall displays, breaking scenes of seaside delights, shattering the careful illusions of Whitecap.

There was no thought to their search, no reason, just the maddening attraction to the residual stink clinging to Gus's armored ass.

"They're searching for you," Rogan explained, his jawline quivering. "Only you. I watched you shoot them, with the automatic weapons. I bet… I bet that was fun."

Gus frowned.

"No?" Rogan asked. He quickly changed the subject. "When you climbed into the ductwork, you surprised me. Surprised me even more when you… when you pulled out that dead tech. I … knew that man. To see him. I think… I think his name was…"

Rogan's shoulders trembled.

"*Chris!*" he blurted with a wild, lingering chuckle, stopping only when Rogan realized Gus didn't join in.

"Sorry," Rogan apologized, suddenly serious. "That wasn't as funny as I thought it was."

"No, it wasn't."

"In any case… the zombies… they're following you… by scent. By smell. I mean… you… smell badly."

"Sorry," Gus said. "Guess I'm in the right spot. How about you give me one of your no-stink sticks?"

"Certainly."

Gus didn't go for one, however. "So you've been waiting here, leading me along."

Rogan's trembling eased, just a bit. "I've been waiting… for someone… to come along. Anyone… to come along. I've been waiting. To turn over this… all of this… to what's been left over. I've been waiting for… you. I think. And your… companions."

Gus wasn't sure he understood. "What?" he finally got out.

Rogan fidgeted in his wheelchair. "We've had terrible things happen here. Terrible things. I was… I was the only one… left alive. I was… with a security team… when the breakout happened. And the virus spread. Like… like a fire."

Gus listened as a growing horror crept through his frayed nerves.

"The virus…" Rogan explained. "There are…. degrees to the virus. Ah, no. *Waves*. Yes. Waves. There was the first outbreak, like a mushroom cloud, so to speak. Those you disposed of by shooting in the head. The only way. The… *cinematic* way. But then, what we later learned, was that there was an unnoticed *second* outbreak. If a zombie was shot in the head, there was a chance that the corpse, during its decomposition, would… *spore*. That the virus would pollinate the air in a last-ditch effort to survive… its dead host. Only a small percentage of the corpses… but if you were anywhere near that five percent… before an air current could disperse it, and you breathed the spore *in*…"

Gus could only stare, and in that stretching silence, he whispered, "What?"

"A second wave of undead. Driven to spread the virus through bloody contact, just like the first. But if you were wounded or bitten, it would take control of a person much faster. Within seconds. *Seconds*."

Rogan cocked his head. "That's the trouble with weaponized strains…With the splicing and the mixing… there are so many levels to testing. So many variables to consider. And so many unknowns. You never really know the final outcome. Not without the proper protective measures, the proper control groups. When we got word that the first virus escaped… that was the beginning of the end. Why we came to Whitecap in the first place. To wait it all out. We even developed the TI serum, just in case, formulating it on what we knew about the initial strain. But even that… was a mistake."

Gus thought of Wallace. "Some people changed."

"Some changed, indeed," Rogan giggled, then grew serious. "We hoped the serum would immunize, and it did. But… it also… mutated. A percentage. In all honesty, the TI serum was rushed. A frantic solution that… we hoped would protect our people… against that first terrible strain. There were no control groups. Only subjects. There was no choice in the matter. Not for active military personnel. We were… we were told… were ordered…to tell them anything. Tell them it's a cure, but report. Record. Everything. Through authorized channels. Take further samples if and when necessary. So… they received the first doses because… they were going out there, you understand. Outside. They needed something. To protect them. They were the first test group."

Computers continued to whisper in the background, filling the silence between the two men.

"I knew one," Gus said. "A soldier from here. A special soldier. He was turning into a zombie, but he still… talked like a guy. Until the end."

"He retained his identity?"

"While I knew him."

"Fascinating." Rogan's jawline began to twitter. "He was an exception. One of Whitecap's soldiers… infected… the whole bunker. That's what happened here. He'd been injected with TI. Then one day, while posted in the med lab, he went full-on zombie. Went from a person… to zombie… in a heartbeat. He bit a nurse. Who bit a doctor. Who bit a waiting patient. One bit one and they became two. Two infected two more. Four infected four more, and so on. From there, it was a frenzy. Carnage."

Rogan's teeth chattered. "Less than a day. A day. Ninety percent of the populace had been turned. The security team I was with. There was a fight. We lost." He chuckled. "We didn't want the infected getting out. Couldn't let anyone in. Some of the soldiers… set explosive charges. Blew the entrance. To prevent anyone from entering. That worked. There were still zombies running around, some even *spored*… which infected the remainder of the soldiers. Two days later, I was the only one left. Secured myself in the upper levels. Here. In security command. Watched the undead… roam the corridors. I watched the madness…. I saw the PM walking about the lower floors with his family. Hunting for survivors. It was horrible. Horrible."

Gus took a deep breath, trying to forget his own experiences with the undead. He knew about horror. He knew about it very well.

"Then, someone came knocking," Rogan said with a giggle. "Or rather, digging. I watched." He pointed at the screens. "Watched it all, as the… knocking… the digging… the *grinding* drew the remainder of the zombies to the main entrance. Everyone. Everyone that could walk. Then the door was opened. Like a plug, in a bathtub. They all flowed out in a gush. Then the fighting started. I couldn't see. The cameras on the outside didn't work for me. I couldn't get them to work. They were broken. Or I didn't know the codes. So I waited. Waited for… whoever… when the door was opened.

"Except no one came. And I was left alone. Again. Except… Whitecap was clear of its zombies. This… all of this… is a paradise compared to what's out there. And I've been waiting. Hoping someone… worthy… would come. Before I die. To tell them what happened. And what might happen. From here on out."

That got Gus's attention. "What might happen?"

"While the zombies roamed Whitecap, I noticed some retained their… vigor… more so than others. Those same zombies, when… sustenance grew sparse… they would devour any of their dead cousins."

The very thought screwed up Gus's face. Then he remembered. "Those zombies," he asked. "Could they die like regular people? Like, being shot in the chest, as well as the head?"

Rogan thought about it. "I never noticed. Did you?"

"I did."

"Interesting. In truth, the spore zombies aren't truly dead. I've seen them… void themselves. They're just… infected. Perhaps your zombies were produced by inhaling spore? Or they were bitten or wounded by spore zombies?"

Gus thought of the masked douchebags and their weaponized mindless. "Maybe."

"Those were my thoughts…" Rogan added. "Behind the ones that… seemed to retain their speed. For a longer period of time. In any case, while the virus is certainly running out of material, it's still out there. And might very well be out there for a while yet. Until all are destroyed. Or decompose… into nothing. In any case, spore or not, they're still zombies. And you led a considerable… *pack*… into the kingdom."

Gus's helmet seemed to tighten around his skull. "Yeah. Guess I did. Sorry about that."

"Who are those people…?"

"They're with me," Gus answered. "We… we were running from a bunch of crazies who—who might be using zombies as shock troops."

That silenced Rogan. His jawline resumed its quivering. "That… is disturbing."

Gus nodded that it most certainly was.

"But… I didn't mean… those people on level five," Rogan pointed out. "I know they're with you. I meant *them*."

He pointed to the computer monitors.

One of the great mysteries after the fall of civilization was where the government went after fleeing the collapsing capital. Most believed the Prime Minister would be whisked away to a secret bunker, deep under the earth. There, he would hunker down and wait out the end of the virus with his family, supporting staff, and a few selected friends. During his isolation, the PM would plan for his return, with whatever security forces remaining, in order to re-establish law, order, and government.

There were plenty of such bunkers south of the border, owned by governments and mega-corporations, but accessing them was a challenge. First, a person had to know the location of the installation, as such information would be classified. Then, there was the understanding that the bunkers were heavily fortified topside, with all manner of defensive measures in place to deter unauthorized individuals. Those measures included armed forces with orders to shoot trespassers on sight. Even if an intruder could sidestep the security considerations, they still had to bypass the main doors, sealed up and built to withstand nuclear blasts.

Finding and accessing a bunker south of the border was out of the question, however, since the radiation belt after the reactor meltdowns prevented individuals from either country from crossing over.

So, when the Vulture walked through the main doors of what was obviously an extensive installation, his mind was whirling with possibilities.

Who might be inside?

What was inside?

And were there weapons?

Initially, the Vulture didn't expect anyone to be inside the bunker, since the doors were wide open. The Leather had passed a veritable field of withered dead—hundreds of corpses leading up to the cavern entrance and within. None of those bodies had belonged to the Leather, however, and that lifted the Vulture's hopes even more.

The mindless that had been cut down on the bunker's threshold had been shot, however. By guns. Perhaps a lot of guns. Which meant ammunition. The Vulture wanted weapons. Automatic weapons. Military-grade. And the ammunition to go with it. Commodities that had all been savagely used up.

It all meant power.

Dozens of the Leather swarmed forward into the enormous garage, their crossbows raised and ready. They stepped over the fallen carcasses of the recently shot mindless, threading their way to open concrete. The Vulture wandered in behind them with a handful of his own personal guard. Military guns and ammo would be a prize. The Vulture would take any other supplies in the absence of weapons, but for now, he wanted the weapons. He wanted the death from above.

The size and scope of the garage impressed him, and he wondered just how big the bunker was. The outer defenses had taken considerable damage, and the main doors were obviously opened for a reason, but otherwise the bunker's innards appeared fully functional. There were lights. Lights meant power. Power meant a source, just waiting to be discovered and accessed, and the Leather had minions capable of carrying out repairs if needed.

Under the ceiling's fragmented lighting system, which resembled great glaring saucers, the Vulture slowed to a stop. His personal guard of a dozen or so stopped as well. The Vulture inspected the nearby building—a security bunker within a bunker. He then studied the abandoned vehicles scattered throughout the vast parking area. Trucks, sedans, even a pair of backhoes, and, God almighty... a *limousine*. In the shadows, the vehicle resembled a sleek black automotive shark.

The Vulture shifted ever so slightly, exchanging neutral glances with the Bronze, but they both knew what the other thought.

The Dog Tongue would be pleased.

Even if they didn't find any weapons or supplies, the bunker itself was a prize. It was an honest-to-God secret base, with its doors wide open. A platform to prepare and launch more strikes into the new world.

The thought of others knowing about this base troubled the Vulture, however. Several of the mindless had been cut down in the enormous corridor leading to the garage. The living dead had cornered survivors in the security booth, evident by the bloody prints still on the laminated glass. A vicious patchwork of skin fragments and hair stuck to the surface, indicating that whatever had been inside that mini-bunker had greatly agitated the mindless. That mess practically covered the entire length of the glass.

The Leather set up a perimeter around the checkpoint, their loaded crossbows aimed outwards. Some of them used the little carts as cover, while a handful inspected one cart left in the middle of the lane. The Vulture ignored his minions' maneuverings. He marched over to the security post and halted when a Leather held up the first of three discarded battle rifles. 'ST1X' was stamped on the shoulder stock, along with 'BELGIUM MADE' and a string of serial numbers.

The Vulture took the offered rifle and studied it. He placed it against his shoulder and looked down the sights. He turned towards his personal guard and aimed at his accompanying meat puppet, who was on his knees. The meat grew still, very much aware of the weapon.

This particular puppet, the one who had called himself Top Gun, had done well killing one of the escaping islanders, and the Vulture had rewarded the man by not stashing him back into the trunk of a car. He still wore the mask and gag, but after making the kill shot, the Vulture decided to take him along. A nearby lesser held the meat puppet's rifle, just in case it was needed again.

Despite the meat puppet's obedience and obvious worth to the cause, he was still a meat puppet.

The Vulture squeezed the trigger with an audible click.

The meat puppet tensed, his eyes blinking behind his mask.

The Vulture handed the weapon over to an underling and took a second weapon. He shouldered it and aimed again, right at the prisoner's head.

Click.

The meat puppet slumped in relief.

The Vulture handed that weapon over, his fingers wiggling for the third. When he got the last gun, he noticed the full magazine on top.

He took aim again.

The meat puppet slowly shook his head, not believing how his day was going.

The Vulture stared down the sights and, at the last second, fired a raging blast *over* the head of the prisoner. The meat puppet flinched, grabbing his head, right where it was supposed to be.

Muffled chuckles erupted from the nearby Leather watching the scene. The meat puppet lowered his shaking hands and nodded, appreciating the joke for what it was.

The Vulture did not hand over the weapon. He turned away from the cowering slave and approached the security checkpoint, a long booth soiled by the touch of the mindless. The booth's door was locked, and the Vulture noted a security keypad nearby. He studied the screen for a moment before pressing a thumb on an important-looking button.

Nothing happened. Until a voice said, "Please enter your authorization code now."

The Vulture ignored that. He stepped around to the glass and wiped a bloody section clean. He peered inside, seeing very little of interest beyond the bloody paw prints marring the window. Then he saw the ceiling, and the drooping grate revealing a man-sized opening.

"Get back," the Vulture ordered, and his minions pulled away from the security bunker. Seeing what their leader was about to do, most took cover behind the scattering of vehicles or the corners of the booth.

The Vulture took aim at the glass, dead center, and fired.

A dazzling line pummeled the surface, the light show winking out after contact. Those shots crackled back into the garage in other directions, causing the Leather to duck. The glass remained intact. The Vulture ceased firing, letting the weapon hang at arm's length. He sighed, then proceeded to the shut door, where he took aim at the keypad.

He didn't fire, however.

After a few thoughtful seconds, he lowered the gun. Blowing out the device wouldn't help; it'd probably only make it more difficult to open.

The Vulture met the Bronze's listless eyes. "Go in. If you find any more of these…" he held up the ST1X, "make use of them. Capture the girl. The others are disposable."

Orders received, the Bronze hefted his executioner's axe. The hammer hung from his belt. He nodded and lumbered forward, following the blood-spattered trail that led into Whitecap. The mindless had followed their prey's scent to the checkpoint but then lost the trail. So they'd taken the only path into the compound in an attempt to pick up on it again.

The Vulture turned away from his menacing henchman and studied the door once again. He then looked over at the carts.

"See what works," the masked leader said to a lesser, gesturing at the vehicles. "Then go back and bring me Carson."

<h1 style="text-align:center">42</h1>

"Those guys," Gus said, watching the tall masked man with the battle axe strut towards a ramp, "are fucking assholes. Shitty-assed, skid-marked assholes."

The chittering of Rogan's jaw picked up speed.

Gus compared the progress of the mindless to that of the advancing killers with the medieval weaponry. His balls almost dropped off when he saw the one with the bird mask pick up the ST1X. When the freak fired the weapon, Gus could only shake his head.

"They've been on our ass ever since they tried killing us on a little island," he said.

"A little island?" Rogan repeated.

"A summer camp."

"Ah."

Gus waved a hand. "Don't you have, I dunno, guns or something? In case fuckheads get inside?"

"We do, but I couldn't access them." Rogan shivered in his wheelchair.

Gus watched him, knowing there was something seriously wrong. "You okay?" he finally asked.

Rogan chuckled. "I most certainly… am not okay."

With a mechanical whirling of gears, the wheelchair rolled towards the light.

Gus straightened.

Rogan's face was a fluttering, twitching rictus of pain. His complexion was red, as if he'd absorbed far too much sun, and pieces of his skin were peeling away like bark off a birch tree. His facial hair was non-existent, and his teeth, though fair, were the color of amber.

Joshua Rogan certainly did not look okay.

Some changed, Gus remembered him saying. "You got a shot of TI?"

"I self-administered a shot… of TI," Rogan admitted. "And every other serum in its final testing stages. As I said, I was with the security team. Whitecap had been overrun. It was decided that I should… inoculate myself. Just in case. I was the one who found patient zero. And that was… after the fact. After… Whitecap had fallen. And I was the only one left. I found out by… watching recorded security feeds from the med lab. Sadly… that was after I'd taken the shot. Multiple shots. I'm afraid I was of the mind that more was better than less."

"Jesus Christ, Joshua," Gus whispered.

The computers continued their chirping in the background.

Rogan shrugged. "It was… a momentary lapse… of reason. Brought on… by panic. I've been changing slowly… at first. But… things seem to be progressing rapidly. I don't know what the final stage will be, but I don't think it will be… flattering."

His jaw shook at that, and a raspy wheeze of a giggle left him.

"But I do think… I'm taking the change… well."

Gus cringed. "You're going to have to wear more deodorant, Josh. This ain't working anymore."

Rogan appeared genuinely puzzled at that, before squeezing his eyes shut in understanding. "Pass me one of those. Please."

Gus hesitated before doing as asked.

"Thank you," Rogan said. With trembling fingers, he popped the cover off and extended the stick.

"You wanna do that later?" Gus asked. He nodded at the monitors. "We got other things to do here."

"Just wanted to show you," Rogan said. "What I've been… eating. All this time."

And to Gus's horror, Rogan bit into the deodorant as if snacking on a chocolate bar. The research assistant chewed loudly, enjoying the mouthful. He sized up the stick before licking around the edges of his bite.

That was a sight Gus knew he would remember in his dreams.

"It's not…" Rogan explained, "as bad as you might think."

Gus shook his head. "Yeah."

"I wasn't always like this, of course. It was just… cornflakes didn't do it for me anymore. I used this brand and, one morning, when I decided… to put some on…"

"You decided to eat it."

A guilty-looking Rogan inspected the stick, and for a moment, Gus thought the man was going to lose it.

"Yes," the research assistant finally said, with a surprising amount of control. "Yes. Exactly that."

"Why the sudden urge to eat deodorant, Josh?" Gus asked.

"I've pondered that myself. The smell drew me in. Smell is closely associated with taste, you know. Regardless, it's what I crave these days. What keeps me… going. Without question…a side effect. Of the multiple TI shots. The ample food provisions here… no longer appealed to me. Considering what I… could be ingesting… I think… this is acceptable."

Rogan looked at Gus. "I'm not… a bad person," he explained. "I saved… you. After all. And I'll save your companions. On condition."

Gus knew he wasn't going to like it. "What's that?"

"I'll… tell you later." The research assistant smiled, then said, "I've exhausted the med lab's supplies of chemicals… trying to cure myself. Turns out… I'm not a very good scientist. This place… is yours. It's perfectly safe. Any spore that… might've been active has long dispersed and perished. We've established that it can't survive long. In that form. If you wish… Whitecap, and all within her…is yours."

Gus stared at the sick man.

"If you… can repel the barbarians," Rogan finished with a sick smile.

"You got any weapons?"

"None."

"Don't you have an armory or something?"

"Three, in fact. With a surplus of munitions. But I don't have the authorization."

"Or the codes," Gus finished for him.

"Or the codes." Rogan half-shrugged. "I'm sorry."

"That's okay. I'm not that great a shot anyway. You have anything else? Pipes or heavy wrenches? Axes? Bats?"

Rogan stiffened in his wheelchair. "Bats?"

"Bats?" Gus asked with hope. "You have any bats?"

"We have… a batting cage. In the LE section of the complex."

"What's LE?"

"Leisure and Entertainment."

"Oh. Okay. So you have bats there?"

"Aluminum ones."

It took Gus a second to absorb that.

"Where?" he finally asked.

43

Carson lay in the trunk of one of the cars.

It was dark, and his legs hurt like unholy fuck. The Leather had taken a hammer not only to his toes, but to his knees as well. He wasn't a doctor, but the way those ten little piggies had popped apart… well, he figured the shivers he was feeling were from the onset of some serious infection.

The worst day of his life was venturing out to Matheson by himself and getting caught by those masked cocksuckers. He should have killed himself before letting it happen. The only thing worse than his current physical pain was the knowledge that he had doomed the rest of the islanders to an existence of servitude. Or death. Or worse.

Carson wasn't a particularly pleasant man, nor was he particularly optimistic, but he tried to be fair. Thought things evened out on their own if you gave them time, though he didn't always have the patience to wait. This time, however, as his lower legs throbbed, and a disturbing cold gripped his lower back, he didn't think things were going to even out. Not this time.

Sooner or later, they're going to open this trunk, he thought before the hurt of his ruined legs tried to short-circuit his tortured brain. And when they did, he was going to claw for the nearest set of eyes or balls he could find.

Just so they knew there would be no breaking him.

Just so they'd kill him. And that would be the end of it.

So when he heard what sounded like a muffled grunt immediately followed by cries of distress, Carson lifted his head and paid attention.

A short scream of pain, then a crinkling of bone.

Someone growled and huffed, as if throwing a punch. The smack of bare fists and a curt grunt followed, then a startling slam of meat upon thin metal.

Another scream, and that sound was snuffed out.

Then nothing.

Wires of light bled through the trunk's seams, but not enough to see anything. Carson's eyes were wide yet saw nothing. He heard plenty, however. A low shambling step, of someone moving around outside.

The steps grew louder.

Carson blinked, wondering what the hell was going on out there, and heard nothing more. Until a weight landed on the rear bumper of the car, causing the vehicle to sag.

"Hey!" Carson shouted. "Hey!"

The weight lifted from the rear bumper.

"Hey! *Who's out there?*"

No answer. Nothing for the longest time, or so it seemed to the trapped man.

Then the release of the lock.

The trunk popped open, allowing precious light to enter. From nearby headlights, but light all the same.

A shadow stood over him, blocking the glare, but what flared around the figure was blinding enough for the mechanic. He shielded his eyes and was so surprised that he'd forgotten his original plan.

"You Carson?"

A woman's voice.

He peeked out from behind his hands. "Yeah."

Carson squinted, studied her from chin to chest, where his voice failed him.

There was a bloody hole close to where the heart should be.

"Well?" Collie asked. "You want out of that fucking trunk or not?"

*

Some twenty minutes later, the EV returned with Carson in the backseat. The driver steered the machine straight on through, causing the Leather inside the entry tunnel to jump out of the way. Heads turned as the EV drove by, slowing to a stop outside of the locked security room.

The Vulture appreciated that kind of loyalty.

The driver, wearing a bulky leather jacket and generic zipper mask, got out of the vehicle and with a grunt pulled Carson onto the floor. The Leather dragged the mechanic by his arms to the Vulture.

That it was a woman, no one cared. There were several in their ranks, equally as vicious as their male counterparts. Or ever more so.

The Vulture ignored her as she propped up the crippled man against one leg.

"Open this," the Vulture said to Carson, indicating the door's keypad.

His features contorted, Carson looked from the Vulture to the door. "I can't reach it," he seethed.

The driver manhandled the mechanic upright, but failed to get him any higher. A second Leather stepped in, and together they got him onto his knees.

Which were broken.

And Carson wailed upon impact.

The Vulture sighed in frustration. He glanced around, looking for a chair before setting his sights on his last meat puppet.

"Bring him here," the leader ordered two of the Leather. They brought Top Gun face-to-face with the Vulture.

"Hands and knees," the Vulture instructed, and the two Leather made certain the meat puppet obeyed.

The Vulture turned to Carson. "Sit on him."

The mechanic's pained face twisted into a question.

"Sit," the Vulture whispered, close to losing patience. He hefted the automatic ST1X as a warning.

Carson screamed as he was positioned on top of Top Gun's back. The Leather who had fetched Carson from the trunk steadied him, then produced a straight-blade combat knife from her boot. She placed the knife to Carson's ear, gripping the blade underhanded, as if about to pick away at a block of ice.

No one gave the knife a second thought. In fact, the Vulture approved of the gesture with a single nod.

Carson's head hung low, very much aware of the blade at his ear. Sweat ran freely down his profile, and he lifted his gaze to consider the keypad.

"I can't open this," he said.

"Open it," the Vulture said calmly.

"You need a code."

"Then break the code."

Carson shook his head. "I can't break the code. I'm just a mechanic."

Silence then, as the Vulture stared at the back of the mechanic's head. "Then bypass it. Take the thing apart. Or be blown apart."

With that, the masked leader pointed the ST1X at Carson's back. Carson fumed and fidgeted, while the female Leather kept him on his human bench.

"I don't even have a fucking screwdriver, you moron," Carson rumbled.

The female Leather reached down with her free hand and grabbed the mechanic's wrist. Keeping him in place with her other (with the blade now at his collar), she extended his hand to the keypad and flattened it against the lower edge of the console.

The Vulture watched her force him into position. "If he doesn't do anything in the next five seconds, you may cut him."

The female Leather didn't appear to hear him. Still holding onto Carson's wrist, she stepped out from behind him, as he no longer needed her for balance. Her hand slid up the back of his and paused for only a second… before she punched in a series of numbers on the keypad, the bright characters stretching across a digital display.

A confused Vulture looked at the female Leather.

In the same second, the security door slid open, whereupon the female Leather spun and punched her knife through the Vulture's neck. There was a choking spurt of blood, a reedy gasp of air, and even though the Vulture wore a mask, there was no mistaking the surprise in the man's eyes.

And in the split instant before his knees gave out, the driver grabbed the ST1X, flipped it about, and unleashed a killer light show.

Six of the nearby Leather were cut apart in an instant, their bloody torsos flung back by the unexpected burst.

Collie dropped back to the doorway and lit up three more of the Leather, blowing apart their heads in a startling display of tracer fire, rags, and brain matter.

That drove the remainder of the pack to take cover. Collie released two more short bursts. Dozens of bullets flashed and crackled across the hide of one of the EVs in a charred line, the force of the blast shoving the vehicle a foot away.

Carson fell with a yell, tumbling off the meat puppet who was still on his knees while screaming, "*Oh Jesus! Oh Jesus!*"

Collie swung the weapon upon the puppet.

"I'm not with them!" the man pleaded.

She wavered, but only for a split second. Shadows were moving in the garage.

"Get him in there!" she roared as she shot a Leather popping up from behind a parked vehicle. The masked man flew backwards as if he'd been hit by rockets, his crossbow flying from his fingers.

One of the Leather swung his crossbow around the corner of the security booth and fired.

The bolt grazed the material not a hair away from Collie's left ear.

She blew her attacker's hands off at the wrist, and the man fell back, screaming.

The freed meat puppet grabbed Carson by the shirt collar and fell into the booth. Collie followed, releasing another burst as she shuffled inside. She got one foot across the threshold when a crossbow bolt nailed her to the doorframe.

The impact surprised her, stunned her even, and she released a grunt. The bolt had sunk into her chest, to the fletching. She slid down the wall just a bit, hearing the scree-scraw of a barbed head dragging over the booth's steel hide. There was no pain, just the brief disorientation of being knocked off-balance.

Two Leather rolled out from behind EVs, while a dozen more popped up from behind the vehicles where they'd taken cover. Collie lifted her battle rifle with one hand and blew away one figure before strafing right and shredding two more in shocking burps of meat and fabric. The remainder of the crossbowmen once again dove for cover.

But those already on the floor took aim.

One bolt took Collie in her knee, dropping her to the concrete. A second bolt pierced her chest, breaking a rib and puncturing a lung right up to the shaft's flights. A third bolt zapped her left shoulder, rocking her back.

The remaining Leather shouted.

Carson and that human stool hauling him into the booth were screaming at her. Collie caught some movement through the wide pane of laminated glass. Shadows darted along the face of the booth, just barely visible through the sheet of gore.

A Leather wielding a medieval spear appeared around the corner, poised to stab.

Collie whipped up the battle rifle and drew an explosive line up the figure's center. Bloody firecrackers erupted from his back.

"Get in here!" the human stool screamed at her.

She tried to stand when a bolt nailed her right shoulder.

She spun with the impact and took two more missiles to the chest, each one driving her against the doorframe. Another bolt missed her face by an inch, while two more bounced off the booth. Everything was becoming slippery. She attempted to lift the rifle, but her right arm refused to respond, and she knew in an instant it was as fucked up as her left.

Two Leather popped up behind an EV, already aiming those jacked-up medieval needle-spitters.

Collie knew she couldn't get either one in time. So she slid her ass across the doorframe, into empty space, and let the impact of those two incoming bolts blast her backwards—into the booth.

She landed on her back.

"Jesus Christ!" Carson screamed.

Two leather-bound bastards holding, of all things, battle axes appeared in the open doorway.

Collie couldn't lift her rifle up when she was standing, but now that she was flat on her back she had no issue angling the gun upwards a few inches. She blasted the attackers, cutting both across the knees, causing them to collapse and grab for stumps that gushed scarlet.

"*Hit that button,*" she shouted.

The man-stool launched himself at the door controls. He hit the red button.

The door slid shut, just as the shadows outside converged upon the closing portal. They didn't make it. The booth was once again secured.

His hands shaking, the man-stool pulled off his mask, revealing a lightly bearded face that had completely shit itself of all color.

Someone smashed a club against the laminated glass, and all three of them flinched.

Collie pulled herself to a sitting position. "I'm getting fucking tired of these nut sacks."

She discarded the ST1X and crawled toward Carson, who wormed his way out of her path. She flicked a switch on one of the computer terminals and hauled a wheeled office chair over to sit on. She collapsed onto the furniture with a gasp. A considerable amount of blood spattered the white floor as she leaned over a keyboard.

The monitor demanded security clearance.

"Authorization," Collie seethed in a furious voice. "You want a code?"

Her fingers nimbly punched in a series of characters. The monitor flashed red, and next to the terminal a plastic cover popped up, revealing a second red button—one specially made to withstand a heavy impact. A klaxon blared to life overhead, warning all individuals to move their asses. The remaining Leather surrounding the booth glanced up at the mechanical sound.

"Here's a fucking code for you," Collie said. She hammered the waiting button with the ball of her fist.

The world outside the booth erupted into cleansing flame.

For a full ten seconds.

The figures battering the glass fell away as if the floor had been yanked out from under them. There was no screaming from beyond, only that muted roar of fire jetting from unseen vents above and below.

"Decontamination box," Collie wearily explained to the two men staring. "'Course, the doors are usually closed when this happens. And I… skipped hosing them down with heavy sanitizer. Figured a shot of the red and heavy was better. Thoughts?"

Carson didn't reply.

The human stool beside him didn't say a word, either.

"Good," Collie said. She eyed one, then the other, and then noticed the crossbow bolts sticking out of her body. She inspected the flights and focused on the human stool.

"You're one of the slaves?" she asked.

"Yeah," he said, rubbing his eyes.

"You gonna give me a hard time?"

The man met her eyes. The ST1X was on the floor, within easy reach if he wanted it. There were even a few rounds remaining.

"Not me," he muttered in pure mental exhaustion.

The flames continued washing the window and the parking garage outside.

"Thought so," Collie muttered.

And went back to watching the fire.

44

Gus hurried along a concrete hallway, a hidden passage that linked several of the underground amenities in the commercial sector. A single rail of light overhead lit the way, illuminating a bare concrete floor and walls. Every fifteen feet or so, the ceiling light winked on as he raced along. Rogan would be watching where he could, the assistant explained, but the back passages didn't have the same extensive surveillance system in place. He also mentioned that his memory was failing him. He promised Gus to do everything in his power to help him repel the barbarians, as the assistant kept referring to them, but for the most part… Gus was on his own.

Which was fine, Gus figured.

He'd been too damn reliant on Collie anyway. Too quick to follow. Not that Collie was a bad person to follow. She was the best. But now… she was gone, and Gus realized he had to start thinking for himself rather than wait for orders.

The thought of her made his heart ache, and his throat clutched until it hurt. Unable to wipe at his eyes because of his helmet's visor, Gus blinked away the sadness. Collie would not approve.

The lit floor below him stretched out ahead about a dozen paces. Gus felt like he was chasing a moving void that was always just out of reach. Rogan told Gus not to worry about his own safety. There were only two ways into the security command center. One was the secret elevator that Gus had used. The other was through a series of stairwells that linked the many levels of the bunker.

And when Gus left him, two steel doors closed, sealing the assistant within Whitecap's inner keep.

The lighting ahead exposed a stairwell stamped with the block characters

'A7' on the wall. He hurried down the seven flights of stairs, all the way to ground level, and by the time he reached 'A1', his legs were aching dearly. His treacherous foot was in full revolt, and the other one wasn't too happy either.

Gus hung off the steel railing, his shoulders lurching, and stood at an intersection. The steps continued below, and if he leaned out over the railing, he could just make out 'B1'. Those steps would take him deeper underground, under the ground entrance, and he could only guess at what was kept down there.

He studied the three wide passageways open before him. The C-area corridor was to the right of the stairwell. That would take him back to the underground paradise he'd walked through earlier, except this time he would be backstage, in the 'Authorized Personnel Only' sections.

Barbarians, he thought.

Forcing himself into a jog, Gus left the stairwell behind and forged ahead, the lights flicking on as he labored along, puffing like a steam engine. Black double doors passed by, leading to the shopping sector and woodlands he'd seen on the other side. Across from each set of doors was a techy-looking area filled with computer terminals, filing cabinets, and doors leading to, presumably, additional storage areas. A single sliding door with a keypad granted access to those rooms, but a couple were opened.

Gus rushed by them all.

"Where the hell's… one of them… goddamn buggies?" he rasped, slowing to a forced march and grimacing with every step. The helmet and body armor weren't as heavy or claustrophobic as his firefighter's gear, but it was every bit as hot. Hotter since he was inside the temperature-controlled innards of a mountain fortress. Whatever thin layers of body fat he might've stored over the winter were quickly melting.

Doors came and went, some spaced apart only a few meters, others more than thirty.

He was getting close now. Very close. Rogan said he would have to go back the way he traveled, then follow the lit hallways until he reached the batting cages.

Rogan. Poor bastard. All alone this whole time, living in what was essentially a giant grave. Bound to a wheelchair and munching on, of all things, deodorant sticks.

That made Gus stop in his tracks.

Well, shit, he thought. When he put it that way, how could the guy *not* be just a little insane?

I'm not… a bad person," the assistant had said. *"I saved… you. After all. And I'll save your companions."*

Gus walked on a few more steps and faced the doorway marked 'Batting Cages'. There were two bolt locks on his side, both unlocked, and when Gus tried turning the knob first, it didn't move. A second later there was an audible click, and the door opened.

I'll be watching where I can, Rogan had also said, just before Gus left him. Whatever surveillance cameras the bunker had were expertly hidden. Gus didn't see anything that resembled a black, overturned snow cone.

He turned the doorknob and cautiously stuck his head inside.

Two lonely lights barely lit up six cages, six distinct lanes divided by netting. Gus realized he was at the rear of the batting area, opposite where the balls would be belted. Three pitching machines were aimed at their respective home plates, one of which was located about ten feet away from him, standing like a silent sentinel cannon. Another three machines were parked in a distant corner to Gus's left. An artificial turf covered the floor, and lawn chairs were just visible at the other end, providing onlookers a place to perch while they waited their turn.

Or whatever. Gus couldn't give a fuck about the particulars. He wanted the goods, and he saw them. Mounted on a gray wall, on the left side of the batting area. The bats stood tall and proud and beckoned him like Olympic torches. Most were colored, from bright orange to glow-in-the-dark green.

Gus then saw the clear glass, which ran the length of the room, right behind where the spectators' chairs were set up.

"Why, Lord?" Gus whispered at the ceiling. "Why do you save my ass, only to kick it back into the shitter? Time after time? I mean… fuck."

Keeping abreast of the netting and the shadows, Gus discovered his second wind as he walked past the individual batting lanes. Halfway through, he discovered the middle lane wasn't enclosed at all, and actually led to the front of the batting area.

He turned the corner, eyes on the glass wall, and eventually reached the bat rack. Wood and alloy bats were firm to the touch. Numbers flittered by, designating weight of each bat. He stopped at a plain gray aluminum slugger, with the number '8' above it. The plainness of that length of metal, soon to be head splitter, attracted him.

Gus took the bat and held it samurai style. It was a good weight. Just under two pounds, yet powerful, and ready to smash.

"Sorry, woodies," he muttered to the others. "I've found Miss Right."

A light flickered on outside the cages from the main walkway, and a shadow raced up to the glass. A floppy hand, boneless from the wrist up, smashed against the clear partition, and sent oily rivulets shooting in all directions. The thing pressed its face against the surface, flattening a cheek, and stretching the skin around a milky eyeball.

An eyeball that slowly split open from the pressure.

Gus grimaced at the sight.

His grimace deepened as more undead (he discovered he had a problem with thinking of these things as alive) caught up and joined the first one at the window. He didn't know how they'd tracked him through what he suspected should have been an air-tight bunker. Maybe the smell afflicting him got sucked up into an airduct or something. In any case, they'd found him. The rest of the pack charged right up to the window and crashed into it like the mindless monsters they were. No more than three dozen of the creatures.

Gus held his bat across his pelvis and glowered at the hateful things.

Then he remembered where he was.

And what was with him.

He retreated, keeping to the shadows, and stopped in a corner with the discarded pitching machines. He studied the black mesh enclosing each designated batting lane. The mesh extended upwards, where it was suspended in an intricate lattice consisting of more rope and support rods hanging from the ceiling.

It was the finest netting Gus had ever seen in his life.

He approached the midway point and rested for all of ten seconds, while his plan took form.

All the while, the mindless tracked him, pounding upon the glass.

He would have to work fast. Very fast. And, even then, he'd have to kill them as if he were in a supercharged game of whack-a-mole, because they would be pissed. Super pissed. And flailing, maybe even desperate.

Excitement began to build as Gus walked up the center lane partitioning the six batting cages, three on either side, towards the main entrance.

This would be close. So very close.

He eyed the door controls. There were two buttons, clearly marked, along with a third one labeled "lock."

The zombies moved toward the entrance, ready to intercept. They were shifting, pawing, piling onto one another, a terrifying multi-legged amoeba of flesh and bone. Eyes watched him. Teeth snapped. Fingers dragged over the surface of the glass, some bursting under the extreme pressure. More faces pressed up against the glass, which was becoming a nightmarish smear of skin and blood.

"Careful what you wish for… bitches."

Gus hefted the bat and tapped the door control.

The portal swung inward.

The scrum of zombies fell forward in a gush, landing in a noisy, howling sprawl. The ones pushing from behind fell over them, as they, in turn were shoved from behind.

Gus didn't wait for them to rise. He was already at the end of the middle lane and turning right, back towards the corner filled with pitching machines, bypassing and staying clear of all those fine batting meshes just hanging in the wind.

The first few zombies to stand charged forward, heedless of Gus's more precise route, and charged after him at an angle—going *through* the netting. The first lane collapsed with an alarming crackle, the mesh falling over at least four gimps. That cleared the way for the rest, but even as the others charged forward, their feet became entangled. One runner avoided the trapped few until a zombie caught under the mesh attempted to rise.

Pulling the net backwards.

Which yanked the charging zombie off his feet and onto his face. That ugly spill tripped up two more right behind him, and they went down in a savage heap.

Gus backed himself into the corner and watched the mayhem.

Mindless raved and trudged over the netting, stomping over the ones trapped underneath. That heaving mess slowed them until they reached the second batting lane. They trundled forward, their fingers stabbing through the mesh. More than a few digits were bowed backward until snapping. The mindless lurched into the netting and the combined weight pulled the support lattice down from the ceiling with a clatter. More zombies were entangled, until the whole floor resembled a spidery oil spill. Those still trying to rise hampered the charge of those free, until, ultimately, they all went down.

Which opened the way for the last of them… and those that got past their struggling companions ran face-first into the netting of the *third* batting lane, yanking a final layer of mesh from the ceiling. The whole area became a thrashing, seething marsh of rising and falling bodies, becoming increasingly entangled with every passing second. In every instance where one zombie attempted to stand, the surrounding chaos pulled the thing back down.

It was glorious.

Gus waited until the foremost of the mindless got within range—a man with the netting pulled tight over his head and screaming through a mouthful of mesh. Gus broke open his skull with one swing—that unsettling crack of metal on bone serving as a starting pistol. When the creature went down, Gus retreated to the bat rack, while the entire floor attempted to follow him.

They could not.

It was a chaotic, lilting tug of war, with no unity beyond being ensnared in the net. Zombies would stand only to be yanked off their feet when others trapped underneath a section would rise. Those covered in mesh would inadvertently drag the net over others. All the while, the lattice of rods and ceiling hooks—pulled down by the mindless—became an anchor, slowing the undead even more.

Gus picked his second target and bashed in its skull. He killed a third, then a fourth, avoiding stepping onto the net itself.

Plenty of zombies remained.

"Fuck me," Gus muttered, realizing just how many were after him. The sight of all those trapped gimps deflated his initial elation of a successful plan. It was going to take *time* to slaughter them all. And energy.

Thanks, Lord, he mentally projected.

Taking a deep breath, he smashed the next head.

<h1 style="text-align:center">45</h1>

Roughly three dozen of the Leather followed the trail of the mindless. Blood streaked the walls in gruesome bar codes, while thick spatters of gore coated the floor.

It was as if a bleeding mob had squeezed their collective asses through a narrow passage. As the Leather delved deeper into the bunker's hidden realms, overhead lights automatically switched on. The Bronze strode behind the advancing Leather, surrounded by a handful of minions. His mask barely acknowledged the artificial splendor of the bunker's indoor beach or shimmering night sky. He didn't care for the shop façades or the numerous sport and entertainment attractions.

He wanted the prize.

For the Dog Tongue.

The Bronze gripped his executioner's axe in one fist. Somewhere in this subterranean maze was a little girl. The little girl was important. Very important to the Leather's plans of expansion. The bunker, however, had the potential to be even more so.

There were weapons to be found.

He could smell it.

But before the Leather could devote time to finding those weapons, he had to contend with the task at hand. So, they followed their unleashed hounds, keeping just enough distance from the mob, and let the mindless do the thing they did best.

Find the meat.

The entrances leading to the bunker's amenities were locked, and one of the Leather with a bat actually clubbed the glass—to no effect. The Bronze barked at the minion in a rare display of anger. They needed to employ stealth, not brute force. There was no need to smash anything. Not on this particular hunt.

Something caught the Bronze's attention, however.

The place was *clean*.

Despite the deluge of bodies leading up and into the bunker, this section was *cleared* of the dead. Which puzzled him.

The lights continued to switch on for the Leather as they strode past elaborate sets resembling beach fronts draped in shadow.

Shops, the Bronze noted. So many *shops*. As if the living believed reconstructing the old world would have any benefit. The old world was gone. Forever. Those who believed otherwise were either dying or already dead.

The Leather ahead stopped and gathered before a shoe shop.

The Bronze saw why.

One of those small golf carts had been jammed through the glass front. Glass pebbles covered the floor. Displays had been either flipped or pushed aside, as if a tank had rolled through the aisle, bursting it completely. Toppled boxes spilled sneakers and packing paper onto the floor, leaving a trail to the rear of the shop.

The Bronze signaled for his minions to wait while he studied the scene. After a moment, he crawled over the cart and stood within the shop. No lights came on, so the executioner readied his axe and headed inside. The Bronze took two steps and paused, cocking his head, listening. Nothing sprang at him from the dark. No one challenged him.

He explored further, pushing through the clutter, dislodging a few boxes as he went.

The trail ended in a back room, where another surprise waited. The overhead light came on as he entered, revealing an open doorway filled with four dead people—their heads either partially destroyed by gunfire or blown off entirely. Blasted soot covered the door frame and nearby shelves, as if an entire can of black paint had exploded. The bodies were stacked unevenly over each other, perhaps shot as they attempted to clear the door.

The Bronze studied the scene carefully. His minions gathered behind him, every bit as curious. Hefting his axe to his shoulder, he leaned outside.

The light overhead came to life.

The tall man leaned one way, then the other, before stepping into a cinder block corridor.

Ah, the Bronze thought.

Bodies filled both sides of the hall, long since dried and gone the way of leather, right up and into the darkness on either end. Most of them were facedown and dressed in casual clothing, but a few of them wore the blood caked remains of uniforms. Heads were opened in the back like melons split by axes. Dead hands clawed at the air. Lower legs and feet stuck up as if the zombies had been shot from behind.

The Bronze spotted something at the very edge of the light, which made it an easy matter to choose which way to go. The Bronze made his way through the corpse-flooded corridor, while the rest of the Leather followed, shadows drifting after a shadow, threading through the ankle-deep crust of dead matter.

The Bronze stopped and, after a moment, tapped the edge of his axe on the helmet of a dead soldier. The man was lying on his back with his neck half-removed, which the Bronze thought odd. A rifle lay to one side, and the magazine on top of the weapon was empty.

The overhead lights illuminated the next ten feet, and there were more deceased zombies.

Perhaps the soldiers were retreating from a group of charging mindless. Perhaps the soldiers were advancing, reached one spot, and were forced to return. Neither scenario explained the golf cart smashed through the window, but that didn't overly concern the Bronze. He'd discovered something here. The corridor was not like the ones outside. This place felt more secretive, and the Bronze very much enjoyed discovering secrets.

Secrets meant power.

The Bronze stalked down the hall, discovering clumps of dead things mangled by gunfire. There were more weapons, and the Leather collected all of them. One of the masked men picked up a grenade, no bigger than a golf ball, and stashed the explosive device in a chest pocket.

Then, for some reason, the automatic lights stopped switching on.

The Bronze halted, lifting his head as if smelling gas. Readying his axe again, he shuffled forward, disappearing into that cauldron depth, his boots scuffing on concrete and cloth. Feeling his way along, the Bronze moved over a pile of debris in the hallway. Jagged edges and cold pipes grazed the big man's frame, but he passed by it all.

A light came on, some thirty feet away. That cone revealed the edges of a substantial blast that had taken out not only a good chunk of the corridor, but quite a few of the mindless. What really got the Bronze's attention, however, was another clump of legs sticking out into the hall. He walked toward them and discovered that the bodies were preventing a sliding steel door from closing. Upon further scrutiny, two of the dead lay on top of another soldier. A huge hole had replaced the man's face, leaving only his lower jaw and upper brow. The man had collapsed on his weapon, which had fallen, lengthwise, into the machine-cut grooves of the sliding door.

The Bronze peered ahead, and his eyes widened.

The concrete ended, and the corridor became a tunnel of perfectly rounded ribs of steel. A red light flashed, whirling in a continuous pattern over pipes and finishes of chrome. Bodies littered the floor, dozens of bodies, both military and civilian. All dead, by headshots.

The Bronze proceeded deeper, turned to his right, and counted two more steel doors, each a foot thick and wide open. There was a side passage, which opened into a large room. He proceeded to enter, and overhead lights once again automatically switched on.

The sight straightened the Bronze's spine.

Guns.

Whole racks of guns and countless ammunition caches. Weapons of a futuristic make that stunned the masked man. There were *rows* of gunracks, stacked on top of one other, stretching well back into the dark. To the right were open lockers, containing complete sets of body armor and even bulletproof shields.

Long dead mindless covered the floor.

And that was just one room. The doors were wide open, as if someone didn't have time to close them. A number of the Leather gathered at the Bronze's back, and he gestured that they take what they wanted. Their black outfits gleamed as they stepped into the armory.

The Bronze, however, returned to the main corridor and pressed on. Ten feet. Twenty. A single red light swirled over steel and support struts, as if this section was under continuous alert. The corridor ended in a pile of mindless, gunned down upon the threshold to another chamber. There were more inside, but the dead didn't interest the Bronze.

Computer terminals filled the room. Huge monitors hung from ceilings. Cords and wiring drooped in black coils. The main level had three multi-level tiers all descending from it, like a mythical giant's stairway to a lower floor. Computer workstations lined those tiers as well, and a single set of stairs split them right down the middle. There were open manuals everywhere, as well as undisturbed coffee cups, tablets, and half-filled water bottles. A few stuffed animals peeked out from between workstations.

A blinking light caught the Bronze's attention.

There, on a raised platform, in the middle of a series of computer terminals, was an elevated plate. Two separate glass covers sat side-by-side, each one protecting a linear keypad and a keyhole.

A green light blinked just to the left of the ominous twins.

The Bronze knew enough about computers to wake the system. He reached for the nearest keyboard and tapped a key. Hard drives whirled to life. Overhead, the red lights switched to white. A huff of hydraulics and the entire center was resurrected, causing the dozen or so Leather accompanying him to become restless.

A moan caught the Bronze's ears.

And below, in between the terraced workstations, a huge white spider crept into view. It crawled out into the stairway running through the tiers. Except it wasn't a spider, it was a hand. Attached to a wrist.

The Bronze stopped at the head of the stairs to get a better look.

A gray length of arm lifted weakly before flopping onto the floor.

The Bronze descended slowly, approaching it. As he drew closer, he could see the arm was dressed in a technician's uniform. The clothing was ripped in places, bloodied as if the person had been mashed by a speeding car. The man's legs came into view, but they ended in rags and were useless. A dirty-blonde head of hair lifted and the face beneath smiled.

Except one side of the mouth had been ripped off to the jawline, where the strip of missing skin continued to the ear.

The zombie greeted the living with a slow, exaggerated nod.

The Bronze split its head with one chop.

The undead creature flopped to the floor and remained motionless, delivered to its final death. The Bronze nudged the skull with a boot and then cleaned it off on the uniform.

From up top, one of the Leather waved.

The Bronze retraced his steps back to the main platform, searching for any more infected lurking in between the other workstations. There were none. The minion that waved to him pointed at three live monitors, ones that had powered up after being awakened from sleep mode.

The Bronze stopped in his tracks. His eyes narrowed and he had to remember to breathe.

Two of the screens showed detailed information that would take time to process. The third screen, however, needed no such effort.

That one offered a live feed of a missile silo, and the single rocket poised and ready within its metal sheath.

46

"All right," Collie said after removing the last of the bolts from her wounds. "That's all good."

Carson was propped up against a cabinet with the battle rifle aimed at the human stool. The cleansing fire of the decontamination chamber had stopped, but scorch streaks marred the bulletproof glass. Once she had the bolts out, Collie removed her leather duds she'd forcefully appropriated from one of the dead cock-knuckles. Her own clothing was underneath, but it was in a sorry state.

"Ohhhh," Collie groaned, inspecting her chest wound while adjusting her own shot-up ass against a cabinet. "Gonna need a shitload of surgical tape for this one."

"How are you even alive?" a wary Carson asked.

"Keep your eyes on him," she ordered softly.

"Sorry."

"S'okay. And to answer your question. No fucking idea. Well. I might have a theory, but all you need to know now is… that I'm still me. Still rational-thinking, secret squirrel shit me." Collie looked at the man-stool then. "You got a name?"

"Top Gun."

That caused her to scowl in amusement. "What? Fuck off, that's not your name."

"That's what they call me."

"I'm not fucking calling you *Top Gun*, so get that outta your head now. What's your real name and don't make me ask twice."

"Milo."

Collie's face went slack. "You're shitting me. From one extreme to the other? Milo's your name?"

He released a tired smile and nodded. "Milo Trasher."

"He's the one who shot you," Carson said, nodding at the man. "I heard them going for him. Telling him what to do."

That information visibly uneased Milo. He chuckled, a breathless sound that might've been the last bit of air shaken free of his lungs, and suddenly he was very attentive.

"You did this?" Collie asked.

"They forced me to," Milo quickly explained. "I had no choice."

"You shot me from a hundred meters out? On a moving vehicle?"

"They would've…" Milo bit his lips, his eyes darting from the automatic cannon in Carson's possession. "They would've hurt me. Just like him. Or worse. Believe me."

"You still didn't have to shoot her," the mechanic said.

"And wind up like you?" Milo demanded. "I don't know her. Don't know any of them. All I knew was that if I didn't shoot, some psycho with a hammer was going to smash in my ear."

"Why they got you dressed up like that?" Collie asked.

"They do this to all their slaves. They call them meat puppets. Which is pretty much how valuable they are to them."

"So you know about these knobs?"

"Yeah. I know about them."

"Who are they?"

Milo sighed. "They're called the Leather. A small army of… well… organized crazies from back west. Past Saskatchewan. Maybe past the Rockies."

"And what are they doing out this way?"

Milo shrugged. "Picking up the leftovers. Conquering. Claiming the land as their own. Medieval shit."

Collie considered the man before him. Carson's expression softened, but only a little.

"Top Gun, eh?" she finally asked.

Milo nodded warily.

"That's something you get from the army?"

That made him blink. "Yeah. Actually."

"So you're CF?"

"Yeah. About seven years. Then I became a gym teacher."

"How old are you?" Collie asked.

"Thirty-nine."

"Jesus. And you were in the Forces? What part?"

"Infantry."

Collie's expression lightened. "Ahhh, a cowboy. What regiment?"

"Patricia's."

"Ohhhhh, a *dirty* cowboy."

Milo nodded with a sorry smile.

"A vicious princess," Collie added with a mild note of appreciation. "I like you already. You're not a lawn dart, are you?" She looked at Carson. "That's paratrooper to you."

Right then, a light on the terminal flashed. Collie got up, hobbled over to the computer station, and tapped a few keys. The two men quieted as Collie reached for a headset and put on the device.

"This is—"

"I know… who you are, Captain Jones," the voice interrupted. "So please. Listen carefully. We have an extremely dangerous… situation… developing…"

<h1 style="text-align:center">47</h1>

The last of the mindless lunged at Gus in a flash of teeth and hooked fingers.

The unexpected attack surprised him, and the mindless, still caught in the batting cage's web, crashed into him. Gus staggered back until his feet were on green flooring. He straightened and saw that the netting still held the trapped zombie, but the creature, through sheer power alone, had managed to pull itself forward a few feet.

"You got me that time," Gus said, and bashed in the thing's head. The mindless went down in a heap, suddenly boneless. Gus moved around the edge of the netting before finishing the job with two more strikes.

After that, he retreated a few steps until his back hit the glass.

He'd done it.

Sweet Christ and honey-tipped titties, he'd done it.

But his shoulders dearly ached from the effort, and he could chop his fucking foot off at the ankle, it was bothering him so much. He'd put the kibosh on the mindless hunting for his ass, however, so that was good. Nothing moved in the batting area that wasn't him, and that alone filled him with relief.

"Thank you, Lord," Gus whispered. "Thank you very much."

Then he remembered the ones who had unleashed the mindless in the first place. They were still out there, the *barbarians*, and it probably was in his best interest to find them.

Before they reached anything important.

The light outside the window began to flash. When he glanced at it, the light stayed on.

"That you, Josh?" he asked, but Rogan did not answer.

Though bone-weary and aching, Gus lumbered towards the batting cage entrance. He hurried outside to the main hall and waited.

The lights remained on.

"You there…?" a voice crackled overhead, causing Gus to jump.

"I'm sorry," Josh Rogan said. "As I mentioned before. I'm research. Not security. And I never had to… use the speaker system before. Not while I was alone. I'm learning as I go."

"S'okay," Gus said. "I don't—"

"Listen carefully," Rogan interrupted. "And don't bother asking questions. I can't hear you. I can see you, but that's it. You've killed off the zombies in your area, but there's a bigger problem now."

"All right," Gus said, realizing at that moment the assistant couldn't hear him.

"A group of those… skid-marked assholes… have found an armory," Rogan continued. "A very important armory. One that must've been opened by a guard. This particular armory… isn't far away from Whitecap's nuclear arsenal."

Nuclear what?

"I think… the arsenal is secure," Rogan explained. "I *think*… but if anyone does a search of the area, they may…eventually find the keys. Then it only stands to reason… that they have someone who can access the weapons. Perhaps activate them."

Gus had heard enough. He started pointing.

"Yes, yes, follow the flashing lights," Rogan said. "I've taken the… the liberty… to summon reinforcements. For you."

As promised, the lights in one section of the underground promenade flashed repeatedly. Gus forced himself into a run, heading towards them.

A short time later, Rogan told him to stop.

Gus stood before the wrecked front of a shoe store, where a golf cart had crashed though the front window. Shattered glass twinkled like diamonds upon the floor. The sight of crushed boxes, scattered footwear, and toppled displays all suggested an army had marched through the shop.

He had no idea where, however.

"Please wait," Rogan informed him. "Reinforcements… are on their way."

"Who?" Gus asked aloud, and then he remembered Rich Trinidad carrying a private gun collection. But if it was Rich Trinidad, what had happened to the islanders escaping through the secret hatch? Did they make it?

Some fifty-plus meters out, the walkway lit up one section at a time, as a lone figure approached.

Body armor. Carrying a handgun.

Gus's eyes narrowed at the advancing figure, sensing something familiar.

The figure waved as he jogged through an unlit area where perhaps the lights needed to be replaced. The shadow slowed to a walk, coming closer, the light flashing off the visor.

"Hiya honey," Collie said.

The heart-stopping realization that it was indeed Collie standing before him robbed Gus of all speech. His arms dropped to his sides as he simply beheld her from head to toe and back again. She let him have his moment.

Then he rushed forward and embraced her.

Their helmets clacked off each other, and his body armor pressed against hers, but Gus didn't care. He had her in his arms and didn't want to let go. Collie hugged him back and held on as if he were a rock in stormy waters.

"I thought you were dead," he said.

Collie's hug lessened. "Yeah," she said near his ear. "About that."

She released him and he did the same a second later. Red-eyed, and clearly in stunned disbelief, Gus simply stared at the woman.

"We—*I*—have a problem," she said.

Gus shook his head, not understanding.

"I was shot through the chest, Gus."

That horrific memory replayed through his mind, the blast erupting out her back in black and white. His lower legs went weak, and his guts crystalized.

"Right through," Collie continued. "One shell blew my heart out my back. And yet… here I am."

"You're… like Wallace," he whispered.

Collie didn't answer right away. "We'll talk about this later. If there is a later. Right now, we got rats nibbling on the powerlines."

"Collie… Josh said this place had nukes."

She didn't hesitate. "Yeah, it does."

"How the hell does it have nukes?"

"We always had them. Just never told the public. One of the government's best kept secrets, really."

Gus's head was swimming.

"We don't have a lot, mind you," she explained. "Just enough to play that card if we needed to. To ruin someone's day."

"Jesus, Collie."

"I'll tell you all about it later. After this next part. Come on."

She pointed her sidearm, which he recognized as the Sig he'd left in the EV.

Collie entered the shoe store, and Gus followed.

48

"*Just wait a moment,*" the disembodied voice announced overhead. "*Reinforcements are on their way.*"

The words blared from the security center's speaker system, hooking the Bronze's attention. Others glanced at the ceiling, searching for the source, while those standing guard near the entrance immediately tensed and took aim at the corridor beyond.

"*Wait a moment,*" the voice said, suddenly wary. "*Damn these controls. Captain. Captain Jones. We might have a problem.*"

49

"What problem?" Collie asked, poised to proceed into the back corridor beyond the shoe store.

Gus was just about to comment that he'd run through a tunnel system on the other side, when Rogan spoke again.

"I might've broadcasted that last thought… throughout the entire complex. I'm so sorry. I never had to… to use any of this equipment before. I'm just—"

"A research assistant," Gus finished with him, drawing a look from Collie.

She looked to the ceiling and drew an imaginary knife across her throat. "Stay off this line from here on end. Don't call us. We'll call you."

Gus wasn't sure if Rogan heard her or not, but the assistant immediately shut up.

"What do we do?" he asked her.

"We're going to be even *more* careful," she answered. *"That's* what we do."

*

The Bronze directed half his minions through the corridor while the others remained around their leader. The Leather took up positions within the tunnel, standing or crouching on one knee, partially hidden behind the steel ribs of the single corridor leading to the armory and beyond. Guns were readied and aimed.

All attention centered on the passageway ahead.

*

Collie advanced into the lit corridor, her gun in both hands. She stepped over the corpses littering the floor and quickly outpaced Gus, who staggered along as if he'd downed a two-fer of Molson's beer.

Which wasn't a bad idea, he decided, still reeling from the one-two punch of Collie being alive, but in a state like Wallace, and then the revelation that the country had in its possession a small and exceptionally well-kept secret nuclear stockpile.

We don't have a lot, mind you, she'd said. *Just enough to play that card if we needed to.*

Collie stooped at times, extending a hand and patting down the bodies. "Picked clean," she whispered to Gus.

That little bit of knowledge didn't do anything for him, either. He knew the leather freaks had weapons, but he was hoping to pick up something along the way. As special with a weapon Collie might be, he didn't think she was capable of squaring off against a small pack of gunmen with just her prized Sig.

Collie held up a hand and Gus stopped.

She reached down and picked up a battle rifle, much like the ST1X he'd used earlier, but a much smaller design.

"KR3," Collie whispered. She inspected the empty magazine. "Dry, though."

"What's a KR3?"

"Belgian ball breaker. Medium-range bang stick for security forces. Not quite frontline, but it'll rip you a new one just as fast. Bet they left this one because it was empty. Mine now."

She holstered her Sig and braced the KR3 against her shoulder. "I like the old German-made HKs myself. But that's pillow talk."

Gus smiled uncertainly.

"Now," she said, studying the floor. "If we can just find a magazine. Full or partial is fine by me."

"This place is a grave, Collie."

But she didn't comment. She crept down the corridor, staying quiet, and Gus tried to emulate her. He got the quiet part down, but Collie was outpacing him as if she were levitating over the bodies. A short distance away, she eased herself into a section with no lighting overhead. Gripping his bat, Gus followed.

In that pocket of darkness, Collie crouched and searched a body. When Gus got close, she held up a straight magazine so that he could see it.

Then she loaded it into her weapon, readying it with a metallic snap.

They pushed on, exiting the dark area in silence. Up ahead they saw the open doorway, and the bodies preventing it from closing.

Collie dropped to a crouch and, without looking, wiggled a few fingers at Gus for him to get down. She then took aim.

Gus hung back behind her, holding onto his bat, watching her. *Collie's back*, his brain shrieked, overjoyed. His heart was racing. She was becoming like Wallace, however, and that chummed his initial rush of happiness into a pulp of uncertainty. He glanced at the dead bodies nearby, then at Collie. The thumping in his chest grew all the stronger. A coldness gripped his innards and gave them a painful squeeze.

Becoming like Wallace.

He remembered Wallace.

Collie suddenly fired, and tracers scorched through shadows. A dark figure Gus had missed entirely flew backwards as if yanked by an invisible cane. Collie crouched lower and fired two more bursts. Someone croaked a note of pain, as if jamming a toe into the corner of a couch. A figure flopped facedown and didn't move.

Collie advanced, staying low, weapon leveled and ready.

Gus lurched after her, his grip tight around his baseball bat.

They reached the open doorway, and Collie fired again. Someone fell in the corridor beyond.

Then bullets screamed back.

Collie pressed herself against the wall, behind a section of steel girders bowed like whale bones. She squeezed herself in tight, while Gus fell on his chest—right behind two corpses lying on another soldier.

"Stay where you are," she ordered, before spinning around. Bullets ricocheted off steel, exploding like aerosol gas cans chucked into a fire.

Collie shot one gunman through the face.

She nailed another through the chest, whipping the black-vested torso around before blowing out the back of his head—and the front of his face.

A third Leather sprayed and prayed, sticking his weapon around a girder while remaining undercover. Collie adjusted her fire with a click, took quick aim, and removed one hand at the wrist.

That got the shooter screaming.

He lumbered away, and Collie let him go. Chrome flashed beneath a spinning red emergency light. Into that, she advanced, just a few steps inside the open doorway. Gus looked up in time to see more of those Halloween freaks creeping up the corridor, emerging from around corners and leapfrogging from steel rib to rib, towards the two of them. They fired as they advanced.

Collie squeezed herself behind a support strut. She hunkered down, presenting a small target, and didn't retreat despite the approaching shadows. She leaned out and killed the two attackers, violently lighting both targets up, before ducking behind the curved strut.

Whereupon she placed her KR3 down and smoothly extracted her Sig.

She cocked her helmet at Gus, as if this was just a regular day at the office. He smiled back, but it was brief. He crawled ahead, over dead things, and reached the door.

Where he saw the thing keeping the door open.

The barrel of an automatic rifle.

The exact kind Collie had used.

But the weapon was in a slotted groove, suggesting that if he took the damned thing, the door might close. Collie didn't need a new rifle, however. She needed ammunition. He pawed at the bodies, forcefully shoving them forward, creating a low barrier of sorts. He needed to know if the weapon was the same as hers. When he pushed the last body onto its side, his face lit up… for about two seconds. He realized more work would be needed to extract the magazine.

Because he didn't have a clue.

Ahead, Collie whirled and fired two shots.

Someone fell. Others took cover. There were plenty of wraiths filling the corridor, however—moving, shifting, pressing ahead with grim concentration, firing as they advanced before taking cover behind the many steel ribs holding up the ceiling.

Collie shot a calf sticking out from behind one of those ribs, and as the guy pitched forward, she finished him off with a bullet to the face. Another stepped around a strut, and Collie shot him twice, driving him back where he fell, both ankles fluttering in the air.

But those masked crazies did not relent.

Daring not to lift his head, Gus's fingers hooked and clawed at metal. He found a short, rectangular switch and tweaked it left and right before finally shoving it upward.

The magazine cleared.

Gus pulled it free.

"Collie," he called out over a frenzied burst of return fire. He held up the magazine as far as he dared.

Then he tossed it at her.

Collie caught the magazine, checked it, and put away her sidearm before going for the KR3. She inserted the mag, readied the weapon, and paused for a few split seconds.

Then she returned fire.

There were no bursts this time, just the surgical snap of a trained marksman with battle experience.

In seconds, she gunned down four more targets.

"Thanks," she said, before whirling around the girder and storming ahead.

Gus jumped up and rushed to her last place of cover.

*

Gunshots rang out from beyond the missile room—or what the Bronze thought of as the missile room. The concerning thing was the storm of gunfire—a devastating hail of killer shot that lit up the red-shaded corridor like spent chain lighting…

Then nothing.

And no more than two seconds later, the *return* fire commenced.

Grunts of pain percolated the air, and those sounds were brief and final.

After the first few rounds of gunfire ceased, the Leather remaining with the Bronze were impassive, their masks hiding all emotion. They were hunched over and waiting to enter the fight, having discarded their crossbows for more modern weaponry.

During the next volley of intense gunfire—an exchange resulting in even more deaths—the Leather still didn't show any emotion, although frustration was bubbling within the Bronze.

Another extended exchange of bullets, and more of the Leather cried out in pain, further breaking their inhuman silence that made them so unnerving.

That resulted in a few looks from those within the missile room. Rifles were hefted a little higher. A head turned here and there. One individual rolled his shoulders before glancing nervously about.

All the while, the raging firefight drew closer.

Leather-clad gunmen came into view then, turning the far corner, firing as they retreated.

Retreated. They were *retreating*. Worse still, there were only a *handful*.

The Bronze's eyes narrowed.

He'd sent almost *two dozen* Leather into the corridor.

His hand tightened upon a formidable machine-gun pistol he'd acquired in the missile room, a short-barreled monster that he had chosen over his axe. The executioner's weapon rested against a desk.

Outside, even though the Leather had taken cover in amongst those thick steel supports, the advancing shooter had still managed to score hits.

A Leather had his head torqued to the left in a shocking burst of gore, and the rest of him collapsed in a heap on the metal floor. Another Leather took a shot dead-center, was backed up to a wall, only to have his throat blown out in an awful smack of bone against metal. One of the minions placed his back against the bulkhead and then stuck only his rifle out into the corridor, firing blindly at the unknown assailant. He emptied the weapon and pulled back to reload—when a single shot ricocheted off the *opposite* wall in a frightening spark. The Leather's unprotected head snapped back in a bloody puff of skull matter.

That unnerved the onlookers in reserve, causing several of them to visibly flinch.

They were being routed. And in the narrow confines of the corridor, they were being routed *back* into the missile room. That simply would not do. The side passage to the armory was thirty feet away. If the Leather lost that, then they would lose everything else.

But who was killing them off so damn easily?

The Bronze was a heavy. A back breaker. A snapper of spines and a hacker of heads. He was a harbinger of terror, held in the same terrible esteem as the Dog Tongue's dreaded Inflictors. No task was out of the question. Nothing scared him. Nothing disturbed him.

But damn if he wasn't feeling uneasy at that exact moment.

He considered one of the Leather, the one that had picked up the small grenade. He strode across the floor and grabbed the man's coat. The Bronze forcefully extracted the grenade from the minion's pocket and shoved him away. With grenade in one hand and machine cannon in the other, the tall masked man marched into the corridor.

It was time to end this firefight, before he lost the rest of his pack.

*

After her dazzling trick shot, Collie took cover behind a strut and shook her head at Gus. He'd seen what she'd done, even saw the dead-arm flop and body-drop after that killer spark of a ricochet.

What was it that Wallace had said about Collie? Gus couldn't remember exactly, but it was frightening. Gus knew what she was capable of with a knife. And a rifle for that matter.

They were perhaps twenty strides from a corner, and the corridor around them was choked with the long-since departed and the more recently dead. Collie had already swapped her weapon out twice, picking the rifles off the floor from where their dead owners lay. Gus was on his feet, peering ahead and behind, in case one of the masked fuckers might've been playing dead. He didn't think they were, but he had to do *something* to make himself useful, even if was just being ready to smack a bastard upside the brain pan. Collie was using the fallen rifles as she advanced, but there weren't any more. Not that he cared. She was a fucking Olympian when it came to shooting.

"Gus," she said, after her last shot. "Stay behind me, okay? We're heading for that corner. That's where the armory is, and the war room after that."

"Where the nukes are?"

"Yeah, but don't worry. They can't do anything with them. There are codes and keys, which they don't have. Not yet, anyway, but if we let these fucking chuggernuts root around down here *long* enough… you never know what shit they might get up to."

She let that thought go.

"Ready?" she asked.

Gus nodded.

She held up a hand and counted down on her fingers. Three, two, one…

She stepped out around the bulky rib of the corridor and immediately had her ankle *grabbed* by one of the not-so-dead freaks upon the floor. The action was so startling, so unexpected, that it caught both of them completely off-guard. She twisted in that grip, slipped, and fell. Gus froze for all of a split second, wavering on what to do.

Just as the tall menacing shade that might've just been released from a medieval dungeon stepped out into the open.

With his arm cocked back, poised to throw.

50

The Bronze threw the grenade.

51

In that whirling klaxon of red light, the black ball hurtled forward. It was considerably smaller than a zombie's head, and it was moving much faster than Gus would have liked.

He knew what it was.

What it *had* to be.

And that unlocked his split-second paralysis.

Acting on reflex alone, he rushed forward—and swung his bat.

And *connected*, sending that explosive nugget *back* towards its owner just as the figure darted back behind the corner.

The grenade bounced off the wall.

*

And landed right at the feet of the paralyzed Bronze, and the remainder of his forces....

*

The explosive detonated in a dragon's belch of fire.

A flashing gout of flame and smoke filled the corridor in an instant, swamping it with raging heat. The force flung Gus backwards, but even as he was falling, he glimpsed the charred husks and body parts of dead men bouncing off the corridor walls.

Then he was flat on his back and gasping.

52

His ears rang, a pure bell tone that seemed to stretch its note forever.

Collie loomed over him, gripping his shoulder. She was shouting, but he didn't hear anything.

Then she stood back and fired at something on the floor, one short burst that startled him.

Not waiting around, she strode forward, towards that rolling cloud of smoke.

And just like that, she was gone.

The ringing in his ears died away, and Gus closed his eyes.

*

A shuffling presence summoned him back. A buckle came undone, and there was a strained grunt, followed by the ripping of a shirt. It wasn't his, though, but that sound of fabric being torn asunder was close.

Gus opened his eyes. Turned his head.

Collie was there, black-eyed and savage, with a beard of gore dripping off her pale face, lowered over one of those masked men.

She felt his stare and glared his way.

Gus's eyes closed again, but he heard her frenzied scrambling to get to him. A second later, he felt her bloody breath on his face.

*

"You okay?" she asked.

Gus came to and cringed, seeing her without her helmet, her face less than a foot away from his.

"Do I look that bad?" she asked.

No gore dripping off her chops. No wild look.

"You look fine," Gus replied.

"I don't feel fine. But, guess what?"

"What?"

"We're still alive."

Those words sank in.

"We're still alive," Gus agreed dreamily.

Collie reached out and placed a palm on the side of his battle helmet.

Gus covered her hand with one of his own.

53

Some time later, Collie and Gus returned to Whitecap's decontamination zone, where they relieved Carson of his guard duty. They were surprised to see that the crippled man had passed out from his pain, his weapon resting on the floor. Milo "Top Gun" Trasher was sitting just across from him, and he actually greeted Gus and Collie upon their return.

When asked why he didn't try to escape, Milo shrugged and answered, "Got no place to go."

Milo was later escorted under guard to a nearby cellblock, where he agreed to remain as sole occupant. Along the way, he didn't protest or complain. Instead, he apologized for shooting Collie, and for firing on their group back on the highway, back at the recharging station.

They left him sitting on a bunk with a blanket and a crapper clean enough to drink from. Or so Gus thought.

Bruno, Cory, little Monica, and the rest of the islanders never made it out of Whitecap. They met up with Collie and Gus at the storeroom on the fifth level, but upon opening the outer hatch, a steady stream of water flowed in from the opening. That elicited an "Oh yeah" moment from Collie. She went on to explain that the passageway led up under a small pond. Nothing so bad to flood the tunnel, but enough to hide the exit. She figured the seals must have leaked over time.

Which she later apologized for forgetting to point out.

Upon securing the missile room and the nearby armory, Collie met with a delighted Rogan. Gus wasn't present when they talked, guessing it was secret government shit, but since he knew about the nukes, he wondered what other secrets Whitecap might be hiding.

That night, however, Collie elected to return to her home, or what was her home, in the living quarters sector of the bunker. She didn't invite Gus, nor did he ask to join her, as much as he wanted. That place was hers and Wallace's, and he wasn't about to disrespect the operator's memory by sleeping with his wife, in what was once their bed.

There were plenty of other places to sleep for the night.

Carson was taken to a nearby infirmary and given enough painkiller to drop a bull. Whitecap's other guests had much more comfortable accommodations. The islanders were assigned their own rooms for the night, along a street that resembled a narrow back road in the country, complete with a mix of real and artificial greenery. As added security, if folks wanted, they could lock their doors. Collie encouraged it, in fact. Just to be on the safe side.

Gus left his room unlocked, and slept on a couch, not wanting to sleep in another person's bed, even though the home was relatively well kept. He supposed that would change in time, if he chose to live here. That got him thinking about what would happen to the place.

And Collie.

The next morning was interesting. Each domicile had electronic screens built into the walls, to replicate windows. At seven o'clock, Gus woke up to the sight of a sun rising in the distance, over a wooded hill. Soft piano music, of all things, drifted in from unseen speakers. Pleasant morning music that Gus initially considered turning off… but didn't. Instead, he stayed on the couch, and stared at that feed of a breaking dawn. He didn't know if it was live or not, but he appreciated the moment for what it was.

It seemed the entire section of Whitecap was no longer in screensaver mode.

The group later gathered in a cafeteria, around one of the larger tables. All the ceiling lights and screens were on, displaying an autumn outdoors and trees rustling in a breeze. Collie entered the cafeteria without her battle helmet on. She did wear a new pair of sunglasses, which took up a good portion of her face. When she noticed his stare, she smiled.

Collie later directed Bruno and Rich Trinidad to the kitchen, where she accessed an impressive pantry full of preserved food. They ate frozen omelets, waffles, bacon, hash browns, and even had, of all things, ketchup—although the ketchup tasted a little vinegary to Gus. Canned fruit was even on the table—peaches and pears.

Collie did not partake, excusing herself to check on the food stores as well as the contents of the freezers. When Bruno and Cory finished cooking, she took a plate of food back to Carson.

After breakfast, however, she returned to the cafeteria and stopped at their tables.

"How's everyone doing?" she asked, standing behind Monica who'd finished off a bowl of dried cereal and powdered milk.

They answered they were doing just fine, but the faces had questions. Gus had his own.

"You're probably wondering what the situation is?" Collie asked.

"Yeah, we are," Sarah Burton piped up.

"Well, as you know, with the help of the resident custodian, Mr. Rogan, we've determined that the individuals assaulting Whitecap are no more. In short, we got them all."

A moment of silence then, which became a series of satisfied nods.

"So…." Sarah began. "What happens now?"

"Well, Whitecap is essentially secured. I'm going to make a few more passes to ease my own mind. There's still some cleaning to do. Removal of bodies and so forth. But I've been assured by Mr. Rogan that there's no biohazard risk to us. Or whoever volunteers to help clean up the mess. After all that, you have a choice. Along with the other residents of Tancook. There's a pretty sophisticated bunker up here. Air filtration systems, water purification systems. Compost, farming."

"Farming?" Bruno asked.

"Indoor farming. There's a seed vault containing most everything you'd want to grow. The thing was designed to be a second vault like the one up in Spitsbergen. The Doomsday Vault."

That widened some eyes.

Collie continued. "Fish tanks, which are at full capacity, so I understand. Living quarters, which you all had a taste of last night. Gyms. Firing ranges. Storefronts. Libraries containing pretty much every book, film, and song ever made. Top off all that with practically unlimited power."

"Holy shit," someone muttered, and Gus realized it was his own mouth.

"So, yeah," Collie summed up. "Everything you need right here. The armories are off limits for now, but they'll be made accessible in time. Think of this place as an underground five-star hotel. All paid for by your tax dollars."

That left them speechless.

"We'll need to go through it all," Collie went on. "Make sure all the dead are cleared. But after that. It's here. Under a mountain, given, but… it's here.

Ready and waiting. We'll need to send someone back to our folks at Tancook. Let them know what's going on. I'll be selecting a couple of volunteers, but I don't think that'll be a problem. Not when you know *how* you'll be getting there."

"How?" Rich Trinidad asked.

Collie smiled. "You'll see. I'm keeping that a surprise."

"You've been saying that ever since we left home," Cory said. "After all this? Let it out."

"All right. I haven't checked to see if they'll start, but the PM had three limos. I spotted a couple in the main garage. Those things are armored, top-of-the-line monsters. Able to run on solar, as well as energy derived from tire friction, brake application, and other sources I either forgot or don't know about. Anyway, they don't need any gas is what I'm saying."

That was met with quizzical stares.

"Top speed I think is only fifty or sixty klicks an hour, but, hey, I don't think anyone here will mind. Not when you see the interior."

Gus squirmed. He didn't care about the transportation. He was hoping to hear about something else.

Thankfully, however, Sarah Burton, God love her, got to the point.

"What about you?" she asked pointedly. "You don't look so good."

Collie flashed a crooked smile. She adjusted her sunglasses, and there was something offsetting about it. "Don't you worry about me. I'm fine. I do have a few things to do, but none of that concerns you. We'll talk again later. Maybe meet here around lunchtime. 'Til then…"

She looked for Gus and beckoned him with a finger.

They stepped away from the group. "Come with me. We need to see someone."

He nodded, fidgeting, close to bursting. Collie gathered up a metal serving tray of food and then headed for the main walkway. As soon as they were out of hearing range of the group, he asked, "All right what's going on with you?"

Collie faced him.

"Out with it. Come on."

She checked on the others. "Yeah, sorry. Let's walk. Not far, because I need to feed Milo, but I'll tell you everything you want to know. And some shit you probably won't want to know."

They started walking.

"So yeah, turns out… I'm something of a mutation. Just like Wallace. Go figure. You sleep with a guy, share some DNA, and turns out, it'll change you."

That robbed Gus of all words.

"Rogan said that it was probably just percentages, but, yeah, whatever was turning Wallace, well, some of that rubbed off on me. Aren't you glad we didn't do anything more than just snuggle?"

"Collie," he said, the misery strong in his voice.

"Sorry, shitty joke. But, again, even Rogan isn't certain. He said it might have just been coincidence that my TI injection did the same to me. He doesn't know what the timeline might be for me. Might be the same for Wallace. Might be longer. Or shorter. Right now… I can feel just a twinge in my joints. Just a twinge. Might've been when I was shot, though…"

Gus stopped her, his eyes stern.

"All right," she sighed. "Sorry again. I'm out of practice here, but I never was one to sugar coat things. I don't… have much time left. And the mission has changed. It's no longer about finding survivors. Well, it is, but… you'll see."

Gus reached out and gripped the woman's shoulder. He stared at her, holding back the sadness welling up in his throat. His solemn gaze, and the visible attempt at control, and seeing it fail, wilted Collie's own expression.

They slowly embraced, and held each other for a long time, while nearby screens showed sailboats gliding across rolling waters.

*

They arrived at Milo's cell about twenty minutes later.

His butt was planted on the bed, amidst a snarl of gray and white blankets and sheets. He was naked from the waist up, baring a lean upper body that might've been lashed by whips at one point. He had thin, sandy-blonde hair, but his face was aged, with dull hazel eyes.

"Morning," he said. "That for me?"

"Yup." Collie placed the tray of food on the bed. "And we want to talk."

"Before, after, or during?"

"Up to you."

Milo studied the breakfast. "During, then. Haven't eaten since yesterday, and that wasn't much."

"They didn't feed you in that outfit of yours?" Gus asked, not entirely pleased with the guy. He'd shot Collie, after all. And one of their pickups not so long ago.

Milo considered the question. "They weren't my outfit. You guys shot up my outfit. Not that I minded. They were assholes. Mostly. These guys here?

They were bigger assholes. Much better organized."

"You called them the Leather?"

Milo sat back. "They called themselves the Leather. For obvious reasons. They still call themselves the Leather."

Gus exchanged looks with Collie.

"There are more?" she asked.

Milo studied the food on the tray and rubbed his jaw. "You know they stick ball gags in your face. They took mine out after I shot you."

Gus tensed at that.

And Milo picked up on it. "Sorry about that. I mean, I had to do it, but again. Sorry." He took a deep breath before continuing. "There's more of them. Lots more. Though, honestly, you took out a good chunk. I wouldn't be surprised if you got close to half. Doubtful, but I wouldn't be surprised."

"Go on," Collie said, folding her arms and leaning against the wall.

Milo didn't meet her eyes. Instead he picked up his breakfast and began picking at it. "We… my outfit… did freelance work for the Leather. They like to stick with their costumes and such. Intimidation, I suppose. But they would hire us to go out and, well, get in among the locals. Infiltrate. Especially the bigger targets. With smaller groups or individuals, it was more like catch, cage, and bring back alive. They were always looking for new people to bring into their gang. They'd supply us. Mostly gas. Food. The usual. Not so much firearms, though. They stuck to the more, ah, medieval shit. Mostly 'cause they ran out of the modern stuff, I think."

"You would catch people?" Gus asked in disbelief.

Milo didn't answer right away. "Yeah. I could say I was getting tired of it all. Especially the crew I was with. Especially with the Leather and what they did to their victims. But, truth of it was, I stuck with it. Because, if I left, the crew I was with? Well, they would've killed me outright or turned me over to the Leather. One or the other. And the Leather was worse."

Milo cocked his head. "I got a dirty past. I know it. Not proud of it. So, whatever you decide. I'm willing to take my punishment. I'm thinking it ain't going to be anything worse than what you saved me from."

Gus rubbed the back of his neck, a sudden unease tensing him up. They may have found this nice bunker, but something told him that things were going to get a lot worse.

"So, yeah," Milo said after a time. "Thanks. I'll happily stay in here for the rest of my days. I like this better than what I just came from."

"You say there are more?" Collie asked. "Of the Leather?"

"Yeah."

"Out west?"

Milo nodded. "Not sure where, exactly, but I know of a couple of Leather towns."

"Leather *towns?*" Gus blurted, but Collie held up a hand.

"So why were all these fuckheads out this way?" she asked.

"Conquest," the soldier said simply. "Can't get down into the states. The radiation belt will cook you from the inside out. You guys obviously haven't been out west, so I'll tell you… it's empty. Just ghosts and bones, and things on the verge of falling down. It's ripe for the staking of claims. And the Leather? They're in a staking kinda mood. All led by a guy called the Dog Tongue."

Gus took another disbelieving pause before shaking his head. "Christ almighty."

"Yeah," Milo said. "Sorry to be the bearer of bad news and all. I'm not saying you got lucky, but… you did take on pretty much the biggest clan west of the Rockies. And won. That counts for something."

Collie straightened. "How long before they notice they've gone missing?"

"No idea. I don't know how they did their communications."

"Dog Tongue," Gus repeated.

"Dog Tongue," Milo said. "Yeah. These Leather shits? They worship the guy. Yeah. He's a regular West Coast warlord. All that."

"Did you know about the mindless?"

Milo's brow scrunched. "The zombies? Yeah, I did. Didn't know how many those bastards had of them, though. Yeah, anyone who didn't… assimilate… got changed over. Least that's what me and my crew speculated. Really, they're all over. Some say they're around because of the radiation belts. One week in and that's that. You're deep-fried. Into one of those."

Collie and Gus traded looks yet again.

"Look," Milo said. "You got a good thing going here. Chances are the Dog Tongue won't find you. Won't find this place. Besides, you have the guns to defend it if he ever did. It's a big country. Lots of places to hide when you know how."

"We could do that…" Collie said. "But then, Dog Tongue just continues to do what he's doing."

"Yeah," Milo admitted. "He does."

"And you already said he's in a staking mood?"

"Yeah. He's working his way here. Leather-controlled towns are set up along the way. Heading all the way to the coast."

That hooked Gus's attention.

"The coast."

"Yeah. Why, you guys from back east?"

Gus didn't answer him, but he motioned for Collie to leave with him.

"Seeya cowboy," Collie said, following Gus out. "Enjoy the eats."

"Thanks. And… hey."

They paused in the doorway.

Milo took a moment, chewing over the words. "Again. I'm sorry. Really."

Collie closed the door and locked it. She placed her back against it and regarded Gus.

"You heard all that?" she asked.

Gus nodded.

"What do you think?"

He couldn't answer.

"I'll tell you what I think. We could hide here and let this Dog Tongue go on with his staking. Odds are he won't find us. But… he will find Tancook. Eventually. Our people are already on the coastline."

"Yeah," Gus agreed, very much not liking where the conversation was going.

"My mission, originally, was to find survivors and bring them back. Not to leave them to some fucked up gluebag who's watched too many *Mad Max* movies."

"Yeah."

"I can't let that happen, Gus," Collie said. She pushed up her sunglasses, revealing her eyes. Once blue, but now cracked with startling streaks of gray. "And, while I'm around… I won't."

"Collie…"

She held up a hand, and that familiar smile returned. "I'm on my way out. I'm done. I'm finished. But I like Ollie's thinking. Go out doing something, rather than sitting down and waiting for it to happen. That's how I'm going to go out. Doing something."

Gus looked her in the eyes, and his faltering voice betrayed his unease. "What are you gonna do?"

Collie didn't hesitate. "I'm gonna find this Dog Tongue," she said, her voice as hard as iron. "And kill the miserable blue-balled sonnavabitch."

About the Author

Keith C. Blackmore is the author of the Mountain Man, 131 Days, and Breeds series, among other horror, heroic fantasy, and crime novels. He lives on the island of Newfoundland in Canada. Visit his website at www.keithcblackmore.com.

DISCOVER
STORIES UNBOUND

PodiumAudio.com